**Miranda smiled, blue eyes twinkling.
"Would you kill for someone you love?"**

"Of course not." Huh. That came out smoother than it should have.

Miranda looked contemplative, but then, too much plastic surgery could do that. "I'd like to think I would, but I doubt I could."

"Hopefully you'll never have to find out. Have a good day, Miranda."

The woman replied, but Audrey didn't quite make out the words—she was too busy thinking about that question.

No, she wouldn't kill for someone she loved.

Not again.

IT TAKES ONE

AN AUDREY HARTE NOVEL

KATE KESSLER

REDHOOK

www.redhookbooks.com

Copyright © 2016 by Kathryn Smith
Excerpt from *Two Can Play* copyright © 2016 by Kathryn Smith

Cover design by Wendy Chan
Cover images copyright © Shutterstock
Cover copyright © 2016 by Hachette Book Group, Inc.

Redhook Books/Orbit
Hachette Book Group
1290 Avenue of the Americas
New York, NY 10104
www.HachetteBookGroup.com

Printed in the United States of America

RRD-C

First edition: April 2016

10 9 8 7 6 5 4 3 2 1

Redhook is an imprint of Orbit, a division of Hachette Book Group.
The Redhook name and logo are trademarks of Hachette Book Group, Inc.

The Hachette Speakers Bureau provides a wide range of authors for speaking events. To find out more, go to www.hachettespeakersbureau.com or call (866) 376-6591.

The publisher is not responsible for websites (or their content) that are not owned by the publisher.

Library of Congress Cataloging-in-Publication Data:
Names: Kessler, Kate, author.
Title: It takes one / Kate Kessler.
Description: First edition. | New York : Redhook, 2016.
Identifiers: LCCN 2015041636 (print) | LCCN 2015049704 (ebook) | ISBN 9780316302500 (paperback) | ISBN 9780316302487 (ebook)
Subjects: LCSH: Police psychologists—Fiction. | Women psychologists—Fiction. | Family secrets—Fiction. | Murder—Investigation—Fiction. | Threats of violence—Fiction. | BISAC: FICTION / Suspense. | GSAFD: Mystery fiction. | Suspense fiction.
Classification: LCC PS3611.E8456 I8 2016 (print) | LCC PS3611.E8456 (ebook) | DDC 813/.6—dc23
LC record available at http://lccn.loc.gov/2015041636

ISBN: 978-0-316-30250-0

My appreciation goes out to these people without whom I couldn't have written this book, and so it's for each and every one of you:

To Devi, for taking a chance, and being so incredibly supportive.

To Miriam, for always being in my corner.

To Dr. Chris Fletcher, for being part of the process. Thank you so much!

To my sisters, for always being there for me no matter what.

To my favorite ginger, for the conversation that led to this book.

To my friends, for understanding and putting up with all the crazy. I love you all.

To Steve, for everything. Absolutely everything. I couldn't do this without your love and support, and occasional kick in the butt.

To all the girls in trouble out there. I hope you find your way out.

And to W. You survived and you thrived. You forgave the unforgivable and found peace. You are strength and grace incarnate.

CHAPTER ONE

"Would you kill for someone you love?"

Audrey Harte went still under the hot studio lights. Sweat licked her hairline with an icy, oily tongue. "Excuse me?"

Miranda Mason, host of *When Kids Kill*, didn't seem to notice Audrey's discomfort. The attractive blonde—whose heavy makeup was starting to cake in the lines around her eyes—leaned forward over her thin legs, which were so tightly crossed she could have wound her foot around the opposite calf. She wore pantyhose. Who wore pantyhose anymore? Especially in Los Angeles in late June? "It's something most of us have said we'd do, isn't it?"

"Sure," Audrey replied, the word forcing its way out of her dry mouth. "I think we as humans like to believe that we're capable of almost anything to protect our loved ones." Did she sound defensive? She felt defensive.

A practiced smile tilted the blonde's sharply defined red lips. "Only most of us are never faced with the decision."

"No." That chilly damp crept down Audrey's neck. *Don't squirm.* "Most of us are not."

Miranda wore her "I'm a serious journalist, damn it" expression. The crew called it her Oprah face. "But David Solomon was. He made his decision with terrible violence that left two boys dead and one severely wounded."

It was almost as though the world, which had gone slightly askew, suddenly clicked into place. They were talking about a case—a rather famous and recent one that occurred in L.A. County. Her mentor, Angeline, had testified for the defense.

It's not always about you, she reminded herself. "David Solomon believed his boyfriend's life was in danger, as well as his own. The boys had been victims of constant, and often extreme, bullying at school. We know that Adam Sanchez had suffered broken ribs and a broken nose, and David himself had to be hospitalized after a similar attack."

Miranda frowned compassionately—as much as anyone with a brow paralyzed by botulism could. "Did the school take any sort of action against the students bullying the boys?"

Audrey shook her head. She was on the edge of her groove now. Talking about the kids—especially the ones driven to protect themselves when no one else would—was the one place she felt totally confident.

"A teacher suggested that the attacks would end if the boys refrained from provoking the bullies with their homosexuality." *Asshole.* "The principal stated that there would hardly be any students left in the school if she suspended everyone who picked on someone else." *Cow.*

"Why didn't the boys leave the school?"

Why did people always ask those questions? Why didn't they run? Why didn't they tell someone? Why didn't they just curl into a ball and die?

"These boys had been raised to believe that you didn't run away from your problems. You faced them. You fought."

"David Solomon did more than fight."

Audrey stiffened at the vaguely patronizing, coy tone that seemed synonymous with all tabloid television. She hadn't signed on to do the show just to sit there and let some Barbara Walters wannabe mock what these kids had been through.

Maybe she should thank Miranda for reminding her of why she'd dedicated so much of her life to earning the "doctor" in front of her name.

"David Solomon felt he had been let down by his school, his community, and the law." Audrey kept her tone carefully neutral. "He believed he was the only one who would protect himself and Adam." What she didn't add was that David Solomon had been right. No one else in their community had stood up for them.

Miranda's expression turned pained. She was about to deliver a line steeped in gravitas. "And now two boys are dead and David Solomon has been sentenced to twenty years in prison."

"A sentence he says is worth it, knowing Adam is safe." David Solomon wasn't going to serve the full twenty. He'd be out before that, provided someone didn't turn around and kill him in prison.

Miranda shot her an arch look for trying to steal the last word, and then turned to the camera and began spouting her usual dramatic babble that she used in every show about senseless tragedies, good kids gone bad, and lives irreparably altered.

This was the tenth episode of the second season of *When Kids Kill*. Audrey was the resident criminal psychologist—only because she was friends with the producer's sister and owed her a couple of favors. Big favors. Normally, Audrey avoided the spotlight, but the extra money from the show paid her credit card bills. And it upped her professional profile, which helped sell her boss's books and seminars.

She'd studied criminal psychology with the intention of helping kids. In between research and writing papers, she'd started assisting her mentor with work on criminal cases, which led to more research and more papers, and a fair amount of time talking to kids who, more often than not, didn't want her help. She never gave up, which was odd, because she considered herself a champion giver-upper.

Thirty minutes later, the interview was over. Miranda had had to do some extra takes when she felt her questions "lacked the proper gravity," which Audrey took to mean drama. Audrey dragged her heels getting out of the chair. It was already late morning and she had to get going.

"Don't you have a flight to catch?" Grant, the producer, asked. He was a couple of years older than her, with long hipster sideburns and rockabilly hair. His sister, Carrie, was Audrey's best friend.

Only friend.

"Yeah," she replied, pulling the black elastic from her wrist and wrapping it around her hair. She wrestled the hairspray-stiff strands into submission. "I'm going home for a few days."

His brow lifted. "You don't seem too happy about it."

She slipped her purse over her shoulder with a shrug. "Family."

Grant chuckled. "Say no more. Thanks for working around the schedule. Carrie's been harping on me to be more social. Dinner when you get back?"

"Sounds good." There was no more use in stalling. If she missed her flight, she'd only have to book another. There wasn't any getting out of the trip. Audrey gathered up her luggage and wheeled the suitcase toward the exit.

"See you later, Miranda," she said as she passed the older woman, who was looking at herself in the mirror of a compact, tissuing some of the heavy makeup off her face. Audrey would take hers off at the airport. She hated falling asleep on planes and waking up with raccoon eyes.

"See ya, Audrey. Oh, hey"—she peered around the compact—"you never answered my question."

Audrey frowned. "I'm pretty sure I answered them all."

Miranda smiled, blue eyes twinkling. "Would you kill for someone you love?"

"Of course not." Huh. That came out smoother than it should have.

Miranda looked contemplative, but then, too much plastic surgery could do that. "I'd like to think I would, but I doubt I could."

"Hopefully you'll never have to find out. Have a good day, Miranda."

The woman replied, but Audrey didn't quite make out the words—she was too busy thinking about that question.

No, she wouldn't kill for someone she loved.

Not again.

It was an eight-and-a-half-hour flight from L.A. to Bangor, with a stopover in Philly. It was an additional two hours and change from Bangor International to Audrey's hometown of Edgeport, on the southeast shore of Maine. She was still fifteen minutes away, driving as fast as she dared on the barren and dark 1A, when her cell phone rang.

It was her mother.

Audrey adjusted her earpiece before answering. She preferred to have both hands on the wheel in case wildlife decided to leap in front of her rented Mini Cooper. It was dark as hell this far out in the middle of nowhere; the streetlights did little more than punch pinpricks in the night, which made it next to impossible to spot wildlife before you were practically on top of it. The little car would not survive an encounter with a moose, and neither would she.

"Hey, Mum. I'll be there by midnight."

"I need you to pick up your father."

Something hard dropped in Audrey's gut, sending a sour taste up her throat that coated her tongue. Could this day become any more of a cosmic bitch-slap? First the show, then she ended up sitting next to a guy who spent the entire flight talking or snoring—to the point that she contemplated rupturing her own eardrums—and now this. The cherry on top. "You're fucking kidding me."

"Audrey!"

She sucked a hard breath through her nose and held it for a second. *Let it go.* "Sorry."

"I can't do it, I have the kids." That was an excuse and they both knew it, though Audrey wouldn't dare call her mother on it. In the course of Audrey's knowledge of her father's love affair with alcohol, never once had she heard of, nor witnessed, Anne Hart leaving the house to bring her husband home.

"Where's Jessica?"

"She and Greg are away. They won't be home until tomorrow." Silence followed as Audrey stewed and her mother waited— probably with a long-suffering, pained expression on her face. Christ, she wasn't even home yet and already everything revolved around her father. She glared at the road through the windshield. She'd take that collision with a moose now.

"Please, babe?"

Her mother knew exactly what to say—and how to say it. And they both knew that as much as Audrey would love to leave her father wherever he was, she'd never forgive herself if he decided to get behind the wheel and hurt someone. She didn't care if he wrapped himself around a tree. She *didn't.* But she couldn't refuse her mother.

Audrey sighed—no stranger to long-suffering herself. "Where is he?"

"Gracie's."

It used to be a takeout and pool hall when she was a kid, but her brother, David, told her it had been turned into a tavern a few years ago. Their father probably single-handedly kept it in business.

"I'll get him, but if he pukes in my rental, you're cleaning it up."

"Of course, dear." Translation: "Not a chance."

Audrey swore as she hung up, yanking the buds out of her ears by the cord. Her mother knew this kind of shit was part of the reason she never came home, but she didn't seem to care. After all these years, Anne Harte still put her drunken husband first. What did it matter anymore if people saw him passed out, or if he got into a fight? Everyone knew what he was. Her mother was the only one who pretended it was still a secret, and everyone let her. Classic.

Rationally, she understood the psychology behind her parents' marriage. What pissed her off was that she couldn't change it. Edgeport was like a time capsule in the twilight zone—nothing in it ever changed, even if it gave the appearance of having been altered in some way. When she crossed that invisible town line, would she revert to being that same angry young woman who couldn't wait to escape?

"I already have," she muttered, then sighed. Between Audrey and her husband, Anne Harte had made a lot of excuses in the course of her life.

Although seven years had passed since she was last home, Audrey drove the nearly desolate road on autopilot. If she closed her eyes she could keep the car between the lines from memory. Each bump and curve was imprinted somewhere she could never erase, the narrow, patched lanes—scarred from decades of abusive frost—and faded yellow lines as ingrained as her own face. The small towns along that stretch bled into one another with little more notice than a weathered sign with a hazardous lean to it. Long stretches of trees gave way to the odd residence, then slowly, the houses became more clustered together, though even the nearest neighbors could host at least two or three rusted-out old cars, or a collapsing barn, between them. Very few of the homes had lights on inside, even though it was Friday night and there were cars parked outside.

You can tell how old a town is by how close its oldest buildings are to the main road, and Ryme—the town west of Edgeport—had places that were separated from the asphalt by only a narrow gravel shoulder, and maybe a shallow ditch. Edgeport was the same. Only the main road was paved, though several dirt roads snaked off into the woods, or out toward the bay. Her grandmother on her mother's side had grown up on Ridge Road. There wasn't much back there anymore—a few hunting camps, some wild blueberries, and an old cemetery that looked like something out of a Stephen King movie. When *Pet Sematary* came out there'd been all kinds of rumors that he'd actually used the one back "the Ridge" for inspiration, though Audrey was fairly certain King had never set foot in her mud puddle of a town in his entire life.

She turned up the radio for the remainder of the trip, forcing herself to sing along to eighties power ballads in an attempt to lighten her mood. Dealing with her father was never easy, and she hadn't seen him since that last trip home, years earlier. God only knew how it was going to go down. He might get belligerent.

Or she might. If they both did there was going to be a party.

Gracie's was located almost exactly at the halfway point on the main road through town. It used to be an ugly-ass building—an old house with awkward additions constructed by people devoid of a sense of form or beauty. The new owner had put some work into the old girl, and now it looked like Audrey imagined a roadhouse ought to look. Raw wooden beams formed the veranda where a half dozen people stood smoking, drinks in hand. Liquor signs in various shades of neon hung along the front, winking lazily.

She had to park out back because the rest of the gravel lot was full. She hadn't seen this kind of crowd gathered in Edgeport since Gracie Tripp's funeral. Gracie and her husband, Mathias, had owned this place—and other businesses in town—for as long as Audrey could remember. Gracie had been a hard woman—the sort who would hit you with a tire iron if necessary, and then sew your stitches and make you a sandwich. She and Mathias dealt with some shady people on occasion, and you could always tell the stupid ones because they were the ones who thought Mathias was the one in charge.

Or stupider still, that Mathias was the one to be afraid of.

Audrey hadn't feared Gracie, but she'd respected her. Loved her, even. If not for that woman, Audrey's life might have turned out very differently.

She opened the car door and stepped out into the summer night, shivering as the ocean-cooled air brushed against her skin. Late June in Maine was a fair bit cooler than in Los Angeles. It was actually refreshing. Tilting her head back, she took a moment there on the gravel, as music drifted out the open back door of the tavern, and drew a deep breath.

Beer. Deep-fryer fat. Grass. Salt water. God, she'd *missed* that smell. The taste of air so pure it made her head swim with every breath.

Something released inside her, like an old latch finally giving way. Edgeport was the place where practically everything awful in her life had taken place, and yet it was home. An invisible anchor, old and rusted from time and neglect, tethered her to this place. The ground felt truly solid beneath her feet. And even though she'd rather give a blow job to a leper than walk through that front door, she didn't hesitate. Her stride was strong and quick, gravel crunching beneath the wedges of her heels.

The people on the veranda barely glanced at her as she walked up the steps. She thought she heard someone whisper her name, but she ignored it. There would be a lot of whispers over the next week, and acknowledging them could be considered a sign of weakness—or rudeness—depending on who did the whispering.

She pushed the door open and crossed the threshold. No turning back now. Inside, a country song played at a volume that discouraged talking but invited drinking and caterwauling along. There were four women on the dance floor, drunkenly swaying their hips while they hoisted their beer bottles into the air. Most of the tables were full and there was a small crowd gathered at the bar. Whoever owned this place had to be making a killing. Why hadn't someone thought of putting a bar in Edgeport before this? Drinking in these parts was like the tide coming in—inevitable.

Audrey turned away from the dancing and laughter. If her father was drunk enough that someone needed to fetch him, then he was going to be in a corner somewhere. She didn't doubt that he'd provided quite a bit of entertainment for Gracie's patrons a couple of hours before. He thrived on attention, the narcissistic bastard. How many songs had he shouted and slurred his way through? How raw was the skin of his knuckles?

She found him slumped in a chair in the back corner, denim-clad legs splayed out in front of him, a scarf of toilet paper—unused—draped over his shoulders and wrapped around his neck like a feather boa. He reeked of rum but luckily not of piss. He'd better keep it that way too. She'd toss him out on the side of the fucking road if his bladder let loose in her rental.

John "Rusty" Harte wasn't a terribly big man, but he was solid and strong. He had a thick head of gray hair that used to be auburn and mismatched eyes that he'd passed on to only one of his children—Audrey. Thankfully she'd gotten her mother's dark hair and looks.

Audrey approached her father without fear or trepidation. Her lip itched to curve into a sneer, but she caught the inside of it in her teeth instead. Give nothing away—that was a lesson she learned from her mother and from Gracie. Show nothing but strength; anything else could be used against you.

She stretched out her foot and gave his a nudge with the toe of her shoe. He rocked in the chair but didn't stir. Great, he was out cold. That never ended well.

She reached out to shake his shoulder when someone came up on her left side. "Dree?"

Audrey froze. Only one person ever called her that—because she never allowed anyone else to do so since.

She bit her lip hard. The pain cut through the panic that gripped at her chest as years of memories, both good and terrible, rushed up from the place where she'd buried them.

Not deep enough.

She turned. Standing before her was Maggie Jones—McGann now—grinning like the damn Joker. She looked truly happy to see Audrey—almost as happy as she had the night the two of them had killed Clint.

Maggie's father.

CHAPTER TWO

Jake Tripp reached beneath the scarred wood of the bar and touched the shotgun he kept there. The ammo was in a small drawer to the right. This was the first night since they'd opened that he thought he might actually have to use it.

The moment he'd seen Audrey Harte walk in, he'd known something was going to happen—it always did when Audrey came around. And tonight, not only was Audrey's old man there, passed out, but Maggie was there too, drunk and loud. That added up to too much booze, not enough sense, and way too much history.

If he'd known she was home, and that she'd be the one sent to get her dad, he wouldn't have called Anne. It wouldn't have been the first time Rusty Harte slept it off in his office.

Jake came out from behind the bar—without the gun—moving on a path to intercept Audrey as she approached her father. A few guys turned their heads to stare at her as she passed. Audrey had grown into her looks over the years. She'd always been pretty, but there was a hard edge to it. She was hot but rough—the sort of woman who might give you the sweetest kiss right before tying your balls in a knot. The sort you'd tell yourself was worth it, and then curse when she left you bleeding.

Yeah, he'd had a lot of time to think about it.

He ignored someone shouting his name. Shrugged them off when they made a sloppy grab at his arm. Fucking drunks.

Jake came up beside Audrey at the same moment Maggie squealed her name. Audrey's face changed—a flicker of surprise followed by a hardening of her jaw, a narrowing of her eyes. People said she had "them Harte devil-eyes," which was as much an insult as it was romantic nonsense. Though they did take some getting used to.

Was Maggie actually going to hug her? Audrey took a step back. Jake took that as his cue. He put himself between them—his back to Maggie because she was the safer bet.

"I'll help you get him out to the car," he said, skipping the niceties. The two of them had never had much use for small talk.

Audrey blinked at him. Looking into her eyes—one blue, one topaz—was like looking at two different people. Not just two different people, but two different people who could both look into the darkest part of you without flinching. It was unnerving.

She didn't speak, but she didn't have to. Her nod, stiff and shallow, said more than any words ever could. Maggie tried to step around him, but Jake pushed her back, shooting her a look over his shoulder that would have told anyone else to fuck off.

Maggie smiled.

John Harte was shorter than Jake, but he was built like a bull, and just as solid. Passed out like he was, he was nothing but deadweight. Jake took his right side as Audrey went left. With an arm about each of their shoulders, and their own arms around his back, they hauled John out of the chair.

Christ, he was heavy! John's steel-toed work boots dragged on the plank floor. Jake glanced at Audrey; she was focused on the exit, but her cheeks were flushed and her nostrils flared. Determination. He knew that look. She would have grabbed her old man by one foot and dragged him out of there on her own if she'd had to. It wouldn't have been pretty, but she would have done it. She couldn't have changed that much over the years, and he knew the only reason she'd accepted *his* help was because she just wanted to get the hell out of there. She could have just as easily punched him in the mouth.

And he'd seen what Audrey could do with those deceptively delicate-looking fists of hers.

Someone laughed when they came out onto the porch. "Night, night, Rusty," he said, snickering.

Jake shot him a glance. It was Albert Neeley. His beer-glazed gaze was unsteady and his knees were slightly bowed. He looked like a drunk bullfrog. "Get your ugly ass off my porch, Neeley. You're bad for business." He jerked his head toward the door. "Last call."

When they reached the bottom of the steps, Jake looked at Audrey. "Go get your car. I'll wait with him." They sat her father down on the rough-hewn wood. Harte's head smacked against the railing. He snorted but didn't wake up. Audrey looked as though she wanted to grab her old man by the hair and try it again.

A cigarette butt landed on the gravel a few feet away from where Jake stood. He glanced up to see the front door close. Last call was taken seriously in this town, and the bar and waitstaff would be overwhelmed with the demands for more beer, more rum, more whiskey, and, occasionally, more wine. He ought to be inside helping out. He ought to be in there encouraging them to drink more. If he was a better man he'd be in there collecting car keys so none of them wrecked their vehicles on the way home. Most of his regulars drove better drunk than sober—years of practice. What he really ought to do was install beds out back and charge for them. Instead of any of those things, he was babysitting one of the town's more notorious drunks on the front step because he'd do just about anything to know that he and Audrey were friends again. His grandmother always said that one good friend was all a person needed. But Gran's standards had been high. To her, a friend would help you dig a grave. A *good* friend would help you put the body in it.

His first memory of Audrey Harte was from when he was about five years old. She and her parents came to Gracie's—which had been a takeout back then—and got ice cream. It was summer, and he would be starting school that fall. Audrey had been watching him and some other kids play, licking her ice-cream cone as her parents talked to some friends. His brother, Lincoln—almost seven and old enough to know better—knocked the ice cream out of her hand, sending it splattering on the hot gravel of the parking lot. Audrey didn't cry. She kicked Lincoln as hard as she could— right in the nuts. He fell into the puddle of ice cream. Only then did Audrey get upset about losing her treat. Jake went in and asked his grandmother for a new cone. She'd given him one for himself too, and he and Audrey sat at one of the picnic tables, eating in silence. Lincoln glared at them both but kept his distance.

When his mother took him and his siblings away a year later, Audrey was the only person he missed. And when his mother returned him to his grandmother with the remark, "He's your problem now," Audrey had been the first friend to welcome him back.

Christ, the first time he got arrested had been with her. Twenty years ago. Just before he'd started to think of her as a girl.

A red Mini Cooper pulled up in front of him. Audrey climbed out of the driver's side and came around to open the passenger door.

"Is that cardboard?" Jake asked, glancing inside at the seat. She shrugged. "Found it out back. I needed something in case he pisses himself." The statement was delivered with absolutely no emotion—just flat matter-of-factness. "It's a rental."

"Smart," Jake replied.

Audrey snorted. "Smart would have been missing my flight." And then, as she bent to collect her father again, "You running the place now?"

"Yeah." He came around to Rusty's other side. "Lincoln helps out." Why had he bothered to tell her that? She probably didn't give two shits if his brother was employed or not.

They managed to get her father into the car and onto the remains of the rum box. "It's like moving a corpse," he joked.

She didn't laugh. She looked at him, though—right in the eye—before stepping back. "Yeah? How many corpses have you moved?" That didn't make things awkward at all.

Jake shut the door, then tugged on the handle to make sure it was latched. "Want me to follow you? Help get him into the house?"

"No. Mum wouldn't like that." She sighed. "Thanks, though."

Jake nodded. "Mine was the same way. I never understood it. Not like it was her fault Dad was a drunk." The one thing that wasn't his mother's fault.

Audrey nodded. "Well, thanks again." She hesitated, then looked up. He swallowed. Went still as her gaze met his. Those damn eyes. "Good night, Jake."

He opened his mouth...

The door to the bar flew open. "Dree! What's your damage?"

Maggie. Of course. She was the punch line to the cosmic fucking joke that was his relationship with Audrey. Jake took a step back to watch the drama unfold. It wasn't the most honorable thing, but he wasn't going to get between them again—that would be begging for trouble.

Soft, blonde, and tottering on four-inch heels, Maggie was everything Audrey wasn't. She'd come back from wherever they'd locked her up as loud and brash as Audrey had turned quiet and focused. Then, she'd stopped partying for a long time and ended up married to one of the town's pride and joys—Gideon McGann. This was the first time Jake had seen her drunk in a long time. Her lipstick was smeared, giving her a vaguely Courtney Love look.

"Are you *seriously* not going to talk to me?" Maggie demanded as she staggered down the steps. "After all we've been through?"

A few people had followed Maggie outside, which Jake took to mean that she'd announced her intent to confront her old friend before heading out. She was still a drama queen.

Audrey frowned. "I didn't come here to talk, Maggie. I came to get my father. You and I can talk later. When you're sober."

Maggie's eyes snapped wide open, but her gaze was still unfocused, giving her a creepy doll-like appearance. "Don't you play all sanctimonious with me, Audrey Harte. I *know* you." She jabbed a skinny finger in Audrey's direction. "I know things about you no one else in this town knows. I could *ruin* you."

Audrey laughed. Jake winced at the sound. "You're welcome to try," she challenged. "But I think we're past that, don't you?"

The air between the two women practically crackled with tension. Jake stared at them along with the rest of the gawkers. No one else spoke. That was Edgeport for you—a town of fucking watchers, like birds lined up on a telephone line. Watching and squawking. So long as you avoided getting shit on, you were okay.

Maggie lurched closer, heels turning on the gravel. Jake imagined her ankle snapping and almost smiled. She stopped right in front of Audrey. In her sandals she was still an inch shorter than her old friend. Her lip quivered. "Come inside and have a drink with me. Just one."

Audrey shook her head. "Sorry. I can't."

Maggie's fingers trailed up Audrey's bare arm. It was a strangely flirtatious gesture. "Yes, you can. Your father will be fine. It will be like it used to be."

"No. It won't."

The blonde pressed closer. How many of the guys watching were sprouting hard-ons? Jake wondered. There had been a time when he would have given his left nut to be part of an Audrey and Maggie sandwich. Now, he found it a little unsettling. It wasn't about being sexy; it was about dominance.

And Maggie had yet to realize that she wasn't alpha anymore.

"I've missed you," Maggie cooed. "Missed my girl. Come on, have a drink with me. Or I'll tell Jake how much you cried the night I fucked him."

Jake flinched. Fourteen years and it was still a top five regret. Top two.

Audrey glanced at him before turning her attention back to the other woman, her face like stone—emotionless. "Bit of a moot point now, Mags." Her voice was eerily calm. "I'm sure you've already told everyone you could about that night. Once you could talk again."

Maggie leaned her head closer and whispered into Audrey's ear. Jake couldn't hear what she said, but it was bad enough for Audrey to give her a shove—hard. Maggie stumbled backward, arms cartwheeling until she landed hard on the steps, her legs splayed. Fortunately she wore shorts, otherwise they would have gotten more than an eyeful—as it was he saw more than he wanted. No one moved to help her. No one said a word. No one would.

Maggie grinned at Audrey. "There's my girl." She cackled. "I knew you were still in there. You want that drink now?"

For a second, Jake thought Audrey was going to go for her throat. Instead, she stomped around the front of the Mini Cooper, yanked the driver's door open, and climbed inside. Gravel flew into the air as she drove away—a pebble struck Jake in the shoulder. It stung.

"Jesus Christ!"

Jake turned. Maggie's husband, Gideon, had arrived to take her home. It was about time. Jake had called him almost twenty minutes ago. He had his daughter, Bailey, with him, and her boyfriend, Isaac. Bailey was a pretty little thing, with hair darker than her father's, and big eyes. In fact, standing there, her face taut with disgust as she stared at her stepmother, she reminded him a lot of Audrey when they were young.

"Maggie, what the hell is wrong with you?" Gideon demanded as he bent down to pick up his wife off the steps. He tugged her shirt down over her exposed midriff as he shot Jake a look that was half-apologetic, half-accusatory. "Sorry about this, Jake."

Jake shrugged. "Nothing to apologize for, man. I just didn't want her trying to drive herself home."

"I appreciate that."

"Dree pushed me," Maggie said, face blotchy and red as her unfocused gaze finally made it to her husband's face. "She shouldn't have done that."

"Hush," Gideon instructed, his tone gentle. "You won't be so upset tomorrow. I bet Audrey will be happy to see you then."

Jake arched a brow. *Yeah, good luck with that.* He glanced up to see Matt Jones—Maggie's brother—on the porch, smoking a cigarette and watching him with a narrow gaze. Jake stared back. The day he backed down from a weasely prick like Jones was the day his grandmother rose from the grave just to slap him in the head.

Binky Taylor—a town institution who was pushing eighty—stepped up beside him. Binky was one of those old men who had a filthy mind, a dirty mouth, and a heart of gold and figured any combination of two out of three made him charming. Most of the time it was true.

"There's some unfinished business 'tween those girls," he announced, as they watched Gideon put Maggie in their car and hand Isaac the keys to Maggie's vehicle for the teens to drive home. The dust from Audrey's departure still lingered in the air.

Jake laughed. "No shit."

Binky spat tobacco juice onto the ground. The glistening glob just missed Jake's foot. "Be interesting to see what happens if one of them decides to finish it."

She was shaking.

Audrey's fingers ached as they clenched the steering wheel. There was a violent churning in her stomach that she hadn't felt in years. A twisted boil of anticipation and hot sick that prickled the soles of her feet and the back of her skull.

Maggie.

They'd been friends once—best friends. Maggie had been the more dominant, but Audrey eagerly followed her lead. Maggie talked Audrey down when she got angry. Maggie made things happen. She knew just what to say or how to act to get exactly what she wanted. That was an amazing power as far as Audrey had been concerned, and it made Audrey realize that manipulation was a far better motivational tool than anger, or even kindness. Then, there was that night with Clint, Maggie's father. Everything changed after that. They were separated for three years, and when Audrey saw her again, Maggie had blossomed into some sort of wildling. Audrey tried to be her friend because she had no other friends, and she and Maggie had a bond, right?

"Fuck," Audrey ground out. In the passenger seat her father snored.

She gritted her teeth.

If anyone had ever deserved to die, it was Clinton Jones. He'd been a lazy, miserable, mean drunk who thought fucking his twelve-year-old daughter was his God-given right. It had been going on for a year before Maggie confided in her. Maggie's mother wouldn't listen, broken as she was. Even Audrey had found it hard to believe that anyone could be so evil, and then she'd seen it with her own eyes.

She sucked in a breath, forced herself to relax. She eased up on the gas pedal and flexed her throbbing fingers. No one ever had the sort of power over her that Maggie had. She was thirty-one years old and Maggie could make her feel seventeen with just a look.

She'd spent three years in a juvenile correctional facility because of what they'd done. She and Maggie had gone in—to different facilities—as friends, but they'd come out so very different. Or at least Audrey had. Maggie hadn't liked that. She hadn't liked that Audrey had found her voice and would speak up for herself, or that she'd acquired the sort of confidence that had come from building physical strength and ability. Or that she'd finally realized that she was smart, and that education could be her ticket out of the life she'd been born to. As soon as Maggie figured out Audrey had a crush on Jake, she pursued him like a DEA dog following a trail of coke. Jake was the one Audrey wanted for herself, and Maggie used him to show Audrey that no matter what she did, or what she wanted, Maggie was *always* going to have things her way.

Of course Jake had to witness her great homecoming. And this wouldn't have all the trappings of a freaking made-for-TV movie if he hadn't retained that rough, pretty-boy edge of his. He still dressed like he was from another era, still had that way of looking at her like he knew what she was thinking. Audrey could have punched him in the mouth for being nice while everyone else stood around gawking and whispering.

No, that wasn't honestly why she could have hit him. He'd broken her heart, just when she'd gotten brave enough to offer it up, and that was why she wanted to knock his teeth down his throat. Back home for less than half an hour and already she wanted to punch people.

She almost missed the house. As it was, she had to hit the brakes hard to make the turn, kicking up gravel as the Mini tore up the driveway.

She pulled up to the front steps and stopped the car. When she got out and opened the passenger door, her father was still out cold—and he hadn't pissed himself. Hooray for small favors.

He wouldn't budge. He probably had close to a hundred pounds on her, and no matter how much she might wish the contrary, she was not strong enough to haul him on her own.

"You fucking piece of shit," she snarled, panting from exertion. If "Daddy Issues" had been a college course she would have gotten a PhD, and she didn't mind admitting it. Everything terrible that had ever happened in her life could be traced back to the man drooling in front of her. Oh, and she knew she was too old to blame him for how fucked-up she was now. As an adult she had the reason and means to curtail that behavior and be the person she wanted to be—all the textbooks told her that.

But that didn't mean she didn't want to kick him. Hard.

Audrey climbed back into the driver's side, wiggling herself around so that she sat facing the passenger seat. Using the steering wheel and seat back for leverage, she set the soles of her shoes against her father's side and pushed. He lolled to the side. She pushed again. His torso fell out the door. One more shove and the rest of him followed. He hit the ground with a grunt and rolled to the foot of the step, where he came to a stop on his stomach.

There. She had picked him up and brought him home. Unless he rolled onto his back there was little chance of him choking on his own vomit, and it was summer, so there was no chance of him

freezing, though at the moment, she wouldn't be all that heartbroken if he did.

She tossed the cardboard on top of him and reached out to
bring the passenger door to a close.

Then, she started the car again and pulled out of the drive. The
one nice thing about growing up in a secretive, closeted little town
like Edgeport was that there were plenty of places for a body to
hide.

Audrey.

In all her life Maggie had never loved or hated someone so
much. Just the sight of her old friend had been enough to make
her heart pound and her temper spike.

Audrey always wanted to save her. Like she needed saving. Like
Audrey was so much *stronger* than she was. She'd come back from
juvy changed, and Maggie's relationship with her died a slow,
horrible death after that. She knew the exact moment it ended—
when Audrey caught her with Jake. She still had scars from it.
If she had to choose the biggest mistake of her life, it was sleeping with Jake Tripp. It was supposed to have driven Audrey back
to her, not further away. She'd underestimated how much Jake
meant to Audrey, and overestimated her own ability to influence
her old friend.

At the time she'd taken some comfort in the fact that she had
the power to make Audrey react so violently. But then one day
she'd realized that it hadn't been her power at all. It had been
Jake's, and he'd used it to make sure Audrey got as far away as she
could—from both of them. The lousy bastard.

Still, she hadn't completely lost her influence. Just a few little
whispered words and Audrey had almost gone over the edge.

Maggie was going to have bruises in the morning from the steps, but it would be worth it if she could make Audrey come to her. She had missed her more than Audrey would ever know. The night they killed Clint, they'd sworn to always protect and never betray each other.

"Guess I fucked that one up," Maggie muttered, staggering through the sand. Good thing she'd taken her shoes off in the camp.

Audrey Harte: the one that got away. She'd done practically everything Maggie asked, but never really what Maggie wanted. No matter how hard she tried, Maggie couldn't bend her. Couldn't keep her. Audrey had left as soon as she could, leaving Maggie on her own—as though she could run away from everything they'd been through together.

As though any amount of distance could change what they'd done.

Audrey had saved her. And Maggie would be fucked if she'd forgive the bitch for it.

She swiped at her cheek with the back of her hand. Shit. She was crying. Pathetic. She should go home, go to bed and sleep, but Gideon was being an ass. He didn't want Bailey—his daughter, not hers—to see her "like this." Like Bailey was some sort of fragile idiot. She loved Maggie, and Maggie loved her.

Or as much as she could love anything. She'd never been very good at it. She always seemed to drive away the people she loved most.

Maggie stopped and looked up. The moon swam in and out of focus above her, surrounded by an ocean of stars. The tide was on its way out, leaving a glossy sheen on the smooth rocks and the smell of salt on the air. This beach was her safe haven and always had been. When they were children she and Audrey came down here every morning they could and spent the entire day, swimming and playing in the sea with Jake and other local kids—and some who were staying at the campground. They'd been the color of walnuts, the pair of them, their hair encrusted with salt and bleached by the sun.

Behind her she heard the crunch of shoes on the sand. Gideon, probably. He didn't like it when she wandered off on her own, especially when she was drunk and driving. Controlling bastard. If it wasn't for Bailey, she would have left him long ago. He was so *boring*. There was no fire in the man at all. Never once had she feared he might say something mean, or hit her. God forbid he ever got rough during sex.

"What do you want?" she demanded, turning around. She moved too quickly and the world shifted before her eyes. A blurry outline of a person wavered before her.

Maggie squinted, and the face came into focus. "Did you follow me?"

There was movement, fast and dizzying. Pain exploded inside Maggie's head. She fell to her knees with a guttural moan that rang in her own ears. She looked up as warm blood ran down the side of her face. She looked right into the cold eyes of her attacker.

"I'm sorry," she whispered, tears stinging her eyes. She held up her hands in supplication. "I'm so sorry."

But then they swung again. Maggie's skull came apart, and there was nothing.

CHAPTER THREE

Her father was still in the dooryard when Audrey returned home an hour and a half later. She'd been tempted to go to the beach, or maybe the camp, but that would mean driving back Tripp's Cove, and past Gracie's old house. It was a journey she wasn't ready to make just yet. So she'd driven back the Ridge and parked by the river until the fight drained out of her. Now, she was just exhausted.

She got out of the car and approached her father. "Oh, fuck." She put her hand over her nose. He'd pissed himself. Son of a bitch. She'd kick him in the kidneys if she didn't think it would make him wetter.

Audrey glanced at the keys in her hand and sighed. Running off again wouldn't change anything, and if he woke up on his own, he would probably stagger into the house and pass out on the sofa or bed—soiling either one with his sour funk. He wouldn't be the one who had to clean it up later either.

She crouched next to him, barely flinching at the stink now that it had registered—the nose never forgot a smell like booze, sweat, and urine; it was a unique bouquet. Familiar. Almost reassuring.

Her father drooled on his sleeve, face smooshed up against his arm. She could turn the hose on him, but he'd probably start screaming and wake up her mother—and the neighbors. Never mind that there was an entire field and a barn between them and the nearest house.

Headlights cut through the night, fixing her in their blinding glare. A minivan came up the drive as Audrey shielded her eyes. Slowly, she rose to her feet, blinking away the dots that always made her think of gasoline the way the colors played on the backs of her eyes.

The van parked beside the Cooper. The overhead light came on when the driver opened the door.

Jessica and Greg.

Oh, hell. The night just kept getting better and better. Maybe Maggie could stop by and tell her every detail about what it felt like to have Jake inside her as well. That would be the icing.

"Hey, Audrey," her brother-in-law said, getting out first. He always looked at her as though she were a puppy he thought might bite his hand if he held it out to her, but he was determined to try anyway. "Welcome home. Everything okay?"

Before Audrey could answer, the passenger door slammed shut and Jessica came around the front of the vehicle. She'd cut her hair into a cute chin-length style since the last bunch of family photos her mother had e-mailed her. She was frowning, but that was nothing new. "What's Dad doing on the ground?"

"It's good to see you too, Jess." Audrey fought the urge to fold her arms over her chest. That was a defensive posture and she wasn't going to show any weakness in front of her older sister. "He's on the ground because he's passed out in a puddle of his own piss."

Jessica's frown turned into a scowl. "You planned to just leave him there, didn't you?"

"No," Audrey lied. "I was just trying to figure out how to get him inside. It's not like I can fireman-carry him." Also, the idea of draping his piss-soaked body over her shoulders was beyond revolting.

"I'll help you," Greg offered. Jessica had him well trained.

"He's wrecked and he stinks," Audrey said. "You don't want to get that on you."

He smiled, blue eyes crinkling at the corners. The fact that Jessica hated her never seemed to affect how Greg treated her. "I'm not planning on dirty dancing with him."

"Fair enough. I'll take his feet."

Her sister got the door. Her nose wrinkled as Audrey, arms wrapped around their father's knees, staggered past.

"That for me, or him?" Audrey asked.

A cool blue gaze locked with hers. "You're the one with the psych degree—can't you figure it out?"

"Doctorate. I have a PhD, not a 'degree.'"

That cool gaze went completely glacial. "Yes, I know. I'm reminded of it every time someone asks Mom how you're doing."

People asked about her? "Huh."

It had always been a sore spot with Jessica that Audrey was able to obtain the education she had. Unlike her little sister, Jessica hadn't had the benefit of a sponsor. Getting that education hadn't been easy; Audrey had taken as many courses as she could through the school year, and summer classes as well. She volunteered for everything she could, cramming as much knowledge and experience as she could into her eager brain. Knowledge was synonymous with freedom, and freedom meant she didn't have to go back to Edgeport unless she wanted to.

Or was emotionally blackmailed into it. She could be back in L.A. right now, asleep in her bed. Not lugging a farting sack of deadweight up the steps and into the house where she'd grown up too fast, her older sister behind her—probably ready to plunge a knife between Audrey's shoulder blades.

"Oh my lord!" Anne Harte cried as her husband was half-lugged, half-dragged into the kitchen. She rushed toward them, stopping short just a few feet away, her face contorted in a second's worth of disgust; it never lasted long. "Take him to the sunporch."

Of course she'd pick the room the farthest away from the kitchen. Why couldn't she have a couch in the kitchen like Audrey's grandmother had? Her shoulders were already feeling the strain of carrying her father, but once this was done, hopefully she'd be able to relax.

"I'll get him some clean clothes," Jessica suggested.

She'd better be prepared to put them on him, Audrey thought, because she wasn't going to.

"I'll get them," their mother said. "You take care of the kids."

The kids. Kids Audrey had never seen in person. The amazing grandchildren to whom her mother referred as "probably the only ones I'll ever get," and of whom she regularly e-mailed Audrey photos.

Her toe caught on the threshold to the sunporch, almost sending her crashing to the floor. Wouldn't that be a perfect ending to the night—landing in her father's pissy lap. With her luck she'd fall face first.

"God, he's heavy," she remarked. She and Greg had a good hold on him, but still his butt sagged toward the floor.

"Most of it's skull," Greg replied.

"And that chip on his shoulder."

"That too. Lift."

Audrey lifted her father's legs as much as she could, shoulders burning. They half-dropped, half-laid him on the small couch that used to be a bed for a dog they had when Audrey was young. It was a good place for her father to sleep it off, and not far from the downstairs bathroom.

"Should we take his boots off?" Greg asked.

She shook her head. "Nah. It will be better if he thinks he got here on his own. He wouldn't bother to take them off."

"Better for who?"

Her gaze moved from her father to her brother-in-law. God, she was tired. "Everyone who likes to pretend there's nothing wrong."

Greg's blue eyes glinted with understanding. Did he have a drunk in his family too? "Can I help you bring your bags in?"

"That would be great, thanks."

Her mother was in the living room, gathering up toys and putting them in the trunk by the TV. That was Jessica she heard upstairs then, along with a sleepy little voice. Why didn't they just leave the kids for the night? Wouldn't that be better than dragging them out of bed? She wasn't going to ask—it would just be an invitation for her sister to remind her that her PhD *wasn't* in child psychology. And what did *she* know about being a mother?

Outside, Audrey opened the trunk for Greg. Then she removed her carry-on and bag from the backseat while her brother-in-law collected her suitcase.

"Did you have a good flight?" he asked as they approached the house.

"Not bad."

"And the show? It's still doing well?"

"It is."

He stepped in front of her. She had to jerk back to avoid colliding with him. "Look, I know it's been years and we barely know each other, but your sister is going to quiz me on you later, and if I don't have answers longer than two words for her, she's going to be pissed."

His expression was one of such mock pleading that Audrey couldn't help but smile. "Really? You have to know the idea of irritating her thrills my inner child."

"I know there's a lot of hurt between the two of you."

She shot him a dry glance as she opened the door to the house. "You should go into psychology with that keen sense of observation."

Greg crossed the threshold into the house before her. "But it takes so long to get a PhD. Nice of you to throw that in her face, by the way."

Heat filled Audrey's cheeks. Jessica had gone to a local college and worked at a doctor's office. She'd wanted to go into medicine but hadn't the grades or money to achieve that goal. That was probably the second-biggest reason she despised Audrey as she did.

"I know it was low," she confessed, closing and locking the door as they both stepped into the porch. "But the fact that her life didn't turn out the way she planned is no more my fault than my plethora of fuckups is hers."

"You and your clinical mumbo jumbo." He grinned over his shoulder. "You want me to take these upstairs?"

"I'll take them, thanks. Just set them down out of the way." He did, and Audrey set the bags she carried on top.

She straightened to find her mother and sister standing there. Her mother had a baby in her arms, while Jessica carted a sleeping five-year-old who was missing a sock. Her husband took the little girl from her.

This was the first time Audrey had seen her sister's children. It was a little more painful than she'd ever expected. She stood there dumbly, staring as the five-year-old—Isabelle was her name— dropped her head onto her father's shoulder. Long, thick lashes parted, and for one heart-pinching moment, Audrey found herself looking into her own eyes.

"Heterochromia," she murmured. "She has it too."

Jessica shot her a sharp glance. "It doesn't mean she's like you."

That probably should have hurt more than it did. "Well, yeah, it kind of does. At least a little bit." Her sister looked as though she were going to pop any second.

"Girls," their mother admonished with a sigh of long-suffering, handing the baby to Jessica. "Please. Not tonight."

Neither of them argued.

"Who are you?" Isabelle asked, watching her with a familiar intensity. So far, the kid had yet to do anything to back up Jessica's theory. She had Audrey's eyes, her bluntness, and her watchfulness.

Please don't let her be like me. Taunting her sister with it was one thing, but reality was another.

"That's your Auntie Audrey," Greg explained. "Can you say hello?"

Another yawn. "Hello. You're pretty."

Audrey smiled. It was hard not to. "Thank you, so are you."

"Okay," Jessica interjected. "Time to go."

So, she wasn't going to be allowed to get to know her nieces while she was home. It was probably better that way. Better not to get attached. God knew when she'd see them again, and eventually their mother would tell them about their awful Aunt Audrey and they wouldn't want anything to do with her anyway. It would be less painful if she just never got to know them.

Jessica slung a flowered bag full of diapers, formula, and onesies over her shoulder while balancing the sleeping baby in her other arm. She kissed their mother's cheek and walked past Audrey without so much as a sideways glance. It was a good thing she had that baby or Audrey would give in to the temptation to kick her feet out from under her.

Suddenly, Jessica stopped. "What is this?" she demanded, pulling a photo from Audrey's bag, turning it so both Audrey and their mother could see it. It was a photo of what David Solomon had done to one of his boyfriend's attackers. It was clinical and graphic and lit by a harsh flash.

Audrey snatched it from her hand. "It's work."

Jessica glared at her. "Just like you to leave that somewhere a child could see it."

She was not going to take the bait. Wait. Yes, she was. "Your child wouldn't have noticed if you hadn't stuck your nosy hand into my bag and pulled it out. That photo could have been of kittens and unicorns and you still would find fault with it."

Her sister's eyes narrowed. Audrey's right hand curled into a fist. *Give me a reason.*

A look of panic passed between Greg and her mother. "Come on, babe," Greg said in a gentle tone. "Let's get the girls home."

"What sort of person would do something like that?" Jessica asked, jerking her chin at the photo in Audrey's hands. The baby stirred against her shoulder, rubbing tiny fists across her squished-up face.

God, that bait was so tempting. Of course she rose to it. "A young man society failed."

It was almost like a physical strike, the moment when their gazes actually locked. Jessica smirked at her. "That's a phrase they use when trying to defend a monster."

Audrey frowned. "They who? *CSI: Nebraska*, or one of those other shows you watch?" For someone who claimed to abhor violence, Jessica watched a lot of procedurals. Audrey knew this because she often stalked her sister's Facebook page when she had too much to drink, and Jess had a lot of posts about the shows and their "hunky" cast members in her feed.

The shorter woman bristled. "Are you mocking me?"

She thought *that* was mocking? "I'm saying that TV doesn't paint an authentic picture of forensic psychology. Not all monsters are obvious."

"I think I know a monster when I see one," Jess shot back. If her meaning were any more clear it would be a sheet of glass breaking over Audrey's head.

The room went dead silent—as though all the breath and life had been sucked out of it. Audrey's mother and Greg were completely still—frozen, cringing statues waiting for the inevitable blowup.

But it was Isabelle's wide-eyed and fearful face that changed everything. Audrey knew that expression—she'd worn it many times at that same age when she couldn't understand why her father acted the way he did, when he scared her.

Audrey turned to Jessica, met that hateful gaze. There would be no changing it. Her sister thought she had every right to hate her, and it wasn't Audrey's place to say she didn't. "If I'm your measuring stick, Jess, you really don't know monsters. Not at all." Then, to her mother, "I'll take my bags upstairs. Greg, it was good to see you. Good night, Miss Izzy." She smiled at the little girl and got a hesitant smile—and a wave—in return.

She took her larger suitcase and carry-on up the stairs to the room that had been hers for as long as she could remember. Jessica's room had been turned into a quilting room, but Audrey's room was exactly as she'd left it before going to college. It was lavender and black—a great bruise of a room that was as painful to be in as it was to look at. So many memories. So many regrets.

Her mother had made the quilt and shams on the bed by hand—and the curtains that hung in the window, indulging her younger daughter's ghastly taste in decor. It had been an effort to make everything okay. To make Audrey okay.

It hadn't worked.

She could live with her sister's hatred. She could live without knowing her nieces. She could live without ever coming back to this place again, but she could not live with her mother thinking that she was somehow to blame for the fact that at thirteen years old, Audrey, who was no stranger to the local police, had helped kill a pedophile—a *real* monster.

She put her carry-on on the desk and rolled her suitcase over to the closet. She wanted to take a pill, crawl into bed, and put this day behind her. She was exhausted, and it was only a few minutes past eleven, L.A. time. Normally she'd be reading, watching some TV, or out with acquaintances. This kind of weariness had nothing to do with what time it was, and pretending otherwise would only be a futile lesson in denial.

If nothing else, that doctorate of hers had provided a heap of self-awareness.

After laying out clothes to wear to the birthday party—why had she agreed to an almost-weeklong visit as her mother's birthday present?—Audrey washed her face, moisturized, brushed her teeth, and slipped into a tank top and cotton shorts. She was just folding back the unnecessary quilt when her mother knocked on the door.

"Can I come in?"

Audrey straightened. "Sure."

She watched as her mother approached. When had she gotten so tiny? She'd never been a big woman, but she'd lost weight. It made her look older. Or maybe she looked just as she ought to, and it was only Audrey's memories of her that said otherwise, and no one looked the same in their sixties as they did in their forties—not without help.

Her mother was still attractive. In her youth she'd been known as one of the prettiest girls in the area, though years of living with Rusty Harte had taken their toll. When she smiled, though—all cheeks and sweetness—the whole world smiled with her, just as Audrey did.

"Look at you," her mother said. "I see you in this room and think you're still seventeen, but you're a woman. A beautiful, successful woman."

Audrey's eyes prickled. If she started crying it would be the icing on the burnt shit-brick cake of a day. "Thanks, Mum. Sorry about the thing with Jess."

Her mother waved a slender hand. "Jessica isn't happy unless she's angry about something. Thank you for picking up your father. Was he happy to see you?"

"He was unconscious when I got there." She hated having to tell her that.

Anne's lips thinned as she nodded her head—just once. "Did you run into any old friends?"

Audrey hated having to answer that even more. She could lie, but people would be talking about it tomorrow. There was always talk. You couldn't pick your nose in this town without someone having something to say about it.

"Jake. And Maggie." Just saying her name was a lesson in rage management. It had been so long since she'd felt that kind of anger.

The invisible string holding her mother's back straight snapped. Her shoulders sagged. "Oh, Auddie. I...I never thought. I'm so sorry."

Audrey shrugged. "Maggie grabbed me and I shoved her. I'm only telling you this because I know you'll hear about it tomorrow."

"Anyone who says anything will be asked to leave. It's my damn birthday, and I won't have anyone gossiping about my baby girl."

Oh, hell. "It's okay, Mum." She sniffed. "Do you need help with Dad? Because I'm wiped. We filmed today, and then with the flight and Maggie and Jess...I just want to go to bed."

Her mother came closer, opening her arms. Audrey braced herself as those same arms wrapped around her—as strong and comforting as she remembered. She closed her eyes and held her breath. She hadn't seen her mother since last fall, when they'd met up for a long weekend in New York. She could probably spout a dozen theories, quote studies, and postulate on the effect of maternal affection, but it would all be shit. Her mother's arms around her felt as wonderful as they did terrible, and it had nothing to do with her mother, and everything to do with herself.

She couldn't help herself; she hugged back. She would always hug back, and hope that she didn't apply so much pressure that she cracked her mother's ribs. For a moment, she let herself feel, but only for a moment. Then she let go. And stepped back.

"Good night," she said.

Anne smiled—maybe it was sad, or maybe it was just tired. "Good night. Pancakes for breakfast."

Audrey's lips stretched into a mockery of a smile. "Sounds great."

At the door, her mother glanced back at her and blew her a kiss. Then she was gone, the latch clicking behind her.

Audrey sank to the bed, gripping the edge of the mattress with white knuckles.

She never should have come home.

She woke to the smell of pancakes and coffee. For a moment, the world was good and exactly as it should be.

But then she looked up at the black ceiling and lavender walls and remembered where she was.

"Fuck," Audrey rasped, sitting up. She dragged her fingers through the wild tangle of her hair. She should have left it tied back when she'd gone to sleep.

She sighed and threw back the blankets. As soon as she was out of the bed, she turned around and made it back up, so that no one would ever know it had been slept in. That particular habit had been hard learned in Stillwater—the facility that had been her home for three years. It was one of the few that actually stuck. That, and where to punch someone so the bruises didn't show.

After changing into her running gear—if she was going to eat both pancakes and birthday cake in the same day, she was going to have to work for it—she went to the bathroom, made an effort to smooth her hair, and twisted it into a bun on the back of her head. She pulled on her sneakers before running downstairs.

Two things struck Audrey as she entered the kitchen: Her father was at the table in his bathrobe with a huge orange cat on his lap, and the kitchen looked nothing like she remembered. The walls had been painted a rich cream, the cabinets were dark, and all the appliances were stainless steel. There was even a butcher-block island. The table and chairs looked new as well—or at least, new to her. What other changes had taken place? And if they could do all of this, why couldn't they paint her room so it didn't look like a damn hematoma?

Her mother was at the stove, dressed in jeans and a blouse. Her highlighted brown hair hung neatly around her shoulders. She even had some makeup on. "Hey, sunshine," she said as she flipped the pancake in the pan before her. "Grab some coffee. Breakfast is just about ready."

Audrey went to the counter, grabbed the biggest mug she could find (the one she'd made for her mother twenty years earlier in a pottery class), and filled it with coffee, cream, and an unhealthy amount of sugar. When she had it as pale and as sweet as she liked it, she raised the cup and took a drink. Heaven.

She turned toward the table and stopped short. Her father had lifted his head from his magazine and was staring right at her.

He wasn't a bad-looking man, her father. He wasn't going to make *People*'s Sexiest Man Alive any time soon, but he wasn't ugly. He was, however, scruffy and weathered. His once ruddy hair and beard were mostly gray, and the lines around his eyes and across his brow had deepened. But his stare—one eye brown and the other blue—made her feel like he saw things inside her that she never let anyone see, even when bloodshot and tired. It was stupid, she knew that, and not just because people couldn't actually see inside one another. But she had those same eyes, and she'd gotten her fascination with understanding people somewhere.

"Hi, Dad," she said finally. This wasn't awkward or anything. He probably had her shoe prints on his back.

"Hi back atcha, kid. Thanks for dragging me home last night."

Audrey nodded. That would be the end of the discussion. It always was. She'd tried talking to him about his drinking once. He'd looked her dead in the eye and informed her that he didn't have a problem, and who the fuck did she think she was to point a finger at him?

"Here you go, Auddie," her mother announced, setting a plate of food on the table.

She stared at it. "You expect me to eat all that? Mom, that's enough food for three people."

Anne waved a hand at her. "Just eat what you want and I'll feed the rest to the crows."

"Goddamned crows," Rusty murmured, before taking a slurp from his coffee mug. His wife put her hand on his shoulder. He reached up and took that hand in his own, pressing his lips to her knuckles. It was an oddly intimate gesture—and completely out of character for them both. Audrey tried not to stare, but she couldn't help it.

She pulled out a chair and sat down before the monstrous feed her mother had dished up. Four pancakes, hash browns, eggs, and sausage. The eggs had been cooked in the sausage grease, the pancakes in rich butter. She was going to die of a heart attack before even taking a bite.

Her father handed her the maple syrup. It was in a whiskey bottle, of course. He always saved his empties for syrup in the spring.

Audrey unscrewed the cap and tipped the bottle over her plate. So. Much. Sugar. She hacked into the stack of pancakes with her fork and shoved the layers into her mouth.

"Oh my God," she practically moaned.

Her parents laughed. It was the most bizarrely "normal" moment she'd ever experienced in that house, and it was cut short the moment the phone rang. Her mother went to the living room to answer it.

"Someone calling about the party," her father supposed, seemingly oblivious to the cat snoring on his lap. "She was supposed to let Jess take care of all of it, but that didn't last long."

Audrey swallowed another bite of carbohydrate heaven—this time with a bit of sausage speared on the end of her fork. "I'm not surprised. Does she still buy all her own Christmas gifts?"

"Mostly, but I still manage to get a few surprises in. I'm pretty sure the bracelet I got her for her birthday is going to be a dim second to having you home."

All that flour and sugar started to turn to a heavy brick in Audrey's gut. "Dad..."

He held up his hand. "I know. The 'why don't you come home more' horse has been beaten so much it's nothing but dust and an old hoof. I'm not trying to give you grief, just saying thank you for making this special for her."

Audrey frowned. What was his angle? Was he sucking up to her because he felt bad about her having to pick him up? Probably not.

Rusty cleared his throat and took a drink of his coffee. "Bertie said you and Maggie had words."

So much for breakfast. "It was nothing. She was drunk." She

scowled. "And Albert Neeley's a nosy old fool who doesn't know when to keep his mouth shut."

"I will not argue with you there." A pause. An assessing look. "You okay?"

Why was everyone so unnaturally interested in her mental state? She hadn't been the one to go to the psych hospital. "Fine." She pushed her plate away and her chair back. "I'd better go for my run if I want to be ready in time for the party. Tell Mum not to feed my breakfast to the crows."

She had one foot outside when her father called after her, "Hey, kiddo?"

Audrey turned her head.

Rusty smiled. "Next time you kick me out of a vehicle, could you do it in your bare feet?"

Audrey arched a brow. "You should just be grateful the car wasn't moving."

The door closed behind her.

CHAPTER FOUR

Jake was drinking coffee on the front porch, reading an old, dog-eared paperback, when he heard a car coming down the dirt road toward his house. He glanced up—a plume of dry gray dust hung over the tops of the trees that lined the road as a familiar blue SUV came around the bend. It was traveling fast—faster than the limit posted in increments along the main road all the way to the beach and back.

The vehicle didn't slow down until it was in his driveway, where it jerked to a stop. Jake set his book on the table beside him, took his bare feet off the rail, and stood, hands in the pockets of his jeans.

The door of the SUV flew open and his sister jumped out. She was pale, green eyes wild.

"Yance?" Jake came down the steps, the wood warm beneath his feet. "What's wrong? Is it Alisha?" Next to his sister, his niece was one of the few family members he actually liked. Loved, even.

Yancy stopped in her tracks and looked at him, dazed. "Lish? No. Jake…there's…there's a dead body on the beach."

"What?" He crossed the small expanse of smooth gravel between them. "Take me."

Seconds later they were tearing back the road, pebbles pinging off the sides of the vehicle.

Jake turned his head toward his sister. "Who is it?"

Her hands gripped the steering wheel so hard her knuckles were white. When she glanced at him, the SUV swerved to the right, hitting the loose gravel.

"Road," he said.

Yancy yanked the wheel, putting the vehicle back on the smooth track. He should have driven. She was too freaked out. "I don't know who it is. One of the guests found her."

He dragged his fingers through his hair. "Fuck." They'd be lucky if every cottage didn't empty out by noon.

"Tell me you're not thinking about business when someone is dead on our land."

"I'm thinking about Edgeport." It wasn't a complete lie. The Tripps had owned the entire cove for almost three hundred years, but beach access had always been shared with the town, and no one had ever died on it that he knew of. This was going to be talked about for the next fifty years regardless of the circumstances.

She glanced at him. "Edgeport's survived worse situations than a body on the beach."

"*Our* beach. Found by one of *our* guests."

She made a face. "Sometimes you're coldhearted. You know that, right?"

"Yeah. I know." Jake turned to the window. "Wonder who I got that from?"

Yancy didn't respond—he knew she wouldn't. Their mother was the one subject upon which the two of them never agreed, despite Marianne Tripp having eventually abandoned all of her children.

Though the road was gravel, it was well traveled enough to be hard packed and smooth in places worn by car tires. The drive out to the point—where the resort was—was smooth as long as Yancy kept off the shoulder. Jake made sure of it, often patching any ruts or potholes himself. The six-mile journey was quick. His sister drove down the access road to the beach. Locals often used the road to have picnics or swim—not that the Gulf of Maine was all that swimmer friendly. The water was cold, sometimes rough, and close enough to the Bay of Fundy that the tidal range was just shy of twenty feet. There'd even been great white sightings in the past few years. A local man had actually caught one last summer. That wasn't enough to deter locals, who were used to swimming in the chilly waves, but most guests who checked in to the cottages and main building of the Cove Resort preferred the heated outdoor pool.

"The woman who found the body," he said as they neared the end of the access road. "Offer her family a free night—two, even. See what it would take to persuade them to stay."

His sister shot him a look he chose to ignore. She was all heart, without an ounce of sense when it came to business. Happy guests were return guests, and he hadn't built an old campground into a very lucrative hideaway to let a corpse fuck it up.

The SUV came to a stop. Jake jumped out and came around the front of the vehicle, squinting. He hadn't brought sunglasses, and the midmorning sun was already fairly bright—and warm—more so than usual for late June.

That should make the body nice and ripe.

Yancy joined him and pointed up the beach. "She said it was up there, by one of the fire pits."

Jake nodded. He'd built each of those pits himself and knew exactly where they were located. "I'll go look. You go back to the main building and call the cops."

She glanced up, her gaze locking with his. "You don't want me to come with you?"

"You don't need to see a corpse. We don't know what kind of condition it's in." He hadn't been able to protect his little sister from the world when they were younger, and he knew he couldn't do it now, but he had to try.

It might have been his imagination, or the sun in his eyes, but he thought she turned a little gray. "Okay, sure. What should I tell them?"

"That a guest claims to have found a body and where. Oh, and tell them I'll be at the site when they arrive."

Her head turned in the direction she'd pointed. "Do you think it's someone we know?"

"I'd bet money on it." And he never played fast and loose when it came to money. "Go, now. I don't want the cops asking why it took us so long to call."

She nodded and jogged back to the vehicle. Jake started up the beach, keeping to the gravel to avoid the cluster of larger rocks closer to the bank. Tiny particles of stone, worn smooth by centuries of tidal tumbling, slipped through his toes, danced warmly over the tops of his feet. He used his hand to shield his eyes from the harsh glare of the sun.

He walked for a few minutes, the breeze ruffling his hair. Dead bodies had their own particular bouquet, but he didn't smell anything but beach. He didn't even see the body until he was almost on top of it—a large length of driftwood partially concealed it.

It was a woman—blonde, slim but hippy. She wore a pink T-shirt and tiny denim shorts that had been further molded to her backside by salt water. He couldn't see her face, but he didn't need to. It was Maggie. He knew from the butterfly tattoo on her left wrist. Her head had literally been bashed in. Her skull looked like broken porcelain; blood and brain clung thick and wet around the fragments. There was no way this could have been an accident—one strike didn't do that much damage. Whoever had hit her, they'd done it more than once.

"Fuck," he muttered. Maggie could be a real bitch, but who would want to off her? And with that much rage? There was only one person he could think of.

Audrey.

It hadn't been her—and that wasn't his dick talking. If Audrey hadn't killed Maggie that night long ago on this very beach, she wouldn't do it now. She had too much to lose, and she was too smart to do something like this. This was sloppy. Whoever had done it probably got a lot of blood on their hands. There wasn't much left on Maggie, though.

The tide was already on its way back in, but high tide wasn't for another few hours. The sand all around Maggie was still slightly damp, as were her clothes. At high tide last night she'd been at least partially submerged, which probably washed away a good amount of any evidence left behind.

He ran the tidal chart in his head. The tide would have been high around two o'clock that morning—a couple of hours after Gideon dragged Maggie home and Audrey left with her father. The waterline on the shore showed how far the waves had gotten to the bank—about a foot past Maggie's head. She'd probably been killed where she lay, or not far from it. He searched the area with his gaze. No discernible footprints, but then he would have been surprised if there were, given that there was more gravel than sand along that part of the shore.

Not far from her body—above the waterline—was a rock the size of a softball. It was a soft blue shade, and the dried blood on it could have been mistaken for red clay if it weren't for the clots and hair stuck to it.

She'd been killed the same way she and Audrey had killed her father. Everyone in town knew they'd bashed Clint's head in like one of those piñatas at a kid's birthday party. There was no way the cops weren't going to suspect Audrey of doing this. Christ, maybe he was giving her too much credit and she really had. Regardless, he pulled his cell phone from his pocket and swiped his finger over the screen. He took photos of the wound, the rock, and the entirety of Maggie's body, careful not to disturb the spot any further. He didn't dare turn her over. The last thing he needed was the staties taking a closer look at *him*.

Should he call Audrey? Warn her? He didn't know her number, but Anne's birthday was scheduled for that afternoon at the hall. He could call there.

He hesitated. If he warned her, she wouldn't be surprised when the cops talked to her, and only guilty people didn't look surprised when the cops showed up. From the way she had looked at him the night before, she wouldn't appreciate the heads-up.

His phone rang. Up until a few years ago, cell reception had been shit in the area, but then a cell tower went up and made annoying the fuck out of people that much easier.

It was Yancy.

"Did you call the police?" he asked.

"They're on their way."

"Thanks." He turned his back to the sun—and to Maggie. "Don't come down, and close the gate. The beach is closed."

"Who is it?" Her voice was slightly high, anxious.

"Not sure," he lied. If he told Yancy it was Maggie, it would be all over town within the hour. His sister was a sweetheart, but she couldn't keep a secret if her life depended on it.

"What do you mean you're not sure? Are...are they missing their face?"

"Just close the beach, Yance." He disconnected and put the phone back in his pocket before turning to look at the body once more. He sat down on the driftwood and studied every inch of the scene in front of him, before coming back to the ruined skull, smashed into fragments.

"Jesus, Maggie," he mused, raking a hand through his hair. "What the fuck did you do?"

* * *

The community hall had a small kitchen with a stove, a refrigerator, a coffeemaker, and a large carafe for hot water. Audrey stood at the counter with its chipped Formica, measuring out scoops of coffee and dumping them in the coffeemaker basket. She did this as slowly as possible, dragging what should have been a two-minute task into one that took five. The longer she spent in the kitchen, the less time she had to spend in the next room where her mother's party was just getting under way.

Her sister had gotten there an hour before Audrey and their mother in order to finish decorating. That wasn't a surprise. Jess would have gotten up at five in order to avoid asking Audrey for help—and so she could take all the credit for the party. She was welcome to it. Audrey didn't want any responsibility for those god-awful streamers and gaudy balloons.

She closed the lid on the coffeemaker and pressed the start button to begin brewing. The water for tea had been taken care of. All that was left was to start taking food out to the table that stood the length of the entire side wall. Paper plates and plastic utensils were already out there, on the bright pink tablecloth, along with plastic cups for cold drinks and thicker paper ones for coffee and tea. There was so much color on that table—pink, green, yellow, white, and blue—that the only sane explanation for it could be that Jess had found a bunch of leftover Easter products on sale. Either that or she was color-blind.

Taking food out—especially if she took only one thing at a time—would require more time spent in the kitchen, looking busy. That worked. She picked up a plastic-wrapped tray of sandwiches and started for the door.

Jessica suddenly appeared at the threshold, as though she'd been lying in wait. It wouldn't be at all surprising if she had been.

"What are you doing?" she demanded.

Audrey glanced down at the sandwiches, then back up at her sister's face. "I'm absconding with the egg salad, of course. You know how I feel about egg salad."

Jessica's cheeks flushed. She snatched the platter out of Audrey's hands. "You can't take that out there."

"Why not?" Audrey challenged. "Because people will think Crazy Audrey poisoned it? Give me a break, Jess." She'd be hurt if her sister were capable of hurting her. All Jessica ever seemed to do was piss her off. The psychologist in her knew it was a coping mechanism; the brat in her stuck out her tongue.

"Because I don't want you touching the food. It's that simple."

"You know, you should really see someone about these paranoid delusions you seem to have where I'm concerned. It's not healthy. Fine, you don't want me handling food? I'll go greet people at the door and ask if any of them have any antipsychotics they could spare. That will freak them out."

The sandwiches were thrust back at her so fast and hard that the edge of the platter dug between her ribs. "Jesus, Jess!" She managed to grab the dish before it fell. "I was joking!"

Her sister leaned in, face red, blue eyes glittering. "If you ruin this day for Mom...," she began.

Audrey set the sandwiches on the stove and stepped forward so they were only inches apart. "You'll what? Make me sorry?" Her gaze searched the other woman's face for even the smallest bit of love or affection. There was none. "You really think you can make me any sorrier than I already am?"

"I don't think you're sorry enough!" her sister hissed. "You ruined our lives, and then you just went away, leaving the rest of us to suffer!"

"I went to a correctional facility, not summer camp."

Jessica's face contorted into a sneer. "And then you went to college with all that money Gracie Tripp gave you."

Audrey frowned. "I can't believe you're still pissed about that. I didn't ask her for help. It's not like you didn't get to go to college too."

"Community college. It's hardly the same thing, is it, Miss PhD? You helped kill a man and I paid for it more than you did. Do you know how many times people have turned away from me, or whispered about me, or gave me pitying looks because of you?"

Okay, this was quickly escalating to a point neither of them should go to—not at a party for their mother. Because if Jessica kept talking, Audrey was going to punch her in the face.

She took a deep breath. "I'm sorry if what I did affected you. I'm sorry people treated you differently." She didn't bother to remind her sister that people turned away from her as well. And she wasn't going to stand there and make excuses for having done something that was mostly inexcusable. She was, however, going to give her sister something to chew on other than bitterness.

"What would you do to someone who hurt Isabelle?"

Jessica's face darkened into an expression that was so much their father, so much herself, that Audrey almost stepped back. But she didn't. "I protected my friend, and that's one less monster you have to worry about coming for your girls. You heard the rumors about him." There had been stories that other girls in the town had been molested by Clint, but only one had come forward, and she hadn't testified at the trial.

"Am I supposed to thank you?" her sister asked. "Because I'm not going to."

Audrey shrugged and picked up the much-abused egg sandwiches once again. "Do what you want. I've had to live with what I did, Jess. I'm sorry if you have to live with it too, but neither of us can change it." She stepped around her sister. She only made it two steps.

"Would you?" Jess's voice was low, and a little too hopeful for Audrey's conscience. "Change it?"

Audrey looked back over her shoulder and met her sister's gaze. "Yes." And when her sister's expression softened, she added, "We wouldn't have gotten caught."

Dear Audrey,

It feels weird, writing you a letter you'll never read, but my shrink thinks it will be "cathartic" for me, so here I am. How are you? God, that's so stupid of me to ask questions you won't answer. That you *can't* answer.

I miss you. If you could read this you probably wouldn't believe me, but I do. No one knows me like you do, especially not at the Fairchild Academy of Cosmetology. What a pompous name, huh? It's hardly Stanford, but I'm good at it. I like it, and when I'm making someone beautiful, my head is quiet. Silent. God, it's *so* awesome. Remember when we'd do each other's hair and makeup? Your mom would let us play at her vanity, and we'd pretend we were movie stars. It was so long ago, but I miss that too.

I'm sorry about what happened with Jake. I just wanted you to see that he wasn't good enough for you. He's a fucking jerk. I don't know why you'd want him anyway. You deserve someone who will treat you better. You deserve to be loved, Dree. Everyone does.

Even me.

Audrey slumped against the wall. "Kill me."

They were only an hour into the party, which was to last another three hours. There'd already been so many people coming by that they had to start on the second cake. Audrey had inhaled a piece of each. She'd needed the sugar to deal with the half dozen or so people who had braved talking to her. The conversations had been awkward, obvious bids for information. Some had seemed more sincere than others—and she'd give them props for being reasonably polite—but basically they all wanted to know how debauched her life was in the evil, glossy den of purgatory that was L.A. And they wanted to see just how Anne Harte's "problem child" had turned out.

One of them—who exactly, she couldn't remember—had actually asked her if everyone in L.A. "did the cocaine," like it was a dance or a tax form.

Her younger brother, David, grinned and handed her a cup of coffee. The two of them were just inside the kitchen, right in the doorway so Jessica couldn't accuse them of hiding. "Suck it up, sunshine. It's about time you had to suffer like the rest of us."

She took a sip from the cup. God, it was good. "So, I'm being punished for seven years between visits?"

"You know it." He took a drink of his own coffee. He was about six feet tall with reddish-brown hair and hazel eyes that had rings of blue. He was twenty-eight and apparently had a boyfriend, though the mystery guy wasn't with him this trip.

It had never occurred to David to hide any aspect of himself growing up, and while Audrey had gotten into more than a few fights defending her little brother, she wouldn't have had him any other way. She adored him, and he was the one member of their family, other than their mother, whom she made an effort to see on a fairly regular basis. He often visited her in L.A. and she would visit him in New York, sometimes with their mother, and sometimes without.

David never looked at her with disappointment or wariness. When he came out, he thanked her for making it easy for him. "I fell in love with a boy—not like I killed somebody," he'd said to her the next time they'd talked, and Audrey had burst out laughing.

"If you loved me," she said, cradling her coffee, "you would walk out there and kiss some man on the lips—like Binky—give them something other than me to whisper about."

Her brother raised a finely groomed brow. Seriously, he had better eyebrows than she did. How could anyone in this town ever ask their mother when he was going to find the "right girl" and settle down?

"Binky? *Please.* But if that Gideon McGann shows up, I'll consider showing you just how much I love you, Auddie." He was the one who started that nickname. It had been one of the first things he said when he began talking.

"I'm surprised his wife hasn't shown up," she commented, taking another drink, wishing she had some espresso vodka to dump in her cup.

David stood beside her, almost shoulder to shoulder, so that his back was flat against the wall as well. Out of the corner of her eye, she saw him turn his head toward her. Audrey kept her gaze front and center so no one could sneak up on them. "You think she'd be that ballsy?" he asked.

"I know she would be, but it all depends on what she thinks would get under my skin the deepest—if she shows up early and stays for the whole thing, or if she lets me think she's not coming at all and then shows up right when I think I've escaped her."

"That's crazy."

Audrey smiled into her cup, equal parts grim, rueful, and amused. "That's Maggie."

"You sound almost wistful."

She glanced at him, still smiling. "Crazy sums Maggie and me up pretty well."

He shrugged. "You'd know. Are all psychologists as fucked-up as you?"

"God, I hope not."

"David?" came a raspy female voice. "What are you doing hiding away in the kitchen?"

Audrey resisted the urge to slam her skull against the wall. It was Jeannie Ray, notorious gossipmonger, shameless bigot, and occasional extortionist. She had to be almost seventy-five, but she dressed like she was twenty, chain-smoked, and hit on any male with even half a pulse.

Her brother plastered a fake smile on his face. "Jeannie! How's my favorite flirt?"

She fluttered into the kitchen like a butterfly on acid, all flowy fabric and big sleeves, and snatched David into her death-grip embrace. Audrey wrinkled her nose at the odor of fabric softener, rye, and stale cigarettes.

"You get more and more handsome every time I see you!" the older woman exclaimed, squeezing his left ass cheek before letting him go. "And who's this with you? *Oh*."

There was nothing like hearing a touch of dread in someone's voice when they recognized you. The old bat had accused Audrey and Maggie of killing one of her cats after they'd been arrested. She said it proved they were serial killers. The cat had obviously been hit by a car, and neither of the girls had been old enough to drive. Besides, they would have killed Jeannie before harming an animal. The old hag shouldn't have let her cats outside.

Audrey forced a smile. "Hi, Jeannie. Always a pleasure."

She was a hard-looking woman, old Jeannie, and the look she gave Audrey didn't make her any more attractive. "Yeah." Then she turned and walked away.

David glared after her. "Bitch."

Audrey smacked him in the arm. "She'll hear you."

"I don't care." He sounded pissed, and his jaw was so tight it twitched. "She can't talk to you like that."

"She can and she did. You giving yourself a stroke about it won't change any of it." Audrey took a drink. "Just let it go."

"Seriously?" He looked at her like she was nuts. "You're okay with being treated like that?"

Audrey shrugged. "I don't care what Jeannie thinks of me, or most of this town, for that matter. They lost my respect a long time ago." When they didn't even try to stop Clint Jones from molesting his daughter.

For a moment, her brother's gaze roved her face as though he were seeing her for the first time. "You really mean that."

She snorted and took another drink. "I mean it right *now*. Ask me again tomorrow and I'll probably be crying over the fact that no one likes me." God, some pills would be fabulous. Just a little something to take the edge off. Xanax maybe.

David's eyes narrowed. "You are so fucking weird."

Smiling, Audrey glanced at him as she entered the kitchen. He followed her. "You don't know the half of it, Davy."

"God, I hate it when you call me that."

Her smile widened—became more genuine. "I know." And then, "Come on, Mom will be opening her gifts soon. We need to brave the throng."

"Look at you being responsible and considerate."

Audrey rolled her eyes at him and set her cup on the counter. "Systematic desensitization." When he gave her a blank look, she explained, "It's a kind of therapy—exposure to something unpleasant to overcome the negativity associated with it. Like gradually working up to touching or holding a snake to overcome your fear of them."

"That's how you think of our mother's birthday party?" Jessica demanded from the door.

"Fuck me," Audrey muttered. This was punishment for all her sins. It had to be. She sucked in a breath, exhaled, then turned to her sister. "No, that's how I feel about this *place*."

Jessica opened her mouth, but David stepped forward. "If Mom's going to open her presents, we should go out."

For the baby of the family, her brother was astonishingly good at defusing tense situations between her and Jessica. Maybe it was because he was the only boy, and so damn cute.

Or, maybe she and Jessica wanted to stop fighting, and he helped them do that without either of them having to admit defeat. Regardless, Audrey could have hugged him for it.

They walked in single file out into the main room where their mother was surrounded by family, friends, and those who were neither but still part of the town and therefore obligated to attend out of either a sense of community or a need for fresh gossip. Or for free food. Judging from the curious looks shot in Audrey's direction, she was a scandalous bonus.

They'd look at you like that even if you'd been a good girl your entire life. Relax.

Her mother had just started opening the pile of gifts set out on the table before her. She wore a white straw hat that people were decorating with the ribbons and bows from the unwrapped gifts. One more reason Audrey was never going to allow people to throw her a birthday party ever. So far the presents were nice, though. Someone had given her a pretty scarf and someone else had given her a gift card.

"What did you get her?" David whispered.

"A Coach bag she put up on Pinterest."

"The pink one?"

It was rose, but she didn't bother to correct him. "Yeah."

He grinned. "I got her the matching wallet."

Audrey returned his smile as she slipped her arm around his back and gave him a squeeze.

Suddenly, Jeannie jumped to her feet from the chair she'd been perched upon like a vulture on a battlefield. "Oh my God," she cried.

Everything stopped. A chorus of "What is it?" filled the room.

The old woman's face was white as the knuckles of the hand holding her cell phone. "They found a body on the beach back at Tripp's Cove." She turned that vulture-like gaze on Audrey. "Maggie McGann's been murdered."

CHAPTER FIVE

Although she would never say it out loud, Detective Neve Graham was surprised that someone hadn't killed Maggie Jones-McGann a long time ago.

"Drink?" Jake asked. They were in the main reception building of the fancy resort he'd built on the former site of his family's campground.

She turned toward him, hands on her hips, not caring if he noticed the damp darkening the pits of her T-shirt. It was hot. Jake wasn't the scarecrow he used to be in high school. He was lean but muscular. She remembered him being fast and surprisingly strong. He could have easily bashed in Maggie's skull. "Are we commiserating, or celebrating?"

"*We're* thirsty," he replied, popping the top on a can of soda that he'd taken from a small refrigerator. He shut the door with his dirty bare foot, watching her with a guiltless gaze through the hair that fell over his forehead.

"What is it with you and your aversion to shoes?" she asked, meeting that gaze. She'd wondered about that for years.

He didn't even blink. "I'm averse to them."

So, Jake Tripp was a bastard, but he hadn't killed Maggie. He wouldn't shit where he ate. More to the point, if he had killed Maggie, no one would have found her. Jake knew every square inch of the mud puddle known as Edgeport, and since his grand-mother's death, he owned a lot of those inches.

This was Neve's first homicide in Edgeport—her first within thirty miles of her hometown. When she'd joined the state police's Major Crimes South unit the year before, after several years in the NYPD, she'd never dreamed that she'd be investigating the murder of someone she'd known most of her life, even if it was someone she wasn't surprised to hear was dead.

Fortunately, most of the people in Edgeport never truly accepted Neve and her family, so she had no trouble looking at them all with suspicion. It wasn't so much that she and her brothers were half-black. It was because their family hadn't roots in the community that extended back a century or more.

"Is it true that Maggie had an altercation with Audrey outside Gracie's last night?" Her mouth was dry, little grains of sand in her teeth. She should have taken him up on that soda.

"Where did you hear that?"

She arched a brow. He knew how the town worked. And she would be the one to ask questions, thank you.

"Fuck," he muttered, and took a drink. If eyes could be belligerent, his were looking for a slap. "They had words."

"I heard Audrey got violent."

Hazel eyes narrowed. "Maggie was being an ass. Audrey gave her a shove and Maggie was so drunk she fell."

Neve studied him. His tone was neutral, his posture relaxed, but Jake Tripp knew how to lie even better than he knew the town. Still, she believed him to an extent. Audrey had always been a scrapper, so "violent" took on a different connotation with her.

"You seem to have an adverse effect on those girls."

One dark brow lifted. It was a mocking look she'd wanted to slap off his face more than once in their youth. "Don't you mean *women*?"

She drew her shoulders back, her gaze locking with his. "Don't yank my chain, Jake."

"Don't talk cop to me, Neve." He set his soda on the counter and braced his palms on the granite top. He did have nice forearms. He could look intimidating when he wanted—which was what Neve always figured Audrey's attraction to him was all about. "If there's something you want to ask me, just ask."

Okay, fine. "What *really* happened between Maggie and Audrey last night?"

"Maggie was drunk and being a bitch. Audrey was just trying to get Rusty into her car and home. Maggie followed her outside." He ran a hand through his hair and grimaced. "You know what she's like."

"Yeah," Neve said before she could stop herself. "We both know what Audrey is like too."

Jake made a face that she took as an insult to her intelligence. "You and I both know Audrey is too smart to kill Maggie after a public spectacle—especially by bashing her head in."

Not that Audrey wouldn't kill Maggie, just that she wouldn't be stupid about it. Neve wanted to believe in her innocence, but she hadn't seen Audrey in a long time. "She almost beat her to death that night at the camp."

"That was different."

"How so? Because they were fighting over you?"

He glared at her. "Not over me. I wasn't any prize."

"Because of you then," she amended. "I heard Maggie taunted Audrey with that last night."

"Who told you that?"

She didn't respond—curious to see if he could guess.

"Fucking Bertie Neeley." He sighed and shook his head. He had guessed correctly "She did, and Audrey looked like she couldn't care less."

"She cared that night at the camp, though."

Jake lifted his soda. "Your memory's fucked-up. And that was a long time ago. She was a kid then. We all were." He didn't meet her gaze.

Hm. He still had a thing for Audrey. Interesting. "I know."

"Audrey didn't do this."

She held his gaze. There was nothing but conviction in that stare. Neve hoped Audrey appreciated his belief in her. "You think I don't want to believe that? When my family moved here, my brothers and I were the only black kids in a twenty-five-mile radius, and Audrey Harte was the first person who made me feel welcome. When Matt Jones called me a nigger, Audrey walked right up to him and slapped him in the mouth."

Jake smiled. "Audrey never met a bully she didn't stand up to."

Neve couldn't help but smile as well, even though she knew it showed bias. The expression was fleeting. "She had the juvenile arrest record to back it up. I don't want to think it, Jake, but I have to investigate just how much Audrey 'stood up' to Maggie last night. Whether I think she's guilty or not doesn't matter."

It had been years since Neve last saw Audrey, and she knew how much people could change over the course of a few years, but Audrey was successful now. She'd always been determined to make something of herself—something more than what this town expected of an angry girl who seemed addicted to getting into trouble. Would she seriously put that career in jeopardy by killing Maggie just because of an old grudge? It didn't make sense.

Or, maybe that temper of hers had gotten fired up and she'd smashed in Maggie's head in a fit of rage. Unfortunately for Audrey, both theories were fairly easy to entertain.

Neve grinned as a memory surfaced. "Remember that time she got into a fight with Duger?"

He laughed. "Who could forget?"

"I bet Duger hasn't." Duger's real name was Scott Ray—Jeannie's nephew. He'd always been a prick. And one day when Neve and Audrey were in seventh grade, Duger called Maggie a slut. No one knew at that time that Clint had been molesting her, so when Maggie burst into tears, Duger was pretty proud of himself. Not so proud when Audrey tackled him to the grass, straddled him, and used his face as a punching bag. She'd made him cry, mostly out of anger, but still.

"Did Maggie have words with anyone else last night?"

Jake thought about it. "Matt didn't seem too happy with her. He was slithering around the bar last night."

"Her brother?" When he nodded, she said, "That's nothing new. Anyone else?"

He shook his head. "Not that I remember."

Neve took one of her cards from her pocket. "Here's my cell number if you remember anything. Or you can reach me at Mom and Dad's."

"You staying in town for a few days?"

She nodded. "It's easier than driving back and forth. Not so easy to keep Dad out of the investigation."

"You can use the old cottage if you want. It's not fit to stay in, but you can set it up as an office if you need."

"Okay." She drew the word out as she looked at him. "I'd thank you, but I get a feeling you're not doing this out of the goodness of your heart."

He smiled and picked up his can of cola. "I rarely do anything out of the goodness of my heart. If you use the cottage, then my guests don't see cop cars parked on the road, and you have separate access to the beach. Do your job and get the hell out as soon as possible."

Her eyebrows rose. "I'm sorry, Jake. Is my trying to find Maggie's murderer going to inconvenience you?"

He didn't even blink. "Yeah. I've already had one cottage check out. And as soon as you're done with the woman who found her, I'm going to lose another."

"Next time I'll see what I can do about having the murder committed someplace you don't own. Or do you own the whole town now?"

Before Jake could answer, his cell phone rang. He pulled it out of his pocket and checked the screen. "Fuck." He ran a hand through his hair. "It's Gideon."

Fuck was right. Neve closed her eyes. "We haven't notified him yet."

"But he knows." Jake's jaw was clenched so hard the muscle stood out beneath his cheek. "God damn Yancy. I'm not going to take this call."

"Don't," she agreed, not bothering to ask why Yancy would spread the word before the police could talk to Gideon. She ought to have told Jake's sister not to say anything, but Neve had forgotten where she was. *Shit.* "I'll go there now. Was it the house number or his cell?"

"House." Jake shoved the phone back into his jeans. He looked older when he was angry—harder. Yancy was going to catch hell when he saw her.

"I'll go there now." Neve hesitated in the doorway. "Hey, Jake?"

He turned toward her. "Yeah?"

She allowed herself a little smile. "When you see Audrey tell her I said hi." She was going to have to talk to her soon herself, but not until she had a clearer picture of what had happened on that beach the night before.

His frown deepened. "You'll probably see her before I will."

Neve chuckled. "Yeah. Right." She closed the door before he could reply.

*   *   *

Maggie was dead?

Not just dead. *Murdered.*

That wasn't possible. Maggie was a force of nature. She ruined people, destroyed everything she touched. People didn't hurt her, she hurt them. That someone could have effectively ended the person whose dark shadow hovered over more than two-thirds of Audrey's life seemed impossible. How could Maggie have died without her knowing? She ought to have felt it—the cutting of the invisible string that bound them together. Some kind of release. *Something.* A little something to precede the shock she felt now.

"Auddie?" It was David's voice. It was also David's face she saw looming in front of her when she finally got out of her mind and back to reality. His face was pale, his gaze worried. "Are you okay?"

"Yeah," she lied, her voice a hoarse whisper. She didn't know whether to cry or burst into "Ding Dong! The Witch Is Dead." "Everyone's staring at me, aren't they?"

"Some," he replied. "The rest are speculating on the details. You look like you need to sit down."

"No. I'm okay." She pulled her shoulders back and straightened her spine just to prove it.

Jessica swooped in like an angry, starving tiger "Did you know about this?"

Audrey opened her mouth, but David beat her to it. "How could she possibly know about it?" he demanded in a rough whisper. "Now back off—this isn't the time or place for public family drama."

For a moment it seemed as though Jess might push it, but she backed down instead. Audrey watched her stomp away, back to the epicenter of the speculating crowd, which was growing bigger and bigger.

"Did you *know* about it." Her brother made a sound of disgust. "What does she think, that you and Maggie shared some kind of psychic link so you would know if the other died?"

"Dave," Audrey whispered, taking his hand in hers, "she's afraid I did it."

His eyes widened, but his mouth thinned. "Bitch," he muttered.

She tried to give him a reassuring smile, but it felt wrong. "She's not the only one in this room wondering."

People were looking at her—she hadn't imagined that, and it didn't surprise her. She and Maggie were the most notorious duo Edgeport had seen since Horace Adams killed his wife, Wanda, and then himself back in 1976. If she were one of these people, she'd watch her too, just to see her reaction to the news of her former best friend's death. She'd also apply all her training in criminal psychology to that scrutiny, looking for any sign of guilt in a person whose criminal record was common knowledge in the local area.

Leave it to Maggie to get killed during the first weekend Audrey had been home in years. And of course they'd had a public exchange the night before. She'd suspect Maggie of staging the whole thing if she weren't dead.

Dead.

An image of Clint flashed in her mind—skull caved in, eyes blank. His big hands still. Audrey's hands trembling. Blood on Maggie's cheek. All that blood...

No, not going there.

"Are they sure it's Maggie?" she asked when her mother approached. Anne didn't even look upset that her party had been ruined. She wore that serene expression that she always wore when things were bad. It was her particular brand of stoicism. Never let them see you vulnerable.

Gentle arms closed around her. "That's what the network's saying."

The "network" was what her mother—and the rest of Edgeport—called the four key gossips of the town, who always seemed to know who was doing what: Jeannie Ray, Flora Martin, Angie Pelletier, and Yancy Tripp. Angie and Yancy were the youngest members of the quartet. Angie had been a year ahead of Audrey in school, and Yancy was a year or so younger. She'd moved back to town—and in with Gracie and Jake—just before Audrey left for college, so she didn't know her that well, but the others she knew as well as she'd ever want.

"It could be just gossip. It might not be her." Later, she'd think about why it meant so much to her that Maggie not be dead, but at that moment, all Audrey wanted was a little hope.

Her mother continued to hug her but pulled back so she could look her in the eye. "Sweetie, Jake identified her."

Audrey blinked. Maggie was really dead. And Jake had seen the body. Did he think she did it? "I need to go," she whispered.

"No." Her mother shook her head. "You're going to stay here, with me. You're going to let everyone see how upset you are by the news of an old friend's death."

"Mum…" She drew a deep breath and let it out. "I don't want them staring at me."

Blue eyes narrowed under a frown. "Yes, you do. You need to let them see you upset, because everyone knows that you and Maggie had words last night, and the only person who was with you after that was too drunk to give you an alibi." Her father had been at the party earlier but only lasted a half hour. There were too many people in attendance and too little booze for his comfort.

Alibi. "Of course they think I did it." So nice to know the whole room thought as little of her as she suspected.

"They wouldn't be stupid enough to say so in front of me, but I've no doubt tongues will be wagging the minute they're out of earshot."

Dazed, Audrey nodded. Of course the town would talk about her. Whether they thought her innocent or guilty didn't matter; they just thought her killing Maggie made a good story.

She looked up over her mother's shoulder and caught Jeannie staring at her with that narrow, lightly jaundiced gaze. There was no doubt that the old bitch thought her capable of killing Maggie. She watched Audrey with blatant interest, looking for some sign of guilt.

Audrey swiped a finger under her eye, as though wiping away a tear. She was a brilliant liar when she wanted to be, and she could fake it convincingly enough.

As a summoned tear trickled down her cheek, Audrey again made eye contact with Jeannie and held it until the woman looked away. Then she brushed the tear from her face. As if she would ever let them see her honestly cry.

That should give the network something to talk about.

Fourteen.

That was how many phone calls Audrey's mother had gotten since they'd arrived home a few hours earlier. There were also five messages on the voice mail that she hadn't listened to yet. With the exception of a scant few, all the callers were looking for gossip—or clarification of it. Had she heard about Maggie? And how was Audrey dealing with the news? The latter was basically code for, "Hey, did your psycho daughter smash Maggie's skull like a teacup?"

As if her mother would know, or admit to it if she did.

When the phone rang for the fifteenth time, Audrey answered. "Yes, we heard about Maggie, and no, I didn't do it." Then she hung up.

"Audrey!" her mother admonished.

She shrugged and shut the ringer off. "Let voice mail take over. We can check it later for legitimate calls. You don't need to spend what's left of your birthday defending me." Truthfully, her mother looked exhausted, and Audrey hated thinking she'd contributed to her fatigue.

"I'll defend you till I'm dust." But Anne sank down onto the sofa with a tired sigh.

Her father had gone out, and fortunately Jessica and her brood had chosen to go home rather than breathe the same air as Audrey. David had gone with her so he could "see the girls," but Audrey knew he was trying to run interference between his sisters. It was quiet in the house.

"Make you a cuppa, Mum?"

"If I drink any more tea today I'll float away." She yawned. "I think I might call it an early night."

It was just after seven. Audrey frowned. "Are you feeling okay?"

Her mother smiled sleepily. "I feel blessed to have so many wonderful and exhausting family and friends. But after a late night and early morning, this busy day has wiped me out, babe."

"Okay. Do you need me to do anything for you?"

"Feed the cat?"

That was easy enough. "Sure."

"Then go out for a while. Go see some friends."

Her brows rose. "Mum, I don't have any friends. Not here."

Anne waved her hand. "Oh, stop. You have plenty of friends. People ask me about you all the time—and not because of your colorful past."

That was one way to describe it. "There's no one I want to see."

A lazy smile curved her mother's mouth. "Not even Jake?"

"Especially not him." The night before at Gracie's had been the first time they'd spoken since Gracie's funeral seven years earlier. They'd reconnected after the service, but once she flew back to

L.A. he apparently forgot about her again. If he wanted to see her, he knew where to find her.

Soft laughter followed. "You know what they say about protesting too much."

"Yeah—it's usually because some crazy person doesn't know what they're talking about."

Anne's smile faded, the worn creases of her face easing into gentle lines. "Is there really no one you'd like to see?"

She couldn't bring herself to tell her mother that the only person who would have been glad to see her was Maggie. "Actually, there is one person I'd like to visit."

Delight was too mild a word to describe her mother's expression. She wasn't naive. She just refused to believe that her husband or one of her kids could be that broken. "Your father went out for a bit. Maybe you'd check in at Gracie's before you come home?"

Ah. She ought to have seen that coming, but it still struck a bitter chord. "Sure." Then she gave her mother a hug and went to the kitchen to feed the cat.

Leaving the house wasn't as hard as she thought it would be. There wasn't a horde of angry townsfolk waiting to kabob her on their pitchforks, and there weren't any police cars parked on the road. Night was falling, and it was quiet. *So* quiet. It was unsettling. Maggie was dead, and her killer was out there somewhere.

And her mother had practically forced her out of the house with a murderer at large. What the hell was up with that?

From her parents' doorstep she could hear the water. She could smell it too, mixed with the scent of freshly mowed grass and a breath of pine. Her father had been splitting wood recently. It was a nice night—cool enough that her light sweater and jeans were perfectly comfortable.

A june bug buzzed near her ear. She jerked back with a small cry. She'd gotten one stuck in her hair once—she could still feel it buzzing and squirming. Another brushed her cheek. She ran down the steps, out of reach of the front-door light where the little sticky bastards congregated on the screen door. How could she have forgotten about the bugs?

Audrey jumped into the Mini and started the engine. Regardless of what Maggie's killer was doing at that moment, getting out of the house was the best thing she could have done. She hadn't realized just how restless she'd been. She needed a little time alone to process what had happened to Maggie without worrying if anyone was watching.

She turned left out of the driveway, onto asphalt that had been patched so many times it was more tar than anything else. It followed a vaguely meandering route to the center of town—the heart of the metropolis that was Edgeport. It would take more than a blink to miss it, but not much more. Gracie's was busy already. A Saturday night on the edge of tourist season with a juicy scandal to speculate over.

It was morbid, really. On a purely logical level, she understood the basic human need to defy the sticky fingers of death by listening to—and repeating—all the gory particulars of a nasty end. Make it a good enough story and it would be hours before the person who had sat across from you wondered if maybe you had motive. It might not take as long for you to wonder the same thing about them.

About a mile past Gracie's, on the opposite side of the road, was the long dirt road known to all as Tripp's Cove. The first Tripp to settle in the area had claimed a huge tract of land that stretched from a bend in the river all the way to the beach and then a fair distance both east and west. The Tripps were the only family who had retained all their original land, and who had gone on to accumulate more. Though there were stories that not all of that new land had been achieved through legal means.

Audrey steered onto the road, keeping her eye out for deer. Or moose. Or bears. There was a good chance of seeing at least one of the three, and she'd rather not run into one of them in a car that, while cute, struck her as the sort of thing that might crumple like a tin can upon impact.

There were a few houses along the first mile of road, but after that they were few and far between, until there was only one, followed by several miles of forest and wild blueberry land. At the end of the road was a fork, one tine of which led to the beach, and the other to what used to be Tripp's Campground. It was a resort now, her mother said. A main building surrounded by private, luxurious cottages. Apparently it was Jake's doing. His grandmother would be proud of him for making something of the place. Then again, old Gracie would be just as likely to hate it for being "new."

Just past that last house, on the opposite side of the road, where there was a field that eventually fell over a tall cliff, stood a tiny stone church with stained-glass windows and a bell spire that hadn't held a bell since before Audrey was born. The story was that some local kids kept breaking into the church and ringing the bell in the middle of the night. No one was surprised when the bell actually fell on one of the kids, breaking his leg. After all, old man Tripp had warned the town that the bell and its mechanism were old and fragile. He'd been terribly upset that someone had been hurt and even paid the young man's medical bills. He'd done it all with a kind smile on his face. Jake used to say that the old man probably wore that same smile when he tampered with the bell so it would crash down upon the next "little bastard" who dared to ring it.

There wasn't an actual road to the church—just a culvert and two tracks of ruddy dirt through the grass. She followed the path to its end and parked. When she stepped out of the car, the sun hung just above the horizon, painting the sky in shades of orange, pink, and purple. There was even a touch of crimson. She stood and stared at it for a few moments. Had sunset always been this beautiful? Because she was sure she would have counted it as one of the rare good things about her hometown.

Tearing her gaze away from the waning day, Audrey continued on through grass that could stand to be mowed, to the low stone wall just to the left of the church. The wrought-iron gate held a worn plaque that simply read TRIPP CEMETERY. She opened the gate and walked through, into the stone garden that held the mortal remains of almost every Tripp who'd ever lived in Edgeport, including Jake's father, Brody, who had died a few years before Gracie.

She immediately found the grave she sought—the headstone looked brand-new next to the moss-covered, crumbling slabs that leaned over some of the other plots. As soon as she found it, she sat down beside it. Even she had enough respect for the dead not to plunk her ass down right on top of them.

"Hey, Gracie," she said, brushing loose grass off the monument. Gracie Tripp. Honored Wife. Devoted Mother. Beloved Grandmother. She would have known all of this even if it wasn't set in stone before her. She added her own silent eulogy to the list: *Savior and Patron Saint of Wayward Delinquent Girls.*

If not for Gracie, Audrey's life might have taken a vastly different turn.

"Maggie's dead." The words caught in her throat, all blunt edges and sharp corners. "It's so weird to think that she's gone. I thought she'd live forever just to spite me, and then the crazy bitch goes and gets herself killed. I think she took a piece of me with her. It feels like she did." The tears she'd so callously summoned earlier that day forsook her, leaving her eyes parched and hot. Audrey wasn't one to use the word "crazy" loosely, but if anyone ever fit the definition, it was Mags.

They'd met in elementary school, when Maggie's family moved into town. New kids were a rarity in Edgeport, so everyone was curious about the pretty blonde girl who didn't have ancestors among the founding families. She was downright exotic to Audrey, who at that point had never been any farther away from home than Portland. Maggie was from another state—New Hampshire.

On her first day at school, Maggie had walked right up to Audrey, whose friends were mostly boys, and told her she had pretty eyes. No one had ever complimented her eyes, which she'd been so self-conscious about. She and Maggie became inseparable after that. Until they killed Clint, that was. They'd been taken away from each other then, until Audrey had been released. The Maggie she had known was not the Maggie waiting for her when she came home from Stillwater. It had taken Audrey a while to realize that, and by the time she had it was too late—the claws were in deep. Ripping them out had been a painful and bloody process for both Maggie and herself.

The sound of a four-wheeler lifted her head. At the other end of the field—at the edge of the tree line—she spotted someone on one of the machines. They were missing a headlight. They paused there, as though watching her. Maybe surprised to see a person in the Tripp family graveyard, or waiting for a companion. After a moment they turned around and tore off into the trees again. Probably a kid who took the wrong trail on his or her way to a party.

Audrey stayed by the grave a little while longer—until the sun was nothing more than a smudge of orange on the horizon, and the trees seemed to gather more thickly, as though slowly closing in to swallow her. Then she got up, dusted herself off, and walked back to her car, batting at the mosquitoes buzzing around her head.

A few minutes later, and just back the way she'd come, she pulled into the driveway of a house in which she'd spent a lot of time when she'd been younger. Gracie had always kept the Queen Anne–style house white, but now it was a warm eggshell with slate-blue trim. The front steps had been replaced, as had most of the windows and the front door, but the old porch swing was still there. Though now the swing was painted the same blue as the trim.

There was a light on inside, and an old pickup in the drive, but it was Saturday night and someone was dead, so the chance of finding anyone at home was slim. Most of the town would be gathered at places where they could get the latest news and speculate until they couldn't tell what was truth and what wasn't.

Audrey hesitated. She shouldn't be there. Where the hell was her pride?

Fuck pride. There was a chance she had one friend left in this town, and she was standing on his porch.

She raised her hand and knocked.

The door opened, jacking her heart rate. She really hadn't expected anyone to answer.

Jake stood in the doorway, tall and lanky. He wore black jeans and a gray T-shirt with black suspenders. Mussed brown hair fell over his forehead, almost in his hazel eyes. He needed to shave, but scruffiness made him look edgier—not that Jake Tripp needed any extra edge. Funny, but she couldn't remember when he'd gone from being that sweet little boy who got her a new ice-cream cone to the man looking at her with wariness in his gaze.

"Hi," she said, slipping her hands into the pockets of her jeans. This was more awkward than seeing him last night.

He braced his forearm on the doorframe. She noticed he still wore his grandfather's watch. There was more than a foot and a half of empty space between them, but it felt like less. Standing at the threshold, he was even taller, looming over her. If she stepped up, right into his face, what would he do? Push her away? Recoil? Laugh?

She waited for him to say something else, or ask why she was there. He said nothing—just watched her. *Shit*. What had she expected? That he'd welcome her with open arms? Until last night it had been years since they'd last seen each other.

Finally, he spoke. "If you're looking to confront Yancy, she's not here."

Audrey frowned, turned her attention back to him. "Why would I . . . ?" Oh, right. It had been Yancy who had texted Jeannie at her mother's party, delivering the news of Maggie's death. "I'm not here to see your sister. I'm here to see you."

"Are you." It wasn't a question. His gaze searched her face, his expression unreadable. "I should probably invite you in, then." He stood back, gesturing with a sweep of one long arm for her to enter.

She took a deep breath before crossing the threshold, but once she was inside it all came whooshing out in a surprised gasp. The house looked somewhat similar to how she remembered it, but it had been completely renovated. Gracie had liked colors like sage and butter yellow. That was all gone now, replaced by rich shades of plum, gray, and slate. She followed him into the kitchen where the wainscot had been stripped down to its original wood, and stained espresso, as was the floor. It would be too dark were it not for an abundance of mellow lighting.

He caught her staring. "It's been a while since you've been in the house," he remarked, turning on the burner under the teakettle on the stove.

"It's incredible," she murmured, not caring that her awe was so transparent. "Did you do this?"

"Most of it, yeah. I'd give you the tour, but my cleaning lady doesn't come until Monday."

She turned to him with a smile. "A cleaning lady? Careful, Jake, or the town will think you're high-feeling."

He grinned. Oh, that grin. She didn't want to think how many pairs of panties had dropped because of that smile. "Too late. 'That Tripp boy thinks too much of himself for where he came from.'"

From what David had told her, Jake had single-handedly saved the town from ruin. The resort brought in money, as did Gracie's. Plus, he'd purchased the small store and gas station, and two other businesses. He employed a lot of people and had gotten involved in the annual summer lobster festival. "I can only imagine what they say about me."

"They don't," he said. "At least not in front of me."

She couldn't tell from his tone if that was just a simple, inno-cent statement, or something more. "Well, they were talking ear-lier today. Jeannie actually asked me point-blank if I'd been to the beach since I got home."

"Jeannie's a vindictive, bored old cow." He opened a cupboard. "What kind of tea do you want?" The shelves were full of various brands—all loose leaves by the look of the number of tins.

Gracie would be so proud of that tea cupboard. "Do you have any Earl Grey?"

"If I didn't Gran would come back and haunt me until I did."

"She liked her tea."

"Almost as much as she liked her rye."

Audrey smiled at the memory of Gracie and the little glass of whiskey she had every night before bed. She glanced around at the large kitchen, marveling at the whole thing—smiling at the old wringer washer in the corner that was obviously there for decora-tion now, but she remembered Gracie using it when Audrey had worked at their campground that summer before college. The old woman had claimed that the "new machines" didn't clean clothes as well.

Then she noticed the shoes by the door—women's shoes. Something pinched in her chest. Jesus Christ, she was in her thirties. She was too old to still be carrying a torch. "I'm sorry, do you have company?"

He glanced over his shoulder and saw where her gaze had gone. "Those are my niece's. And no. It's just the two of us."

Like it used to be. At one time the thought would have filled her with youthful hopefulness that he would kiss her, or touch her— anything. Now...it was just good to see him, regardless of how deep the water under the bridge that spanned their relationship.

He'd been the first one to welcome her back after Stillwater. He never asked about her time there; he just went on being her friend. If she wanted to talk, he listened. Maggie, on the other hand, had seemed to constantly ask her questions she didn't want to answer. Maggie hadn't liked that Audrey hung out more with Jake than with her. When they'd been younger the three of them had spent a lot of time together—and with other kids of the town. The campground had been something of a hangout, and when they were older they moved their parties to the camp across the road.

She ought to have known that when Maggie stopped teasing her about her longtime crush on Jake it was a warning of things to come. Maggie hadn't slept with Jake because she liked him. She'd done it to make a point, and that point had been to teach Audrey her place.

And then Audrey beat Maggie into hers.

"I'm sorry for being curt with you last night," she said.

He shrugged. "You had Rusty to deal with. I get it."

Silence settled between them. It wasn't uncomfortable, but it wasn't easy either. It was...uncertain. While the tea steeped, Jake got out a plate and filled it with cookies from a jar on the counter.

"Tell me you didn't bake those," she said before she could stop herself.

"If I had, I wouldn't share them with someone as dubious sounding as you." He set the plate on the table. "Alisha made them. Yancy's girl."

Ah. The niece. "How old is she now?"

"Fifteen going on thirty. You still take milk and sugar?"

"Yes, please. Has she gotten into any trouble?" In her experience fifteen was a rough age for most girls. More specifically, the years between twelve and fifteen. God knew they'd been rough for her. And every year since, come to think of it.

"Not much yet, but it's coming. A couple of older boys tried getting her drunk a few weekends ago at a party." He poured the tea into cups. "I'll be polite and say they were of amorous intent."

The muscles of Audrey's stomach clenched. "Did they hurt her?"

He paused in the middle of stirring sugar into one of the cups to look at her. "No, but it was pretty clear what they had in mind."

"What stopped them?"

Jake stirred the other cup. "She called me."

A smart and lucky girl. She had met so many who hadn't had an uncle, father, or brother to call. Worse, she'd seen so many cases in which one—or more—of the three had been the abuser. "What did you do?"

He set the cups on the sturdy antique table that had been in the house since before either one of them ever stepped foot in it. "I took a page from Gran's book. Sit."

She lowered herself into the closest chair. "And?"

Jake sat across from her and dunked a cookie in his tea. "I took them into the woods, handed them each a shovel, and had them dig two deep holes about the size of a steamer trunk. When they were done I told them that those were the holes I'd bury them in if I ever heard of them trying to hurt another girl." He shoved the tea-soaked cookie in his mouth.

Audrey choked on a laugh. Rural justice had long been the code by which many lived in Edgeport. It had left a sour taste in her own mouth, but she admired Jake for how he'd handled it. "And they didn't report you because then they'd have to own up to what they'd done."

He shrugged. "If you don't take care of the people you love, no one else will."

His sharp gaze was a little too focused on her. She took a sip of tea. It was fabulous. "Is it true you found her?"

There was no need to say who "her" was. "No. A guest at the cottages did. I went to check it out and stayed until the police came. Neve was one of them."

"Neve Graham?" At his nod she continued, "I thought she moved to New York."

"She did. She's back."

Audrey nodded. She and Neve had been friends when they were younger, and her father, Everett, had been one of the officers who investigated Clint's death. He'd actually been the first on the scene, and the first to suspect that the two of them had planned it. If she thought about it too much, it still pissed her off that the adults they'd gone to for help hadn't done their job, leaving two young girls to act out of desperation. Her mother had talked to her father about it, and Rusty hadn't wanted to believe his drinking buddy was a monster.

Audrey's mother thought Maggie had lied, because she'd caught the girl lying before. Maggie's own mother had slapped her for suggesting such a thing. How could she have been with Clint so many years and not realized what he was? Especially after Maggie's older sister died suspiciously before the family left New Hampshire?

What other choice did they have but to kill him? If she could go back she'd do it again, but she'd never admitted that to anyone. It was bad enough that she'd revealed to Jess that she wished they hadn't gotten caught. But then, how would she have turned out if she hadn't been sent to Stillwater? Killing Clint was the cherry on the top of her delinquent career of theft and violence, convincing the judge that Audrey needed to go to a detention center for agreeing to help Maggie, who believed killing her father was the only way to escape him. Maggie had stood up and told the judge how she planned it, how she'd asked Audrey to help, and how sorry she was for getting her friend in trouble. That sweet speech, and her psychological assessment, had gotten her sent to a psychiatric hospital rather than detention, because it was obvious she suffered from years of abuse.

Gracie had clucked her tongue and maintained that in her youth, what Audrey and Maggie had done would have been considered rural justice, and that would be the end of it. The old woman used what influence she could to get Audrey sent to Stillwater, a center with a stellar reputation, and one of the highest rehabilitation rates in the country. It had been considered progressive at the time. These days more and more facilities were trying a "rehabilitation rather than incarceration" approach similar to Stillwater's, and it was working. Mountain View, a juvenile facility up north, had closed because alternate programs had been successful in rehabilitating young offenders.

It was funny in a twisted sort of way that Audrey had gotten the worst of the deal but came back to Edgeport in better shape than Maggie had. Whatever they'd done to her in that hospital, it hadn't helped her.

Or maybe Maggie just couldn't be helped. Sometimes damage ran so deep it was as much a part of a person as their DNA.

Knowing as much of Audrey's past as she did, there was no way

Neve wouldn't question her about her encounter with Maggie the night she was killed. She'd probably already talked to Jake about it. Christ, she should have stayed in L.A.

"I didn't do it," she said, breaking the silence that had fallen between them.

"I know."

He meant it—she could tell. There was nothing in his posture, tone, or expression that indicated he was anything but truthful. That's what had really brought her to his door. They had always accepted each other exactly as they were. That was a wonderful, terrible thing that made each of them far too vulnerable to the other.

The phone rang—shrill and demanding, violating the emotionally fraught moment Jake got up from the table to answer it. "Yeah?" Audrey heard the voice that answered but couldn't make out the words. "You're fucking kidding me... No. I'm on my way." He hung up.

Before Audrey could ask, he said, "There's a fight at Gracie's. I have to go sort it out."

She stood up. "I'll follow you. I told Mum I'd check if Dad was there."

"Oh, he's there," Jake replied with a laugh. "Who do you think started the fight?"

CHAPTER SIX

Rusty Harte never met a fight he didn't like, though some wouldn't return the sentiment.

When Audrey pulled into Gracie's parking lot behind Jake's truck, the first thing caught in the glare of headlights was her father. His shirt had come untucked from his jeans, and blood from a cut on his forehead trickled down his face. He had one big hand wrapped around Albert Neeley's throat as he bent the smaller man over the hood of a rusting-out Toyota.

Audrey parked in the middle of the drive, right behind Jake. If someone wanted her to move they could take it up with him. She climbed out of the Mini and slammed the door, slipping her hands into the pockets of her jeans as she strode toward her father and the crowd gathered around him, cheering and jeering like they were watching lions devour the entrails of hapless Christians. Some of the onlookers fell silent as she and Jake approached, their gazes ranging from curiosity to open hostility. Audrey knew most of them—had grown up with either them or their children—and was well enough acquainted with each to not care much what they thought of her.

She glanced at Jake. He gave her a nod, answering the question she hadn't voiced. He understood her so well there was no way he could have been ignorant of her feelings for him when they were kids, the bastard. He'd known what he was doing that night at the camp with Maggie. He'd known how it would hurt her.

The crowd parted for her, which prevented her from scratching the itch to push her way through. Audrey moved to stand beside her father, cautiously leaning against the fragile shell of the car that looked as though it might crumble beneath Albert's and her combined weight.

"Bit early for a brawl, isn't it, Dad?"

His gaze stayed fastened on the man whose throat would bear his handprint for the next few days. "As good a time as any." His hair, which had gotten a little long and shaggy in the years since she'd last seen him, fell around his face. He wasn't florid, and his eyes were focused. Audrey frowned.

Rusty Harte was actually sober. Or at least mostly so.

"I can't argue with that logic, but you know how Mum hates you fighting."

"She wouldn't mind this time."

Ah. If she hadn't guessed at the reason behind the fight already, she'd definitely figured it out now. "I don't need you to defend my honor, you know. Never mind that not even you could take them all on. All this is doing is making Albert here certain that I got my particular flavor of crazy from you. Isn't that right, Albert?"

Albert nodded—as much as a man could with a hand big enough to suffocate a moose wrapped around his neck. His bloodshot eyes were wide-open as they rolled toward her, his face a mottled red.

"Let him go, Dad."

He shook his head. "You don't know what he said."

"I don't care," she replied honestly. "No offense," she added, glancing at Albert.

"None taken," he rasped.

"She was being sarcastic, you stupid bastard," her father growled.

There had been times in her life—and this might very well become one of them—when Audrey actually liked her father. She put her hand on his arm. He might be getting older, but there was no denying the strength beneath her fingers. "Let him go. Please. For me."

The tension in his arm eased, then released. Her father removed his hand from Neeley's throat and stepped back, surprising Audrey as much as Bertie. It took the other man a few seconds to realize he was free and react accordingly. He scurried out of harm's way like a mouse escaping an owl.

"You're welcome," Audrey called after him.

"All right," Jake said in a loud, clear voice. "Show's over. Go back inside and drink, or go the hell home. I don't much care which."

There were mutterings and disgruntled noises from the gathered crowd, but they all did as he commanded. Audrey watched them go with an emotion she couldn't quite name. Amusement? Awe? Disbelief? Apparently Jake had also inherited his grandmother's ability to make people do exactly what he wanted. Behold, the power of the barkeep.

"Not you, Neeley," he called as the man placed a foot on the bar steps. "You're cut off for the rest of the night. Go the hell home."

The older man turned. He looked horrified. Audrey thought he might actually cry out in physical pain at Jake's banishment of him. She thought she knew every expression an alcoholic could make, but that was a new one.

"Because of her?" Neeley demanded, jerking his thumb at Audrey. So much for him not wanting to offend her, asshole.

"No. Because of him." He nodded at her father. "He always

pays his tab, and he tips better than you do. Plus, I'm going to buy him a drink, and who knows what he might do to you once he's gotten a few under his belt."

Neeley's expression hardly changed, but Audrey saw it. Everyone who knew her father knew what sort of man he was. Some thought him better than he was, and others worse, but they all knew that breaking up a fight between him and someone else only worked if they were physically separated. If they stayed in the same room, Rusty was eventually going to kick Neeley's ass. It was a violent form of OCD. He just couldn't seem to help himself. Tomorrow, however, he'd be back to slapping Neeley on the back and buying him a beer.

Slowly—and with substantial grace for a drunkard—the man backed down the steps. It might have been comical on any other night. "I'll just be on my way then."

No one spoke. The three of them just stood there and listened to gravel crunch beneath Neeley's boots as he walked away. He lived not even a quarter mile down the road, which was good, because Edgeport didn't need any more career drunk drivers than it already had.

"You coming in, kid?"

Audrey turned toward her father, but her gaze went immediately to Jake, who watched her with a passive expression on his angular face. What was it about him that burrowed so far under her skin that she could feel it in her bones? His hair was a mess. He dressed like an old man from the thirties, avoided shoes whenever possible, and threatened to kill teenage boys. Those traits did not add up to attractive, but he was—to her, at any rate.

Jake shrugged—the only sign that he even noticed her staring at him. "Yeah, why not? I'll buy you a beer too, Aud."

The grown-up inside her screamed that drinking with her alcoholic father would cause nothing but trouble, and trigger all kinds of emotions and memories she didn't want to revisit, but the kid in her—the one who used to cry because he'd rarely come with her mother to visit her in Stillwater—wanted nothing more than her daddy's attention. It was why she'd committed most of her crimes. She may not like him much—sometimes not at all—but she loved the bastard.

God, she was so *textbook*.

But more than that, she owed her father something for defending her, didn't she? How many fights had he gotten into after her arrest? Her trial? How many people had said purposely hurtful things to him, to her mother, or Jess and David? She had very few regrets in her life, but leaving her family to face the social fallout that followed her actions was one of them.

"Make it a rum and Coke," she said, as they started toward the tavern door.

"Still on that, are you?" Jake asked. "I thought once you became a big-shot TV star you'd switch to Cristal."

Audrey frowned. "TV star? Are you high?"

"Rum was your grandfather's poison of choice," her father remarked from between them. "He had just poured a smash when his heart stopped. Didn't even get to take a drink, the poor bastard."

"He died the way he lived," Audrey replied without thinking. "There are worse ways to die than in front of the television with a drink in one hand and a steak in the other." In actuality, her grandfather had the steak *knife* in his hand, but that didn't sound as good when she told the story to people. She rather liked them having the image of the old man sitting in a chair with a medium-rare slab of meat dripping down his cold, stiff fingers.

"Wood chipper." Rusty nodded. "That's got to be worse."

"Only if you're alive when you go in," Jake expounded. "Feet first and you're going to feel it for a long time before you're dead."

Her father nodded again. "I always heard you should put 'em in frozen. Less mess."

Audrey stopped them at the top of the steps to the veranda that wrapped around the building. Was she in some kind of twilight zone? "Can we not talk about terrible ways to die, please? Someone might hear, and people in this town think I'm crazy enough as it is."

"Get over yourself," Jake said with a scowl. "No one's talked about you in years."

Was she supposed to be offended or relieved? "You don't think they're talking about me now? My father was defending my honor, for fuck's sake."

"Language," Rusty singsonged with a smile. "My darlin' girl, you used to not care what people said about you. Why now?"

"Because—" She stopped, and swallowed, mouth suddenly dry. "Because this time I didn't do anything wrong." The two men—oddly enough the only two males from whom she ever wanted anything emotional—stared at her, as if she'd sprouted a huge horn in the middle of her forehead, and somehow it was their fault. Maybe she shouldn't have been so honest.

"Can we go in for that drink now?" she asked, breaking the awkward silence. "I'm thirsty."

"You're damn right we can," her father enthused, giving her a squeeze. Audrey almost—almost—leaned against him, but he pulled away before she could do something so stupid.

Jake held the door. Audrey cringed at the loud country music as her father waltzed in like he owned the place. This wasn't a good idea. She should just go the hell home, but she wanted the gossips and people of this town—people who knew her—to see her out and around. She wasn't going to hide from them as though she was guilty. Her mother had been right to make her leave the house.

Jake grabbed her arm as she passed him. Their gazes locked and held. "It's okay to care what they're saying about you, so long as you don't start to believe it."

Audrey tugged her arm free. "I know who and what I am, Jake. I don't need anyone to tell me "

He smiled. "You're cute when you're a bitch, you know that?"

She couldn't help but laugh. "Fuck off, Tripp."

He leaned down so that his mouth was near her ear—so close she could feel the heat of his breath. "It's good to have you home, Aud."

If she turned her head just a little bit, she could kiss him, but that would be stupid. And probably a lesson in rejection. Instead, she patted his shoulder. "I wish I could say it's good to be home, but so far *you've* been the highlight of the trip." Any drier and she'd be spitting sawdust.

"You poor thing. Get your arse inside. Your father's probably had two already."

"He pays you, doesn't he? For the booze? You weren't lying when you said he paid his tab?"

He eyed her curiously, a tilt to his head. "What would you do, pay it?"

"Well, yeah." Never be in anyone's debt—it was a habit she'd tried to keep ever since Gracie paid for her schooling.

His eyes narrowed. "Didn't you tell me that your father never had to face any consequences for the things he did? You said everyone else in his life took the responsibility for him. I'm not going to tell you if he has a tab or how much it is. You paying it wouldn't change a damn thing—he'd just run it up again."

He was fucking with her head. That was *her* job. "Someone's been reading his *Psychology for Dummies*."

Jake leaned back with a smirk. "I don't need a book to understand *you*. Never did."

"I've got a freaking PhD and I still don't understand you."

Hands in his pockets, he rocked back on his heels, his smirk fading. "Liar." He walked away.

Audrey watched him go, letting him get a few steps ahead so she wouldn't be tempted to snap at his bait. Fortunately, he looked almost as good from the back as he did from the front—skinny ass and all—so it wasn't a hardship. If it was anyone else she'd wonder why he was so prickly with her when he had been the one to break her heart, but he was right—she didn't need a book to understand him either. He'd practically held the proverbial door open for her to leave Edgeport by sleeping with Maggie. She conceded when he called her home for Gracie's funeral, but she wasn't going to be the one to apologize. She'd slam that door on his fingers first, and hope that it hurt.

He was right that there were obviously people who couldn't give a sweet flying fuck about her and her past. A few heads turned at her entrance. A few stared; others turned back to their beer. A lot of them were young—young enough that she didn't recognize them, but obviously old enough to drink. It made sense that they wouldn't be interested in her; they didn't know who she was and they didn't care. And yes, it irked her.

Perspective sometimes cast an unflattering shadow.

Her father sat at the bar, so she hopped up onto the stool beside him. His posture was relaxed, but it wouldn't take much to set him off again. Violence was cathartic—like a good cry, only with blood instead of tears. She understood it. Sometimes the only way to let all the emotion out was to hit something. Or someone.

Behind the bar—where his brother, Lincoln, poured draft— Jake said something to a young bleached blonde woman wearing a tight tank top. She smiled up at him like he was some kind of god, bestowing his munificence upon her. He grinned back and touched her bare arm.

Suddenly, Audrey felt the need for a little catharsis.

Jake turned his head and looked at her as he lifted his hand from the girl's tanned skin. Audrey arched a brow. Stupid to be jealous, but she was. She knew it wasn't rational, but he was like a splinter under her nail that had burrowed deep and festered, poisoned her blood. That made him *hers*.

The blonde set a Sam Adams in front of her father. "Here you go, Rusty."

Her father grinned, all grizzled charm. "Thank you, Donalda darlin'. You remember my daughter, Audrey? Sweetheart, Donalda's Reggie LeBlanc's youngest."

"Hi," Audrey said, trying to look at least passably pleasant when confronted with such stereotypical youth and beauty. "I think I went to school with your brother Jimmy."

The girl looked at her with wide brown eyes. "Wow, hi! I think I was seven or eight when you left for college. Nice to see you again." Then she bounced away to tend to a customer at the other end of the bar who called her name.

Lincoln looked up from the tap. He had the same hazel eyes as Jake, but any other similarities between them were found in mannerisms rather than physical features. With his dark hair hanging loose about his shoulders, Lincoln was one of those guys who could actually pull off dressing like a rock star and not look like he was trying too hard. Unfortunately, he knew it, and worked it.

"Audrey Harte," he said with a grin, holding out his hand. "Look at you."

Audrey slipped her fingers into his, squeezing his hand before letting go. "Good to see you, Linc."

He shook his head, hair glossy beneath the bar lights. "Jay said you were home, but he didn't mention that you'd gotten even more gorgeous." He turned to her father. "You and the missus do good work, Rusty."

Rusty laughed and waved him off. "Go flirt with someone else, boy."

Lincoln grinned, swinging his attention back to Audrey. "Hopefully I'll see you again before you take off."

She nodded. Nothing like attention from the older brother of the guy who rejected her to make a girl feel pretty. "I'm home for a week."

Jake tapped his brother on the arm with the back of his knuckles. "Carl's trying to get your attention."

"Got it." Lincoln shot Audrey another grin before returning to work. She grinned back.

Jake poured what looked to be a lot more than an ounce of dark rum in a glass, tossed in some ice, and topped it up with diet cola. He set the glass on the scarred wood in front of Audrey, and then dropped a cherry in it. "I'm going home," he said, jaw tight. "You two try to stay out of trouble."

"We make no promises." Her father smiled. "Thanks for the beer."

"And the cherry," Audrey drawled. Jake looked at her a moment before a mockery of a smile curved his lips. He nodded as though they'd just shared a private joke, and then he was gone. What had she expected? That he'd thank her for gracing him with her presence?

Her father turned his head toward her. "Never could understand what you saw in that smug bastard."

Lifting her glass, Audrey clinked it against the bottle in his hand. The cherry bobbed like a tiny red bomb just dying to explode. "Neither do I, Dad. Neither do I."

It was Sunday morning and her father wasn't hungover—a sight Audrey didn't remember seeing ever before. He usually binged on the weekends. Sobriety didn't make him any more open to Jesus, however.

"I'm not going to goddamned church," he informed her mother, his cheeks flushing with good old-fashioned Irish defiance.

"John!" his wife exclaimed, setting the butter dish on the table so hard Audrey thought it might break. "Language!"

"I'm not going to *fucking* church," he amended, odd-colored eyes glittering. "The rest of this town might be a bunch of Sunday-morning hypocrites, but not me."

John Harte had never been much of a churchgoer, but this outburst was overly angry, even for him. It was like he had a personal beef with religion. Then again, Audrey didn't remember her mother being a regular attendee. Things had definitely changed since the last time she'd come home, because her mother was all decked out in a pretty pale yellow dress with matching heels. She had put on a little makeup and had the purse Audrey had given her for her birthday over her arm. She probably had the wallet David bought her in there too.

"I'm going," Audrey interjected. No thanks to either of her siblings. David, the little bugger, had been smart when he flew back to New York earlier that morning. No doubt he'd done it to escape church duty. He'd be back next week for July Fourth weekend, so Audrey would be able to get revenge before returning to L.A.

Her father shot her a look that said she'd just proved his point. "Good for you." Then, to her mother, "You do what you need to do, Annie, but I'm out."

Her parents stared at each other, the air between them seeming to buckle under the intensity. Audrey looked from one to the other and back again. "What the hell's going on?" she asked.

Her mother's lips thinned as she turned away from her husband. "You and I are going to church." Then she brushed past John as though she'd rather die than touch him.

Audrey followed her, pausing beside her father. "Dad?"

He waved her away with a negligent flick of his wrist. "It's okay, Auddie. Just a difference of opinion. You're a good girl to go with her."

"Who are you and what have you done with my father?" Then, "And when did you add 'fuck' to your vocabulary?"

"Only about, oh, fifty-five fucking years ago." He gave her a slight smile. "And no, we're not discussing it—you're our kid, not our therapist. Get out of here; your mother's waiting."

"You know, I never could understand what she sees in you, you smug bastard."

A twinkle lit his eyes—topaz and aquamarine. "Neither do I."

The most ridiculous urge to hug him struck her as she walked toward the door. She didn't give in. This conflict of love and anger she felt toward her father was old news. She would be careful to remember that, so she didn't buy into the good, only to get hurt when he slipped into bastard mode. She walked by him, through to the porch, and out to the dooryard where her mother sat in the passenger side of the Mini Cooper.

"You don't want to take your car?" Audrey asked as she opened the door. Her mother never let her drive.

"No. I've decided I want you to chauffeur me."

"Okay." She didn't ask any more questions, since it was obvious her mother was not in the mood for conversation. People rarely stayed the same their entire lives, and her mother was in her sixties—it made sense that she'd changed some habits in the seven years since Audrey had last been home, even in the months since they'd met in New York. Still, it was weird to discover that time hadn't just stood still in Edgeport while she'd been off living her life in L.A.

But church? The only time Audrey ever remembered going as a kid was Easter and Christmas—before Stillwater, that was. After that she never went to church at all. This would be the first time in more than fifteen years. She was only going now because it obviously meant something to her mother that she did.

Hopefully the place wouldn't burst into flames when she walked in.

The United Church of Edgeport wasn't fancy—white with dark trim and a steeple with a bell that hadn't rung in at least fifty years. It had been built by the town in 1920, when the town minister declared the Tripp family a godless bunch and refused to preach on their land anymore. Apparently, old Elias Tripp— Jake's great-great-grandfather—took to preaching himself, and the town was divided between which church to attend for several years, until Elias dropped dead at the pulpit during a particularly inspired sermon. He was buried in the Tripp graveyard, and the little church was used only for Christmas celebrations and Tripp family weddings after that. And funerals, of course. Gracie's had been held there, the crowd spilling out into the field.

When she'd been young and stupid, Audrey had fantasized about getting married in that church.

The gravel lot was full, and there were cars parked on the grass, their dusty tires flattening the dark green blades.

"Busy spot," Audrey commented as she parked next to a battered pickup that was three different shades of faded blue underneath an unhealthy amount of rust.

"Church is always full after a death," her mother replied.

Maggie.

Somehow—for at least a few hours—Audrey had forgotten that her old frenemy was dead. Murdered—probably by someone in the town. The killer might even be inside the church.

She pulled the keys from the ignition. "Did you bring me here so people will think I'm innocent?"

"It won't hurt."

"Murderers go to church, Mum. Either to throw suspicion off themselves or as a way to stay close to their crime."

Her mother didn't even look at her. "Well, today you're going because I want to remind people who you are. You are my daughter, and you are not a murderer."

"Except they all know that I am."

"Don't say that. You were a scared little girl."

A scared little girl who had put a grown man in the ground, but she didn't remind her mother of that. She remembered the look on Maggie's face when she realized her father was dead—not something she wanted to think about. She didn't want to think of Maggie at all. Not alive, and certainly not dead. If she didn't think about it, she didn't have to face it. "We'd better go in."

There were a few people milling about at the entrance, chatting. Binky Taylor, wearing his best boots and work pants, tipped his cap to them as they climbed the wide, shallow steps. Albert Neeley's wife, Mary, stood just inside the door, talking to Jeannie, who shot Audrey a glare as she passed.

"Someday, Jeannie," she warned, "your face is going to stick like that."

Anne grabbed her by the hand and pulled her into the dim interior of the foyer. They stood right in front of the door to the lower level where the kitchen area, choir robes, and bathroom were. The door had been painted a butterscotch color when Audrey was a kid. Now it was plain stained oak. Very pretty. In fact, all that old paint was gone. It must have been a hellish job.

Her mother's cheeks were flushed. "That was very rude."

"I'm pretty sure Jeannie can take it—and that she deserved it. When did they strip the paint off the woodwork?"

A frustrated sigh filled the air between them. "A few years ago. You are so much like your father. I swear, sometimes I just want to smash your heads together and see if it makes either one of you any less determined to make yourselves social pariahs."

"I'm sure it's some kind of personality disorder. Probably one that hasn't any treatment. You should trust me on this—I'm a *doctor*."

"Smart-ass." But there was a hint of a smile on her lips.

"Wonder what side I get that from." Audrey turned on her heel and started up the left-side stairs to the upper floor where services were held. The old runner had been replaced, but the wood still creaked in the same old places. At the top there was a small landing with a door on either side, one for each staircase.

Audrey balked at the threshold. The church was full—death tended to bring everyone together, as her mother had said, and everyone would be hoping to hear the latest word on what the police thought had happened. Walking into that felt like taking her life into her own hands—stupid and reckless. Careless. It was like the stained-glass windows were slides and she was the specimen trapped between them to be viewed under a microscope. It was paranoid thinking, but not totally irrational, she told herself. It wasn't as though the people of this town wouldn't have reason to wonder at the coincidence of Maggie being killed during her first trip home in years.

Her mother took her by the hand once again and pulled her inside. Anne held her head high as she marched Audrey to a center pew. People noticed them, of course. Luckily there was enough conversation going on that the noise became one incomprehensible drone. If Christ himself walked in singing show tunes, she doubted she would have heard it. They sat down almost halfway into the row, her mother picking their placement exactly, as though good seats mattered in church.

Audrey turned her attention toward the pulpit, her gaze lighting on a familiar profile to her left and a couple of rows in front of her. Neve. It wasn't hard to recognize her: Her mother and brothers were still the only black people in Edgeport. Her father was white, but his size and rugged appearance made him hard to miss as well. Eighteen years ago he'd been intimidating when he'd questioned herself and Maggie about Clint's death. Those years hadn't done much to soften him. The sight of him made her heart jump nervously—a little girl's reaction to a big, rugged cop who'd looked at her as though there was something wrong with her.

There'd been something *wrong* with the whole fucking town.

Deep breaths. Sometimes anger felt good—cleansing. This was one of those times, but sitting in church, in front of the town's most pious and judgmental, looking like she wanted to gut someone, wasn't going to win her any friends.

The choir came in and took their seats in the front of the church. The reverend—Donna Whittaker, who'd been the local minister for almost twenty years—was right behind them. Her hair was totally gray, her face lined. Judging from the woman's pinched expression, Audrey went ahead and made the assumption that the years hadn't made her any more pleasant to be around. The sermon was going to be thirty minutes of torture mixed with a couple of mournful hymns. If she had something long and sharp she'd rupture her eardrums and save herself.

Murmurs rose behind her, but Audrey didn't look—she didn't want to see all those faces staring back. She barely turned her head to look as someone slid into the pew and sat down beside her.

It was Jake. All that fuss suddenly made sense. She'd bet her favorite pair of Miu Miu pumps that he hadn't set foot in this place since…well, ever. If the place hadn't burst into flames by now it probably wasn't going to. Yancy and a girl Audrey assumed was her daughter sat down beside him. Yancy cast a hesitant glance at her. Audrey smiled automatically—a habit formed over years of trying to put people at ease. Then, she turned her attention to Yancy's brother, sitting there in black pants and a white shirt, looking like butter wouldn't melt in his damn mouth. His hair was reasonably neat. He even wore shoes. He'd neglected to shave, though.

"What are you doing here?" Audrey whispered.

Jake turned his head, his expression all guileless innocence. "Were you hoping for Lincoln?"

Was he jealous, or just being a dick? "No."

"I wanted to see Reverend Donna's eyes roll back into her head when she sees you."

"How did you know I would be here?"

He shrugged. "I had a feeling." He leaned closer, so that their shoulders touched. "Ten bucks says she starts speaking in tongues."

Audrey choked on a laugh. Her mother elbowed her, shooting Jake a dirty look. He smiled sweetly in return. "Good morning, Mrs. Harte. You look exceptionally lovely today."

Anne's eyes narrowed. She looked as though she'd bitten into something bitter. "Thank you, Jake. I hope you don't plan on making my daughter giggle throughout the entire service?"

Jake didn't look the least bit offended. "No, ma'am."

It was the immovable object meeting the unstoppable force. She was saved from having to decide who was which when Reverend Donna began her sermon.

"Good morning, friends. It's good to see so many of you here today, though I know many of you are here in the hope of making sense of yesterday's tragedy. Sometimes it's difficult to have faith when faced with such terrible violence—we wonder how a kind and gentle God could allow one of His flock to murder another." She looked right at Audrey. Didn't she? It was hard to tell with the light reflecting off the minister's bifocals just where her gaze struck.

"But I can tell you, my friends, that it wasn't God who allowed Maggie McGann to be cut down so early. It was the work of the Devil. God gave us free will, and while most of us choose to live a good and Christian life, there are those who are beyond God's reach."

Audrey's jaw tightened. She couldn't tell if the woman was talking about her, or if it was just her own guilty conscience raising its voice.

"In these dark and trying times, we must come together as a community, to heal and comfort one another. I know it's difficult to practice love and compassion when fear and anger make us look at our neighbors with suspicion, but we must try to open our hearts so that those who have darkness in theirs will come forward and ask forgiveness."

Yep. Reverend Donna was talking to her. Audrey met the older woman's gaze without shame. She was not going to "ask forgiveness" for something she didn't do.

"Let us bow our heads and pray," the reverend went on. "Pray for the soul of our departed, Maggie McGann, that God will lift her up and welcome her into His kingdom. Pray for her husband, Gideon, stepdaughter Bailey, and her brother, Matthew, that they find comfort and strength in this sorrowful time. And pray that the shadow that has fallen over us will soon be lifted, and that those who are lost will find their way back to God. Pray that the prodigal will seek redemption, and that we, like the father in that story, will offer the same love and forgiveness. Let us pray."

Reverend Donna bowed her head and began to pray. Audrey couldn't bring herself to do the same. She sat there, dumb and frozen. The prodigal? It didn't take much to figure out who *that* was. She'd had meaner things said to her in life, and certainly with less eloquence, but never with such conviction. It was as though the woman had already weighed her soul and found it damnably lacking.

Warm fingers closed around hers. She looked down to see Jake's hand wrapped around her own. When she lifted her gaze to his face, he didn't look at her. He kept his gaze fastened on Reverend Donna, and if looks could kill, the woman would be lying on the pulpit hemorrhaging from the ears.

And then her mother took hold of her other hand, lacing their fingers together in a tight weave. Audrey sat there, held in place by two of the very few living people whose opinion of her truly mattered. The realization brought the hot sting of tears to her eyes, but she blinked them away so they couldn't stream freely down her cheeks without her hands free to wipe them away.

She made it through the service somehow. When everyone stood to sing the selected hymns, she made certain to sing along. Jake stood silent beside her. He didn't sing, even though she knew he could. He didn't bow his head. He stood there, hands in his pockets, staring a hole in Reverend Donna, whose only sin had been to preach forgiveness.

Afterward, when it was finally over, Audrey escaped outside while her mother stopped to talk to several older women, each of whom fixed her mother with sympathetic gazes while ignoring Audrey altogether. Jake, she noticed, leaned against the hood of Reverend Donna's car—the same car she'd driven for as long as Audrey could remember—arms folded over his chest. It was a position she'd seen him adopt more times than she could count, waiting for her to come out of the house so they could pick up as many friends as his old car would hold and head off to wherever the party was. Only back then he waited with a smile.

Was he seriously going to give a minister a hard time for spouting her ideas of Biblical charity and guilt? No doubt he could quote the Scripture just as well as she. Gracie had been big on knowing her Bible—mostly so she could turn it around on people who used it to judge her or those she loved. She'd said it was a dangerous weapon in the hands of the small-minded, and that she and her brood ought to know how to defend themselves.

A man stepped in front of her. "You got a lot of nerve."

She stiffened, rearing back from the invasion of personal space. He was wiry, not much taller than she was. Life had left a lot of heavy traffic on his face, but he wasn't even thirty. Matthew Jones—Maggie's younger brother. Fabulous. Just who she needed to have in her face reeking of stale sweat with a hint of beer-vomit. His blue eyes were bloodshot as he glared at her.

"Coming back here. Walking around like you're something special. A *lot* of nerve after what you did."

"I don't want any trouble, Matt," she said, carefully. And she really didn't want it in front of almost the entire town from a guy who had been in and out of jail since he was sixteen and smelled like he'd been drunk for a week.

His nostrils flared as he sucked in breath. "You should have thought of that before you killed my father."

"Clint?" Did she look as dumbfounded as she sounded? This was about that child-raping bastard rather than his sister? That was—what was the clinical term? Oh, yes—*fucked-up.*

"Don't you say his name!" Spit flew. Audrey barely managed to dodge it. "The two of you took him away and ruined my life. My sister got what she deserved, and I hope you do too." With that, he pivoted on his heel and stomped away, weaving slightly.

Maggie got what she deserved? That was pretty harsh, even for someone he blamed for ruining his life.

"Audrey."

Off-kilter, she turned, not at all surprised to see Neve walking toward her. First Matt and now this. Maybe she should take up praying after all.

Neve's long, tight curls hung around her shoulders, glossy and bright despite the overcast day. She wore a pretty tangerine dress and flats but still managed to look as though she could kick the ass of anyone who presented the challenge.

Audrey sighed and tried to muster a sincere smile. "Neve. Hi."

The other woman—who was even more gorgeous than she'd been in high school—opened her arms and came in for a brief hug. Audrey hugged back, but it was stiff. She hadn't expected such a warm greeting.

"What was that about?"

"Just a friendly welcome home."

"I bet." Neve released her and stepped back. "I don't want any of them speculating about our conversation," she explained in her low, smooth, no-nonsense voice.

"So this isn't just a friendly hello." It wasn't really a surprise, but it was still disappointing.

"I wish it was." Her russet gaze was direct, easily meeting Audrey's. "I'm investigating Maggie's death."

"And you heard that she and I had words at Gracie's Friday night."

Neve nodded. "I did. You may have been one of the last people who saw her alive."

A wry smile twisted Audrey's lips. "Maybe even *the* last—is that the implication here?"

The other woman's expression never changed. "I try to avoid implications. Would you be willing to meet me tomorrow and give a statement?"

If she told her no it would only make things worse. Better to get it over with if she couldn't avoid it. "Sure. When?" It might have been Audrey's imagination, but her old friend seemed to visibly relax.

"Around one or two? Jake's letting law enforcement use an old cottage on his land as a base so we're not running back and forth all the time. I figure meeting there would be better than me showing up at your parents' house."

"It is, and I appreciate it. Thanks. Which cottage?" There used to be a lot of Tripp houses in back of that cove. Who knew how many were still standing?

"You should remember it—it's not far from the camp. The little blue one."

Bitterness bloomed on her tongue. It would be that one. Maggie was probably getting a pedicure in hell laughing her ass off knowing that even dead, she could still stick it to Audrey. "I know it. I'll meet you there shortly after one."

"Great." Neve turned to go but paused mid turn. "For what it's worth, it's good to see you."

"You too."

Then she was gone—striding across the gravel to climb into her father's SUV. Everett Graham held the door open for his only daughter, but his gaze was fixed on Audrey, and it was obvious that he thought she was trouble. He was probably right, but she wasn't a scared little girl anymore. Audrey stared back, until he finally turned away and climbed into the vehicle. It wasn't much, but after the past couple of days, she'd take winning a staring contest against a hardened cop as a victory.

"What did she want?"

Was a moment of peace too much to ask? Audrey turned. Jake stood in front of her, frowning.

Lying to him didn't occur to her. Neither did telling him to stay out of it. "She wants to talk to me about Maggie, of course."

"When?"

"Tomorrow."

He frowned. "Come by the house tomorrow night. There's something I want to show you, but I promised I'd watch a movie with Alisha tonight."

"Just so there's no confusion, I'm not going to show you mine after you show me yours." *Ugh.* Stupid thing to say.

Surprise lit his angular features. Then he smiled, slow and sure, as he rocked back on his heels. "You know, when you sound so sure like that it just makes me want to prove you wrong."

Audrey's heart tapped her ribs. She gave him a coy smile. "You're welcome to try, Tripp." And then she brushed past him to intercept her mother, who had been walking across the gravel toward them, because no one wanted their mother to know they were still hung up on the town bad boy.

Although maybe this time she'd get the balls up to do something about it.

If she wasn't arrested first.

CHAPTER SEVEN

The cottage's blue paint was flaked and peeling, the windows covered with a dusty haze. It was early Monday afternoon, and Audrey stood at the foot of the rickety steps that led to the door, cursing herself for hesitating. She hadn't been in that cottage since the night she walked in and found Maggie and Jake naked on the old sofa. Good times.

The camp, as they called it, was another building not far away in the dense forest. That was where she'd spent most of her free time after getting out of Stillwater. She and Jake had become friends again when she returned—he'd even gotten her a job at the campground his grandparents owned. The flat grass and fire pits had been replaced by simple but luxurious cottages and a main building. The resort was lovely—Gracie would probably hate the look of it but love the profit it generated. The blue cottage and the camp were the only landmarks of Audrey's youth that remained.

She would have set fire to the blue one then and there if there hadn't been people in it.

The door opened to reveal Neve in a snug T-shirt and jeans. "Takes you back, doesn't it?" she asked. "Come see what I found." She stepped back into the dim interior, leaving the door gaping. Waiting.

No more putting it off. Audrey climbed the lopsided steps and hesitated only a split second before crossing the threshold.

It took a moment for her eyes to adjust to the lack of sunlight. Even though the curtains were pushed wide, there were only two windows in the main room. Both of them were open, letting in a pleasant breeze that almost succeeded in chasing away the musty smell of disuse.

"It's in better shape than I expected," she commented, her gaze traveling around the room. "It looks different." So much for it remaining unchanged.

Neve offered her a can of soda from a cooler on the plywood counter. "Jake brought some of his grandmother's old furniture in just after you moved to California. We had a huge bonfire with the old stuff. He took an axe to that old sofa—it still took forever to burn."

"I'm surprised it didn't go up in a blaze after all the booze spilled on it." She popped the top on the soda. He burned the sofa, huh? Her brain could run in so many different directions with that.

"And other things," Neve added with a grimace as she leaned her hip against the counter. "You should have left for school a week later—you could have seen it for yourself."

"Another week would have driven me crazy," Audrey confided. "I had to get out of here."

Neve's almond-shaped gaze sought hers. "Did you ever talk to her again after that?"

"Her" didn't need to be named. "Before Saturday night? She tried talking to me at the funeral." There was no need to put a name on that either, because she'd only returned for one.

"Tried?"

"That day was about Gracie, not Maggie and me. When she tried to engage I told her it wasn't going to happen and walked away."

Rounded brows rose. "That's harsh. What happened between the two of you?"

Audrey's eyes narrowed as she peered over the top of the can. "You don't know? I thought everyone knew."

Neve shook her head, looking her dead in the eye. "Maggie never said. Then again, it's hard to speak with a broken jaw."

It was an innocent enough remark—nothing but simple fact—but it felt heavier. Tricky.

She lowered her drink, despite the dryness of her mouth. The only people who made eye contact that intensely were cops and psychopaths. And in Audrey's experience, both were especially good at deception. "You know exactly what happened. You just wanted to see if I'd tell you the truth. Maybe engage in a little malingering?"

"Maybe," Neve replied with a shrug. "I guess you see a lot of that in your line of work."

"Yeah, I do, but mostly from teenagers." She set the soda on the scarred top of an old kitchen table. "It wasn't a proud moment for me, you know. I hadn't been out of Stillwater long—you're familiar with the place?"

Her old friend nodded, curls bouncing. She'd always had fabulous hair. "I've been there a couple of times since I got transferred. Reva Kim is very protective of her girls."

Audrey smiled. "Yes, she is. The facility does a good job with the girls who go there, and the education part of it is amazing."

"That's why old Gracie Tripp called in so many favors to get you sent there."

That wasn't exactly a secret either, but the reminder of all that Gracie had done for her hit Audrey sideways, knocking her off-kilter for a second. Her smile faded. "She did. Academically I flourished, but it was still a correctional facility, and every girl there, regardless of where they fit in the social strata, was there for a reason, and there was a lot of violence and pain. Anger. God knows I was full of it." *I still am.*

Neve folded her arms over her chest and crossed her right leg over the other. She wasn't comfortable with the conversation, Audrey could tell. Fair enough—Audrey wasn't comfortable either. "So, you beat Maggie senseless because you came out of Stillwater angrier than you went in?"

"No. I beat her up because she fucked the boy I loved just to teach me a lesson."

Dark eyes widened. Maybe that had been a little too honest of a response. Audrey went on. "She was mad that I was going to be leaving for school. Mad that she couldn't manipulate me like she used to. Sleeping with Jake was the best way she could think of to get my attention."

"She got it, all right. Apparently she got it again Friday night."

Audrey rubbed the knuckles on her right hand. There was still a scar from Maggie's teeth across the second one. "She was drunk and in my face. I pushed her, nothing more. She was still there when I left."

"Where did you go after leaving Gracie's?"

"I took my father home."

"Did you stay there?"

"No. I went for a drive."

Neve straightened. "Seriously?"

"Look, it's not like I knew Maggie was going to get herself killed. An alibi didn't occur to me. I was upset at her, and at my drunk-ass father, and I went for a goddamned drive." She sucked in a deep breath. Losing her temper wouldn't do her any favors, not when it was her damn temper that made her such a fabulous candidate for Maggie's murderer.

"Did anyone see you?"

"Wendell Stokes might have. I drove back the Ridge." Wendell had to be in his late eighties now, but unless he'd changed drastically in the years she'd been gone, he still kept a ledger of every vehicle that drove past his place. He was paranoid, even for a man who made moonshine. There were rumors that the woods around his house were laced with booby traps and that he couldn't sleep unless he had a shotgun in the bed with him and a box of shells under his pillow.

A little smile curved Neve's full lips. "To the falls?"

"Yeah. I sat in the dark for a bit, listened to the radio. Then I went home. Mum was up, so she can back that up."

"I'm going to talk to her—just so you know."

Audrey thought on that for a moment—and the frank way her old friend looked at her. "Am I the only person of interest?"

"You know I can't tell you that."

"You can tell me something. I mean, holy hell, Neve. Maggie might have been a twisted bitch, but at one time I would have done anything for her. I spent three years in Stillwater for her. My sister hates me. Everyone talks about me. I had to go across the country just to get away from what I did for Maggie. I might have resented her, but I couldn't kill her—not after all we've been through." That was over now. She and Maggie would never go through anything ever again. There was no more Maggie.

Audrey grabbed at one of the mismatched chairs and yanked it out from under the table. She fell into it, as limp kneed as a rag doll. "I can't believe she's dead." She laughed—a horribly harsh sound. "I can't believe you think I did it."

Neve sighed. "I don't *want* to think you did it, but it's my job to check out all the possibilities, and you're a possibility." She crossed the floor in a few quick strides and pulled out the chair next to Audrey, turning it so they sat facing each other. "Maggie's injuries are very similar to Clint's. The person accessed the beach through the woods, so they knew the area. And we found one bloody footprint that coincides with a woman's size ten."

"There are lots of women with size ten feet—or men with skinny size eight."

"She wasn't afraid of her attacker. There's no sign of her putting up a fight."

"None of this proves it was me, Neve. In fact, just the opposite. If Maggie saw me coming at her she'd back up, no matter how drunk she was. At least out of reach. Getting close at Gracie's was just for show."

"I know. It's all circumstantial. I shouldn't even be telling you any of this."

"And yet you are."

She shrugged. "This is too close to home to be a normal investigation. You have to admit that you have motive to want Maggie dead."

Audrey made a face. "What motive? That she pissed me off? If being annoyed was motive for murder, most of us would be serial killers. Seriously, if I was going to kill Maggie it would not be the same way Clint died."

Neve tilted her head. "The way you and Maggie killed him, you mean. Clint Jones didn't just die."

That pushed a button. "I *know* how Clint Jones died, and I don't remember seeing *you* there. He was a pedophile, a rapist—and probably a murderer—that this entire town knew about and never lifted a finger to stop."

Neve didn't argue that. "Who did he supposedly murder?"

"Maggie's older sister. She died before they moved here. Maggie thought Clint had molested her too, and killed her to keep her from telling."

"I never heard that." Neve sounded dubious. Fucking cops.

"Maybe you heard that Clint was in the process of raping Maggie when I arrived at her house that night? Ask your father—he'd know the results of the rape kit they did at the hospital. Maggie and I both had to have one." Clint had only made a grab for her once, when he'd been drunk. Audrey reminded him who her father was and he never even looked at her again.

Neve's gaze flitted away. "I'll check the case files."

Audrey tilted her head at the other woman's tone. "I'm not the only one in this room with daddy issues, I see."

"I didn't ask you to come here for therapy."

"Good, because I think we'd need way more than an hour."

Neve blinked. Then a smile curved her lips. "Hostile much?"

Time for a new tactic—and a deep breath. "If I close my eyes I can still *see* it—Clint on top of her, his white, hairy ass quivering with every thrust. I can hear the disgusting things he said to her. What kind of man tells his own daughter what a sweet pussy she has?"

Now she had Neve's attention. Audrey leaned forward. "What Maggie and I did might have been wrong, but there's never been a day that I've regretted putting Clint Jones in the fucking ground. He hit me, you know. Punched me hard in the face. Said he didn't care who my father was. He deserved to die. Maggie, though… she was messed up, but I had no reason to kill her, Neve. Not one."

She arched her damn eyebrows again. "Not even the fact that Maggie was writing a book about that night?"

Audrey shook her head. She couldn't have heard her correctly. "What?"

"She was jealous of your success. Everyone knew it. She hated that you had made something of yourself and had that TV show. She was overheard at Gracie's one night saying that she was going to tell the world what really happened the night Clint died, and then the world would see you for what you really were."

Audrey stared at her, her heart lodged so hard in her throat that she couldn't speak. She laughed instead. "That's ridiculous."

"Yeah? So nothing happened that night that the two of you forgot to tell? Or maybe that the two of you agreed to lie about?"

"Like what, Detective?" Audrey was careful not to lean back in her chair or cross her arms. She kept her posture relaxed rather than defensive. "We confessed. What else could there possibly be to tell?"

Neve drummed her fingers on the rough tabletop. "Supposedly, something you'd kill to keep quiet. Some truth you don't want to get out."

"No," Audrey replied in a firm tone, wishing she felt as certain as she sounded. "Because the *truth* is already out. I hit him once and Maggie finished the job when he turned on me. That's what happened."

The other woman stared at her for a long moment. Audrey stared back, unflinching and cool. Her heart rate hadn't even accelerated. Her posture was easy and open, as was her expression. She knew she didn't look or sound like a liar.

But she was.

Dear Audrey,

As much as it hurt, there's a part of me that wants to thank you for breaking my jaw. The doctor reset it, and I think it made a big difference in my looks. I can't stop looking at myself in the mirror. I don't care if it's vain, I love my face now. I'm sorry you never got a chance to see it before you left for L.A.

I want to share something with you. Yeah, I know you're never going to see this, but I need to tell someone, and I'd rather tell a fake you than anyone else. When I went to the hospital after we did what we did, I found out I was pregnant. How's that for a huge cosmic fucking joke? Fourteen and pregnant by my own damn father. It's like a backwoods nightmare. I didn't keep her, obviously. Sometimes I wonder about her. She'd be almost four now. I know giving her away was the right thing to do—I can't even keep a cactus alive—but there are days when it doesn't feel right. As far as I know she turned out okay despite being her own sister. Weird, huh? I'm glad she's with people who will love her, because I don't think I could have. Loved her, that is. Not the way I should. I wouldn't be able to look at her without thinking about how she came to be. What would I say if she asked who her father was? No kid deserves that. I didn't want to hate her, or have her hate me. It was probably wrong of me to even have her. I should have had an abortion, but a nurse at the hospital got me in touch with a pro-life group. Yeah, that's right. Pro-life. I like to imagine your reaction to reading that. Anyway, I had her and then I let her go. I just wanted you to know that. No one else. Maybe someday I'll give you this stupid journal—put it in a box and send it to you in L.A. I'm so jealous that you're living there now, making all your dreams come true, you fucking bitch. Would it kill you to send me an e-mail? Or a postcard? I'm not greedy, I just miss you. And I would like to know where to send this journal when it's finished. I'm putting a picture in it for you. This is the best place for the only one I have of my baby. They let me name her. Her new parents probably named her something different, but I wanted you to know that I named her Audrey.

Approximately three-quarters of a mile out on Tripp's Cove was a small island called Minerva's Folly. It was Tripp land, named for Minerva Tripp, who cheated on her husband, Angus, in the summer of 1792 with Davin Harte. When Angus found out, he banished her to the little island to live out the rest of her days. He thought it was punishment, but Davin was a sea dog and often rowed out to meet with his lover, who was thrilled to no longer have to look at her husband's miserable face. Unfortunately, that face was the last thing Minerva and Davin ever saw, as legend had it that Angus took a little boat trip out to the island and shot them both. He claimed to have found them dead when he arrived, but since he buried the bodies on the island—and because his personality was even more miserable than his face—no one ever questioned him.

Jake and Lincoln used to camp out on the island, near the stone foundation of Minerva's cottage. It was also where they met their hashish supplier from Nova Scotia, who also arrived by boat. Jake didn't have much need for drug income anymore, but Lincoln still occasionally made a late-night journey out to the island, which was then followed by a flurry of after-hours visitors to his apartment above Gracie's.

"I don't care what you do," Jake had told him. "Just don't do it in my house." That applied to all of his "houses." Linc shrugged and that was the end of the discussion. He could deal in his apartment, but not the bar.

The Cove Resort offered guided sea kayaking trips out to Minerva's Folly July through September. Every June, Jake took a trip out to make sure the old foundation and well were still roped off, and that his guests weren't going to find the decaying corpse of a French-Canadian drug trafficker who had gotten stoned and fallen to his death on the rocks. It was a quick paddle—about an hour or so round-trip, unless he had to battle the current. He spent another hour inspecting the island and the ruins of Minerva's cottage. He didn't need to take that long, but he did because he enjoyed the quiet.

He had just returned home after his annual inspection to find his niece, Alisha, and her friend Bailey McGann watching a movie in his living room. Each girl was sprawled on one of the two sofas, with a bowl of potato chips in her lap and a soda within reach.

"Don't you have a TV at home?" he asked his niece. Normally he liked having her around, but if Audrey actually showed up he wanted to be able to have some privacy.

She grinned at him—all round cheeks and bright blue eyes. She looked a lot like Yancy except for her eyes. They were the only good thing her useless father ever gave her. Her hair was dyed a light blonde, but it looked good on her. She did not look her age, and that scared him. "Yours is better. Besides, Mom has a guy over. Can I stay here again tonight?"

"Yeah," Jake replied without hesitation. "What guy?"

She cast an anxious glance at her friend. "Matthew Jones."

Maggie's brother. No wonder she was concerned about saying his name in front of Bailey, but her concern was misplaced. The other girl didn't even blink. In fact, she didn't seem to even be listening. No, it was Jake who hated hearing it. Jones was bad news, but then that entire family had been seriously fucked-up for a long time.

"She seeing him now?" He kept his tone neutral. Bored.

Alisha shrugged, absently chewing on the hood-lace of a gray hoodie at least two sizes too big for her. "I guess. He's been over a few times."

Which meant Yancy was sleeping with him. His sister had a good heart, but shitty judgment where men were concerned. The bigger the loser, the harder his sister seemed to fall.

His niece glanced at the TV. "You got a call while you were out."

Jake frowned. "On the house phone?" No one but banks and telemarketers ever called that number.

"Yep."

"Who was it?"

Alisha hesitated, casting another glance at the vacant Bailey. "Audrey Harte."

It was like throwing a switch, the way Bailey came to life at the mention of Audrey's name. "Audrey Harte? You know her?"

Jake nodded. It wasn't a question that needed an answer. "What did she want, Lish?"

His niece wasn't looking at him, but at Bailey. "They were more than friends."

Jake's frown turned into a scowl. "No we weren't."

The snorting noise that came out of her made him want to send her home, Yancy and her weasel of a hookup be damned. "Please, Uncle Jake. She beat up Maggie when you slept with her. Girls don't do that unless one messed with the other's guy."

He was never—*ever*—Audrey's guy. He would remember if he had been.

Bailey's eyes were wide as they suddenly saw him in a whole new light. It was disconcerting. Creepy even. Teenage girls were only slightly less unsettling than ventriloquist dummies in his opinion. "She beat up Maggie?"

Fuck it all. He shot Alisha a look that had her shrinking into her ridiculous hoodie. She had her mother's discretion, that was for fucking certain. Jake turned to the other girl. "That doesn't mean she had anything to do with Maggie's death."

She made a face. "*Sha.*" If his grandmother were still alive the girl would have been verbally flayed six ways from Sunday, Monday, *and* Tuesday for talking to someone older than her that way. "Maggie talked about her all the time. I just never knew they'd fought over *you.*" She looked at him in that coy way that only teenage girls could—like she was intrigued by the fact that he might actually be a sexual person. Or a prize to be won.

Jake held her gaze. "They didn't fight over me." Because of him, but not over. It was the second time he'd had to make that distinction since Saturday.

"But they did fight?"

"Of course they did!" Alisha retorted before he could. Then, with a sideways glance at him, "Didn't they?"

God help him. Her mother's mouth and her father's brains. He was going to have to make sure he spent a good amount of time with her this summer, give her some of the opportunities and guidance his grandmother had given him. They'd start with the importance of listening to gossip but not repeating it. "They did," he replied. "Now, what did Audrey say when she called?"

"She said you could call her at her mother's if you still want her to come over." Wide blue eyes turned to almost complete circles. "Are you *sleeping* with her?"

Now they were both staring at him. "What in the name of sweet fuck makes you think that would be any of your god-damned business?"

His niece smirked. "So you're not."

Maybe she didn't need any lessons from him after all. "Fuck off, kid." He turned around, left them giggling behind him as he went back to the kitchen. If he had to choose between a chain-saw vasectomy and spending the rest of his life dealing with teenage girls, he'd put a new chain on the Husqvarna and find something to bite down on.

There was a cordless phone in his bedroom, but in the kitchen it was still the push-button that had been there since long before he'd been born. It was a horrible shade of yellow his grandmother had called "marigold," and the buttons were so badly worn that half of them stuck and you could scarcely make out the numbers.

He could dial the Harte house from memory, but he hesitated for a moment, his brain blank. If he made this call, he was going to be putting himself in the middle of a murder investigation. He didn't need the cops looking too closely at his business and his comings and goings. For that matter, he didn't need the town watching him either. Or Lincoln.

But this was Audrey. Aud. Until that night at the camp she'd been his best friend. His only friend. She was the only person who had ever seen him cry, and how he felt about her was a strange dichotomy of love and anger even Merriam-Webster couldn't define.

His finger pushed one button and then another. His mind might be faulty, but his muscle memory wasn't. He braced his forearm along the width of the cupboard beside his head and leaned into it as he listened to the ringing.

"Hello?" came a voice in his ear.

He closed his eyes. For a moment he was eighteen and calling her to see if she wanted to go for a drive. He said what he always said: "It's me."

"Your secretary told you I called?" Laughter in her tone.

"That was my niece."

"Yeah, I deduced as much."

Deduced. Like she was Sherlock Holmes. He picked at an ancient sticker on the side of the phone. "You want to come up?"

"If the invitation still stands."

"It does." Jake glanced at the clock. "Have you eaten?"

"No."

"I'll cook."

Silence for a beat. "Okay. When should I come up?"

"Whenever you're ready. I'll start on dinner now."

"See you in a bit, then."

He hung up, a smile tugging insistently at his lips. He went to the fridge and pulled out leftover roast chicken, vegetables, and butter, then gathered the rest of what he needed from the pantry.

Within a few minutes he had chicken and vegetables cut up and in a bowl. Then he started in on making piecrust.

Alisha wandered out into the kitchen, an empty glass in her hand. "What are you making?" she asked, pulling a bottle of soda from the fridge. For the first few months after she and her mother moved back to Edgeport, they'd lived with Jake and he cooked for them almost every night, teaching Yancy most of the recipes.

"Chicken pot pie," he replied, flouring the rolling pin.

"Great-Gramma's?"

He smiled at the hopefulness in her tone. "Yep."

She came to stand beside him. "Can I help?"

Jake hesitated. Then he made the mistake of looking in her eyes. The kid had had him wrapped around her finger since he first laid eyes on her. He had taken Yancy to the hospital when she went into labor. He was with her in the delivery room. "Get the pan from the cupboard."

Alisha practically danced with glee, fool that she was. Jake shook his head at her as he rolled out the pastry.

A few moments later, Bailey appeared—she must have heard them laughing. The two of them were covered in flour—thanks to Alisha.

"You staying for dinner, Bee?" Jake asked. Only because of Alisha. Having her around would only make Audrey uncomfortable, and he didn't want the girl hearing any of their conversation.

"Thanks, Jake, but no. I called Dad. He's coming to get me. You two look like idiots, by the way."

Jake reached into the flour bag, pulled out a handful, and threw it at her.

"Asshole!" she cried, laughing.

God, she was a pale kid—dark circles under her eyes. Losing Maggie so violently had to have been hard on her, even if they weren't terribly close. She smelled like hash—something he was going have to ask Linc about. He'd told his brother twice that dealing to the local kids was not a smart business choice. Don't shit where you eat, as his grandmother used to say.

His grandmother would have looked at this girl and said something like, "You all right, my dar?" Jake didn't ask. It wasn't his business or his problem, and that sort of question often came with consequences he had no interest in facing—like sobbing little girls. When Alisha didn't try to persuade her friend to stay, he wondered if maybe his niece was a little more perceptive than he often gave her credit for.

A vehicle pulled into the drive a few minutes later. Alisha answered the door because Jake was arranging pastry in a baking dish.

"Hey, Mr. McGann," she said.

Gideon smiled wearily as he ran a hand through his graying brown hair. "How many times do I have to tell you not to be so formal with me, Alisha?"

She shrugged. "Till calling you by your first name feels right, I guess."

Jake smiled to himself. There was a little Gracie Tripp in the kid after all. "I'd shake your hand but..."

His old friend waved him off. "I don't mind being left out of your flour bath." He brushed his hand over his daughter's white-dusted hair so gently Jake almost felt embarrassed to have seen it. "You have everything, sweetie?"

Bailey nodded, leaning into him. Jake looked away. Witnessing vulnerability always felt like peeking in windows.

Another car pulled into the yard. Shit.

Gideon glanced out the screen door. "Is that Audrey?" he asked quietly.

"Yes," Jake replied. He waited. Gideon probably wasn't going to make trouble, but grief did strange things to people. He knew that. After his grandmother died, he'd done a host of things he'd rather not remember.

Audrey knocked on the doorframe and let herself in before anyone could intercept. The door smacked shut behind her just as she looked up and saw who Jake had for company. She went as still as a deer in a jacker's headlights.

"Hello," she said.

"Hi," Alisha and Bailey chorused.

Gideon inclined his head. "Go wait for me in the truck, Bailey."

"But..." Her voice trailed off as she apparently realized her father meant business. "Okay. See ya, Jake."

"See ya, kiddo." He wiped his hands on a dish towel, just in case he needed to use them on Gideon. "Lish, walk her out."

The girls hurried outside, both of them looking at Audrey like she was some kind of celebrity.

"Gideon," she said softly. "I don't want any trouble."

"And I don't mean to give you any," he replied. "I know you wouldn't hurt Maggie. That you didn't."

Jake's gaze narrowed. He *knew*, did he? Knew it like Jake himself knew it? Or because he'd been the one who bashed his wife's head in?

Audrey seemed just as puzzled. "You do?"

Gideon, who had known both of them for most of their lives, nodded. "Maggie talked a lot about how she regretted the way things went between the two of you. I know she was rude that night at Gracie's, but she planned to apologize to you the next day. Regardless, you"—he swallowed—"*hurting* her after that little tussle just doesn't make sense. It's like a bad movie plot."

The sound Audrey made might have been a sob—or a laugh. "Well, it's starting to feel like I'm starring in that movie, but thanks. I appreciate that."

"Actually," Gideon began, clearing his throat, "I was hoping I might beg a favor?"

Audrey's brows shot up. "Oh?"

He raked his hand through his hair again. "I don't suppose you would consider talking to Bailey?"

"In what capacity?"

"Professional."

Jake spooned the bowl of vegetables and chicken into the pastry shell. He hadn't seen this coming.

Audrey shook her head. "I'm not a clinical psychologist—I do assessments and interviews for research and court cases." She was an occasional expert witness, assistant, and sometimes consultant, but she did *not* give therapy. Mostly because sometimes the wrong words came out of her mouth. "Besides, I'm a person of interest."

"I don't care. I've seen your show. And your mother's told me about your work. My daughter's not herself, and I don't know what to do."

"She's grieving." Jake noticed that she looked at Gideon as if weighing the fact that he ought to be grieving as well. He wasn't— at least not like a husband should.

"It started before Maggie died. Please, Audrey. I've tried to get her to talk to someone else, but she says there's nothing wrong."

"Maybe she's telling you the truth." It sounded weak.

"She's gone from the top of her class to close to the bottom, and she smells like Lincoln—no offense, Jake."

"None taken," Jake replied. Of course Gideon had noticed the drugs—he'd smoked enough of them in his own youth.

Had he ever noticed that same smell on Maggie?

Audrey was quiet, her indecision plain on her face. He could almost read her thoughts: She was reluctant to talk to the girl in case it came back to bite her on the ass, but that part of her that had always cared more about everyone other than herself wanted to help. She was going to cave. She always did. It was that white-knight complex of hers that got her in trouble more than her temper.

"I'll talk to her," she told Gideon, who looked so relieved it was almost sad. "But you have to let Neve know you asked me to do it—and that I resisted. Agreed?"

"Of course. Thanks so much." He reached into his jeans and pulled out a card. "This is my cell. Call me when you're ready and we'll set something up. I really appreciate this."

She nodded and took the card. "I can't promise she'll talk to me."

"I think she will. She's asked about you a few times already. And she's heard Maggie's stories about you."

"Hmm." Her smile looked more like a grimace.

Gideon said good-bye and left, leaving Jake and Audrey alone for the few moments it would take for Alisha to return.

"That was good of you," Jake said. "Probably not smart, but good."

"Well, I can't let the girl go around smelling like Lincoln, can I?" She slid the card into the pocket of her jeans.

Jake smiled. "You could, but that would just be cruel."

Her lips twitched. "You're covered in flour."

Not so subtle change of subject. "Lish and I were being idiots. Let me finish the pie and I'll go shower."

"Gracie's chicken pot pie?"

"You know it." He almost laughed at the joy on her face.

She didn't ask if she could help—she knew him too well. Instead, she stood not far away, hip pressed against the counter, and watched him work. She didn't speak until he'd put the dish in the oven. "You own half the town, you can cook, you're not ugly, and you play surrogate father to your niece. Why aren't you married, Jake?"

Not ugly? Married? His good humor faded as he straightened and turned to meet her teasing gaze. Was she serious? Or fishing? "What the fuck is that about?"

She shrugged, not the least bit fazed by his sharp tone. "People ask me all the time."

"I don't care about people. You and I aren't *people*."

"You don't get asked because you're a guy. You're allowed to be in your thirties and single. Childless. It's all good, but there must be something wrong with me."

He didn't know where this was coming from and he didn't care. He stepped as close to her as he dared. "There *is* something wrong with you," he said, voice low. "I like the part of you that's wrong. Always have. We're single because no one in their right goddamned minds would have either of us."

She actually smiled. "That's what Gracie used to say. That we were friends because we were too crazy for anyone else."

"She was right."

Jake saw the question in her gaze. She wanted to ask why he'd slept with Maggie. Fourteen years and she was still pissed. Hurt. It wasn't a conversation he intended to have. "I'm going to grab a shower. There's beer and wine in the fridge. Help yourself."

He left her standing there, but he knew she didn't watch as he walked away. She knew he'd be back, and he knew she'd be waiting.

It was what they did.

CHAPTER EIGHT

A few minutes after Jake went to take a shower, his niece returned to the house after her lengthy good-bye with Bailey McGann. Her gaze went wide as it settled on Audrey alone in the kitchen, cleaning up the remnants of the flour fight. Cleaning seemed more productive than replaying every word and look of the exchange she'd just had with Jake like she was seventeen again.

"Where's Uncle Jake?"

"Shower," Audrey replied with a smile, emptying the dustpan in the garbage. She hung it and the broom on the back of the pantry door, where it and all its predecessors had hung on a bent nail for at least half a century. What the hell was she supposed to say to the girl? "It's nice to see you again."

Alisha blinked. "Gramma Gracie's funeral. I remember that you were there. You stood with Uncle Jake."

She hadn't been given a choice. Jake had held her hand like it was the only thing keeping him tethered to the earth. She'd squeezed back just as tight. "I did. Gracie meant a lot to me. My life would have turned out very different without her."

"Yeah, Uncle Lincoln said you were the reason my mother never got to go to college."

Audrey raised a brow. "Lincoln's still full of shit, I see."

The girl laughed. "Yeah. I think he was just trying to make me feel better. Everybody knows she couldn't go to college because of me."

Audrey frowned. "That's not true."

"Yeah, it is," Alisha argued with a defiant lift of her chin reminiscent of Jake.

"Says who?" Audrey challenged.

"Nobody has to say it—I can tell. She had me when she was fifteen."

Crossing to the fridge, Audrey withdrew a bottle of moscato. She set it on the sideboard and regarded it a second. This was unsteady ground the girl had drawn her onto. She remembered when Yancy came to live with Gracie—a scared little girl tossed out by her heartless mother. It had been the summer Audrey left. "Do you really believe your mother regrets having you?"

Alisha lifted her chin. "Yeah, I do."

Audrey studied her. Dyed hair. Makeup. Under that shapeless hoodie she probably wore a tight T-shirt. A little girl trying to find her way into becoming a woman way too fast and desperately, but embarrassed by it. She remembered that feeling. She opened the bottle. "Have you given her reason to wish you'd never been born?"

That defiant jaw quivered a little. "Yeah. All the time, I know it."

"Ever kill somebody?" The question surprised her as much as Alisha.

The girl's mouth opened and closed without sound. And then, "No!"

Wineglasses were in the cupboard by the sink, second shelf, if she remembered correctly. "Then you've got nothing." She took down the biggest wineglass she could find. "I know you've taken on all this guilt and shame, and you blame yourself for everything you possibly can. I know there's nothing more terribly dramatic than your life, and that no one truly understands the depth of your suffering, but let me tell you something about mothers—it takes some serious shit to make the good ones toss aside their kids. If my mother could go through my trial, my time at Stillwater, and everything this shitty town threw at her because of what I did, yours won't love you any less for having set her academic career on hold, especially when she knows what it's like to have a shit mother. You can trust me on that. Wine?"

It was like the girl was on a five-second delay. She blinked, then shook her head. "Mom doesn't like me drinking."

Audrey smiled and filled her glass. "Gracie used to let us drink. If we had too much and got sick, she'd tell us we should have thought of the consequences before." She recapped the bottle. "One other thing—Gracie Tripp would have sent your mother to any school she wanted. If Yancy didn't go to college right out of high school, it's because she didn't want to go. Probably because you were more important. If you want to feel guilty, feel guilty over the fact that she loves you that much. It works for me."

"You're pretty blunt." Alisha hopped up onto the counter, her denim-clad hip only inches from the bottle of moscato. "Do you talk to Uncle Jake like this?"

"Pretty much." And then, "I didn't mean to upset you."

"You didn't. I'd like to hear you talk to Uncle Jake that way, though." The girl grinned. In that moment she looked so much like Jake—and like Gracie—that Audrey's eyes stung. God, she missed that old woman. Gracie had been the only adult—*only*—who hadn't looked at her differently after Clint's death. It was as though she'd seen that part of Audrey before even Audrey had.

She took a drink of the wine, pulling herself together. "How's Bailey taking Maggie's death?"

Alisha hesitated. "Okay, I guess. They hadn't been getting along lately. Maggie had an enormous hate-boner for Isaac. She didn't think he was good enough for Bee."

"Is he?"

"Yeah. He's quiet, but he treats her really well. I think it's because his family's not as well-off as Bailey's."

Maggie ought to have been the last to judge on that basis. Clint Jones hadn't worked any more than he had to. Her mother had worked herself sick and still didn't make enough money to keep them in any sort of comfort. Maggie's clothes had been donation and thrift-store finds.

"I've seen you on TV. Your show's creepy."

Audrey took a drink. "It's supposed to be. A lot of those kids have done terrible things."

"I always find it worse when the kid started out nice—like they were good kids who did something bad to protect a friend or something."

The wine bittered on her tongue. "Yeah. Me too." She met the girl's wide gaze and saw so many questions there. "Doing a bad thing doesn't make you a bad person. People do bad things for the right reasons all the time." *Excuses, excuses.*

"Like helping a friend kill her asshole father?"

"Alisha." Jake's voice had the impact of a bullet shot through a silencer. Audrey jerked back. Alisha jumped off the counter, twisting so that she and Audrey stood side by side.

Jake stood in the doorway in a T-shirt and jeans, hair damp, cheeks flushed from the hot water. He didn't look angry, but he clearly wasn't impressed. His hazel eyes glittered. "What the hell, kid? You couldn't have thought of something a little more subtle?"

Audrey almost smiled. Of course he'd be more upset with *how* she asked rather than the fact that she actually had.

Alisha turned to her, cheeks flushed with embarrassment. She made eye contact, though. "I'm sorry."

"Don't be," she replied honestly. "And to answer your question, yes. Exactly like that."

The girl smiled.

"Go watch TV or something," Jake ordered. "I need to talk to Audrey without you listening in. I'll call you when supper's ready."

There was no argument. Alisha simply left the room.

"Did she upset you?"

"Alisha?" At his nod, Audrey shook her head. "I appreciate her blunt honesty. You don't get a lot of that in this town."

"She's a good kid. Is that the moscato?"

"Yeah. It's good."

"Yancy likes to use it in sangria." Jake went to the fridge and got a beer. He popped the cap and gestured toward the doorway to the rest of the house. "I want to show you something."

Audrey followed him through the old house, smiling as the floor creaked familiarly beneath her bare feet. He'd changed the colors and the decor, but it was still the same house, no matter how you dressed it. He led her past the sturdy staircase, around the corner to the room that used to be Gracie's sewing room. He'd turned it into a den—or an office. The walls were painted a rich navy, the woodwork stained walnut. It would have been too dark were it not for the fact that two of the four walls were mostly windows.

He walked behind the desk. Audrey stood where she was, watching him. His hair, dark with damp, hung over his forehead. He wasn't as tanned as she remembered, and the lighter tone of his skin made the slight flush in his cheeks all the more noticeable. One of the things she'd always liked about him was that glow to his skin. She had gotten so she could tell his mood by his coloring.

That night at the cottage with Maggie he'd been pale when he saw what Audrey had done to her.

Standing there, bent at the waist to look up something on the laptop on the desk, he didn't look much different than he had at eighteen. Obviously, he was older, more chiseled, rougher, but he was still her Jake. And he still hated anything on his feet. She used to joke that he owned only one pair of shoes and they were only for special occasions. She'd loved him back then. It was clearer to her now than it had been at the time.

"Come look at these," he said, breaking her train of thought. Thank God.

Audrey joined him behind the antique desk. It had been his great-grandfather's. She ran her hand over the smooth top. They used to do homework at this desk, go over the schedule for the campground where they both worked. One night, he'd pinned her between him and the desk, and for a sweet, terrible moment she'd thought he was going to kiss her. But he hadn't.

"Look." He opened the top right drawer.

She didn't have to look, but she did anyway. It was empty except for a pencil. There, carved into the bottom, were their initials—hers, Jake's, and Maggie's. Audrey pressed her fingers to the M and the J. They had to be at least twenty years old, those letters. Maggie hadn't always liked including Jake in their time together, but she liked hanging out at the campground and the takeout where he often got them free food.

"Hard to believe she's gone. I keep expecting her to show up wherever I am and bitch at me for not talking to her."

"How'd it go with Neve?"

She shrugged. "Right now I'm all they've got for suspects."

"You're kidding."

Brow arched, she turned her gaze to his. "Yes. I'm making all of this shit up for my own enjoyment."

He didn't seem to appreciate her sarcasm, judging from his scowl. "Neve doesn't believe it, does she?"

She was tempted to ask him what he planned to do about it if Neve did believe her guilty. "She says she doesn't, but apparently Maggie was writing a book about the night Clint died. The *real* story." Had Maggie actually written it down? How much of it?

"What the fuck is that supposed to mean?"

"Her version of events, I assume. Neve didn't know. She hasn't seen it yet—if it even exists." It was going to be inconvenient if it did. God, why couldn't the past stay in the past?

"What are you going to do?"

"Have faith that they'll find the real killer. Don't give me that look. Neve's a smart woman. If anyone can find the truth, it's her." That revelation did nothing to make her feel better. "What did you want to show me?"

He nudged the desk chair toward her with his foot. "Sit. You haven't gotten squeamish on me, have you?"

"You're funny."

"When I sat with Maggie's body before the cops arrived, I took pictures."

"You did what? Fuck around, Jake! If the police find out, you could get in a lot of trouble!" *Fuck around?* She hadn't used that term in over a decade. Three full days in Edgeport and she had already regressed to her teens.

"She was killed on my land." And he took it personally, obviously. "You think I wasn't going to protect my own ass? I wanted to document the scene before the cops stomped through it. Don't you want to know if there's something there that might take their attention off you?"

Audrey shook her head. Of course she did. "Show me."

He touched the screen, opening a file of photographs. Then, he opened one of those. It was of a woman's body on the sand, damp and still. Pale. Her blond hair matted with blood, glinting white bone peeking through the strands.

"Oh my God," Audrey whispered. Jack pushed the chair at her and she stumbled into it. In her mind, she didn't see Maggie. She saw Clint, blood running into his ear, and down his neck. Still. Silenced. The panic of that long-ago moment clawed at the sides of her brain, frantically scrambling to get out. She closed her eyes and forced those memories back. When she opened her eyes again, there was just the computer, showing her photographs of a dead woman. She had detached.

She scrolled through the pictures, but she wasn't a crime-scene investigator. That was why she normally told people she was a criminal psychologist and not a forensic one. Thanks to TV, most people associated forensics with the people who went to crime scenes and gathered evidence, when really forensics could be applied to all aspects of criminal investigation. She could interview a killer and get an idea of their mental state, but she couldn't look at a picture and tell how someone had been killed.

Except that it was obvious that Maggie's skull had been smashed in. It also looked as though her knees were sunk deeper into the gravel than the rest of her, but that only meant that she'd probably fallen to her knees after the first blow, forcing the killer to hit her again, and again, to finish the job.

"What do you think, doc? Crime of passion?"

Audrey glanced up at Jake. He looked at her, not the screen. "It was definitely up close and personal. It takes a lot of rage to hit someone that hard."

He nodded. "Mags did have a way of pissing people off."

She couldn't argue that. "Whoever did this wanted to get up close. Wanted to see her die. That requires a lot of hate. A *lot*."

"If you weren't you, would you think you'd done this?"

She scrolled to another photo taken from a different angle. "I'd want to talk to me, sure. But I haven't seen Maggie since the last time I was home. Haven't had any contact. Her confronting me at Gracie's isn't enough motive for this sort of viciousness."

"But if you met her at the beach and she told you she was going to tell the world what really happened the night Clint died, and you didn't want to let that get out, what would you do?"

Audrey's stomach clenched. "Try to stop her."

"So the question is"—Jake leaned against the desk—"what really happened that night, Aud?"

She held his gaze. "We killed Clint."

"That's it?"

"That's it." She stood up, hands clenched into fists. "I thought you said you didn't think I killed her. No, that you *knew* I didn't kill her."

"I do know you didn't kill her. I'm just trying to understand why someone might believe you had."

She smirked, lifting her hand to massage the taut line of muscle across the top of her shoulder. "Because I played a part in killing Clint I must kill everyone I don't like?"

"If anyone ever deserved killing it was Clint Jones."

Audrey glanced back at the screen. "Apparently someone thought Maggie deserved it as well."

"We just need to find out who."

Her gaze snapped to his. "We?"

One corner of his mouth tilted, carving faint half circles in his cheek. "This is my town. Someone killed one of my people. On my land. I'm damn well going to find out who."

"And here I thought it might be because of how far back we go. Or am I another one of your 'people'? A commodity to be protected?"

"All that money spent studying people's minds, and you can't even be honest about what's going on in your own. Say what you really mean, Aud. Dump the passive aggression and let the hurt out. For once, just say it—damn the consequences."

It ought to have terrified her, but as she stared at him—at the color high in his cheeks—an overwhelming rush of daring filled her. *Fuck it.* "Why did you sleep with Maggie? Of all the girls you could have had that night, why her? *Why not me?*" Heat rushed to her face, but there was no taking it back. She trembled from head to toe, but a weight had been lifted from her shoulders, leaving her so light she might just float away.

Jake straightened, turning his lean body toward her so that they stood face-to-face, only a fist apart. "Because Gran and your mother were afraid you wouldn't go to college because of me, and because fucking Maggie was the one thing I knew would make you leave."

Words had power, and those ones hit with the force of an eighteen-wheeler. Audrey opened her mouth, but no sound came out.

The nasal wail of the oven timer echoed from the kitchen. The pie was done. Jake turned his back on her and strode from the room, his shoulders tense and straight.

Audrey stood there, still and stunned. After a few moments, she glanced back at the photo of Maggie, lying bloodied and lifeless on the beach. It was both a tragic and a fitting way for her to go out.

"He never loved you, you bitch," she whispered. She snapped the lid of the computer shut and followed after Jake, and the smell of Gracie's chicken pot pie.

CHAPTER NINE

The pot pie was delicious—no one had expected otherwise.

"I'm going to regret that second piece," Audrey said, leaning back in her chair. She smiled at Jake. "Gracie would be proud."

He grinned. "She'd say, 'Sweet, my dar, but your carrots be too strong and your tates too weak.'"

Audrey could almost hear her say it. "At the risk of being struck by lightning, she'd be wrong. Not that I'd tell her that."

"I like the potatoes," Alisha joined in, looking between the two of them in the hopeful manner of a girl trying to breach the distance between adolescent and adult. She just wanted to be part of the conversation.

"Gracie was very particular about vegetable consistency," Audrey shared. "Also, she wasn't about to praise anyone too strongly."

"Lest it go to their head," Jake added with a crooked grin.

Alisha leaned her elbow on the table. "Did you like her? Great-Gramma?"

A wave of emotion tightened Audrey's throat. "I loved her."

Jake stood and began gathering up their empty plates. There was still half a pie in the center of the table. "Audrey was the first person I called when Gran died."

"I was?" She couldn't believe it. "After Yancy and Lincoln, you mean."

He was at the sink, his back to her, so she couldn't see his face. "The word 'first' generally means before anyone else. You loved her as much as I did."

Audrey didn't know what to say. She cast a helpless glance at Alisha instead. "It's okay," the girl said. "Mom and Gramma used to fight all the time, and Uncle Lincoln only sticks around long enough to get some money and then he takes off again. I would have called you first too."

"She's sucking up because she wants dirt on me," Jake warned as he put their plates and cutlery in the dishwasher. "Okay, kid, I'm taking Audrey for a drive back the point. You're on your own for a bit."

"Back the point?" Why were they going there? That was where Maggie had been killed.

"You want me to make coffee for when you get back?" Alisha rose from her chair and continued clearing the table. Audrey stood up to help.

"Sure. Don't watch too much porn while I'm gone. It'll stunt your growth."

His niece rolled her eyes before turning to Audrey. "Once. It was *once*, and he won't let me forget it."

It wasn't the most appropriate conversation, but after years of seeing some of the terrible things people did to their kids, or made their kids do to them, she was a little less militant about the things she really didn't think mattered. It was obvious that Jake and Alisha had a great relationship that worked for them, and she didn't pick up any danger signals from it. Jake had his faults, but he wasn't a monster.

"Did your uncle ever tell you about the time he patched into his father's satellite TV so he could watch what Gracie called 'the blue movies'?"

Alisha's jaw dropped, and she let loose a laugh that must have come from her toes, it was so big. Audrey couldn't help but chuckle herself. Even Jake had to grin.

"All right," he said. "Let's go. We won't have daylight much longer. Lish, you're on cleanup."

Audrey followed him out onto the veranda where he shoved his long, narrow feet into a pair of familiar-looking Doc Marten boots that were creased and worn. "Are those the same boots you had in high school?"

"They only got comfortable a couple of years ago."

"I can't believe you still have them."

"Not like they get a lot of wear. We'll take my truck."

"Fine with me." And honestly, she didn't care what he wore on his feet, or how old his boots were. It didn't matter.

"Not worried that I'll kill you and hide your body?"

She paused on the passenger side of the truck and regarded him over the faded hood. "Are you worried that I'll kill you? The odds are stacked in my favor."

"You were a kid—it doesn't count."

Opening the door, Audrey climbed inside. "It counts. Murder always counts."

Jake didn't respond as he slipped behind the wheel. The engine grumbled to life, and he backed the truck out onto the gravel road. It was 7:36—they had an hour of daylight left, tops.

They drove all the way back, veering away from the resort at the end to travel the narrow dirt lane Audrey had taken earlier to see Neve. Where were they going?

"I can't go to the crime scene if that's what you've planned. They find any shred of me there, it's game over. I'd rather not go to prison for a crime I didn't commit." How cool and dry she sounded, like an antiperspirant.

"Give me some credit," he said, keeping his gaze on the road. "We're not going to the crime scene. We're going to the camp."

They'd gone to the camp the last time she'd been home too. The night of Gracie's funeral—after the reception at the house. They'd looked through old photos and other memorabilia from their childhood, drank beer, and cried a little.

She looked out the window as three ATVs roared past, the thick tires kicking up a jet-cloud of dust. "What's at the camp?"

"Probably nothing." Jake checked his rear view. "If those little bastards were on the beach around the resort I'm going to slash their fucking tires."

"You sounded like your grandfather just then."

"Christ," he muttered. "I did, didn't I?"

Audrey smiled. "I saw a four-wheeler the other night when I stopped to pay my respects to Gracie. One of the headlights was burnt out."

"Could have been Isaac Canning. Good kid for the most part. He's Bailey's boyfriend."

Audrey glanced out the window. *So. Many. Trees.* "I can't believe Gideon asked me to talk to her."

"No?"

"No." She turned her attention back to him. After so many years, it felt surreal to be with him. "He shouldn't want me anywhere near his kid."

"Wow. I'm just going to leave that hanging there and let you chew on it for a bit. You're a fucking mess—you know that, right?"

She smiled. "Yeah, but you like it."

He laughed. "Doesn't say much for either one of us."

They drove past the cottage where the police were set up—there were two state-police-blue cars parked outside—to another small building just around a bend in the narrow road. The wood was rough and dark gray from years of exposure. Mismatched curtains made of old sheets and flags hung in the windows, faded almost into colorlessness. There was a patch of "lawn" in the front with a fire pit set in the middle of it. It was surrounded by a ring of old tree stumps of varying heights and widths that served as seats. Audrey had spent a lot of nights gathered around that pit.

"Doesn't look like much anymore, does it?" Jake asked, as he turned the key in the ignition. The trunk's engine grumbled into silence.

"Nostalgia overlooks a host of flaws," Audrey replied, opening the door and stepping out into the waning daylight.

"That's almost poetic. You learn that from a book at your fancy college, or did you think it up all by yourself?"

She gave him the finger as she climbed the steps—or what was left of them. They had a serious lean to the left that shifted to the right with every step.

The key used to be kept in a little compartment Jake had carved into the railing. You had to know where to look to even notice it. Audrey pulled the key out and unlocked the door, stepping into the dim interior.

"Careful of raccoons," Jake cautioned.

"No self-respecting raccoon would be caught dead in this dump." She said it with a smile, because this place had always been a favorite of hers. It smelled of old wood and salt with a side of dust. That last summer there'd always been a layer of sand on the floor, because they'd run to the beach and back almost constantly. The path they took was still visible from the door. Almost every night there'd be a bunch of them back there. Sometimes they drank and sometimes they just had a fire. She'd eaten a disgusting amount of hot dogs and marshmallows those nights. Making up for the summers she'd lost while in Stillwater, she supposed.

The old furniture—wicker chairs and couch, plastic lawn recliners, milk crates and an old wooden table—were still there, though all the cushions and blankets were gone. Probably rotted years ago, or Jake had finally gotten sick of them and set the pile on fire. There were Polaroid photos pinned all over the walls—some blurry, others little more than the glaringly white face of someone who had gotten too close to the camera. Most of them were of similar composition—two or more drunk kids with their arms around each other, grinning like assholes. There were a few that had a single subject as well, and some that were of animals. There were the obligatory shots of people who had passed out at a party, others doing hot-knives with a torch or Coleman stove.

Audrey went straight to where her personal favorites were still stapled. A photo of her by the fire that Jake had taken. One of Jake climbing a tree, and one of the two of them with their arms around each other—Jake looking at her with a smile, her looking at the camera, grinning, unaware that he wasn't doing the same. There was even one of her and Maggie—before things got too rough between them.

"Did you know that Maggie has a drink in her hand in every picture of her on these walls?" Jake mused. "I don't remember a party where she ever stayed even remotely sober."

"Mm." Her gaze roved over other white-trimmed moments of captured time. "She thought she was more fun when she drank."

"And it was an excuse to be a slut."

She turned her head, frowning at him over her shoulder. "Slut-shaming's not a good look for you. Promiscuity is common among victims of childhood sexual assault. If she was a guy you wouldn't have noticed."

"If Maggie had been a guy, she would have been a rapist."

It was a terrible thing for him to say, but Audrey didn't argue, because it was uncomfortably true. "The deck was stacked against her."

"Come on, we all had something that sucked in our lives. Your dad drank, my mother tossed me away. My mother's husband used to beat Lincoln, Yancy got pregnant by a married man when she was fifteen. None of us had it easy, emotionally speaking."

"Clint raped her—that's worse than anything I ever suffered. You too, I imagine. You know, one time he got drunk and threatened to set Maggie and me on fire. We were nine."

"There's not a person in Edgeport who misses that bastard—except for Matt." He moved to stand next to her, also looking at the wall. "Shit, there's you after you put that pounding into Maggie."

Audrey followed his gaze. Sure enough, there was a photo of her walking toward her car, her shirt stained red, face angry and flushed. The sight of her knuckles, red and bloody, made her cringe. She looked wild. Feral.

"I felt a little guilty about that. If you were going to go to town on anyone it ought to have been me."

"Yeah, well, you could have just told me you didn't like me. The evening might have turned out differently."

"That wouldn't have worked."

"Why not?"

His eyes narrowed. "Because it wouldn't have been true. Fuck, Aud, I showered three times a day for a week after screwing Maggie, I felt so dirty. She hit on me a few years ago—just being a bitch. I told her I still hadn't forgiven myself for the first time. She laughed and told me to get over myself—that we'd both gotten what we wanted."

"I'm pretty sure being beaten to a pulp wasn't what she wanted."

Hands in his pockets, he shrugged. "She told me it was worth it knowing that you and I never got together. She said I wasn't good enough for you."

Christ. "That's fucked-up, even for her." Deep inside, seventeen-year-old Audrey thrilled at the fact that there might have been even the smallest chance that she and Jake could have gotten together. It was foolish, but there was simply no heartache like teenage heartbreak.

"Yeah, Mags was a real mess." He frowned, looking over her shoulder. "Who left that out?"

Audrey turned. On the old, battered table sat an old photo album, open. They went to investigate together. While the good pictures made it to the walls, the not so great—or embarrassing—went into the book. It was open to a page that contained mostly photos of Audrey and Maggie. Beside the book was an old ashtray made out of a quahog shell. There were three cigarette butts in it, all stained by shocking-pink lipstick.

"Looks like we're not the first people here this summer," Jake remarked. "Maggie, do you think?"

"That's definitely a shade she'd wear." Peeking out from underneath the album was the corner of a napkin. Audrey moved the book to get a better look. The napkin was small—like the kind bartenders put drinks on—and light pink, and had a pair of puckered red lips in the top right corner, and "Lipstick" printed in a script font in the bottom left. In the center was written the name "Chelsea" and what Audrey believed to be a Bangor phone number, given the area code.

"That's Maggie's writing," she said.

"Lipstick's a lesbian bar."

Her head snapped up. "How do you know that? You hardly ever leave town."

"I'm not a fucking recluse, and I know about it because I dated a girl a while back who liked to go there."

"Why am I not surprised?"

He made a face. "I thought a little girl-on-girl might be fun."

"Was it?" Why was she asking? It was like some perverse part of her wanted to know all about all the sex he had with people who weren't her.

"Not so much. I realized I'm selfish that way. I want all the attention in bed."

Audrey smirked. "I bet you do."

"Hey, I give all of my attention too." He glanced back to the napkin. "What was Maggie doing there? If this is hers, that is."

"Am I interrupting?" came a voice from the door.

Audrey jumped, even though it was only Neve. Jake, on the other hand, remained totally calm. He also picked up the napkin and shoved it into his pocket with the skill and grace of a practiced thief.

"Don't you ever go home?" Jake demanded lightly. "Come over here and tell us what you make of this."

Neve moved toward them. She was dressed in a deep, rich magenta blouse that would have made Audrey look clownish and black cropped pants. Not a wrinkle in sight. She looked at the table. "Someone was here smoking and looking at pictures. So what?"

"We're thinking it might have been Maggie," he told her. "Audrey thinks that's her lipstick, and the album is open to photos of the two of them." He didn't mention the bar, and it was easy for Audrey to follow his lead.

"When was the last time you were here?" Neve asked him—it was as though Audrey didn't exist.

"Thursday."

"It could have been her. Okay, I need the two of you to leave so I can have some guys run through here. Did you touch anything?"

"The photo album," Audrey said. "I picked it up."

Neve shook her head. "Of course you did." Her tone was one of resigned exasperation, as though Audrey were Lucille Ball caught in the middle of a murder investigation.

"That book's got the fingerprints of practically everyone in our age group," Jake reminded them both. "But you're welcome to take it."

"You can get DNA from cigarette butts," Audrey joined in. "Can't you? If it does turn out to be Maggie's then she was probably here the night she died."

"Murdered," Neve corrected. "She didn't die of old age or in an accident. Someone killed her."

Audrey stiffened. "I'm aware of that. I'm the one everyone's pointing their finger at, remember?"

"Okay, we're leaving," Jake cut in. "Knock yourself out, Neve. Just lock up when you leave. You remember where the key is?"

She nodded but didn't speak. Audrey didn't either. She headed for the door with Jake right behind her.

Outside, the sun was fading fast on the horizon. The police wouldn't be able to search the camp that night unless they brought in some lighting. It wasn't until they were in the confines of the truck cab, heading back toward Jake's, that either of them spoke.

"So much for believing I didn't do it," Audrey muttered. "She looked at me like I was already wearing an orange jumpsuit. Are you going to give her the napkin?"

"Eventually, but first there's something I want to ask you."

"And that is...?

Jake grinned. "Want to go to a lesbian bar with me tomorrow night?"

Tuesday arrived wet and gray, carried on a wind that churned the tide into great, murky, whitecapped waves. Neve watched it from the window of her parents' kitchen, a cup of hot coffee nestled in her hands.

"Crime scene's done," she lamented to no one in particular. "If we missed anything it's gone now."

Her father snorted from where he sat at the counter, working on a crossword puzzle. Used to be he wouldn't sit still for more than two minutes at a time. "That Harte girl's worked with law enforcement before. She's not stupid enough to leave evidence behind. This isn't her first murder."

Neve cast a glance at her mother, who gave her head a subtle shake. Neve ignored the warning. "There's no evidence Audrey was anywhere near the beach that night, Dad." She wasn't going to tell him about Jake and Audrey finding the cigarette butts at the camp, or that she was checking tire tracks, footprints, and anything else she could find, in an attempt to figure out who Maggie met that night.

Everett Graham looked up, fixing his daughter with a look that could still intimidate grown men. "Then you're not doing your job."

That stiffened her spine as she poured coffee into her favorite travel mug.

"Ev," his wife chastised.

Neve held up her hand. "You don't have to step in for me, Mama. He can say whatever he wants. Point remains that this isn't his investigation."

Her father, who had gone back to his crossword, scratched his pen against the paper. "I'd have some leads if it was mine."

"No, you'd have a potentially innocent woman locked up and ignore all the evidence." Neve shoved the lid onto her cup and stomped toward the door. "I won't be home for dinner."

As she stepped out onto the veranda, she heard her mother giving her father a hard time, and his gruff protests. There was no arguing with the man, so why did her mother even bother? He would never concede that he might be wrong. A long time ago, Neve had thought becoming a cop would bring her closer to her father, but it had only forced them further apart, as he criticized her every move.

Classic, she supposed.

She climbed into her car without needing to unlock it first. There weren't many people in Edgeport stupid enough to come onto their property with mischief in mind. Her father was still a crack shot and had no compunctions about taking out a thief's kneecap.

The Graham house—a pretty slate-blue farmhouse with cream trim and a wraparound veranda—wasn't far from the Harte property. Both were located in the section of the rural town called "Lower Edgeport," where practically every house had an ocean view and the population doubled in the summer when the cottagers came to roost.

Neve had been almost as eager to get the hell out as Audrey had been.

The narrow main road was a dull gray, with so many tar-filled cracks that it often felt like driving on a thick sheet of soft rubber on hot summer days—not an issue at that moment. Though she'd rather a bouncy ride than a wind she literally had to steer against. There was a spot, closer to the center of town, where the bank dipped to a height of five feet, that was simply referred to as "the Mire." It was boggy and thick with vegetation—a boneyard of driftwood, tossed up by the tide, bleached and pale. In the early spring, when the snow melted, it wasn't uncommon for the area to flood, murky water spreading over the road like an oil slick. On that morning, putty-colored waves broke over the top of the bank, hitting the already sodden ground with a violent splash. "Tidal suicide," Audrey had once called it, back in their teens, when every conversation stank of drama and exaggerated gravitas.

Was she missing what was right in front of her face? Had Audrey killed Maggie in a fit of rage? It was possible, but it still made no sense. Her father was right about one thing—Audrey wasn't stupid. If she had killed Maggie, she would have to have been completely out of her mind. She'd been surprised to hear about Maggie's mysterious book; that was one thing Neve knew for certain. She was by no means a human lie detector, but she was pretty good at reading people.

Her boss thought she'd been a good one to have on this case because she knew the town—because her father had been a big deal. Four days in, and she was beginning to doubt that decision. It wasn't that she didn't believe anyone she knew could be a murderer. Quite the opposite—she knew just how damn dark and immoral Edgeport could be.

So, if not Audrey, then who? She was on her way to talk to Gideon—the husband was always a consideration in these kinds of cases. She'd never really known Gideon to lose his temper, but that didn't mean he didn't have one. From what she'd heard, Maggie had been drinking a lot lately. Historically, when Maggie drank, her inhibitions went south fast, and she didn't have many inhibitions to begin with. And then there was Matt, Maggie's younger brother, who seemed to make trouble with the ease that some people made conversation. Everyone knew he blamed Maggie for his ending up in foster care, and then in juvy. But why kill his sister now? Why not years ago when he would have gotten a lighter sentence? Matt knew how the system worked—he'd spent a good portion of his life in it.

He had told Audrey that Maggie got what she deserved, though.

There had been a photo to go along with the cigarettes at the camp. Tucked between the next two pages she'd found a Polaroid of Maggie at that decrepit table, wearing lipstick that looked like the same color as on the butts. No way to know for certain when the photo had been taken, but in it she was wearing the same clothes she'd been killed in, so it would appear it had been the same night. Had she met her killer there, or had she brought him or her with her? There had been only one set of car tracks, and those had been Maggie's. But there had been ATV tracks all over the place.

And someone had to have taken that photo of her, right? Those old cameras only focused so close. She should have it dusted for prints, but there'd be so many, and none that would conclusively prove anything. Still, she'd get one of her guys to do it.

She needed to check and see if John Harte had a four-wheeler, however unlikely that Audrey would have driven the bloody thing all the way to Tripp's Cove. But whoever killed Maggie had to have gotten home somehow, and Maggie's car had been parked by the camp. Audrey's car had been seen back the Ridge just as she claimed. Old Wendell Stokes had it written in his ledger, but he hadn't seen her drive back out, so she still could have made the trip back Tripp's Cove. She could have parked on the road and walked to the beach.

Aside from Audrey, Matt Jones had been very vocal since his return to town as to how much he despised his sister. Audrey wasn't the only one he'd told that Maggie had gotten what she deserved. Apparently he'd even gone to Maggie's salon earlier on the day she was killed and verbally abused her. Maggie hadn't called the police, though. Since this came to her via town gossip, Neve was going to stop by the salon and ask the staff about it.

And then there were rumors that the McGann marriage had been on the rocks, and that Maggie had been fooling around. Not a surprise.

Neve's brow was set into a permanent frown by the time she pulled into Gideon McGann's drive. He was in the dooryard, loading scaffolding into the back of his truck with the help of Isaac Canning, his daughter's boyfriend. They both turned to look as she got out of the car. It was unmarked, but obviously police, and it had the ability to unsettle the locals. She hadn't been born there, so she was still an outsider. Add the fact that she was darker, her hair a thick, foreign mass of tight curls, and she was sometimes watched with an open hostility that had nothing to do with her job. Though no one in Edgeport was prejudiced, and each and every one of them would be the first to tell you that.

Gideon smiled slightly. He was a gorgeous man, but then she'd always had a bit of a thing for him. A lot of girls had back when Neve had been a teenager. He was a little older, and in addition to working with his father, he'd earned money for college by doing odd jobs around town. For a long time Neve's mother used to wonder aloud if "that McGann boy owns a shirt." Every red-blooded female with a hormone to her name hoped that he didn't.

The Canning kid was perfectly still as she approached, a vague look of panic in his eyes. Normal for his age. Probably thought she was coming for him despite there having been a murder. Teen boys always had a sense of narcissism when it came to their delinquent behavior, the need to brag tending to outweigh the common sense it took to remain silent and uncaught.

"Mornin', Neve," Gideon greeted her. Up close she could see the fatigue around his eyes.

"Hey," she replied. "Are you on your way out?"

"Just loading up the truck for a job later this morning." He must have seen the question in her eyes, because he added, "Keeping busy helps."

A sympathetic smile curved her mouth. "I understand. Can you give me a minute?"

"Sure. Isaac, why don't you go inside and see if Bailey's up yet."

The boy didn't have to be told twice. Probably hoped to get lucky while his girl's father was out of the way.

"He and Bailey been dating long?" she asked as the boy disappeared into the house.

"Almost six months. Practically forever in teen time. He's a good kid."

"He must be if you're putting him to work."

"Well, his own father isn't around, so I try to spend time with Isaac when I can." He smiled. "Besides, he's here all the time—I might as well take advantage of him. But you didn't come here to discuss my relationship with my daughter's boyfriend."

"No. I just have a few questions if you don't mind."

"Not at all."

"Did Maggie smoke?"

"Sometimes when she was drinking, yeah. I saw a pack in her purse last week. Usually she was better at hiding stuff." He didn't sound bitter, or even resigned. He sounded...done.

Neve frowned. "Were the two of you having problems?"

Gideon rubbed a hand over the back of his neck as the wind ruffled his hair. The sky was on its way to a gunmetal gray—an indication that they were in for a storm. "I told her I wanted to separate."

So the rumors were true. "What was her reaction?"

"She was upset, but I don't think she was all that surprised. We haven't been close in a long time."

Meaning they weren't having sex. What sort of woman wouldn't take advantage of being married to a man like Gideon? A long time ago, at a party back Tripp's Cove, he and Neve had made out. She'd been afraid to let it go any further, but looking at him, she had to admit that sometimes she wondered what she'd passed up.

The ending of their marriage explained why he wasn't more broken up about Maggie's death. Then again, maybe he killed her. Being gorgeous wasn't synonymous with innocence.

"Do you have a four-wheeler, Gideon?"

"Two. Your guys already took a look. You need to see them again?"

Neve shook her head. One less thing on her to-do list. "Do you know anything about a book Maggie was writing?"

"You mean her autobiography? I knew about it. I tried to talk her out of it."

"Why?"

Hands in his pockets, he shrugged. "Maggie doesn't...she *didn't* always have a reliable memory."

"You mean she'd embellish or lie about things." It wasn't really a question—she remembered Maggie's penchant for exaggeration.

"Or she'd claim not to remember them at all. That happened a fair bit."

Interesting. Although it was hardly surprising that Maggie lied. Anything had to be better than the life she'd lived—at least most of it. "Was she writing this book on a computer?"

"Her laptop."

"I'm going to need that."

"Sure. Come into the house."

They walked side by side to the steps. When he stopped for her, she gestured for him to go ahead. She wasn't going to give her back to someone, no matter how hot he was, or how long she'd known him.

The McGann household was an orderly one. The kitchen was clean—a couple of pairs of shoes that looked as though they'd been kicked where they lay, and a few dishes in the sink, but that was the extent of any disarray.

Gideon noticed her appraisal. "Lorraine Pettis cleans for me once a week. She was here yesterday."

Neve nodded. She'd have to remember to talk to Lorraine. A cleaning lady had an extremely intimate view of a person's life. "Where's the laptop?"

He drew back. Guilt twanged in her chest. "In the den."

As she followed him out of the kitchen, down a wide corridor, Neve sighed. "I don't mean to be rude, Gid."

"I know. You're just doing your job."

She cringed. Her superiors thought she was the best choice for this case, but they were wrong. She was the worst choice because of her connection to this place and its people. It wasn't going to take long for the town to resent her—more than some already did.

The den wasn't decorated in the same easy style as the rest of the house. It was done in dark red, with black furniture and rich accents.

Modern bordello, Neve thought. It looked like Maggie's style.

On the shiny black desk was a laptop with the lid closed, its iconic apple logo right in the center. Gideon unplugged it and handed it to her. "It's all password protected."

Neve tilted her head as she looked up at him, the computer held against her chest. "You tried to log in?"

His cheeks flushed. "Yeah. A few months ago, when I started suspecting that Maggie was having an affair."

Again the rumor mill proved accurate. "You thought she was seeing someone else?"

"She was really secretive about some texts and calls she got on her phone. My first wife did the same thing when she cheated, so I had red flags going off. One day Maggie told me she was going to the shop, but when I called later she wasn't there. Tami said she hadn't come in at all."

Neve made another mental note to stop by Maggie's salon and talk to her employees later that day, and to check on whether or not her guys had found Maggie's missing purse or cell phone. "She missed work, okay. What did she say when you asked her about it?"

"I didn't ask. I was going to hire an investigator to follow her."

"Did you?"

He shook his head. "I realized that I didn't care if she was see-ing someone else. That's when I knew it was over."

And he just gave up? Just like that? Most people would still be jealous—or pissed. Then again, if he was going to leave her, why kill her? Unless Maggie hadn't wanted to let him go.

"I'll let you get back to work," she said in her most professional and courteous tone.

"I'll walk you out."

As they retraced the route that had taken them to the den, the sound of young laughter drifted down from upstairs.

"If I ever had a boy in my room, my father would have lost his shit," she commented with a hint of a smile.

Gideon grinned. "That didn't stop all of us from trying to get with you, only to be cruelly shot down."

"Shot down?" she echoed as they entered the kitchen. "Is that how you remember it? I remember saying we should slow down and next thing I knew we were back at the party. You should have had more patience."

He laughed. "That's what I get for trying to be a gentleman."

As far as moments went, it was a nice one, if not a little charged. And then he had to go and ruin it. "I've asked Audrey to talk to Bailey. She wanted me to make sure I told you."

"You realize she's a suspect?"

He arched a brow. "Neve, I'm pretty certain *I'm* a suspect as far as the police are concerned."

Her cheeks warmed. "Fair enough. I don't think it's a good idea."

"Neither does Audrey, but I asked her regardless."

There was a look in his eye Neve recognized, having been the only daughter of a protective father. Her protests weren't going to change his mind. "I want to know if Audrey says or does anything to make Bailey suspicious or uncomfortable."

"If she says anything I'll let you know."

She nodded. That was the end of that. "Thanks for the laptop."

He followed her to the door, standing on the step as gravel crunched beneath her feet.

"Hey, Neve."

Her hand on the door handle, she turned her head to look at him.

"I don't think Audrey did it."

"Noted," she replied, pulling the door open and tossing the laptop onto the other seat. "But we've already established that you don't understand women at all." She climbed behind the driver's seat.

He was smiling as she drove away.

CHAPTER TEN

Audrey opened her eyes to find them staring back at her.

"Hi," her doppelgänger said uncertainly. Hopefully. Her soft cheek rested on the opposite pillow, squishing her round face so that her mouth resembled tiny little fish lips.

Audrey smiled. It was impossible not to, despite everything. "Good morning, Miss Isabelle."

"Are you getting up now? Grammie said I shouldn't wake you up, but if you woke up by yourself it was okay. Are you up?"

Even if she needed more sleep, she didn't think it was an option. "I'm up."

"Yay!" She squirmed closer. "Do you...?" Her eyes rolled to the side as she grinned, giving her a look that only small children and lunatics could achieve.

Audrey raised a questioning brow. "Want to build a snowman?"

"No!" Her niece laughed. "Do you wanttogetsomebreakfast?"

"In a minute." This might be the only conversation she ever had with the kid—she was in no rush to end it. She tucked her arm beneath her head. "Is your mom here too?"

Her niece mimicked the position. It was like staring into a mirror and seeing a miniature version of herself. How did Jessica feel about that? She seemed to be good with Isabelle, so her hatred of her own sister hadn't poisoned her *that* much. "No. She's at work. Don't you have to pee? I always have to pee when I wake up."

Audrey laughed. "Maybe a little."

"You should go pee then." She smiled, burrowing deeper beneath the blankets. "I'll wait."

"There you are," came Anne's voice from the doorway. "She finally woke up, did she, Izzy?"

"Yep. Aunt Audrey wants French toast, Grammie."

"She does? Wow, what a coincidence that she wants the same breakfast that you asked for."

"Yeah," Isabelle agreed, jumping up onto her knees. "It is." She tried pushing her hair back from her face but only succeeded in making it more of a mess.

Audrey and her mother shared an amused glace. Isabelle climbed over her aunt and jumped off the bed. "Let's go downstairs—Aunt Audrey's hungry."

"I am," Audrey agreed with mock gravity as she tossed back the covers. "Do you want to help Grammie make breakfast?"

"Can I, Grammie? Can Aunt Audrey and me help?"

"Of course you can." Anne took her hand. "Let's go downstairs and make some coffee."

Audrey was still smiling when she pulled on her robe and headed for the bathroom. She did have to pee after all. A few minutes later she was in the kitchen, watching Isabelle—standing on a chair—measure coffee into the filter as her grandmother supervised.

"She reminds me of you," John said, reading the paper at the table, his glasses perched on the end of his long nose.

"Yeah. Me too. It's a little weird."

"She's a better kid, though."

Audrey arched a brow. "That's not hard. She is only five, though."

"Bah. You turned out all right."

She shot him a look of disbelief. *Really?* He shrugged.

"Aunt Audrey, I made coffee!" Isabelle shouted. "Come see. It looks like it's peeing!"

After inspecting the peeing coffee, Audrey got the egg-soaked bread out of the refrigerator and heated up the electric griddle. She wasn't surprised that her mother had it all ready to go. She probably made French toast for Isabelle at least once a week.

Her mother fried up sausages while Isabelle and her grandfather set the table and got out all the condiments. It was odd to see her father help out—he never used to.

"I want you to eat at least three of those," Audrey informed her mother, pointing at the pan with her fork. "You're too thin."

"I am not, and an extra sausage isn't going to make a difference regardless."

Audrey didn't argue—not in front of Isabelle—but if her mother thought she wasn't too thin, she had body dysmorphia. Had she developed an eating disorder? She used to have problems with acid reflux and indigestion; maybe they had gotten worse.

Once breakfast was ready, the four of them sat down at the table. Isabelle wanted to sit beside Audrey rather than beside her grandfather, which called for a little arranging, but was fun all the same. They stole pieces of one another's food and Isabelle drank her juice from a mug so she could pretend she was having coffee with the adults.

Somewhere between waking up and coffee, Audrey fell in love. It wasn't hard, no matter how unwanted the emotion might be. Jessica was probably leaving Isabelle at the house hoping Audrey would become attached—just so it would hurt that much more when Jessica took her daughter away. If it wasn't for the fact that murder was messy, she'd entertain the idea that Jessica had killed Maggie just to set Audrey up for it.

Hell, if Jessica and Matt Jones got together they could start a club—people whose lives had been ruined by Audrey.

It still didn't make her regret it. Not a bit.

Isabelle had syrup around her mouth when she looked up from her seat beside Audrey. She licked at it with her little pink tongue, but it only pushed the stickiness closer to her nose. "Are you coming shopping with Grammie and me?" she asked. "Mommy's going to meet us for lunch. I plan on having lobster."

She sounded like a forty-year-old in a child's body. "I would love to go with you, but I have to go see a friend." She would like to spend more time with both her niece and her mother, but lunch with Jessica was a pain in the ass she just didn't need.

Anne and Isabelle left after they cleared the table and loaded the dishwasher.

"I'm going up to the store," her father announced. "See the boys. Get the news."

The "boys" were a small group of men in their sixties and older who had nothing better to do than stand around and talk all day. There'd always been a group of them for as long as Audrey could remember. They were like the Hydra—one died and two more took his place. "How many of them think I killed Maggie?" she couldn't help but ask.

"None of them," he replied with a sharp look. "At least no one who's brave enough to say it to my face."

"Well, that's something."

Her tone must have sounded sharper than she thought, because he said, "Nothing ever happens here, Auddie, and when it does, no one knows what to do but talk about it."

"Rationally I understand that, Dad. Still, I'd be a sociopath if I didn't assume at least a little bit of responsibility." In fact, there were times when she wondered if she wasn't one anyway.

He shrugged. "Never could change your mind once you made it up."

Audrey's lips twitched. "Wonder where I got that?"

"Funny. You're a goddamned comedian."

"Yeah, I got that from you too. Have fun with your hen circle. I'm going to go for a run."

After telling her to be careful, her father left as well, leaving her completely alone in the house. It was quiet. It was too quiet. This whole town had a veil of silence hanging over it like a dense fog. They whispered speculation, made judgments with stony stares. Gossip might be a rampant white noise, but the truth was an insidious thing, slithering beneath the surface of Edgeport like a monstrous worm, quietly biding its time, feeding on all the deep, dark things that were never spoken. And Audrey fed it, just like everyone else. Fed it with a secret that had been forced upon her, that she hadn't wanted, and that—someday—was going to rise up behind her and sink its fangs into her back.

"Cheerful," she murmured, shaking off the sense of foreboding that threatened to take hold. Time to get out of the house and go do something. She and Jake were going to the bar in Bangor later that night, but they weren't leaving for another few hours.

Audrey ran upstairs and changed into her running clothes. It was windy and damp out, but she didn't care. She needed to expend some energy. Needed focus.

She drove back the Ridge—a winding dirt road that ran parallel to the river, which really wasn't much of a river anymore. It was where she'd gone the night Maggie had been killed, and it would be a good, quiet place to get in a run without worrying about people stopping to talk to her—because if anyone saw her, they would stop. They'd drive along beside her if she didn't stop as well. Some would be friendly, but others wouldn't, and she couldn't trust herself not to put a foot-sized dent in the passenger-side door of their vehicle.

Home. The one place that filled her with both peace and rage in equal measure.

The first mile or so of the road was dotted with houses. Some were cute little bungalows; others were dingy remnants from the thirties—plain wooden boxes with timbers that sagged under the weight of the history they'd endured. Given the choice, Audrey would take the old girls and their sad lead-pane eyes any day. There was something reassuring about wildflowers and tall grass. Manicured grounds creeped her out. Anyone with those perfectly straight lines in their lawn had to have a body in the backyard. The only thing Wendell Stokes had in his backyard was half a dozen old cars, an old washing machine, and a still. There was comfort in that chaos.

Past this little neighborhood was a several-mile stretch of nothing that eventually turned into one of Edgeport's original settlements. There were still a few old farmhouses back there, but most were long gone, nothing left but a pile of rotted boards or an old foundation. Mostly it was all hunting camps, and one of the oldest cemeteries in the county. At one time the Hartes had owned a lot of land back the Ridge, but it had been sold and divided up over the years. This far back, the Ridge was mostly wild blueberry scrub—acres of it. According to her mother, Jake owned most of it now. Just how much of the town had his name on it? Gracie would be puffed up with pride if she could see what he'd achieved, though Audrey had to wonder if all of it had been completely legal. Probably not.

She parked the Mini in an old driveway that was mostly grass and climbed out. She had a bottle of water and her iPod, and her keys were tucked in a small pocket in her leggings. The rain had let up, leaving the air cool and damp, and the wind wasn't quite so strong back there, buffered by trees and so far from the ocean.

She ran a mile back the road—over slight hills and around bends that followed the river until the road crossed over it via a bridge that had been old twenty years ago. It was practically ancient now. She turned there and ran back the way she'd come, old Nine Inch Nails playing in her ears as she kept her eyes open for bears. Normally they didn't come out of the woods much until the blueberries were ripe, but there was always a chance one might appear. Her grandmother once had one come right up onto her doorstep and scratch at the door as though he wanted to interest her in a copy of *The Watchtower*. Realistically she knew that even if one did come along it probably wouldn't bother with her. She also knew that if it did bother with her, there was nothing she could do about it.

About a quarter of a mile from where she'd parked her car, she spotted a half-ton bouncing along the road toward her. It was going fast, and reckless, with a weave to it that had her getting as close to the edge of the road as she could. She knew drunk driving when she saw it. Most people would probably be alarmed to think of someone being drunk when it wasn't even ten o'clock in the morning, but unfortunately it wasn't all that strange in Edgeport. Dougie Taylor used to have six beers for breakfast every morning. He had a beer in his hand when he was found dead in a ditch in the fall of 2001.

There wasn't a ditch for Audrey to jump into if the truck got too close, but there was a field—and a couple of trees she could climb in case the driver decided to play chicken. It could happen.

The truck passed by, the driver making eye contact. *Fuck*. It was Matt Jones. The truck lurched to a stop and reversed, kicking up wet gravel. A stone struck her shoulder, stinging hard through the fabric of her hoodie. She picked up the pace and glanced over her shoulder to make sure he wasn't coming straight at her. Huge tires tore up the road a few feet ahead of her before coming to a stop. The driver door opened, and out stepped Matthew. He had someone with him, but she couldn't see who.

"Ain't this a piece of luck," he said with a grin as he approached.

She didn't have any kind of weapon except her keys, which meant she was going to have to go for his eyes if she couldn't talk him out of doing something stupid. It would probably prove as futile as asking the sun not to rise.

"I don't want any trouble, Matt," she said, taking a step back.

"That's too bad, 'cause I do." He kept coming closer, fists clenched at his sides. "I've been waiting a long time to *thank* you and Maggie for what you did to me."

"Is that why you killed Maggie? To punish her? And now you're going to punish me?" Her heart punched hard against her ribs.

"Punish you? We're not in elementary school, bitch." His face contorted with disbelief and rage. "I want payback. *You're* the killer. The two of you murdered my father."

"Who raped your sister and used to beat you and your mother unconscious. Don't you remember that?"

He lifted his chin, jaw tense and jutting. "He never laid a hand on Maggie, you stupid cunt. Not like the father in the first foster family they sent me to." Matt's eyes were red and glassy with unshed tears. "He used to come into my room at night. She knew about it, but she never stopped him. But I stopped him. I bit his cock so hard he had to go to the hospital for stitches. Then I ran away. The next place wasn't much better."

"I'm sorry that happened to you, but it wasn't our fault. Maggie and I were just kids defending ourselves. We didn't know you'd be taken from your mother."

"She lost her fucking mind after you killed Dad. Went completely mental."

"You could have stayed with your aunt Joan," she reminded

him. Joan had taken Maggie in. Mostly because Maggie's mother refused to believe the truth about her husband.

"She didn't want me!" He lunged toward her. "She let them take me away!"

It probably wouldn't be smart to remind him that he'd attacked his aunt with a butcher knife and that's why she had him removed from her home.

"What do you want, Matt? An apology? Okay. I am truly sorry if any of my actions had a negative impact on your life. Sincerely sorry. Does that make you feel any better?" God, she wished she'd met up with a bear instead.

He lashed out, grabbing her by the ponytail and hauling her close. He pulled so hard her head tipped back. Audrey's eyes watered from the sudden pain, but she didn't make a sound. He smelled of stale beer, sweat, and hash, and there was a sore forming at the side of his mouth. He used to be a good-looking kid, but now he had the puffiness of a drunk, and the jaundice to match.

"I'll feel better after I show you some of the things he used to like to do to me. Ever been fucked in the ass, Audrey?" Spit rained on her cheeks. Matt tilted his head, a wet strand hanging from his front teeth. "I bet you like it. You won't the way I do it."

"Not going to happen," she told him, anger welling up inside her.

A door slammed, followed by the sound of footsteps on gravel. "Let her go, Matt." She knew that voice, even if she couldn't see him. It was Lincoln. About fucking time he stepped in.

Matt turned his attention to the other man. "Stay out of this, Linc."

Audrey turned her body, drew back her arm, and nailed her fist into his throat so hard he stumbled backward—almost taking her with him when he fell to the dirt. He still had strands of her hair in his fist as he lay there gasping for breath, eyes bugging out like a frog's.

Lincoln was suddenly beside her. He didn't smell much better than Matt had, but at least he didn't seem intent on hurting her. "Shit, I'm sorry. I was passed out in the cab or I would have stopped him. You okay, Audrey?"

She nodded. She wasn't okay at all. She was scared, shocked, and pissed off. What she really wanted to do was kick the snot out of Matt while he was down, until she was calm again. "I'm good, Linc, thanks."

He glanced down at the man on the ground. He and Jake shared a similar enough profile that she caught herself staring. Then he looked back at her. "Would you give me a ride home? I really shouldn't drive—and he's not going to be able to for a bit."

Audrey hesitated. How much could she trust Lincoln? It had to be more than she trusted Matt. "Sure. He shouldn't be driving either." But she really didn't care if Matt wrapped his truck around a tree.

It wasn't a long drive from the Ridge to Gracie's, but Lincoln chatted away during the entire thing. He alternated between moments of deep thought and almost total incoherence.

When they finally arrived at the back door of Gracie's, Lincoln turned to her with a lazy smile that made his intention—and expectations—perfectly clear. "Wanna come up?"

Her smile felt almost genuine. Almost. "Thanks, but no." She suspected her scalp was actually bleeding a bit, and she wanted to report what happened to Neve as quickly as possible. She didn't want to throw the asshole under the bus, but he'd threatened her, and from the amount of rage he had inside, it was pretty obvious that he could have killed his sister.

Lincoln looked charmingly disappointed. Even drunk and in need of a shower he was still a good-looking guy. "Another time."

Audrey smiled. Yeah, that was never going to happen.

"Thanks for the ride," he said before climbing out of the car. Audrey watched him go inside before leaving.

She arrived at Tripp's Cove about ten minutes later and went straight to the little cottage where Neve and the other police were set up. When she pulled up, Neve was just climbing the steps.

"Audrey." She greeted her with that purposely blank expression that only cops and school principals seemed to possess. "What's happened?"

She had to look like hell—flushed and sweaty with a limp ponytail—probably a wild look in her eyes. "Matthew Jones just threatened to rape me."

Brown eyes widened. "Tell me everything. Now."

Audrey did. She told her every detail she could remember about both confrontations with Matt. "I think he meant it, Neve. He was broken a long time ago."

"Do you want to file against him?"

Shamefully, her first thought was to say no and let it drop. She had, after all, ruined the guy's life. But there was also the side of her driven by anger rather than guilt. That side wanted to pay Matthew a visit that night with a baseball bat in hand. That was the Edgeport way. Fortunately, Audrey had learned not to trust her instincts.

"Yes. Can you take my statement?"

Neve nodded. "Just out of curiosity—Matt's behavior; would you say it was caused by mental illness?"

"And a mix of alcohol and drugs. If he was telling the truth, Matt Jones has been abused, manipulated, and suffered more than a kid ever should, and that can do a lot of emotional damage. I'd have to do a full assessment to get an understanding of what all of his issues are, but he's definitely got a few of them. Enough that he's dangerous—to himself and others. I don't have any doubt he would have followed through if I hadn't punched him in the throat."

The other woman arched a brow. "Still a scrapper."

"Self-defense doesn't fall into that category, but yeah, there are some conflicts that can't be solved with talk."

Neve seemed to ponder that a moment. "True enough. Come inside. I'll write up your statement. Also, I want to show you something."

Audrey followed her into the cottage. There were two other cops inside—one wore rubber boots that were covered in wet sand. The other had damp patches on his pants. They stood next to the rickety table, upon which sat a black leather Coach bag. It was wet, dirt and leaves clinging to it.

"That's a waste of a great bag," she commented. Then, her stomach rolled over. "Was it...?"

"Maggie's? Yeah. You know much about what drugs someone who was mentally ill might take?"

"Some. I can't prescribe, but I've studied drugs and what they do, so I can understand the effects on certain conditions. Why?"

Neve opened the purse and gestured for her to look inside. When she did, she spied at least four different prescription bottles. The top one was Xanax. Another was Prozac. Nothing to really blink at, knowing Maggie and her background, though it was a significant dosage. She couldn't read the other two, but there were at least a dozen pills in each bottle.

"What kind of conditions are treated with these sort of drugs, Dr. Harte?"

Audrey would have rolled her eyes at her use of "doctor" had one of the other bottles not shifted and shown her its label. It was an antidepressant. That on top of the other two gave her pause. She wasn't an expert in pharmacology, but she knew enough to be concerned. They weren't hard-core antipsychotics or anything, but she'd heard the names of them before in regard to various disorders. They all bore the same doctor's name, which was at least some comfort—they hadn't come from a variety of sources, so chances were they were actually being taken together for a specific disorder rather than being acquired through different sources to self-medicate.

"There are quite a few, Detective. Some of them can be quite serious." She gestured to the last bottle. Neve used a pen to turn it over. Caffeine? In addition to all of these other pills? She turned her head to look at Neve. "I think you'd better talk to Maggie's psychiatrist."

Jake was in his office at Gracie's doing paperwork when he heard his brother clomping up the stairs to his apartment. It was probably the first time his brother had been home since leaving work the night before. He didn't care what Lincoln did so long as he was showered and sober before they opened for the night. But he did want to ask him if he'd been back to the camp lately, and warn him away from Bailey McGann.

He finished the payroll he'd been working on, saved it, and locked his computer. Then he opened the door at the back of the room that connected to the small foyer with the staircase leading up to Linc's place. His brother would have heard him coming, but he knocked anyway.

"It's open."

Jake walked in, closing the door behind him. He made a face on the next breath. "Jesus, Linc. It smells like fucking puke in here." The apartment wasn't huge, but it did take up the entire second floor of the building. It was a little rustic, but it had a full kitchen and bathroom, along with a bedroom and living room. It had been nice enough when Lincoln moved in, and now it was a mess. Mixing with the smell of puke was stale cigarette and hashish smoke and rotting food.

His brother—a disheveled scarecrow—paused in the middle of lighting a cigarette to open a window. He weaved slightly. "Donalda was up here the other night. Chick can't hold her liquor." He lit the cigarette and took a drag. "I thought I cleaned it up."

There was a pinkish stain on the carpet not far from the couch. It looked like wine—with pizza in it. Jake scowled. He was going to have to shampoo that.

"Dude." Lincoln chuckled, puffs of smoke coming out of his mouth. "What the fuck are you wearing? Those pants look like something Gramps would have worn."

"They were Gramps's," he replied. They were vintage and fit him perfectly. He wore braces with them, over a white shirt. He was even wearing shoes. "I have a meeting later."

Lincoln shook his head, still chuckling like they were kids and his little brother had done something so incredibly stupid that he had to rub his face in it. Jake stared at him. Poor Linc hadn't figured out yet that *he* was the stupid one now.

"I'm going to hire Lorraine to come up here and clean every couple of weeks." He'd pay her enough to make sure the work was worth it.

His brother shrugged. "Yeah, okay."

"Did Morley give you the money?" he asked.

"Some of it." Cigarette hanging from his lips, Lincoln shoved his hand into the pocket of his faded jeans and pulled out a wad of cash. He tossed it to Jake, who snatched it out of the air. "Said he'd have the rest next week."

Jake counted the bills. It was exactly half of what Morley owed. He'd put it in the safe when he went downstairs. "Did he give you any trouble?"

His brother shrugged behind a cloud of smoke. "He whined a bit, but he gave it up pretty quickly. He knows better than to poor-mouth."

"Good. Hey, don't sell to anyone under eighteen. Gideon said something the other day about Bailey smelling like hash. That's shit we don't need."

Another shrug. "Okay." Jake could tell he wasn't happy about it, but if he wanted to keep his job and his apartment he was going to go along—at least until he fucked up again. Linc was a lot like their mother—full of big talk and good intentions, and incapable of making any of it a reality. He'd been among the most pissed off when the entire Tripp clan discovered that Gracie had left all the land and money to Jake. He pretended to be okay with it, but if Jake went to Morley and asked how much money he'd given Lincoln, he wouldn't be surprised to find a couple hundred missing from the count in his hand.

"Have you been back to the camp lately? There were cigarette butts in the ashtray." He didn't mention the lipstick on them. But he'd seen his brother talking to Maggie the night she was killed, and the two of them had disappeared at the same time only to suddenly show up again within a few minutes of each other. Much like Yancy not having much sense when it came to men, Lincoln didn't have any when it came to women. He'd bang anything, and it didn't matter if she was totally insane. He probably preferred it.

"Nope." Lincoln picked up a half-empty bottle of beer from the battered—sticky—coffee table and inspected it before taking a drink. Christ only knew how long it had been sitting there. "Not mine. I haven't been back there for a few weeks."

Jake didn't bother to ask why he'd been at the camp—he most likely didn't want to know. "Okay. I'm going back to the house. You have anything you want taken over?"

"You mind taking my laundry? I can come up and do it later." Lincoln drove a motorcycle, which made transporting anything bigger than a helmet tricky.

A familiar green duffel bag sat open near the door. No puke on it. Jake bent down to pick it up and saw bloodstains on something inside. He pulled it out—it was a light gray shirt, torn on the shoulder. The shoulder hadn't been torn when Lincoln had worn the shirt Friday night at work.

"Whose blood is this?" he asked, unease curdling in his stomach.

His brother looked unconcerned. "The last person I got into it with, I suppose."

"You made somebody bleed and you don't remember it?"

"I remember making them bleed. I just don't remember who they were, or why I did it."

That made absolutely no fucking sense, but questioning him now would be nothing more than a lesson in rage management. Jake avoided rage whenever possible. It seemed in the best interest of everyone if he waited until his brother was totally sober to tear a strip off him.

He turned toward the door. "Whatever. I'm leaving. I'll see you later."

"Mm. Oh, hey—your girlfriend punched Matt in the throat this morning."

Slowly, Jake turned to face him. "Say that again."

Lincoln grinned as he crushed his cigarette into the brightly colored interior of an abalone shell. "She was back the Ridge when Matt and I went back looking for 'shrooms. I don't know what she said to him, but he grabbed her. Then she punched him in the throat and laid him out. It was pretty hot."

Cold crept into Jake's gut. "Matt Jones went after Audrey and you didn't stop him?"

The moment Lincoln realized he ought to have kept his mouth shut was obvious. He immediately took on his innocent face. "I didn't know he was going to hurt her. I was passed out when we stopped. I thought he just wanted to hit on her or something. I mean, she turned out good."

"Good" was not a word Jake would ever attach to Audrey. "Did he hurt her?"

"I don't think so. I asked her if she was okay and she said yeah. She didn't mention anything when she drove me home."

She wouldn't have either. "Where's Matt now?"

"No idea." Lincoln drained the rest of the beer. "I wouldn't tell you even if I knew. Not when you've got that look on your face."

"Fine." He was in no mood to argue. No—that was a lie. He was in every mood to argue. In fact, he wanted to surpass arguing and go straight to hammering his brother's teeth down his throat. He walked out instead.

In the office, he opened the safe and deposited Morley's payment on his loan. Then, he took the duffel bag out to his truck and drove back to the house. Out behind the shed there was an old fifty-five-gallon drum that his grandfather used to use to burn trash. Before going into the house, Jake took Lincoln's shirt from the bag, used his grandfather's lighter to set it on fire, and dropped it into the scorched interior of the drum. Better to destroy it, just in case.

In case the blood was Maggie's.

CHAPTER ELEVEN

Audrey hadn't brought anything suitable to wear to a club with her, so she went with jeans, a black blouse, and flats. She left her hair down and curled it a bit, and put on a full face of makeup. It was the most she'd felt like herself—the person she wanted to be—since coming home.

Her mother and father were in the living room watching a movie—something with John Wayne in it. The two of them were cuddled on the sofa like a couple of teenagers. What was up with all the PDAs? They'd touched each other more these past few days than she could remember them ever doing her entire life.

"You look nice," her mother said with that smile only mothers possessed. "Are you going out?"

Her father turned his head, the lines in his forehead deepening. He was sober, but then the weekend was several days off. "Not with that Tripp kid?"

Audrey ignored him and smiled. "Don't wait up for me. I'm not sure when I'll be home." Bangor was about a two-hour drive, although she had no doubt Jake would shave as much off that as he could.

"Have fun!" Her mother turned back to the television. She looked a little drawn and pale. Her husband stroked her hair absentmindedly, with a gentleness that was almost embarrassing to watch, but from which Audrey couldn't look away. It was so odd to see, especially since he was still frowning at her.

"I'll be fine," she told him.

"That boy's always been trouble," he said. He looked genuinely concerned, and she didn't know what to do with that.

She shook her head as she heard a vehicle pull into the yard. "So have I."

In the truck, Jake looked like he always did—a little old-fashioned, pretty, and a little scruffy. His hair was mussed, but his eyes and lean features were sharpened by the overhead light. "Hoping to pick up tonight?" he asked as his gaze swept her from head to toe and back.

Audrey climbed into the cab and closed the door. "Why? You hoping for some more girl-on-girl?"

He looked at her. "I told you I don't like to share." He put the truck in gear and steered down the driveway, leaving her wondering if he meant that he didn't want to share *her* or share *with* her, and too chickenshit to ask. After years of study, therapy, and self-reflection, she ought to have put away her feelings for him, but they battered her gut like birds thrashing themselves to death. Fear of rejection had always been a weakness of hers—at least in her private life. Professionally she tended to be much more fearless, but when face-to-face with someone who could actually hurt her, she balked.

And it was her own fault for giving him that power.

"Speaking of girl-on-girl," he began once they'd been on the road for a few minutes. "Did you know Maggie was into women?"

"She never said anything to me when we were kids, but that doesn't mean anything. She flirted with everybody. I mean, she said some things when we were younger, but she liked people thinking she was wild and edgy. I think she is...*was* bisexual, because we both know she liked guys."

"Jesus Christ, Aud. Are you *still* hung up on that?"

"No." And that was the truth. "I meant just that—we both know she's been with men. Maybe *you're* the one who's still hung up on it."

A muscle in his jaw clenched—she could see it beneath his skin. "Maybe I am."

He turned on the radio and they spent the next hour of the drive in silence, until a song from their teen years came on, and both of them started singing along. They'd sung together as kids—Jake on guitar, Audrey wishing she could sing as well as he played. When she'd gotten out of Stillwater, and no one knew how to treat her, it had been Jake who showed up at her parents' in his grandfather's truck. He took her back to the camp, and they sang and played and talked until midnight, and then he drove her home.

They'd each been the other's confessor. She'd told him things she'd never told anyone else, and he her, but there were some secrets she couldn't share, and it was okay, because he had his own.

"Jake?" she asked as they stopped at a light. The club wasn't far now.

"Yeah?"

"Thanks for always being my friend, even when I wasn't yours."

He stared straight ahead, the lines of his face taut. A car behind them honked its horn—the light had turned green. Jake swore and stepped hard on the gas. Audrey grabbed the "holy fuck" handle above her window. A moment later, they pulled into a parking lot. The building in front of them had two neon signs. One read: THE FOX & THE BOUND—GENTLEMEN'S CLUB. The other was bright red—the outline of a tube of lipstick, or perhaps a vibrator—LIPSTICK.

He turned the key, and the rumble of the truck collapsed into stillness. "You're welcome," he said.

Touching him seemed like a bad idea, so Audrey unfastened her seat belt and opened the door.

Muted music filled the night air. A dance beat from Lipstick, and something a little raunchier from The Fox & The Bound. The feminist in her wanted to march in and rail against the objectification of women, which seriously pissed her off. At the same time, another part of her wanted to go in and cheer the girls on for bleeding their clientele as dry as dust and owning their sexuality.

She didn't do either. She walked next to Jake as they approached the door of their destination.

"Do we have a plan?" she asked.

"No."

"Maybe we should have called the number on the napkin—Chelsea or whatever her name was—first."

"You want to be the one to tell her the woman she gave her number to is dead? That's a job for Neve, not us."

"Since when do you care about crossing the cops?"

He stopped and turned to face her. "Since you became a suspect."

Of course he would say that. Audrey shook her head. "I am *such* a dick."

To her surprise, Jake grinned. "Yeah, you are. You know, you're taking this whole thing well. Not many people would hold up under suspicion."

She stuck her hands in her pockets, hunching her shoulders. "Don't give me too much credit. I'm here because I'm terrified if I don't prove my innocence no one else will. I'd really rather not have Neve arrest me and make it a Graham family tradition."

Jake reached out and pulled her right hand free, then entwined his own with it. "I'll smuggle you into Canada before I let Neve take you in."

She chuckled. "That's the sweetest thing anyone's ever said to me."

He held her hand as they continued into the club. Audrey didn't pull away or question what it meant. Life was less complicated when she just let their relationship be whatever it was and didn't worry about the rest. She already had enough things to worry about without adding Jake to the mix.

Inside, Lipstick was like most clubs—too dark with a lot of neon and bass lines that rumbled through the floor. It smelled of booze, perfume, and, faintly, sweat. The stage and dance floor were barren. Three tables were occupied by women who looked to be between the ages of twenty-five and forty. They were every size, shape, and ethnicity Bangor had to offer—which wasn't much. It was pretty white, save for two black women and the bartender, who looked to be part Asian. After living in California for more than a decade, it felt bizarre to be surrounded by so much white skin.

Audrey headed for the bar. In a lot of clubs, the music was too loud and the bar too busy to strike up a conversation, but bartenders knew their regulars and knew at least some of their issues. They spent almost as much time studying people as therapists did—with a lot more practical application of the skill.

The woman behind the bar smiled at her as she approached. "Hey there. What can I get you?"

Audrey returned the smile. "Two rum and Cokes and hopefully a little information, if you don't mind."

She got down two glasses and scooped ice into each one before pouring the rum. "What sort of information?"

Jake set a photograph on the bar. It was of Maggie—the sort that looked like a profile photo on a social media site. "Has she been in here before?"

The woman placed two small napkins on the bar before setting their drinks on them. Now she looked at both of them suspiciously. "Why are you asking?"

Audrey jumped in before Jake had a chance. "She's my girlfriend. She's cheated on me before, and I found this in her pocket the other night." She turned to Jake. "Show her the napkin."

He reached into his pocket, retrieved the napkin, and set it on top of the bar. The bartender glanced at it and made a chuffing noise. "Chelsea. I ought to have known. Look, it's none of my business, but no one deserves to get played. Yeah, she's been in here a few times over the last five or six months. Hooked up with someone new every time. I'm surprised it took this long for Chelsea to make a move. She usually goes for the aggressive femmes."

"Yeah." Audrey laughed sharply, still playing the betrayed lover. "Maggie likes someone else to take charge."

The bartender frowned. "Maggie? She told me her name was Audrey."

It was as though the woman had sprayed her in the face with ice water. At that moment it became painfully clear from the bartender's expression that she had been one of Maggie's hookups. "No," she said, her voice a hoarse rasp. "Her name's Maggie. I'm Audrey."

"Oh, hell. Honey, are you okay?" the woman asked. "I think you should sit down. I am so sorry. Look, Chelsea's actually here tonight. You want to talk to her?"

"Yes," Jake said when Audrey barely nodded.

"I'll get her." She flashed a sympathetic look in Audrey's direction. "Those drinks are on the house."

Audrey heard Jake thank her, but her mind was somewhere else, trying to figure out what Maggie got out of using her name. It had served some selfish purpose—Maggie never did anything without a reason.

She took a deep swallow of her drink, draining it by half.

"You're pale," Jake said, close to her ear.

He smelled like spice with a hint of sweet. She wanted to turn her head, speak against the rough stubble on his jaw. Let him hold her. She didn't. "I'm okay. I just wasn't expecting that."

He kissed her forehead—a gesture that almost made her cry. Then, he took the napkin with Chelsea's phone number from the bar and slipped it into Audrey's pocket.

Chelsea was a brunette of medium height with a tough swagger. Audrey had known girls like her at Stillwater. Hell, she'd been one of those girls with their abandonment issues and chips on their shoulders.

"What do you want to know?" she asked, folding her arms over the front of her black T-shirt.

"Did you and Ma—uh, Audrey—get together?"

Chelsea shook her head. "We were going to meet Saturday night. Guess you're why she didn't show, huh?"

"Something like that," Audrey replied. "Have you known her long?"

"Only from seeing her here. I knew she was a player, but it's not like I'm looking for anything serious right now. I thought we'd have some fun and go our separate ways."

That sounded like Maggie. She'd always been promiscuous, but that, as she had scolded Jake about, was unfortunately a common trait among those who had been abused as children. Maggie had also made a habit of playing with people's emotions. "Do you know if there was anyone who had a problem with her?"

"Why?"

Yeah, why? "Because she's been getting texts that upset her and she won't tell me who they're from. I don't want some crazy-ass dyke showing up at my house and boiling my bunny or something." Jake nudged her foot with the toe of his shoe. He probably thought she needed to take it down a notch, but Audrey ignored him. "Is there someone I should be worried about?"

The other woman looked around, as though making certain no one was listening. "Janis White. She hooked up with Audrey last month. She thought they had something special, then Audrey tossed her over. Janis was really pissed. She said she wasn't going to be dropped like garbage. I wouldn't put it past her to send texts. I've seen her get physical with girls before. She's tough. Like, prison tough. She said that's what Audrey liked about her."

Fuck, but it was weird to sit there and hear someone say her name in reference to Maggie. "Aren't you afraid of Janis coming after you for hooking up with her?"

Chelsea shrugged. "I can handle Janis. Audrey, though? She wouldn't stand a chance." Audrey wasn't so sure of that.

"What did Janis go to prison for?" Jake asked. Audrey silently berated herself for not asking first.

"Assault. She put her last girlfriend in the hospital when she found out she was cheating on her."

Audrey and Jake shared a glance. Definitely the kind of person who might kill someone in a jealous rage. "Were you here Saturday night?"

"Yeah."

"Was Janis?"

The other woman thought for a moment. "No. I don't think so. The place was pretty packed, though. She could have been here and I just didn't see her. We don't exactly hang out."

Audrey grabbed a pen and a napkin from the bar. "If you think of anything else, will you call me?" She scribbled her phone number and handed it to Chelsea.

"Sure." Her tone was noncommittal, however, as she stuffed the napkin in her pocket. "Hey, I didn't know she wasn't single. I've been cheated on myself. There's no way I'd do it to someone else. I'm sorry I'm what brought you here."

"Thanks," Audrey replied, surprisingly touched by the sentiment.

When Chelsea left, Audrey turned to Jake. "We need to tell Neve about Janis."

He nodded. "You want me to do it?"

"No. I want to discuss with her why Maggie might have behaved this way, and why she'd be attracted to someone with an explosive temper."

"You know why, right?"

She barely glanced at him. "Yeah, I know." It made complete sense, even if it disturbed her. In Maggie's mind she would have seen Audrey as abandoning her, letting her down like everyone else in her life. Since she'd been abused from a young age, driving Audrey to violence was a lot like love in Maggie's book. Audrey had been her savior, and Maggie had betrayed her. It was all very Shakespearean, and it all came back to Audrey. Audrey and Maggie.

Jake shrugged. "The less I have to interact with the cops the better."

"Yours is a dangerous life, Don Trippilone," she quipped, draining the remains of her free drink. "Our work here seems to be done. I don't want to press our luck. You want to get something to eat, or do you want to stay and watch some girls kiss?"

"Don't you want to hang out and see if Janis shows up?"

"Nope. Let's leave that to Neve. She's going to be pissed off enough, and I'd rather not get attacked by an angry prison-chick." Incarcerated girls had been bad enough.

"As opposed to a crazy-ass dyke?"

She winced. "I was in character."

"Yeah, you spun a good story." He eyed her with something

that looked a lot like grudging admiration. "Who knew you were such a good liar?"

He didn't know the half of it, and she wanted to keep it that way, but she could tell he was already thinking it, wondering what she might have lied to him about. "Admit it, you like it."

He smiled at that.

They left the bar after Jake finished his drink. Audrey did a search for local restaurants on her phone, and they ended up at the Chicago Grill by the mall. Their waitress was a young thing with strawberry blonde hair and wide blue eyes. She gave Jake an extra friendly smile. What was it about him that drew women in? It wasn't his thrift-store fashion sense or mussed haircut. But when he looked at a female with those bright eyes of his and flashed his perfect white teeth, they fell for it. More charm than the devil, her mother used to say about him.

"So, just how much of Edgeport do you own?" Audrey asked, gesturing at him with a fry.

He plucked the fry from her fingers and shoved it into his mouth, so she snagged a piece of pepperoni from his pizza. "You want square miles or a percentage?"

"Percentage."

He thought a moment—milking it. There was no way he didn't know the exact number down to the nearest decimal. "Right now I'm at 22 percent."

"Get out. Seriously?" That was a lot of land. What Edgeport lacked in population, it made up for in area.

Jake made a face at her as he pulled a slice from his pizza. "Yes. Somebody has to breathe a little life into the place—it's been choking to death since the seventies."

"Can't argue with that." She could remember restaurants and businesses that had disappeared when she was a kid. "What made you decide it had to be you?"

He chewed and swallowed the bite he'd just taken. "Ever have that feeling of knowing exactly who you are and what you were meant to do?"

"Yes." It wasn't a lie. She often had that feeling when she did assessments, or research interviews. And she'd had it the night Clint Jones died, but she wasn't about to admit that.

"That's how I feel about trying to save Edgeport. You don't understand that, do you?"

"Your loyalty to the town?" When he nodded, she shrugged. "No, I don't get it, but I know your grandmother felt a sense of responsibility to the town and its people." She'd always suspected that Gracie had helped her out so much because the old girl felt that she ought to have been the one to take care of Clint, not two teenage girls.

"She did. My motives aren't as philanthropic as hers."

"No?" Audrey took a drink of her Coke. His motivation had always been a source of mystery and fascination for her. "Seems to me quite a few people in town have jobs because of you."

"I'm related to most of them."

"So it's nepotism."

"Pretty much, yeah." He tore off a piece of crust.

She shook her head. He wasn't that mercenary. "I don't believe that. Not completely."

"You always saw more good in me than I deserve."

She smiled. "It's a personality flaw."

He leaned back in the booth, chewed, and swallowed. "You were also the only person I'd ever met who wasn't afraid of my grandmother. I figured maybe you knew something I didn't. I wasn't going to argue why we were friends. I just accepted it."

"It was that night at the campground. When those older boys came after Maggie and me." The summer before they'd killed Clint, she and Maggie had gone to the campground looking for

Jake and some of their friends. What they'd found were four older boys—they had to be fifteen or sixteen—who didn't care that the girls were only twelve. She and Maggie had looked older for their age. It was the first time Audrey had ever experienced fear of rape. Looking back, she realized Maggie had exhibited signs of sexual abuse even then, but she'd been too young to see them. It had been Maggie's idea to flirt with the boys. Maggie who told her to pretend she was someone else.

Then Jake had come along. He was only a year older than the girls, but the campground belonged to his family, and he knew where his father kept the shotgun. He took the girls back to his grandmother, who took one look at Audrey's pale face and torn shirt and drove back the road to address the situation. It was late, but she kicked the boys out. She'd been in her sixties at the time, and she faced the four of them alone. Audrey didn't know what she'd said to them, or what she'd done, but they sped out that road so fast a dust cloud clung to the back bumper of their car, and they never came back.

That was the night Jake went from friend to crush, and the night Audrey decided she wanted to be like Gracie Tripp when she grew up. She'd had a savior complex even then, only at that age she looked for it in other people before she finally made it part of her own makeup.

Jake nodded—she could tell he remembered that night too. "I remember how you looked at me." He smiled slightly. "Made me feel like I was a hero or something."

"You were—at least to me."

"And now if a guy lays a hand on you, you just punch him in the throat. Good work, by the way. I'm told it was 'hot.'"

She dipped a fry in ketchup. "You've been sitting on that one all night."

He smirked. "I thought I'd wait to see if you mentioned it."

"It's not exactly something you bring up in casual conversation." She popped the fry in her mouth.

"Nothing you and I say to each other is casual."

True enough. "There was nothing to say. I took care of it. Telling you would have felt like I was asking you to do something about it, and I don't need you to rescue me this time."

"How the hero has fallen." His humorous tone didn't quite ring true.

"You believing that I didn't kill Maggie means more to me than you punching Matt in the face." She jabbed another fry in his direction. "And don't try to tell me that wasn't your first thought when you heard."

"It might have been. I still might do it."

She shrugged, trying to ignore the thrill that buzzed through her. "Whatever turns your crank." The thought of Jake pounding the snot out of Matt over her was electrifying. A stupid fantasy of having an alpha male resort to violence to protect what was his.

Jake winked at her and stole one of her fries. God! Could he read her mind? Or was her poker face just that bad? Or was he just that frigging arrogant that he assumed she still had a thing for him? If she had any balls at all she'd call him on it.

"So tell me all the good stuff I've missed," she said. "Give me the dirt."

For the next half hour he told her stories about people in the town: how Binky Taylor had been seen leaving Jeannie Ray's house in the wee hours, and how Junior Pelletier—a distant cousin of Audrey's—had locked himself in the cellar with a crate of oranges and a twelve-gauge because he thought the apocalypse was coming. He filled her in on who was sleeping with who, who was on the wagon and who had fallen off, who had the most kids with different fathers, and who had fathered most of the same kids. Surprisingly, it was not Lincoln.

"What about you?" she asked. "Any husbands looking to gut you, or barefooted, hazel-eyed kids who don't look anything like the men raising them?"

"Please." He looked disgusted by the very idea. "If I had any kids I'd acknowledge them, whether their mothers wanted me to or not. As for married women, I did that once and I have no intention of doing it again."

"Hiding in closets and jumping out windows when the husband comes home wasn't your style?" *Careful, Harte. Your petty jealousy is showing.*

"I didn't do any of that, but she was so unhappy I felt like I was taking advantage of her, despite the fact that she approached me. I don't like that feeling."

Their gazes locked as silence fell between them. Jake never had been overly promiscuous—at least not to her knowledge. She didn't remember him having any girlfriends either. If she hadn't walked in on him and Maggie she might have wondered if he was gay, but no self-respecting gay man would dress like he did.

Time to change the subject. "Now tell me how you managed to build that gorgeous resort. You talked about plans for it when I was home for the funeral."

"There's nothing really to say. Gran left me a lot of money, but a lot of run-down property too. I managed to get a loan against the land, and I built the resort. I bought some other properties too—got into the blueberry business. And it panned out."

"All of it?"

He nodded. "All of it." But there was a lot of story he left out—she knew because she knew him. He wasn't going to talk up his achievements because he had done things he wasn't proud of in order to achieve them. At his core, Jake was a good man, but that goodness only extended so far. Get in his way, and he'd make certain you regretted it. He wasn't above using the weaknesses of others in his favor. Case in point: He wanted her to go away to college, and it didn't matter that Maggie wanted to hurt her. It didn't even matter than he didn't like Maggie. All that mattered was the fact that fucking Maggie would make certain Audrey walked away—from both of them. He'd gotten what he wanted, and while Audrey's tears and Maggie's blood were unfortunate consequences, they were consequences he could live with.

Living with consequences was something with which she had plenty of experience.

They finished their meal and headed back to the truck.

"Long drive for a little bit of information," she remarked. "Sorry about that."

Jake opened her door for her. "No one's demanded a fucking thing from me tonight. No teenagers, no siblings, no drunks. It's like vacation."

Audrey climbed into the truck. He shut the door and came around to his own. Once they were on the road he said, "So did all of your plans work out? Last time I saw you, you were still in school."

"Yeah," she said, surprised to realize that most of them had. "I never planned on the TV thing, though." She didn't mention that Alisha had told her that he watched it. "I'm not sure how I feel about it."

"You're a celebrity," he teased. "At least around these parts."

"Yeah, that's what I don't like. Too many people remember what happened."

"You were a kid. Your names were never printed."

She rolled her eyes in the dark. "People still know. They talk."

After a moment's silence he asked, "Do you regret it?"

Staring at the lights on the dash, Audrey thought about whether or not she should lie. Make herself sound better. But lying didn't feel right, not with Jake. Because she knew if she outright asked him what terrible things he'd done to achieve his goals, he'd tell her.

"No. I don't regret it at all. I told Jess that I regretted getting caught, but I'm not sure that's true. Stillwater was hard in a lot of ways—brutal, even. But it was still just girls. And we had some really incredible teachers, and therapists that came to work with us. I don't think I would have gone into psychology if not for that place. That's where I met Angeline—my mentor. She came to Stillwater to interview some of us who were in for violent crimes."

"You say her name the same way you say Gran's. With reverence."

Audrey smiled. "She's had almost as much impact on me as Gracie. I've been very lucky in terms of the women in my life."

"Except for Maggie."

Her smile faded. "Except for Maggie." Since they were being honest . . . "That night at the camp destroyed the last bit of innocence I had. It probably sounds stupid, but my crush on you was something pure and sweet—the one thing I had left that made me like any other girl."

"Fuck."

She glanced at him in the dim light. "I got over it." She settled back in her seat. "And really, the two of you did me a favor, didn't you? I went to school and worked my ass off, and now I've got a great job that I love. God knows how I might have ended up if I stayed here."

Silence fell between them, and Audrey didn't mind. It felt like years of tension had been lifted off her shoulders.

It was around two in the morning when they pulled into her parents' driveway. The porch light was on, as was one inside, but the rest of the house was dark. Her parents would have gone to bed hours ago.

Audrey unfastened her seat belt and turned to Jake. "Thank

you for everything you've done for me, Jake. I want you to know how much I appreciate it." Then, on a whim, she leaned across and kissed his cheek before turning and hopping out of the truck.

She'd just shut her door when he grabbed her. She hadn't been aware of him getting out. Audrey gasped as she was spun around and pressed against the warm metal. Jake took her face in both of his hands, his expression dark, eyes bright. She could feel the tension vibrating through him as he held her.

"Me," he rasped, his cheeks flushed. "You would have ended up with *me*." And then his mouth was on hers in a kiss that was anything but gentle. It was hot and damp, and so full of regret and longing that her eyes burned as one hand clutched his back, the other grabbing at his hair. Her heart thrashed against her ribs; her lungs gasped for air. Adrenaline screamed through her veins. She tugged him closer, until a breath couldn't even have fit between them.

When he tore his lips from hers, she made a small noise in protest. Her breath came in ragged gasps, as did his. He kept her pinned between his body and the truck. "Are your parents expecting you home tonight?"

She nodded.

He slid his hand along her cheek; his thumb brushed her lower lip, dragged across the edge of her teeth. "Tomorrow night you're staying with me. I don't care what you tell them." His hand slid lower, down to the neckline of her shirt. He pulled it aside and traced the same route with his mouth, the light stubble on his jaw rough against her skin. "I don't care who fucking knows." His head came back up, and his gaze locked with hers. "We're not waiting any longer."

Another nod.

Jake hesitated, and for a moment she thought he might kiss her again. Instead, he stepped back, and then walked around the front of the truck and got in. Audrey went to the steps and watched him drive away. Then, when her trembling legs refused to do any more work, she sat down hard on the steps and waited for the rush to subside.

She chuckled and shook her head. Then she began to laugh. She had to muffle the noise with her hands so as not to wake her parents, but she laughed so hard she cried, tears streaming over her hands. There was only one thing that could have made the night any better—if Maggie had been alive so Audrey could rub her face in it.

CHAPTER TWELVE

Jake had gotten up at eight, thoughts of Audrey still swimming in his head. Would she show up that night, or would she run away? She could do one just as easily as the other. If she didn't show he was done waiting. Done with her. Even he had his pride.

He took a drive out to the resort to talk to Yancy about repairs that needed to be done before they hit their busy season. She wasn't in the office. There was a sign on the door saying that she'd be back in a few minutes, with her cell number if there was an emergency. Jake frowned. Where the hell was she? Only a couple of cottages were occupied at that moment, thanks to Maggie getting herself killed, but the July Fourth weekend was coming up, and they were booked solid. He needed her at the office taking care of things.

He tried her house next. There was a battered old pickup out front that brought a grim smile to his face. It was as though Fate had delivered the fight he was looking for right to his door. When Fate delivered a gift, it was rude not to accept.

He parked behind the truck and slowly got out. The gravel cool beneath his bare feet, the sun not yet high enough over the evergreens to warm the ground. The stones were smooth, and he walked across them with a lazy stride. Jones wasn't going anywhere anytime soon.

Yancy's house was similar in design to those on the resort property, but larger, and the siding was cream rather than the stone color of the rentable cottages, the trim on the shutters and around the door dark rose rather than navy blue. Lacy curtains hung in the windows, and the entire yard was covered in flowers, shrubs, and decorative trees. It was definitely a feminine house—and suited his sister's generally sweet personality. As Jake passed one of the flower beds, he noticed that it looked as though someone had stomped through it wearing work boots, crushing the delicate blooms into the dirt.

That seemed to sum up Matt Jones in one image.

He knocked on the door and was about to let himself in when Alisha opened it. Her hair was mussed, and her expression sullen. Her blue eyes were smudged with black, as though she'd gone to bed with makeup on. Her face brightened at the sight of him. His chest tightened in response. He loved that kid, more than he ever wanted anyone to know. Eventually, either she or someone else was going to use that emotion against him. It wasn't going to be pretty when they did.

"Hey kiddo," he said, brushing past her to enter the house. "Where's your mom?"

Alisha rolled her eyes. "She's in her room. With the dick."

Normally Jake would have smiled. "Is he okay with you? With your mom?"

She shrugged. "He's creepy, but he hasn't touched me." *Yet.* Alisha could be as silly and light as the next teenage girl, but she was definitely getting better at taking a person's measure. "I think he hits her, but she hasn't told me."

Jake nodded. He put his hand on her head and stroked her hair before moving through the kitchen into the hall. "Yance," he called. "You here?"

Hushed voices answered—one obviously Yancy's, the other low

and male, laughing. Jake's spine stiffened. If Jones thought he was a joke, he was about to learn differently.

His sister emerged from her room. Her tank-top strap hung over one shoulder, and the skin around her mouth and chin was bright pink from whisker burn. She looked sheepish.

"I need you back at the office," he said quietly.

She nodded. "I'll get back right away. I hadn't meant to be gone this long."

Jake hooked one finger under that drooping strap and pulled it up where it belonged. "Change your shirt first, my dar. You've got a love bite."

Yancy flushed. "Sure."

A shadow moved across the hall, and then Jones was there—shirtless in a pair of low-slung jeans that looked as though they'd needed a wash two weeks ago. He was so skinny you could count his ribs, but that wasn't what caught Jake's attention. It was the tattoo portrait of Clint Jones over his heart, with the dates of his birth and death below.

"Cracking the whip, Jake?" the other man sneered. "You don't own her, you know."

"Is that why you had to mark her?" Jake inquired, keeping his voice low. "So I'd know she's yours?"

Jones grinned. He had fairly good teeth, considering. He ran his nicotine-stained fingers up Yancy's arm. "Sure. Why not? You want to be mine, baby?"

Yancy shrugged, moving away from him. He laughed.

"Gross," Alisha drawled, rolling her eyes as she got a soda from the fridge.

Jones moved toward her, shoving Yancy out of his way. His lean face was dark with anger. Jake intercepted fast, grabbing him by the throat and whipping him around so he was bent back over the sink.

"What the fuck, man?" Jones demanded.

Jake kept his hand on the other man's throat, applying steady pressure against his windpipe. "Here's how it's going to go, you sorry sack of shit: If you ever lay a hand on my sister or my niece—if you hurt them in *any* way—they won't ever find what's left of you. It won't be quick and it won't be clean. Nod if you believe I'll do it." At that moment he remembered one of the things he admired most about Audrey. She had killed to protect someone she cared about, and that was a loyalty he wished he could win—and give in return.

Jones's face was red, but he nodded—a jerky movement. Jake held him there a few more seconds, and then let him go. Jones came at him with a wide and violent swing that made Jake grin. He pulled his punch, but still managed to land a solid blow to the other man's throat that sent him staggering backward, coughing and sputtering.

"Jake!" Yancy cried, rushing toward her boyfriend. Alisha stepped to Jake's side. He put his arm around her.

Jones shrugged off Yancy's hands, pushing her away. He held a hand to his throat, eyes watering as he glared at Jake. "You fucking cunt," he whispered.

"This is my property," Jake told him with a smile. "Get the fuck off it."

Jones didn't argue. He continued to glare at Jake as he stomped by in his unlaced combat boots. Jake turned to watch him leave. Jones was not the kind of man he would ever turn his back on. The door slammed behind him, followed a few seconds later by the roar of a truck engine.

Jake moved to the front window and watched as the backwoods little prick had to maneuver his half-ton around Jake's own. Were the situation reversed, Jake would have backed up and tore the front bumper off the other. Jones didn't have the balls to throw down such a challenge. Or maybe he was smarter than he looked.

"I can't believe you did that!" Yancy shouted, tears in her eyes. "Matt loves me and you treated him like dirt!"

He kept his expression neutral. "Your boyfriend threatened to rape Audrey."

The tears evaporated. "You're lying."

He arched a brow and tilted his head. "When have I ever lied to you?"

"Then she's lying. I hear she's good at it." Her expression was sullen. She looked younger than Alisha.

"Jones tell you that?"

"No. He hasn't said a word about her. Jeannie did."

"Then it must be true." What he found most interesting was that Matt hadn't tried to convince Yancy that Audrey had killed his sister. "You don't believe me? Ask Lincoln. He was there and saw the whole thing."

His sister's face turned pale. Jake almost felt bad about bursting her little bubble, but better he did it now than have her turn into Matt Jones's punching bag. His first instinct was to hug her, but his grandmother wouldn't have caved so easily, so he wasn't going to. "Get changed and get back to work, Yance. Fuck whoever you want on your time, not mine."

She shot him a dirty look, but he held her gaze without flinching. She looked away first, slinking back into her bedroom.

Jake turned to his niece. "If she doesn't leave the house in the next ten minutes, text me."

Alisha nodded. "Would you really kill him?" she asked. "If he hurt me or Mom?"

"I would. I'll protect the two of you till I die."

She threw her arms around his waist, her head on his shoulder. "I love you, Uncle Jake."

His throat tightened. "I love you too, kid."

He hoped Matt Jones understood just how much.

*   *   *

It was foolish, being thirty-one and trying to figure out how to tell your mother you weren't going to be home that night. Even more insane was fretting over that when you were probably the top, if not the only, suspect in a murder investigation—a fact of which Audrey was reminded when Neve arrived at the house that morning.

"You got a minute?" her old friend asked.

Audrey poured herself a cup of coffee. "Have you had breakfast?"

"Yeah, thanks. I'll take a coffee, though."

She got another mug from the cupboard and filled it, bringing both to the table. "What's up?"

Neve fixed her coffee with cream and sugar. "Gideon gave me Maggie's computer. I've been reading the book she was writing."

Audrey's heart skipped a beat as she spooned sugar into her own mug. "Is it any good?"

"Honestly? I wouldn't want to be her editor."

She tapped her spoon on the rim of her cup. "You didn't come down here to discuss her prose, though. Did you?"

"No." Neve reached into the messenger bag she'd hung on the back of the chair and pulled out a few sheets of paper. She set them on the table in front of Audrey.

The first page was the dedication page. It read *To Audrey, forgive me.* Audrey arched a brow but said nothing. That was just Maggie being dramatic. The next page had text highlighted on it. "Audrey was my dearest friend, my greatest supporter, and my self-appointed protector. When I told her what my father had done—was doing—to me, it was her idea to kill him."

Maggie, you fucking bitch.

Neve watched her closely. "Is this true?"

Audrey shook her head. "Of course not. I don't know what she hoped to gain by writing that, but if she published it, I'd slap her with a libel suit."

"Tell me everything that happened that day. I know what I heard as a kid, and what you told me at the cottage, but I want to hear it all, because Maggie never said anything about it being your idea, not ever."

Audrey drew a breath, curling her hands around the mug in front of her. The ceramic was hot against her palms, giving her something to focus on. "Maggie told me that her father had been abusing her for almost a year. I couldn't believe she hadn't confided in me sooner, but she said she was afraid I wouldn't want to be her friend anymore. I told my mother, but she never really trusted Maggie and thought she might have been lying for attention."

Neve nodded slowly. "I can understand her concern."

"I can too—to an extent. My default is to always believe the kid. I'd rather be a fool later than know I allowed that kind of sickness to continue."

"Fair enough. What happened next?"

"Mum told Dad, who couldn't believe his buddy would do such a thing, even though he knew Clint often raised his hand to Penny and the kids. Maggie told her mother and Penny slapped her. Looking back, I think she was terrified Clint would silence Maggie the same way he'd silenced her older sister, Beth."

"I checked that out. Elizabeth Jones's death was ruled a suicide. She drowned in the bathtub."

Audrey looked directly into Neve's eyes. "I know. I also know Clint was the only one at home with her at the time."

Another nod. "What then?"

"We didn't think anyone was going to do anything. Maggie said she wished she could kill him, and we talked about ways to make that happen. I never thought we'd actually do it, but I knew

I could if I had to. I was prepared to suffer the consequences if it meant Maggie would be free."

"You had a bit of a white-knight complex, didn't you?" The detective's tone wasn't quite censorious, but it wasn't complimentary either. "Always defending the underdog, fighting bullies."

Audrey shrugged and took a drink from her mug. The coffee was sweet and strong on her tongue. "I did. Still do. I'm not going to apologize for it, if that's what you're hoping. And yes, Neve, I'm fully aware of the motivation behind it. The first person I ever psychoanalyzed was myself."

Neve smiled ever so slightly. "Go on."

"I went over to Maggie's house after dinner that night. We were going to study for a math test. I let myself in—they never locked the door. Her mother and Matthew weren't home, and the house was quiet. When I got to Maggie's room and opened the door, I found her on the bed, naked. Her father was also naked, and he was raping her." She stopped and took a drink of her coffee. She had to pull herself together.

Neve looked horrified. "Christ. I can't imagine what that must have been like."

"It was terrible," Audrey confessed. It was something she would never, ever forget, for so many reasons. "I tried to pull him off of her, but he was a big man. He swatted me away like a fly. I hit him with a stone gargoyle Maggie had gotten at a flea market. That got his attention and he got off the bed. He hit me and knocked me to the floor." She could still feel the force of that blow across her cheek. "He said he'd get to me when he was done with Maggie. He hit me again, and then the next thing I knew, he was lying across my legs, his head bleeding. Maggie stood over him, sobbing. She had the gargoyle in her hand. I took it from her and called the police. Your father was the first to arrive. I still remember the look on his face when he realized what Clint had done to his daughter."

"It's a hard thing for most fathers to wrap their heads around."

"Yeah," Audrey agreed. "I think Dad just didn't want to believe it, even though he knew it was true. He didn't want to think that he'd be friends with such a monster."

Neve cradled her mug in both hands. "Explain to me why Maggie would lie about any of this and try to pin it on you after all these years."

"Really? You knew her. She never needed any other reason than attention. I think she resented the fact that I left Edgeport, and she never forgave me for turning away from her. After all we'd been through, I let her down, just like everyone else. I don't know why she would think to do it now, though. Maybe she was hoping to affect my career. She had this twisted way of thinking that she could hold on to the people she loved through hurting them. No one ever taught her differently."

"You don't think it had anything to do with you beating the shit out of her?"

That was bait she wasn't going to snap at. "It might, but Maggie was used to physical violence—she grew up with it. If you wanted to hurt Maggie, a punch wasn't going to do it." She'd seen it in countless kids who had suffered at a parental hand. "She wasn't vulnerable that way."

The other woman was contemplative for a moment. "I never thought of Maggie as vulnerable."

"We're all vulnerable. Some people just hide it better than others."

"Yeah?" Neve leaned back in her chair with a mocking smile. "What's your vulnerability, Dr. Harte? What's mine?"

Audrey arched a brow. "Seriously?"

The other woman made a "bring it" motion with her hand. "You're the big-shot TV psychologist. Let's hear it."

All right. If that was the way she wanted it... "My greatest vulnerability is the people I love. I would do anything for them, and letting them down terrifies me. Funny, right? Since I let my family down in such a spectacular way. I thought going to school and making something of myself would make up for it."

"Did it?"

"No." But she wasn't going to talk about herself anymore. "Your vulnerability, Detective, is just how badly you want your father's approval."

Neve went perfectly still, and Audrey knew she'd nailed it. It hadn't been hard. As kids, Neve had desperately wanted her father's attention.

"You stopped hanging out with me to please him. You went to prom with the guy he thought you should date. You became a cop, just like him—you even went to New York, where he used to work. You became a detective young and moved back here so he could see what you've accomplished. All you want is for him to tell you you've done good, but he hasn't said it. Instead, he tells you how to do your job and makes you feel like a kid. And even though you know in your heart that I didn't kill Maggie, you're going to keep investigating me because your father is convinced that Maggie and I lied about what happened that night, and he thinks I'm good for her murder. How am I doing so far?"

Neve shrugged. "I've got daddy issues. What girl doesn't?"

Audrey held up her hands. "Hey, I'm president of the fan club. If you need to turn my life inside out to prove something to your father, then knock yourself out, but don't ignore everything else. I can help you with this, Neve. Jake too. No one knows more about what goes on in this town than him. And I know killers."

Dark eyes bore into hers. "I guess you do."

She smiled. "You're going to have to do better than that to provoke me. Whoever killed Maggie was angry—really angry. It was personal, committed by someone who knows about her past.

They had to hit her a couple of times to kill her, which proves intent. The fact that she was found facedown indicates that she fell that way, or that the killer turned her so they didn't have to look at her face. That's remorse. Only someone close to her would have done that."

"How do you know she was found facedown?" Neve asked softly.

Oh, hell. "Gossip. Everyone knows." Technically it wasn't a lie. Everyone did know most of the details thanks to Yancy, but Audrey wasn't going to rat on Jake. "If I had killed her, I would have looked her in the face when I did it. And, I would have tried to cover my ass by burying her somewhere. I wouldn't have left her where she'd be found so quickly."

"There weren't any prints on the rock, and the tide washed away any trace evidence that might have been left behind. You're smart enough to do that."

Audrey shrugged. "Frankly, I would have called Jake. We both know she would never be found once he stepped in." She took a drink of coffee. "I'm sorry if you feel like I've stepped on your toes. I'm just frustrated. I don't want to put my family through this again."

The other woman's full lips curved into a sympathetic smile. "There's that vulnerability coming into play."

She laughed hoarsely. "Yeah. I guess so. Anyway, look, Maggie and I killed Clint, that's the truth. There was nothing to lie about."

"Based on your story, I'd say Maggie killed Clint. You were just trying to help a friend."

"Well, you know what they say about good intentions."

"What I don't understand is why Maggie got out before you did."

"Maggie was mostly in the psych hospital. She was diagnosed

with PTSD, I think. Certainly there were a lot of issues to be dealt with, but they wouldn't have let her out if they didn't think she was okay. I already had a record when we were arrested, so the judge decided I needed some 'straightening out,' as he put it. I kept getting into fights at Stillwater—stuff that delayed me getting out."

"Why?"

No one had ever asked her that. Audrey smiled. If Neve wanted vulnerability, she didn't mind delivering. "I didn't want to come home and face everyone."

Their gazes locked, and then Neve nodded. "I should get going." She stood. "Oh, I wanted to let you know I went by Matt's place last night, but he wasn't there. Nobody seems to know where he's at, so you be careful, okay? No running back the Ridge or any other secluded place."

Audrey held up her hands. "Yes, ma'am."

Neve smiled slightly and let herself out.

Alone, Audrey looked at the pages on the table. She'd gotten so caught up in the past she'd forgotten to tell Neve about Maggie and her trips to Lipstick.

Goddamn you, Maggie. She'd never asked for the secret Maggie had thrust upon her. Now, it was coming back to bite her on the ass. She ought to have known Maggie would turn on her one day—she'd said as much the night she was killed. She leaned in and slurred in Audrey's ear, "I know what you are, killer." And Audrey had reacted. Fortunately she'd only shoved Maggie instead of belting her like instinct demanded.

She was also thankful that Maggie hadn't gotten any further into her poorly written, self-indulgent memoir than she had, otherwise it would be that much more difficult to prove that Audrey hadn't killed Maggie the same way she'd killed her best friend's father.

* * *

Audrey—

I can't believe you came home for *HIM*. You didn't come home for me when Aunt Joan died—or my mother, for that matter. But you came home to bury that old woman? Why? Because she paid for you to go to that fucking uptight university of yours? She bought you, is that it?

I saw you at the graveside with Jake, holding his hand. The two of you looked so cozy, like you always did when we were kids. You came back from Stillwater and suddenly Jake was your new best friend.

I WAS YOUR BEST FRIEND, YOU BITCH!!!!!! ME!! I told the police I killed my father for you, so you wouldn't have to go to jail. We knew they'd go easier on me. I *lied* for you. And how did you thank me? You left me. Just like everyone else has left me. Just tossed me aside like dirt. After all I'd done for you, you ignored me, hardly spent any time with me. I had to fuck Jake just to get your attention. Do you have any idea how debasing that was? God. He said your name when he came. Just to fuck with him I said your name too. I wish you could have seen the look on his stupid face. I knew when you hit me that I mattered more to you than he did. Only someone you loved could have driven you to violence. But then you went away. You went away and you never called. You changed your number and your e-mail. You left me. You were the only person who ever understood me.

But you came home for Jake and that old bitch Gracie.

I'm never going to forgive you for that. *NEVER.*

CHAPTER THIRTEEN

Neve sat on the floor of her bedroom, every clue and bit of information concerning Maggie's death spread out around her. Crime-scene photos, autopsy findings, the photograph of the footprint, pages from Maggie's manuscript that had passages highlighted, and her own notes. No tox screen, though. That took a while. Her laptop sat beside her, open to a Google search on the many kinds of issues and conditions treated by the various drugs Maggie had been prescribed.

Neve had called Maggie's psychiatrist, but it went straight to a service. It was early summer and the long weekend was coming up soon. He was probably on vacation.

The autopsy hadn't turned up any surprises other than human DNA mixed with the booze in Maggie's stomach, so she'd been with a guy that night, and Neve suspected it hadn't been her husband.

Okay, so what else did she have? Maggie had been hit by someone taller than her, which didn't narrow the suspect pool because she was tiny. She'd been hit multiple times and died from the injuries. There were no prints on the rock, but plenty of blood, bone, and hair. The one footprint was smooth, so it had been made by a shoe without a tread. Sand wasn't always reliable, especially when dry, so the best guess was that it was a woman's ten, or a man's eight. That was it. Any other footprints were too messed up to get any information from. There had been evidence of four-wheelers—many of them. Practically everyone up and down the shore owned one.

Maggie's wallet still had money and credit cards in it, so the killer hadn't wanted to rob her. Had the killer dropped the bag, or had Maggie lost it as she staggered drunkenly to the beach? The lipstick in her bag looked to be a match to that on the cigarettes in the camp, but they'd have to test it to be sure. And she was no closer to figuring out if the killer had been with her in the camp.

She looked at her notes. Under "suspects" she had a few names, although Audrey was still at the top. Then Matt, Maggie's brother. He'd been in and out of trouble with the law since he was a kid, and he'd been heavily into drugs and alcohol since his early teens. There were two domestic abuse arrests in his file. He seemed to like hurting women. And he had a huge hate on for his sister. And Audrey.

She had yet to find him so she could confront him about Audrey. He'd been seen around town, but he was hiding out somewhere outside of his usual haunts. She needed to talk to Lincoln too.

That left Gideon. She needed to treat him like a suspect as well, but why kill Maggie when he could divorce her? No, he didn't act like a man in mourning, but he was either the most chill murderer she'd ever heard of, or he didn't feel enough emotion for his wife to put up a fight. It had taken several blows to kill Maggie, indicating that the person wasn't physically powerful. Gideon was a strong guy, used to physical labor. He would have ended Maggie's life much more economically than the actual killer.

She gathered up all the papers and put them back in the file, which she then tucked in her bag, and went downstairs. As luck would have it, her father was in the kitchen, making a pot of chili. "Where are you off to?" he asked.

"I have some people to interview."

"You still haven't arrested the Harte girl."

Neve shoved her feet into her shoes. "No, Dad. I haven't. I prefer to get concrete evidence before I arrest people."

He gave her "the look." She gave it back. Surprisingly, he didn't push it. "Will you be home for dinner?"

That was an unexpected change in tactic. "Yeah. It smells good, by the way."

He looked smug. "It always does."

She left him to his culinary adventures and got into her car. Her first stop was M—Maggie's salon. It had closed for a couple of days when the news broke, but was open again. And since hairdressers were second only to bartenders and priests for hearing people's secrets, talking to the ladies who worked with Maggie seemed a good idea.

When she walked in, Tami Pelletier—a pretty, curvy woman—looked up from the front counter. "Neve. Hey, there. Do you have an appointment?" She checked the book.

"Official visit, Tami, sorry. Do you have a minute?"

The girl's round face fell. "Is this about Maggie?"

Neve nodded.

"Yeah, sure." She turned her head to call over her shoulder, "Carol, cover the front, will you? I'll be back in a minute."

The younger woman took Neve to the back room. "What do you want to know?"

"Did Maggie have trouble with anyone that you know of?"

Tami moved a bottle of shampoo to another shelf. "Not that I'd seen, but she told me that she and Gideon weren't getting along, which was a surprise because he always seemed like a nice guy, you know?"

"Yeah," Neve agreed, "I know. Did she say if the two of them were fighting? Or was she afraid of him?"

"Oh, no. She used to complain that Gideon never fought with her. I think Maggie equated anger with caring, which sounds messed up, but I think she wanted him to fight for her, and he didn't. She didn't much care for Isaac, Bailey's boyfriend, either, but I don't know the kid that well."

"What about her brother?"

Tami's eyes widened as she puffed out her cheeks. "Oh! That guy is such an *ass*. He came by on Friday, being a prick to her. He showed up here one night last week demanding money. He told Maggie it was the least she could do for him. He tried to break into the cash. He hit Maggie when she tried to stop him."

Neve's brows pulled together. There had been nothing about this in Matt's record. "She never reported the assault or the theft."

"Oh, he didn't get any money. Maggie pulled a gun on him. She kept a small pistol in a box underneath the counter. She pulled it on him again on Friday. She said, 'Get the fuck out of here, Matt, or I'll reunite you with Clint.'"

"That must have been tense." And certainly could have been a trigger for Matt to attack her later. "What did Matt do?"

Tami shrugged and reached for a bottle of hair color. "He left. We were all pretty surprised he gave up that easily."

"Or maybe he knew she meant it."

"Maybe. He never came back, thank God."

"Did she have trouble with anyone else?"

"Not that I know of." Tami paused, hair dye still in hand. "She sometimes got texts that upset her, but she got some made her happy too. *Really* happy." The look she gave Neve was pointed to the edge of pantomime.

"Do you know who they were from?"

The other woman peered out the door before gently closing it. "Listen, Neve"—her voice had dropped to a whisper—"I think

Maggie had something going on with someone else. And I think it was a woman."

This was interesting. "What makes you think that?"

"Well, she'd get those texts, but then she'd also spend a lot of time making herself pretty and then leave early. Sometimes she asked me to cover for her. If anyone—especially Gideon—called for her I was supposed to tell them she was with a client, then call her cell and tell her to call the person back. It happened a few times a month. Or, she'd ask me to pretend that we were doing something after work, like going for dinner or hanging out at someone's house."

That definitely sounded like the actions of someone sneaking around. "Why do you think it was with a woman?"

"She bought a lipstick—a bright pink one—that she thought a 'friend' would really like, but then she put the lipstick on herself. One time we were shopping and she bought lingerie I knew wouldn't fit her. She said it was for Bailey, but it was pretty sexy stuff for a teenager. And every once in a while she'd say something that hinted at her swinging both ways—like women being better kissers than men. That sort of thing."

"She never mentioned any names?"

Tami shook her head. "The only woman she talked about—besides any of us, the town, or Bailey—was Audrey Harte. She used to say she regretted how things went between them. Do you really think Audrey killed her?"

Neve forced a smile. That was her cue. "Thanks for your time." She held out her card. "Call me if you think of anything else."

"Sure." Tami looked disappointed that Neve hadn't answered her question. She'd get over it, Neve was sure. Before she walked out, Neve went to the cosmetics display near the front counter and found the lipstick that was in Maggie's purse. She bought one for herself. It was a pretty color.

Back in her car, Neve began the hunt for Matt Jones. He didn't have a permanent address that she knew of. He seemed to bounce back and forth between a camp back the Ridge, Lincoln's apartment, and Yancy's cottage. His rusted-out excuse for a truck wasn't parked behind Gracie's. Ridge Road was closer than Tripp's Cove, but if she were a guy like Matt and had to choose between a musty old camp and a girlfriend who would cook for him, she'd be at the girlfriend's.

Sure enough, that's where she found him—at Yancy's. He was outside, shirtless, loading a lawn mower into the back of his truck. The lawn mower had "The Cove Resort" painted on the back.

"Hey, Matt," Neve greeted him when she got out of the car. "Whatcha doing?"

He looked at her, his narrow face pinching. "What the fuck is it to you?"

Matt had never liked her and she had never cared. He was younger than she was, but he looked older. A life of self-abuse did that to a person.

She nodded at the lawn mower. "If I asked Jake if you were allowed to have that mower in your possession, what would he say?"

He frowned, making him look even meaner and older. "Fuck Jake. Yancy said I could borrow it earlier today."

Almost as if on cue, Yancy appeared on the doorstep. "Hey, Neve. Something wrong?"

Neve smiled at her. "I'm here to talk to Matt about an altercation between him and Audrey Harte that took place back the Ridge the other day."

Yancy shot him an anxious glance. She didn't look surprised, though. Had Lincoln told her? Or had Jake already been by to defend Audrey's honor? God, those two should just sleep together and get it over with.

Matt sneered, not the least bit intimidated by her badge. Then again, he'd always been about the superior color of his skin. "Just had a talk with her, that's all."

"Her scalp bled from you grabbing her."

He spat. "I never touched her. Ask Lincoln. He was there."

Neve nodded. "I'll be sure to do that." She wanted to ask who he thought Lincoln would be more loyal to—Matt or Jake. "Just out of curiosity, where were you Friday night?"

"Here." He looked at Yancy. "Wasn't I, babe?"

"Yeah." Yancy nodded vigorously. "He was here all night."

"Great." Neve didn't believe either one of them, but she wasn't going to get the truth out of Yancy with him standing there. Had he started hitting her yet? Maybe it was still too early in the relationship, but it was coming. Clint Jones had passed on more than just his looks to his son. "Thank you both for your time."

She made eye contact with Yancy. The younger woman glanced away. Such a pretty, sweet woman deserved better than Matt, but a sad number of women accepted guys they *believed* they deserved rather than a guy who treated them with respect.

Neve was just getting into her car when Jake's truck pulled into the yard. She paused, one leg in. There was no way she was going to miss this.

Jake climbed out of the truck. Barefoot as usual. Jeans rolled up like Huck Finn, wearing a ratty old T-shirt. He was lean as hell, but that only made the long lines of the muscles in his arms more pronounced. She knew he was a strong—and tough—son of a bitch.

"You don't listen well, Jones. When I told you to get off my land, I didn't mean it as a temporary arrangement. So, unless you're taking that ride-on back to the resort, take it out of the back of your fucking truck."

Yancy came down off the steps. "Jake, I said he could borrow it." She put herself between the two men. "If you're going to be mad, be mad at me."

Her brother reached out and put his hand on her shoulder. "I'm not mad, my dar." His expression tightened when he turned to Matt. "You need a hand getting it down?"

And that was that. Matt's jaw tightened, and his eyes burned, but he didn't defy Jake. And now Neve had his measure: the sort of man who would hit a woman, or someone he saw as weaker, but not someone who might be an equal or superior. If he ever came after *her* he was going to get a surprise.

Jake walked over to her, his stride steady and sure across the gravel. He had to have soles like leather. "Have you been talking to Audrey today?" he asked.

"No. Why?" There was nothing in his face or tone that gave anything away, so it was just her natural distrust that made her wonder what the two of them had been up to.

"You might want to give her a call today or tomorrow."

"I'll do that. Hey, Jake, I know there's a lot of traffic back this road during the summer, but have you seen anyone who shouldn't be back here?"

"Besides him?" He jerked his head in Matt's direction. "No. But, a lot of people come through here on four-wheelers. I had the trails cut for that reason."

"You don't mind people trespassing on your land?"

"Not when they stay where I want them."

She regarded him for a moment. "I don't suppose you have cameras installed on those trails or around the beach?"

"No, but I'm looking into it now." He looked her in the eye, but then, Jake rarely looked anywhere else. "I'll let you know if I think of anything."

"All right. Thanks. I'll call Audrey."

He nodded and walked away, back to his sister and Matt, and

the drama of the lawn mower. Neve shook her head as she got into her car. What the hell had she been thinking coming back to this fucked-up town?

Audrey waited until seven before leaving to go to Jake's. She'd thought about chickening out, but even her own nerves couldn't stop her from getting in the car. Her mother had gone to bed with a headache, and her father was on the couch watching TV, so it wasn't as though they were going to miss her.

"Hey," she said from the living-room doorway.

Her father pressed pause on the remote and turned his head toward her. He was sprawled on the sofa like a teddy bear that had lost most of its stuffing. "What's up?"

She leaned against the doorframe. "Is Mum okay?"

He blinked. "Yeah. Yeah, she's okay. She's just been tired lately. She keeps forgetting she's not forty anymore."

"So, it's not because of me? And all the stuff with Maggie's... murder?"

His face softened. "No. No, of course not."

"Okay. Good." Though what would she have done if he said yes? "I wouldn't have come home if I'd known this was going to happen. I should have missed that damn flight."

"None of this is your fault, so don't you go around feeling guilty."

She nodded. Easier said than done.

"You going out?"

She nodded. "I'm going to Jake's."

He actually smiled. "Good. I give you a hard time about him, but he's been a good friend to you through this, even if the skinny bastard did break your heart."

"Ha." She dipped her head. "He has been a good friend. He broke my heart so I'd go away to school."

"Yeah, I know. That didn't make it any easier for your mother or me to watch. If he does it again this time he and I are going to have a talk."

"You'll have to sell tickets to that." People would pay. In this town, people would *definitely* pay—and sell refreshments.

He waved a dismissive hand. "Aw, he'd probably knock me on my ass."

Audrey smiled. "Has anyone ever knocked you on your ass, Dad?"

He actually had to think about it. "First time for everything."

Audrey chuckled. In her years of harboring resentment and anger, she'd forgotten that sometimes he was okay. She even admired him on some level. "And on that note, I'm going to go. Don't wait up."

His expression turned serious. "Be careful, kiddo."

She knew he wasn't talking about Jake, but rather Maggie's killer—and possibly anyone else in the town who might mean her harm,—like Matt Jones. She also knew that her father hadn't heard about Matt accosting her, because Matt would be in traction if he had. It was going to happen. Yancy might be the least discreet of the Tripp siblings, but Lincoln was almost as bad. He wouldn't be able to keep himself from bringing it up.

"I will," she promised. She turned away, walking down the hall toward the kitchen. She'd made it only a few steps before she heard the popping of a can. Her father opening a beer. He probably had at least a six-pack under the couch. She really shouldn't be surprised, or disappointed, but she was. Something inside her dropped, and settled heavy in her stomach. So much for that admiration.

It was a lovely but cool evening when she stepped outside. The sun was sinking on the horizon, and there was a light breeze off the ocean. As Audrey unlocked the Mini, she heard an ATV engine start. She turned just in time to see the four-wheeler drive by in the field across the road. It was missing a headlight. Was it the same one she'd seen at the Tripp graveyard? If so, what was it doing way down here? Was it Bailey McGann's boyfriend, as Jake supposed? The rider's face was hidden by a helmet and visor, but the clothes and build seemed decidedly masculine.

It was probably no one—just that Canning kid out for a drive—but unease trickled down her spine. It was an occupational hazard to sometimes see dark intentions where often there were none.

Audrey jumped into the car and started it. She sped out of the yard in the direction the four-wheeler had gone, but there was no sign of it. The driver had probably veered off onto one of the private drives that led to cottages at the top of the cliff. There was one such lane that meandered down to the beach itself. People used it all the time for beach access when the owners weren't about, which was most of the year.

She shook her head. She was being paranoid—arrogantly so. As Jake had reminded her only a few days ago, people in Edgeport did have other things to do than talk about—or plot against—her. She was just trying to redirect her nervousness about what might transpire that night at Jake's. She'd rather think someone was stalking her than admit she was excited. *Hopeful.*

Best-case scenario, they both got a little closure. It couldn't really be anything else, could it? She was going to have to return to L.A. eventually. It wasn't as though they could ever have a relationship. That didn't stop her from speeding the entire way to Tripp's Cove, even though Neve and her statie buddies were probably out and about the town.

Neve had called her earlier—said Jake had told her she might want to. Audrey told her about the napkin, and the trip to

Bangor. Was the cop impressed? No. In fact, she gave Audrey an earful—including a threat to arrest her just to keep her out of the investigation.

"Somebody has to prove I'm innocent," Audrey retorted. "So far you haven't managed it."

"You're not the only person of interest, okay? I'm not ready to lock you up just yet, but keep going off on your own and I will. Understood?"

Audrey gave her Chelsea's number and told her that if she heard anything Neve would be the first one she called. Her old friend actually laughed before hanging up. It wasn't much, but at least it was something to take attention off her. She had to do something. She couldn't just sit there and trust in the process—not when it seemed everyone already thought her guilty.

When she pulled into Jake's driveway, she sat there for a moment, staring at the house that had been one of her favorite places as a kid. So much work he'd put into it, making it his own, but it still felt as safe and warm as it had when Gracie sat on the front porch smoking her pipe, working on quilts set in a frame Mathias had made for her.

This was the place that felt most like home. And she was about to do something that might ruin that forever—or make it mean even more.

Fuck it. She tried very hard during the course of her adult life to not act impulsively. Doing so in the past had always come back to bite her on the ass. But, every once in a while, she gave in. She wanted a new pair of boots but also groceries? Fuck it. She got the boots and ate peanut butter for a few days. Her feet looked fabulous, and she liked peanut butter, so it wasn't that much of a trial. She wanted dessert but her scale said no? Fuck it. She upped her cardio for the next few days. She was all about the gratification and she knew it. Not like she was hurting anyone. At least not anyone other than herself.

She wanted Jake but knew it would probably hurt her in the long run? *Fuck. It.* The sane part of her brain tried to intervene and she shut it out. She'd wanted this too long, and she'd regret it if she let the moment pass.

She opened the door and stepped out, shutting it and locking it before she could jump in and drive away. Her heart pounded in her throat as she marched toward the front door. She'd seen a lot of scary and disturbing things in her life, of which Clint on top of Maggie was one of the worst. She had faced it, and juvy. Hell, she'd faced a TV camera on a regular basis. She could find the courage to do this thing she'd wanted to do since she was old enough to want it.

Through the screen she could see the warmly lit kitchen, but no sign of Jake. She raised her fist and knocked.

And held her breath.

Idiot.

And then he was there, opening the door for her. She stared. He'd shaved. His hair was neat. He wore a plum dress shirt and black pants. And shoes. Old-fashioned dress shoes that suited him perfectly. Her gaze traveled the lean length of him and back up to meet his eyes.

He smiled—that vaguely amused smile that he seemed to reserve just for her. "I thought you were going to stand me up."

She stepped inside. He closed the door behind her but didn't move. They were so close she could smell the subtle amber scent of his soap. Her heart broke out into a sprint. "No."

Jake reached out and took her left hand in his right. "Let's have a drink." He led her down the hall toward the living room. It was decorated in the same rich palette as the other rooms she'd seen—masculine without reeking of testosterone. The furniture inviting, lights warm and muted.

"Rum and Coke?" he asked.

"Yeah. Please." She was actually shaking a little. It was embarrassing.

He went behind the bar in the back corner. Its dark wood shone with a satiny finish. Audrey watched as he mixed a glass for each of them. When he offered her one, she hoped he didn't notice how eagerly she grabbed at it before taking a deep swallow.

He gave her a slight smile. "Sit down. There's something I want to show you."

She took a seat on the dark gray sofa. It was plush and enveloping without feeling like she was sitting in a marshmallow. Jake joined her moments later, sitting next to her—not so close that they touched, but almost. He had a large book in his hands—the kind that looked like a wedding album.

"Gran kept one of these for all of her grandchildren. She also kept one for you."

"She did?" Maybe she shouldn't have been so surprised. She'd known that Gracie loved her, but not that she thought as much of her as her own blood. Blood was important to the Tripps. Blood was everything.

He opened the book so that it rested on both their laps. The first page contained the first newspaper article about Clint's murder that had been printed. There was a photo of herself and Maggie—their faces covered, of course. Looking at it probably should have been more upsetting than it was. It was like looking at someone else; someone familiar whom she couldn't quite place.

"Sorry," Jake said, flipping a couple of pages forward. "I should have remembered she kept some of those."

"It's okay." She looked down at the page he'd found. It was a photo of her at the campground, the first summer she worked there—right after she got released from Stillwater. She wore shorts and a tank top, revealing lean, but developed, muscles in her arms and legs. She was helping someone set up their tent.

"I look like such a kid," she remarked.

"You were."

"I felt ancient."

"Hard time does that to a person," he teased.

Audrey nudged him with her elbow. "You survive a few years in juvy and then we can talk." She turned the pages, smiling at each captured memory. There were photos of her at work, and one of her with Gracie that made her heart ache. They were sitting on the porch swing, and they were looking at each other, smiling, oblivious to the fact that Jake had taken their photo.

"Could I have a copy of this?" she asked. He nodded. "Thanks."

She continued flipping. Gracie had documented so much of her life. Things that Audrey hadn't seen as necessarily important milestones were framed on the pages like each one had been a momentous event. It wasn't until she saw a photo of her standing beside Jake, holding his hand at Gracie's graveside, that she realized he had continued adding to the book after his grandmother's death. Papers she had written and published were stapled to the heavy sheets. There were even photos of her on the set of *When Kids Kill*.

She turned to him. "You've been following me."

"Not literally," he quipped. "But yeah, I've followed your career."

Audrey leaned back against the cushions. "I never would have pegged you as a closet romantic. Or a scrapbooker, for that matter."

"Doesn't take much talent to staple or tape things onto a page. As for being a romantic... that depends on the day."

She smiled. "Show me the book she made for you."

And he did. His book was two and a half times thicker than

hers. It began with photos of Jake as a baby and went all the way up to just before Gracie died. It was so odd to see his transformation from boy to man laid out step by step. She went back to his high school graduation photo. He had finished high school the year before Audrey and Maggie.

"You were so cute," she commented. "All the girls had a crush on you. It helped that you were a total bad boy."

"Bad boy?" He frowned. "I wasn't that bad."

She arched a brow. "You could fight. You had been arrested, were in a band, and you had a car. Trust me when I say that combination of attributes adds up to bad boy."

"I remember the two of us getting arrested together."

"Gracie was so pissed that we tried to break into someone's cottage." It had belonged to some rich guy no one in town really knew. He'd come to town for a few weeks in the summer with an entourage and then disappear until the next year.

"She was pissed that we got caught," Jake corrected her with a grin. "She asked me why we'd done it and I told her we'd just wanted to see what was inside. She cuffed me upside the head and told me to never do anything that wasn't worth the consequences."

"We did a good job replacing the window we broke. What were we, eleven?" Audrey remembered that vividly, because in fixing the window, they'd finally gotten a look inside the cottage. It wasn't as nice as they'd hoped. Maggie had been so upset that Audrey and Jake had an adventure without her, but Clint hadn't allowed her to hang out with them that night.

"I was twelve. I learned how to pick locks after that."

"No doubt at Gracie's knee."

He took the book out of her hands and set it on the coffee table. His body was angled toward hers now, the invisible barriers of personal space breached. "You still think I'm bad?" he asked softly with a crooked grin. "Or am I good?"

She copied the coy smile and raised her glass to her lips. "I'll let you know in the morning."

Jake went perfectly still, a perplexed look on his face. "I've thought about this moment for a long damn time. Now that it's here I don't know how to start."

Feeling bold, Audrey set aside her drink. Then she reached out and wrapped her hand around the back of his neck, pulling his head to hers so that she could kiss him. Their mouths opened, as though the other was some sort of exotic taste their tongues had never experienced. She didn't know how long it lasted—to be honest she was a little light-headed. But when Jake pulled away she let him go. And when he offered her his hand for the second time that evening, she took it. He didn't say anything, but his cheeks were flushed in that way she loved, and his eyes were heavy-lidded and bright. He pulled her to her feet and led her from the room to the staircase, drawing her up to the second floor.

She'd been in his room as a kid, but that wasn't where he took her. Instead, they went to a room at the end of the hall—what had been his grandfather's room. There was a solitary light on, its shade a warm amber. It was a similar effect to candlelight.

Jake led her to the bed—a large four-poster that had probably been hand carved more than a century earlier—and turned to face her.

"Is this what you want?" he asked, the planes and angles of his face highlighted by the dim light. "Don't take this any further if you're going to run away."

A valid request. One he had every right to make. "I won't run if you don't push." Another valid point.

His fingers combed through her hair, then clenched into a fist. He pulled her head back. It didn't hurt like it had when Matt grabbed her. He kissed her neck, licked the hollow of her throat while his other hand worked at unbuttoning her shirt. He bit gently at her ear, kissed the curve of her jaw as he released her hair.

Audrey straightened, her own hands going to the buttons on his shirt. Her fingers felt clumsy—shaky.

They didn't speak. What was there to say?

He pulled her shirt off her shoulders, down her arms, and tossed it aside. She did the same to him. He'd filled out over the years. Still lean, but with defined muscles everywhere. She leaned in and buried her face in the curve of his neck, licking and nipping at his warm skin. He reached behind her and released the clasp of her bra. She stepped back so he could finish removing it.

Jake stared at her bare skin, running warm fingers along every slope and curve until Audrey felt as though every nerve in her body was alive. And then he followed the path with his mouth, lowering her onto the soft mattress, pressing himself along the entire length of her body.

Slowly, they undressed each other, damp breath on heated skin, fingers exploring, tongues tasting. He made her orgasm with his mouth and fingers before rolling onto his back, taking her with him so that she was on top. Her hand slipped between their bodies, wrapping around him, bringing the two of them together like pieces of a puzzle.

They took their time—though she didn't know how they managed to contain more than a decade of wanting. She watched his face—kissed his eyes when his lashes fell shut. Licked his lips. Ran her hands over his chest and throat. His hands curved around her hips—changing their rhythm. Audrey's breath caught, and then she fell forward, bracing her hands on either side of his head.

"Look at me," she said.

His eyes opened. His fingers bit into her hips as she moved faster.

They came together—shuddering, gasping, mindless. Afterward—when she'd rolled to his side—they clung to each other, knowing the other could bolt at any moment.

Silence felt awkward.

"That was like something out of a romance novel," she joked.

"You can call me Fabio," he replied with a loopy grin. He suddenly looked very young and very...sweet. Jake had always been the kind of person who walked both sides of the whole good-vs.-bad spectrum. Audrey walked that same line herself. To have him drop his guard with her, to be vulnerable, was something she'd never considered. And it hit like a brick. She'd been so afraid of being vulnerable to him, she hadn't thought that he might feel the same about her.

"You regret this already, don't you?" he asked, his grin fading. "I fucking *knew* it."

"No!" She threw an arm and leg over him to keep him from leaving the bed. "It's just..."

"Just what?" he demanded. He was wounded and already closing off from her. If she lied, he would know—just as he always seemed to know.

"You're the only person who has the power to hurt me. People in L.A., they don't know me, not the real me. You know that angry girl I was, and you see through who I've tried to be. I don't even know who the fuck I am sometimes, but you...you *know* me. And strangely enough, you still seem to like me."

"Like you?" He laughed. "Woman, that's not the half of it. What's really going through that labyrinth you call a brain?"

"I haven't trusted someone in a long time."

"I make it a habit to never fully trust anyone, but here we are." His gaze narrowed as he watched her. Audrey's stomach clenched. "Is there something you need to tell me? Are you married or something?"

"No." She laughed hoarsely. "Not that."

"Then what is it?"

Every ounce of self-preservation screamed at her not to trust him.

That he could hurt her in so many ways, but the need to let him in outweighed common sense. She had wanted to confide in him—in someone—for years, and she almost had when she came home for Gracie's funeral.

"Aud?" He lifted up onto his elbow. "What's wrong?"

"I'm the one who hit him." She looked him straight in the eye, because she wanted to watch his opinion of her change. "Jake, Maggie wasn't the one who beat Clint to death. It was me. It was *all* me."

CHAPTER FOURTEEN

I know."

Audrey sat up, very much aware of her nakedness as she turned toward him. "How?"

Jake rolled onto his back, one arm under his head. He was obviously more comfortable being nude than she was. "Maggie told me."

It shouldn't have felt like a betrayal after all she and Maggie had said and done to each other, but it did. It was as though a deep, festering wound inside her had been lanced, spilling infection that poisoned her blood. They had made a promise to each other the night they killed Clint—that they would stick to their story forever, no matter what—so long as they were both alive. Audrey had kept her promise.

Jake took her hand in his. "She also told me it had been your idea."

Bitterness coated her tongue as she swallowed. There was a strange prickling in the back of her head. "I think I might be sick." Maggie had betrayed her completely. *Oh, you bitch, you're so lucky you're already dead.*

He sat up and took her face in his hands. "It's okay. No one else knows."

"How do you know that? She could have told everyone who'd fucking listen."

"She only told me because she thought it would drive me away from you, and she could have you to herself again."

Audrey frowned. "How long ago was this?"

"Before you left for Stanford."

Probably that night at the camp. That *awful* night. "You've known the truth for over a decade and you never told me?"

"Gran's funeral was hardly the right moment to bring it up. At the time I thought Maggie and I had hurt you bad enough. You didn't need to know what she'd done."

She pulled free of his hold. "You slept with me knowing I'm a murderer." Christ, which one of them was more fucked-up?

"Yeah. And you know I used to be a drug dealer. You killed to protect someone you cared about, Aud. That's not the same as murder."

She stared at him. His words made her stop and run an assessment in her head. Was he delusional? No. Jake had his own skewed view of the world, but he was very much rooted in reality. He had simply been raised by a woman who took care of her own, and who valued loyalty above all else. Only someone like that could take what she had done and turn it into something heroic. Honorable.

"Maggie lied to the police about which one of us had actually killed Clint because she knew a judge would come down harder on me. With my history of trouble she said they'd try me as an adult."

She didn't regret killing Clint, though it haunted her. The man was a monster who needed to die, and Maggie had at least gone on to have some semblance of a normal life. Yes, they had planned it, but only after Maggie finally confided to her all the terrible things her father had done to her. It might have been Audrey's idea, but Maggie had actually encouraged Clint that night so that they would have evidence of sexual assault when the police came.

Maggie had held her afterward as Audrey shook. She said Audrey was her hero. Her protector. She said she would take the blame because the courts would go easier on her. At the time Audrey hadn't known she was giving Maggie ammunition to use against her later.

She thought she was the only one still alive who knew the truth. She was wrong. Did Maggie's murderer know the truth as well?

"You could have told me," he said.

Audrey shrugged. "We made a promise. I shouldn't be surprised she broke it. Jake, are you sure no one else knows?"

He tilted his head. "Are you serious? The whole town would know if Maggie had told anyone but me."

"True." She wrapped her cold fingers around his warmer ones and squeezed. "Thanks."

He lifted her hand to his mouth and pressed his lips to her knuckles. "There are only two people in my life who ever made me feel worthy and good. One's dead, and the other one is you. I would never betray you, Aud. You have my word."

When Gracie Tripp gave someone her word, she meant it. Her grandson was no different, and he didn't make the gesture lightly.

She leaned forward and kissed him. It was a hungry, desperate kiss, but Jake didn't seem to mind. When he pressed her back into the mattress, he was insistent, rough even. She wanted that ferocity. Needed it.

Afterward, he pulled on a pair of pajama pants and gave her a robe to wear before the two of them made their way down into the kitchen to find food.

The sound of an ATV outside caught Audrey's attention. She went to the door and saw one out on the road. It had one headlight, and a driver who wore a helmet and visor. He had driven the machine into the drive—just enough to be off the road—and sat there, engine idling.

"Jake," she began, a tendril of dread dripping down her spine. Years of having seen the worst of people made her wary and suspicious. "Do you know this person?"

He came over and looked out. "It looks like Isaac."

That didn't raise an alarm in her head *at all*. "I think he's been following me."

Jake glanced at her, frowning. "What?" He walked over to the screen door and opened it. The four-wheeler tore out of the drive backward and sped off down the road, kicking up gravel.

"Maybe he was just turning around," she suggested, but she didn't believe it. How many times had she seen that same four-wheeler since she'd been home? Three times? Seeing it back the cove a couple of times could be dismissed, but him being down by her parents' house couldn't.

"No," Jake said. "The kids know better. I let them ride through my fields and the woods, but my yard is off-limits unless they're coming to see me. From the way he peeled out of here, I don't think that was the case."

"I don't know why he'd want to follow me." She shook her head. "I'm just being paranoid. After that run-in with Matt, I think I'm being stalked."

"Maybe you are." His face was stern as he spoke. "Alisha said that Maggie hated Isaac and tried to keep him away from Bailey. Maybe he decided to take Maggie out of the equation. He probably knows we've been asking questions."

Audrey considered that. "I'd be the last person to ever say teenagers aren't capable of murder. Maybe he truly thought Maggie was going to prevent him from seeing Bailey and snapped. All those new hormones and the inherent shitty attitude of a lot of teens make for a pretty hostile environment. I've seen kids get violent over something far less dramatic than a Romeo-and-Juliet situation." She turned to him. "What's his family like?"

"No idea. But Lish might know. You want to ask her?"

"I think she'd be more likely to be completely truthful with you." Plus, it gave her distance from the case. It might bring more trouble down on her head if she got caught talking to potential witnesses.

She was in this now. If she hadn't realized that before, she knew it all too clearly at that moment. Since the murder she'd thought of herself only as a suspect, but now, after the run-in with Matt, and being followed by Isaac, she was forced to think of herself as something else.

A potential victim.

Audrey didn't spend the entire night, but she stayed for most of it. Jake was still processing what finally sleeping with her meant, and it pissed him off that his brain devoted so much time to it. It wasn't as though anything could come of it. Audrey was going to go back to L.A. as soon as she could, and Christ only knew when he'd see her again. That was for the best, because she still had the foolish idea that he was a good man, and he liked it.

After making coffee, he went to his office in the back of the house and unlocked the filing cabinet with one of the keys he kept in a secret compartment he'd made in the mantel above the old fireplace. In the top two drawers there were dividers labeled "Edgeport," "Ryme," and "Eastrock." The latter two had fewer folders behind them, but the first took up almost all of both drawers. There were scans of every last scrap of paper contained within those folders on a flash drive in his lockbox at the bank, and on a duplicate that was in the custody of his lawyer. Both were encrypted and password protected. He wasn't paranoid, just prepared.

There were people who would be alarmed if they realized Jake had a file on almost every resident of Edgeport, and some in the neighboring towns. They might try to steal their file, or peek into someone else's. It paid to have backup.

He flipped through the files until he found the ones he wanted: Matt Jones, Gideon McGann, Maggie Jones-McGann, Neve Graham, and Isaac Canning. Then he pulled Lincoln's as well, though he already knew most of what was in it. His brother's bloody shirt was gone, nothing but ash in the drum out back, but it wasn't so easy to do away with the nagging suspicion in the back of his brain. Was his brother capable of murder? He had no doubt, but why would he kill Maggie? Motive was the big question, though he could imagine Maggie driving just about anyone crazy enough to want to kill her.

He sat down at his desk with the files and a cup of coffee. He started with Isaac. The kid hadn't been born in Edgeport or one of the neighboring towns, though his family had been there for generations. His parents moved back four years ago, when Isaac was thirteen. His father left shortly thereafter. There had been rumors that after one too many run-ins with the law, his folks decided to move Isaac someplace quiet where he couldn't get into much trouble. Jake laughed at the idea. Anyone who thought small towns were all flowers and picnics had never lived in one.

After making a note to dig into the kid's record—sealed didn't mean gone—he moved on. Neve was next. The only remotely scandalous thing in her file was that she almost ruined a murder investigation because she'd gotten involved with the killer. She hadn't known he was the man she was hunting down until someone made the connection between him and the victim. She went after him and brought him in, but the shame over having been played was what made her decide to come back home. That little tidbit might come in handy if Audrey was actually arrested.

Gideon's file was pretty bland except for his wife's death. The poor bastard. His company was legit, and he seemed to be exactly as he presented himself. Jake made a note to dig a little deeper into his past. No one was *that* good. Hadn't Gideon been caught drinking and driving once? He used to treat getting drunk like a competitive sport. He didn't come by the bar much, and if he did he never drank. That didn't mean he didn't fall off the wagon occasionally, though.

And then there was Matt.

The file was at least an inch thick. The guy had been trouble since he'd been old enough to shoot his mouth off. He had a juvy record—everyone in a twenty-mile radius knew Matt Jones was bad news. Of course he didn't have copies of that sealed record, but he didn't need them in a town where everyone knew everyone else's business. Matt's aunt Joan had to put him out of the house when he attacked her, and he went straight into foster care. His anger, violence, and criminal record grew steadily after that. He'd been out of jail for almost six months, but he would be headed that way again. Or dead. People with his habits tended to have short lives.

If he touched a woman Jake cared about again he'd find out just how short.

Jake picked up the phone and dialed a Warren number. His cousin, Kenny, was a guard at the state prison, the place Matthew Jones had called home before returning to Edgeport.

His cousin picked up after two rings. "Hello?" He sounded cautious—he always did when Jake called.

"I need information," Jake said. "On Matthew Clinton Jones. He was released from Warren about six months ago."

"What kind of information?"

"All of it."

Jake heard his hesitation. "I don't know—"

"Everything."

Another pause. "If I do this, will it count against my debt?"

"If the information is useful."

"When do you need it?"

"Tomorrow."

"Jesus, Jake! I can't—"

"You owe me, Kenny," Jake reminded him calmly, searching through the top drawer of his desk for sticky notes. He grabbed a pad of yellow ones and closed the drawer. "Are you going to renege on that debt?" He let that hang in the air between them. Kenny had more imagination than most of his extended family, so he could easily imagine the consequences. He also knew exactly what was at stake, and Jake thought nothing of letting the secret out. He'd dug his own hole a long time ago—before begging Jake to get him out of it.

"How do you want me to get it to you? E-mail?"

"Yeah, use the secure service. Encrypt the file just to be sure." Kenny was useful—he didn't want him getting caught.

"How much longer am I going to be in your debt?"

Jake smiled coolly. "Until I decide you're not." He hung up and set the phone back on the base. His stomach growled; he hadn't eaten that morning.

Nothing like a little blackmail to work up an appetite.

He was just about to log out of his e-mail—which he'd checked earlier—when he saw a message from Alisha. The subject was: HAVE U SEEN THIS?!?!?! OMFG. He opened it and clicked on the link she provided. It took him to one of those celebrity gossip sites that he despised but his niece loved for some unfathomable reason. Then he saw the article she meant for him to see.

"Fuck," he muttered as he skimmed it. "Fuck it to hell."

Audrey was not going to be happy.

SOFT-HEARTED TV PSYCHOLOGIST IMPLICATED IN SMALL-TOWN MURDER, the article read.

Audrey stared at the screen. The link had been texted to her by David, along with "R U OK?" No one actually spelled words anymore. It was annoying.

She sat down to read it—her legs didn't feel so sturdy at the moment.

Dr. Audrey Harte, frequent guest star of TXT's *When Kids Kill*, has found herself in the middle of a "life imitating art" moment, and it may not be her first. The 31-year-old wunderkind in the world of criminal psychology has been implicated in the murder of her childhood friend, Maggie Jones-McGann, in the tiny coastal town of Edgeport, ME. Sources close to Dr. Harte verified that she was also involved in the murder of Jones-McGann's father 18 years ago…

"Fuck. Fuck. Fuckfuckfuckfuckfuck. *Fuck!*" She almost threw her phone—her arm drew back, but common sense managed to snag hold through the rage before she could break the device that held most of her life. She was not a kid anymore. Her temper was not some wild thing that jumped off the leash when poked.

And what the fuck had they meant by "wunderkind"?

Her mother was suddenly there, in the living-room doorway. "Audrey? What's happened?"

She could lie, but her mother was going to hear about it sooner or later. Tears burned her eyes, but she refused to let them come. Shame gnawed at the pit of her stomach. "Maggie's finally managed to ruin my life. It took the bitch almost twenty years, but she finally got what she wanted." She laughed—harsh and ragged. "Too bad she's not here to see it."

Her mother walked toward her, nothing but love and concern in her eyes. She wrapped her arms around Audrey. "It's okay, babe."

Audrey hugged her back, pressing her cheek against the top of her mother's head. "No, it's not, Mom. It's really not. News of

Maggie's murder has gotten out—websites are running this story."
She handed her mother the phone so she could read for herself.
"The show will know soon if they don't already. So will my boss."
She didn't know what Grant would do with the information, but
her main concern was Angeline. Her boss and mentor knew her
story, but it was different having it be public knowledge. If she
didn't get fired it would be a miracle.

Anne's lips grew tighter and thinner as she read. "I bet that
bitch Jeannie Ray is behind this."

Audrey went still. Her mother didn't swear very often, and
she certainly didn't get angry easily. When she did get angry, you
looked for cover. "She'd be my guess too."

The kitchen door flew open, banging off the wainscot.

"Hey!" Audrey heard her father yell. "What the hell?"

"Have you seen the news?" Jessica demanded. Audrey closed
her eyes. Just when she thought it couldn't get any worse. "Audrey
is all over the web, and now local affiliates are picking it up. It's
like Clint's murder all over again!"

"Affiliates?" John echoed. "What the hell are you talking
about? Who even says affiliates anyway?"

Anne and Audrey walked out to the kitchen.

"You're overexaggerating," Anne said soothingly. "It's not like
that at all. Audrey's done nothing wrong."

Her sister's face was red, her eyes glittering with hate. "You."
She pointed at Audrey. "How many times are you going to ruin
my fucking life?"

Audrey opened her mouth—to apologize, actually—but her
mother cut her off, stepping forward with a finger jabbing the
air in front of her oldest child's chest. "That's enough out of you.
Ever since your sister came home, you've done nothing but berate
her and act as though she ruined your life, when in reality you've
gotten on very well, have a loving husband and two beautiful

daughters. Your father and I don't blame her. In fact, we've carried the guilt of not having listened when she came to us all those years ago, saying that she thought Clint was abusing Maggie. I'm glad that man is dead, and as the mother of two young girls, you ought to be as well. Now, I want no more of this foolishness in this house. Am I clear? If you can't be civil, stay the hell home."

Jessica's mouth fell open. Audrey made a choking noise. Her father shook his head at her. *Do* not *laugh*.

"Now," Anne said, turning to her younger daughter. "I would like you to drive me to my Ladies Auxiliary meeting this morning, please."

"Uh, okay." That wasn't random or anything.

Jessica spun on her heel and walked out, not bothering to close the door behind her. A few seconds later, her car tore down the drive, spraying gravel.

"She'll get over it," John said, and went back to his crossword puzzle.

Audrey touched her mother's shoulder. She could feel bone more readily than before. "Are you okay?" she asked.

"No, but I will be." Her mother looked pissed off—her eyes always turned bright blue when she was angry. "Your father's right. Jess will get over it. Hopefully before you have to go back to L.A."

"That's not what I meant."

Anne shook her head. "Don't you worry about me, bobaloo. I'm good."

Audrey wasn't convinced, but she knew better than to push. "You know, that's a ridiculous pet name."

"It's what my mother called me. I feel bad—you and I haven't spent much time together at all because I've been under the weather. Why don't we go to Fat Franks tonight?"

"Sure. Whatever you want, Mum." Audrey didn't argue because she knew her mother wanted to show her support, and parading

Audrey in public seemed to be the only way she thought she could do that.

Her mother nodded, a determined look on her face. "Good." She patted Audrey's cheek. "This isn't the end of the world, hon."

"I'll take your word for it."

"I'll get my purse."

Ten minutes later, after her mother had brushed her teeth and found her purse, they were in the Mini and on their way to the church where the ladies had their monthly meeting. When they arrived, there were several cars in the gravel lot. Jeannie Ray climbed out of a battered old dark blue station wagon with wood paneling.

Anne jumped out of the car before Audrey could put it in park. Her mother made a beeline toward the older woman, hands curled into fists at her side.

"Oh, hell," Audrey whispered, and jumped out of the car to jog after her mother, but it was too late. Anne had the older woman cornered between two cars.

"What do you want?" Jeannie demanded. Then she looked at Audrey. "She's not welcome here."

"*She's* not staying," Audrey retorted.

Jeannie sniffed and pulled her pale blue cardigan tighter around her thin shoulders. She smelled like Chantilly and cigarettes. "Good."

"Jeannie," Anne began with a cold smile, "you're going to leave Audrey alone. If I find out you were the one who gossiped to the press about her, I'll make you regret it."

Jeannie's pointy chin jutted. "You don't scare me."

Anne took a step closer. "You remember what I know about you, Jeannie Ray."

As Audrey watched, the bitter old crone's eyes widened. Real fear lit their pale depths before she whirled around and scurried away around the front of her car like a rat after the scent of cheese.

"What do you know about her?" Audrey asked.

Her mother smiled. "It wouldn't be good blackmail material if I told anyone, babe." She kissed Audrey's cheek. "You can leave now. Your father will pick me up."

Audrey did as she was told, pausing only a moment to watch her mother stride into the church like she owned the place, oblivious to how the other women watched her. She'd tell them all to go to hell if she thought it would make a difference, but her mother could apparently take care of herself.

Huh. She began to see Anne in a whole new light.

Maybe Audrey hadn't inherited her love of a good fight from her father after all.

Dear Audrey,

I realized something in therapy today. As much as I love you for what you did for me (and you know what you did), there's a part of me that hates you for it. A big part of me. I wanted to escape him (my father) so badly that I couldn't think of any other way out. And there you were, my friend and champion, so ready to do whatever was necessary. You wanted to save me and I wanted saving. But we killed him, Dree. Regardless of him being the monster under my bed—or in it, if you want to get technical—he was my father. There were times in my life when he was good to me, when he was the person he should have been. I know those moments were rare, that most of the time he was a miserable bastard who thought he deserved to fuck me because I was his kid, but when I think of him lately, I remember those few times when he was a good man, and those are the times I regret what we did, and I hate you for taking him from me. And I'm not sure if I can ever forgive you for it.

* * *

Before Audrey pulled out of the churchyard, she got a call from Gideon. She didn't know how he'd gotten her cell number. It was tempting to let it go to voice mail, but she had made a promise to call him that night at Jake's and then avoided keeping it.

"Hi, Gideon," she said, putting it on speaker as she pulled out onto the street—not that there was any traffic on it to be concerned about.

"Actually, it's Bailey. I'm just using Dad's phone because he got your number from Rusty. I mean, your father."

She was going to have to talk to her father about giving out her number. "Okay. Hi, Bailey. What's up?"

"I know we were supposed to wait until you called us, but could you come by sometime soon? I think I'd like to talk about Maggie."

Balls, as her grandmother Pelletier was fond of saying. "I'm almost at your house now. Does that work?"

"Right now?" She sounded heartbreakingly hopeful.

"In a minute or so. Is that okay?"

"Yeah! That's great. See you in a bit!"

Audrey hung up, a queasy sense of dread churning in her gut. She hadn't counseled anyone in years—it wasn't her thing. Since going to work with Angeline, she had spent most of her time doing assessments and research. She'd written papers and spoken to professionals about troubled teens. She'd taken on the role of advocate more than the mantle of therapist. Offering comfort made her uneasy, and the idea of trying to help someone who had probably loved Maggie made it even worse. How could she look the girl in the eye and pretend that Maggie had been her friend?

Her misgivings weren't enough to make her keep driving when she reached Gideon's driveway. She pulled in and parked behind his truck. He met her at the door before she had a chance to ring the bell.

He gave her that smile that used to send all the local girls into a swoon years ago. He was still a good-looking man. She'd never found him attractive, though. "Audrey, thanks so much for coming by. Bailey is so happy you could see her."

It was the perfect thing to say to make her feel even guiltier for not wanting to be there. She forced a smile. "No problem. Where is Bailey?"

"Upstairs in her room. I told her I'd send you up so you could have privacy. I'm actually going out. Can I get you a tea or something?"

Tea. The staple of an Edgeport diet. "Just some water, thanks."

He got a couple of bottles from the fridge and gave them to her. "Thanks again. You have my cell number in case you need me?"

This time her smile was more genuine. He was a caring father. "We'll be fine. Though therapy can be emotional for some people. Don't be surprised if Bailey's a little off when you get home."

His brow tightened slightly. He seemed every inch the doting dad, and it struck her how Jake acted the same way with Alisha. "Off how?"

"She might be very happy or maybe sad. She might even be angry—it all depends what we talk about. However she feels, it's part of the process."

Gideon nodded. "I appreciate the heads-up." He glanced anxiously toward the doorway that led to the hall. "I just want her to be okay."

"You can go. I'm sure all we're going to talk about is how she feels about Maggie's death."

"Mm." He was still looking at the door.

"Speaking of that, how are you doing?" God, she just couldn't help herself.

That got his attention. His gaze whipped back to hers. "Better than I probably should be, and then guilty and sad because it's obvious our marriage was over before she died. I feel sorry for Maggie, but I don't miss her. That's terrible, isn't it?"

Audrey shrugged. "It is what it is. You can't help how you feel. Honestly, Gideon, her death feels like a release to me." She shouldn't have said it, but he didn't seem surprised to hear it. He just nodded again, understanding.

"She wasn't an easy woman to live with, but I don't know why anyone would want to kill her."

She looked at him, reading his face and body language. Was he lying? It sure felt like it. But maybe that was her own opinion forcing itself onto his words. She could think of lots of reasons someone would want to kill Maggie.

"I'm sure we'll find out what really happened soon enough. Neve's good at her job."

At the mention of the cop, Gideon's face brightened. *So that's how it is.* "She is. No doubt."

"Go do what you need to do. Bailey and I will be fine." When he had his hand on the doorknob, she added, "And, Gideon? If you want to talk, you have my number." God, she really did have a white-knight complex.

He smiled. "I just might. Thanks again for coming when my kid called." He opened the door and stepped out, pulling it closed behind him.

Alone in the spacious, modern kitchen, Audrey sighed. A bottle of water in each hand, she walked down the hall to the stairs and climbed to the second floor. There were three bedrooms and a bathroom on that level. She resisted the urge to snoop. Maggie had called one of those rooms hers. Neve had no doubt already been through it, but she didn't know Maggie like Audrey did.

She stood at the landing, staring at the closed doors. Temptation was a bitch.

One of the doors opened, revealing Bailey in a T-shirt and shorts. She grinned when she saw Audrey. "Hi."

The girl had an aura of sweetness about her that was hard not to smile at. "Hi. Your dad's gone out so it's just the two of us. Is that okay with you?"

"Oh, yeah. I prefer it, actually. I love my dad, but he doesn't need to know everything about me, y'know?"

Audrey nodded. She knew. She gestured at the bedroom behind the girl. "Shall I come in? Or do you want to talk somewhere else?"

"No, this is good." She stepped back from the door so Audrey could enter.

As she crossed the threshold, Audrey tried very hard not to laugh. Bailey's room was decorated entirely in lavender and black—with a touch of white. How many other teenage girls had decorated with this same color scheme over the decades?

"Nice room," she commented, taking in the posters and photos and little knickknacks. Some things never changed.

"Thanks. Maggie and I did it last summer." At the mention of Maggie's name, Bailey's face fell. Audrey couldn't help but wonder if Maggie had helped choose these colors. It was egotistical to think it, but then, it was clear Maggie had been somewhat obsessed with her.

Audrey offered her a small smile, and a bottle of water. "I don't know about you, but talking makes my mouth dry as sandpaper."

The girl took the water. "Thanks. You can sit down if you want."

Audrey sat down on the carpet in front of the closet, leaning back against the lavender-and-white-trimmed door. Bailey stared at her a moment before also sitting on the floor, but against her unmade bed.

After a few moments of silence, Audrey said, "What would you like to talk about?"

The girl shrugged. There was something familiar about the way she held herself and the set of her jaw. It was probably a resemblance to her father. "What do people normally talk to you about?"

"Well, normally I spend my days interviewing kids that have either had awful things done to them, or have done awful things. Or both. I usually talk to them about that."

She glanced away, arms wrapping around her legs as she drew them to her chest. "Oh."

Audrey didn't say anything, didn't let anything show on her face, but Bailey's posture said so much that the girl hadn't. She avoided eye contact and closed herself off. Normally, Audrey would already have some of the facts about the teen's situation—their home life, what sort of crime they'd committed, or had been the victim of. She was working blind here.

"Do you have a job lined up for the summer?" It seemed the most banal way to draw the girl into conversation. They'd get to the point eventually, when she was more comfortable with Audrey.

Bailey seemed surprised by the question. "Yeah. Alisha's mom—well, her uncle Jake—hired the two of us to work at the resort. We're going to help clean rooms, tell guests what the best places to visit are—you know. He says we're Customer Service Representatives."

Audrey smiled. Did Jake realize he was in danger of taking on Gracie's patronage of teenage girls? "You and Alisha are best friends?"

Bailey nodded. "She's great. Her mom's nice too—but she's more like a friend than a mom. She's got rotten taste in guys. Ugh. Some of them have been real slimeballs."

"Sometimes women date men they think they deserve."

Wide eyes stared at her. "Yancy's not a slimeball."

"I know she's not, but sometimes we don't see ourselves like others do. What kind of boys does Alisha like?"

"She likes tall, skinny guys. She says she's so picky because she has to date someone who won't be afraid of her uncle."

Audrey chuckled. "Good luck with that."

Bailey tilted her head. "Maggie told me you had a crush on Jake when you were my age."

Her smile faded. "Maggie talked about me?" It really shouldn't be a surprise.

"All the time. She told me that the two of you were best friends, and that you saved her. She told me to never let a guy come between me and Alisha, because Jake ruined your friendship."

Choose your words carefully, Harte. "Jake didn't ruin anything. He and I never dated."

"Because he slept with Maggie?"

"Maggie told you that too?"

"No, Alisha's mom did."

Right. "And people wonder why I moved to L.A."

Bailey laughed. "You forgave him, though. Didn't you? But you never forgave Maggie because she was supposed to be your friend."

A small smile. "Maybe you should go into psychology. Once I understood why they'd done what they did it was a lot easier to forgive."

"I'd never forgive Isaac or Alisha if they slept together."

"Every situation is different."

"So, if Jake didn't ruin your friendship, what did? Was it killing her father?"

"Jesus Christ."

Bailey pulled back. "I'm sorry."

Audrey held up her hand. "No. It's okay. I just...I just haven't talked about this stuff in a long time." She should nip the conversation in the bud, but Bailey hadn't asked anything most of the town didn't already know. And if it meant earning the girl's trust, she could suffer through a little discomfort.

"My friendship with Maggie ended when I came back from Stillwater. I wasn't the same girl I was when I went in. I had focus, discipline. A confidence in myself that I hadn't had before that. Obviously, that didn't extend to guys, but I had changed, and Maggie…Maggie wanted me to be the girl I had been. I couldn't give her that."

"I think Maggie wanted me to be someone I wasn't. She'd get upset when I didn't react the way she thought I should."

Audrey nodded. That was the Maggie she knew. "Did you like Maggie?"

The girl looked away again. "I did at first. She was awesome."

Of course Maggie had seemed awesome. That was the courtship period.

"But then…I don't know. She cheated, and I never forgave her for it. I guess we started to grow apart. The harder she tried, the more I pulled back."

"That's normal behavior when someone is trying to manipulate you."

"Yeah. I guess I never realized that's what she was doing. I just felt like it was all my fault. Everything was my fault. She kept telling me she just wanted us to be close like we had been. I started spending more and more time with friends. I didn't want to be around her. I felt like I couldn't trust her."

Déjà-fucking-vu. Audrey felt that she finally understood why Bailey had wanted to talk to her.

"Do you know who she was seeing?"

Bailey nodded. "I didn't want to say anything because of Jake."

Audrey froze. "She was seeing Jake?"

"*No.* She hated Jake. She was sleeping with Lincoln."

She didn't even want to think about how relieved she was. God, Lincoln was such a dog. Out of those three kids, Jake was the least messed up, and that said something about the other two.

"Bailey, it's okay if a part of you is glad she's gone."

Tears pooled in the girl's eyes, spilling over onto her round cheeks. "I miss her too." She looked at Audrey with such an imploring expression that it broke her heart. "Sometimes I miss her so much." Then she buried her face in her hands and sobbed so hard her whole body shuddered.

Audrey moved toward her, and as she knelt in front of her, she pulled Bailey into her arms. Bailey's own arms wrapped around her waist like a boa constrictor, pressing hard against her ribs. As she stroked the girl's hair, letting her cry it out, Audrey noticed something on Bailey's back, beneath her shirt. Gently, she moved the fabric of her shirt for a better look. The girl didn't notice.

There were bruises—dark and ugly. The sort that often got worse-looking as they healed. Bruises that looked like she'd been punched. Had she gotten into a fight? Or was her earlier protective posture a hint of darker things?

Audrey didn't ask. She didn't want to put the girl through any more upheaval, and she might cut Audrey out if she felt her secret was going to be exposed. Battered kids had a tendency to protect the one who hurt them. The question was, if someone had hit her, who the hell was it?

And how could she make sure it never happened again?

CHAPTER FIFTEEN

Audrey took her parents out to dinner that night at Fat Franks in Eastrock. It was a family-owned place, known for their seafood and eccentric decor. A few heads turned when they walked in, and her father nodded at one table as they passed, but otherwise no one paid much attention.

"I suppose that's one benefit to small-town living," Audrey allowed. "People aren't too caught up in Internet gossip."

Her father shoved a menu at her. "Folks around here still like to get their news the old-fashioned way—in a newspaper or on TV."

"Or from their neighbor," his wife added with a wry smile.

Audrey grinned. It was the first time since she'd come home that her mother seemed more like herself—even with the murder and all the scandal around Audrey's return to town, she managed to be happy and sweet. And her father hadn't gotten shit-faced yet.

The waitress came by and took their drink order. Her father ordered a beer. Audrey ordered one as well as she looked over the menu. Why did she even bother looking? She knew what she wanted. "Hey, Dad, are the clams here still good?"

He looked at her like she'd just asked if the sun was still warm. "The best in Maine."

Just like the sign out front claimed. Audrey closed the menu. "I know what I'm getting, then."

Anne shook her head. "I prefer their flounder."

"Good," Audrey said. "Then you won't be stealing clams off my plate."

Her mother shrugged, but the little smile remained. Audrey was going to have to be diligent in guarding her food.

The waitress returned with their drinks and pulled a pad out of her apron. "What can I get you folks?"

Her mother and father ordered. When it was her turn, Audrey said, "I want a double order of fried clams. Can you double dip those and make them extra crispy?"

The waitress smiled. "Audrey Harte. You and Jake Tripp are still the only people who ever place that order. Nice to see you again, dear." She gathered up the menus and left.

"Auddie?" Her mother asked. "Are you all right?"

Her parents were watching her, twin expressions of concern on their faces. Audrey shook her head. "Sorry. She was just so nice, and...well, not too many people around these parts have been happy to see me."

"That Tripp kid was." Her father took a drink from the frosty bottle in front of him.

"You know his name, Dad. I've heard you use it."

He shrugged. "That was before I knew you were still infatuated with him. Until he's proved himself good enough for my baby girl, I'll call him whatever I want."

"That's bizarrely touching," she informed him. And it was, really. She wasn't sure how to feel about it. Life was easier when she didn't like him.

"Hey, I'm in touch with my sensitive side." He caught his wife smiling at him and reached across the table to squeeze her hand. Audrey swallowed against the lump in her throat. She wanted what they had, and she hadn't realized it until that moment. She wanted someone to love her unconditionally. Someone who loved her so much all of her shit and baggage didn't matter. Someone who saw her at her worst and still thought she was worth having.

The psychologist in her knew this was irrational. Hell, even her irrational self knew it was irrational. Her parents did not have some kind of perfectly attuned marriage. They worked at it. There had to be times when her mother wanted to give up and walk away. *Had* to be. Probably a few times her father did as well.

Her phone buzzed in her purse. She snuck a look at it. Her father would give her a hard time if she took it out. It was a text from Grant. *Audrey, someone forwarded an article to me about you. Is it true? If so, we need to talk. CALL ME.*

She closed her purse. Being fired—and answering his questions—would have to wait. Right now she was going to stick her head in the sand and enjoy seeing her mother smiling and her father sober.

The food came a few minutes later—the clams were perfect. Afterward, they went for a walk along the shore and bought cones of ice cream from the place that had been there since Audrey was a kid. She didn't know the name of it, because it didn't appear to be named anything. The only sign on the building read ICE CREAM and that was it. Audrey asked for a mix of vanilla, butterscotch, and chocolate. The mound of ice cream on the cone was as big as her head. She devoured the entire thing, earning a cheer from her father, who had finished his as well. Gluttony—a Harte family trait.

They arrived home shortly after eight.

"I'm going to take a bath," her mother announced. She'd been smiling almost the entire duration of the evening. That smile soothed Audrey's soul. It was her "everything is all right" smile, and for as long as Audrey could remember, that smile had never lied.

"I'll run the water for you," John said, and hurried off to do just that.

Audrey watched after him, bemused. "Did pod people take him over, or what?"

Anne set her purse on the kitchen table. "Men get more sentimental as they get older, especially the wild ones." She slipped out of her low-heeled pumps and picked them up. "I think your father is realizing his own mortality. And mine. Regardless, I don't mind the attention."

"It's about time he appreciated you."

"Don't be too hard on him dear. He's only human."

That was a subtle hint for Audrey to remember that her house was glass, and there was a whole quarry just outside, waiting.

"Enjoy your bath."

"I intend to. Are you going to Jake's tonight?"

She actually blushed a little—like a damn kid. "Probably."

"He's always cared about you. The Tripps are a rough bunch, but they're loyal. Like wolves. They mate for life."

Audrey chuckled. "You are so subtle."

Her mother patted her shoulder. "I'll see you in the morning."

Audrey nodded. When her mother was gone, she gathered up the overnight bag she'd packed earlier and went out to the Mini. Her cell rang as she tossed her bag in the passenger-side seat. It was a number she didn't recognize. She hesitated. Was it a reporter? She touched the screen.

"Hello?"

"Is this Audrey? The real Audrey? Chelsea gave me your number."

She went still, one foot inside the car. "Janis?"

"Yes."

She pulled her foot out and closed the car door. "Thanks for calling me."

"No problem. Did something happen to the other Audrey?"

Audrey hesitated. "Yeah, something did."

"She's dead, isn't she? I can tell from the tone of your voice."

"I'm afraid so."

There was a pause, as though the other woman was pulling herself together. "Was she really your girlfriend?" Her voice was raw.

"No. But we had been friends. A long time ago she was my best friend."

"Well, you'd better ask me what you want to know."

"Did the two of you meet at Lipstick?"

"Yes. Back in April. We got together a few times. Next thing I know she's with someone else, and she treats me like I'm shit on her stilettos."

"That must have hurt."

Janis laughed—it turned into a cough. *Smoker.* "It didn't tickle. I didn't take the rejection so well—the girls at the club could tell you that."

"They did say you'd gotten physical with other girls."

"Stupid catfights is all. That was one of the things she—the other Audrey—said she liked about me, that I could fight. She liked feeling protected."

Audrey swallowed. Bailey had said that Maggie felt Audrey was her protector. It made sense that someone who had suffered the sort of abuse Maggie had would gravitate toward someone she thought could protect her.

Janis was still talking "...but, after a while, I was glad she took up with someone else. Chick was all kinds of fucked-up."

That was an understatement. "How so?"

"She was moody. One night she'd be one way, and the next she'd be another—if she showed up at all."

That sounded like Maggie. Selfish and flighty.

"She called me about a week or so ago. Said she wanted to see me again. She never showed. Then I heard that she stood up Chelsea too. Why did she say she was you?"

"I don't know."

"What was her real name?"

"Maggie."

"Huh. She told me she used to have a friend named Maggie. I assumed it was an old girlfriend from the way she went on about her. Wonder if she was talking about you or herself?"

"I have no idea. Janis, do you know of anyone who might have wanted to hurt her?"

"Nah. Maybe slap her around a bit, but no one at the club had that kind of hate-on for her. She was a little crazy, and a player, but she was never vicious or cruel. It was just like sometimes she didn't care. I guess that's worse than being vicious."

"What else did she tell you about herself?"

"That she owned her own business, and that she was divorced. She said she was thinking of moving to Bangor. She wanted me to help her move. She was looking for a change of scenery—a new beginning, and I thought I was part of it. Was any of that true?"

"I honestly don't know. Did she ever mention if she was in trouble, or if someone was bothering her? Did she seem afraid?"

"Once. She told me she had done something really bad when she was a kid and that sometimes she felt like the people in her hometown distrusted her and thought she was a terrible person. She never mentioned anyone specifically, although...she did mention being pissed at someone named Isaac. Does that help?"

"It does, yeah."

"Look, I need to go, but if you need any more information, let me know."

"Thanks. Janis, a Detective Neve Graham might contact you as well. She's known Maggie since she was a kid."

"Wait. You asked if someone might want to hurt her, and then tell me a cop might call. Christ, was that her they found on the beach in Edgeport this past weekend?"

"Yes. It was."

"Fuck me. Give the cop my number. I'll tell her whatever I can. Guess I'd better start with where I was on that night, huh?"

"I'd advise waiting until she asks."

"You haven't asked."

Audrey almost smiled. "That's not my job. Thank you for reaching out, though. I appreciate it."

"No problem. I hope you catch whoever did it."

"Me too," Audrey replied gravely before hanging up. If they didn't find another suspect soon, they were going to throw her in jail just to save face.

She was *not* going to be locked up because of Maggie.

Not again.

When Audrey walked into Gracie's, the place was pretty quiet. There were a few tables taken, and Jake was behind the bar, polishing glasses. He didn't look happy.

"Hey," he said when he saw her, his expression softening.

"Hi. Everything okay?"

He picked up another glass. "Neve was just here looking for Linc."

That explained his frown. She hopped up onto one of the barstools. "She found out about him and Maggie, huh?"

"You knew?"

She smiled at the incredulous note in his voice. "Bailey told me when I talked to her earlier."

"How'd that go? You want a drink?"

"Fine, and yes, please. Do you think Neve views Linc as a suspect?"

"I think she'd be stupid if she didn't."

His response didn't surprise her. Jake and Lincoln had never been particularly close. They'd spent years apart after Jake's mother abandoned him at Gracie's, and then Lincoln had been upset about Gracie's will. It was one of those situations—in Audrey's opinion—that was a case of loving the person, but not liking them very much. She could relate.

"You don't think he did it?"

"I honestly don't know." He set a rum and Coke in front of her. "You okay?"

She shrugged and took a sip. Perfect. "Janis called."

"The lesbian?"

"Yes. I don't think she did it, but I'm going to give her info to Neve anyway. It will take her attention off me."

Jake set his hands on the bar. Audrey touched his grandfather's wedding band, which he wore on his right hand. "Neve knows you didn't kill Maggie."

"She *thinks* I didn't do it." She stopped playing with his ring and lifted her gaze to his. She'd feared sex would complicate things between them, but it only seemed to make them more at ease. "The only people who know for certain are me and Maggie."

"And the real killer."

Audrey smiled a little. "And the real killer." Then, after a sip from her glass, "Are you still okay with me talking to Alisha about Bailey?"

"Yeah, sure. You might want to ask Yancy, though."

"I'd rather word didn't get out that I was asking. No offense."

His lips twitched. "None taken. What are you looking for?"

"I'm not sure. I could be wrong, but I think Bailey might have been abused. I hate to think Gideon might have done it, but maybe the boyfriend? Maggie?" There had been something strange about that conversation with Bailey. The kid hadn't told her everything. Who was she protecting?

"Isaac's been in trouble. He always struck me as a good kid, though. Just a little fucked-up."

"That's why I want to ask Alisha before I go digging with Bailey. They're best friends—Alisha might know if there's something going on."

He shook his head. "I hope not."

Audrey sighed. "Yeah, me too." She'd never been abused by anyone she loved, and even though she had seen so much of it in her work, she still wondered how someone could hurt the very person they claimed to love. To a much lesser extent, it was like what Maggie had done to her—inflicting pain under the pretense of caring. Even dead she was still playing games, hitting Audrey in all the right places to cause the most pain. If she lost her job with Angeline...

Jake looked at her for a moment. "Come with me." He put the glass and towel away before opening the bar top and walking through.

She drained her glass in one long swallow and then followed after him. He led her through the small corridor, past the restrooms, to his office. He unlocked the door and steered her over the threshold, flicking the light switch as he closed them both in.

"Are you upset because of the article online?"

Audrey turned to face him, prepared to tell him that she'd had a shitty day and that it was nothing. Instead, she burst into tears. The sloppy, shuddering kind that rendered a woman a screw-faced, wet mute.

Immediately, he was there, wrapping his arms around her. He didn't speak. Didn't try to shush her. He simply rubbed her back as she sobbed into his shoulder.

Finally, she had no more tears to cry. Her nose was clogged with thick, wet snot and her eyes were scratchy and hot. She probably had mascara smeared down her face. This wasn't embarrassing at all.

Jake handed her a bunch of tissues. She wiped at her cheeks, dabbed at her eyes, and then blew her nose.

"Sorry."

He gave her a gentle smile. "Not like I haven't fallen apart on you."

Gracie's funeral. He'd cried on her shoulder that night out of grief. "Thanks. Fuck, I hate crying."

"I don't know of too many people who like it. You feel better now?"

"A little, I guess." More than a little, actually. God, she thought she was being so strong and stoic. She hadn't realized just how much crap she'd been avoiding until she gave herself permission to feel it. What a great psychologist she was. She couldn't even figure herself out.

"Want to talk about it?"

Audrey shrugged. She was drained—as though someone had sucked the life out of her. She couldn't even bring herself to care at that moment—about anything. "My producer wants to talk to me, and I'm front-page news online."

"There you go again, overestimating your importance. Second page at best."

He was trying to make her feel better, she knew that. He was also right. "I'm more famous than you are."

There was a glint in his eyes as his smile grew. "Depends on who you talk to." He leaned back against his desk, fingers curling around the edge. "What's the worst thing that could happen?"

"Other than me going to prison for Maggie's murder?"

"That's not going to happen."

"You can't promise me that."

His expression turned serious. "I know more ways to make a person disappear than you've ever heard of. Even if they are stupid enough to think you did it, you're not going to prison."

It was an arrogant, melodramatic statement, but when he said it, she believed him. "Other than prison, I could lose the show."

"Would that really be so horrible?"

"No." That surprised her, but not too much. "But losing my position with Angeline would."

"Your professor?"

She nodded. "She was." She dabbed at her eyes with the ball of tissues. "She's my boss now."

A frown tugged at his eyebrows. "Isn't she the one you met at Stillwater? She wrote about you, didn't she?"

"Yeah. She interviewed me while I was there. And then mentored me at Stanford."

"She already knows your story. Why would she fire you?"

"I'll be an embarrassment to her."

His frown deepened. "If she thought that was possible she wouldn't have hired you at all. You know, for someone who claims to have no regret for killing Clint, you sure carry a lot of shame for it."

"Regret and shame are different things."

Jake shrugged. "If you could go back in time, would you do it again?"

She didn't even have to think. "Yeah. Yeah, I would."

"Then you'd better accept the consequences, my dar, and face them like the Audrey Harte I know."

Audrey smiled. "My dar. That was what Gracie always said."

"I picked up a few things from the old woman."

"Yeah, you did. Including knowing exactly how to get me to pull my head out of my ass."

"It's an acquired skill."

Her grin slowly faded. "I need to tell Neve about Janis."

"Probably a good idea. Tell her to look into who gave the news site the dirt on you."

She hadn't thought of that—proof of just how off her game she really was. "Mom thinks it was Jeannie Ray. Tore a strip off her earlier."

"Your mother's a lot like Gran in some ways." And then, "I'm getting a copy of Matt's prison file."

Audrey stared at him. "How did you manage that?"

"Called in a favor. He was one of Warren's mentally ill inmates."

"That doesn't surprise me. Clint was physically abusive as well, and if Matt suffered half of what he told me, it's no wonder he's messed up." Her fingers went to the sore spot on her scalp where Matt had yanked on her hair. "Poor bastard never stood a chance."

"That poor bastard threatened you."

"I don't have to like someone to have empathy for them."

"That was always your Achilles' heel."

She straightened. "Excuse me?"

"Always trying to rescue everybody. Birds, cats. People. If someone even remotely looked like they needed rescuing you jumped right in and saved their ass whether they liked it or not. Why do you think Maggie told you about her father?"

She knew where he was going with this. "She didn't tell me what happened so that I'd save her."

He tilted his head toward his left shoulder. "Sure she did. Maggie was a lot of things, but dumb wasn't one of them. She might not have known how far you'd go for her, but she knew you'd do something, even though no one else had. And you did."

"She took the blame for it."

Jake shook his head, hair falling over his forehead. "Of course she did. How else was she going to hold it over you for the rest of her life?"

Had Maggie really played her like that? Years ago she might have wondered if a thirteen-year-old girl was even capable of that sort of long-term manipulation, but she knew just how possible it really was. She'd met many kids capable of such deception over her years of helping Angeline with her research.

She looked Jake in the eye. "She was going to out me in that damn book of hers."

"That was just to get your attention. No one would have believed her. I know you think you're a pariah around here, but this town isn't just a bunch of ignorant, inbred yokels. They know trouble when they see it. Maggie was only tolerated like she was because she got her claws into Gideon and tried to put on a good face."

Audrey's brow puckered. "I've never thought this town was a bunch of ignorant, inbred yokels. It's my home too, remember."

"One you couldn't wait to leave."

Understanding dawned like a shovel to the face. He'd taken her desire to get out personally. "Don't blame me for running when you gave me a good fucking push."

"I came after you once."

Fuck the shovel, this was a sledgehammer. "What?"

He folded his arms over his chest. "I drove out. Gran thought I was in Florida with Linc. I got your address from her book and went to your apartment. I saw you coming down the steps with a guy. He was wearing a red T-shirt and jeans. He was blond. He kissed you and I wanted to kill him, but you looked happy. Really happy." He shrugged. "So I drove home."

That he had done that was insane. And then not to talk to her? The guy had been Kurt, her only real boyfriend at Stanford. He turned out to be a douche, but he'd helped her stop pining for Jake.

She went to him. Reached up and brushed the hair back from his face. Then she lifted up on her toes to plant a soft kiss on his lips. "Thank you."

His gaze searched her face. Audrey had no idea just what he was looking for. "I'm not going to try to stop you when leave this time either."

"I know."

"And I'm not going to chase after you."

"I know that too, but I'm here for now."

Then he kissed her, and for now was good enough.

He cocked his head toward the door. "Help me close up?"

"Sure."

The handful of people in the bar responded pretty quickly to Jake's "last call"—leaving rather than getting another drink. It was a weeknight, after all. She locked the door after Binky Taylor finally hauled himself outside. Then, while Jake counted the cash, she cleared glasses from the tables and started putting the chairs up.

"Leave that for Lincoln," Jake said. "He needs to do something to earn what I pay him."

A few minutes later—after putting the night's profits in the safe—Jake turned off most of the lights and set the alarm, and they left by the back door. He left a list of things to do before opening on the door to Lincoln's apartment.

"My car's out front," Audrey told him. "I'll follow you."

There was a streetlight near the road that illuminated a good portion of the front lot, so it wasn't like she had to walk through the dark. Still, it was a quiet enough night that the hairs on the back of her neck twitched at every sound. Years of urban dwelling had made her distrustful of silence.

She hit the unlock button on the key, picking up her pace as she heard Jake's truck start. She had just reached the Mini when she heard it—the rumble of an ATV. It pulled out of the lane across the road, kicking up a stream of gravel as its front wheels gripped the pavement. With the help of the streetlight she could see it clearly—red, missing a headlight, the driver wearing a full helmet and visor.

Audrey watched it drive away. Had he been waiting for her? She was tempted to go after him, but the four-wheeler pulled into a driveway a short distance down the road.

Gideon's house.

Jake's truck pulled up beside her, so Audrey climbed into her car and started the engine. As she followed Jake back to his house, Audrey made the decision to talk to Alisha.

And then she was going to have a chat with Isaac Canning.

Audrey and Jake were still in bed when her cell phone rang the next morning. Jake raised an eyebrow at the tone. "'Lola'?"

"It's Angeline's favorite song," Audrey replied, diving for the bedside table. The pulse in her throat thumped so hard it actually hurt. Her boss had to have seen the news by now.

"Hello?"

"Good morning," came the familiar and soothing sound of Dr. Angeline Beharrie's voice. "I hope I'm not calling too early. I can never remember the time difference."

"It's earlier where you are, so you don't need to apologize to me. I assume you're calling about the online article." Audrey couldn't stand dragging out the suspense.

"Actually, I'm not. But I do want to know how you're doing up there."

Audrey filled her in on what had happened, as well as what little she'd managed to dig up.

"I truly don't believe they have enough to build any sort of case against you, but I know you're probably apprehensive."

She smiled. "That's underselling it, Angie. The producer from the show—Grant—he's already called. I haven't had the guts to call him back."

"Ignoring him won't change his decision, my dear. You know that. Avoidance is not a viable coping mechanism." Audrey knew her boss wasn't being patronizing, just factual.

"Yes, I know. I was planning to call him today."

"Good. Meanwhile, let me tell you something that may make you feel better. I've had two calls from local news agencies wanting to interview you. Three calls from defense attorneys who want to discuss client assessments with you, and Reva called me last night about a girl she has at Stillwater. When I told her you were in Maine, she asked me to contact you. I know you're on vacation, but would you be willing to drive up and see her? She believes the girl is malingering, but she wants a second opinion."

It took a moment for Audrey's brain to process what it had just heard. "You're not going to fire me?"

"Why on earth would I fire you? I've always known about your past—it's what makes you so valuable to me as an assistant and colleague. At the risk of sounding mercenary, you've just upped our public profile. I have no problem taking full advantage of it—and neither should you."

"I'm not sure what you mean."

"I'll be blunt—you know what it's like to have killed someone. Use what you know to find the person who killed Maggie. Point the police away from you and in the right direction. That will make a much better story, don't you think? Now, can I tell Reva to expect you?"

"Uh, sure." Audrey winced. She sounded like an idiot. "When does she want me?"

"I don't suppose you could go today?"

The Stillwater Facility for Girls was located just north of Orono. With traffic—and there was never traffic, not by L.A. standards—it would be about a two-hour trip. "I can, yes." Any excuse to get the hell out of Edgeport and at least pretend her life was as it normally was.

"Expense a hotel stay if you want, and your expenses. I'm sending Reva your contact information now, and vice versa. I'm also sending you the girl's initial assessment and any additional paperwork. Thanks for doing this. Oh, and, Audrey?"

"Yes?"

"I'm here if you need me. I can be on a plane tonight if necessary. You don't have to go through this alone."

The idea of Angeline showing up in Edgeport with her perfect hair and tailored suits made Audrey smile. It also made her throat tight. "I'm not alone, but thank you. I appreciate it."

When Audrey ended the call, she turned to Jake. "I have to drive up to Stillwater. Want to come? It might be an overnight trip."

Their gazes met. Bringing him to Stillwater was a big deal to her, and she hoped he saw that. The only other people who had ever visited the place had been her parents, and they certainly hadn't been back since she'd been released. Audrey hadn't been back since her release either, though she and Reva sometimes still corresponded because Angeline worked closely with the facility.

"The town won't fall apart without me for one night," he replied. "I'll check in with Yancy and Lincoln. When are you leaving?"

"I'll need to go home and pick up a few things—pack a new bag." She checked her watch. Twelve-thirty? Traffic wouldn't be heavy, even though they were heading into the July Fourth weekend. She'd hoped to fly back to L.A. tomorrow, but that wasn't going to happen. Neve hadn't demanded she stick around, but leaving would feel too much like running. She didn't want to run anymore.

"It's been a week already," she commented. "Since Maggie was killed."

"I spoke to Gideon yesterday. He said they're releasing the body soon. He's hoping to have a service for her next week."

Audrey didn't say it aloud, but she hoped to be gone by then. "Having a funeral will be good for both him and Bailey. It's a necessary part of mourning and closure."

"If you say so, doc." He grinned. "Go, get out of here. Call me when you're leaving."

She arched a brow. "Are you going to let me drive?"

"You don't want to arrive at Stillwater in my beat-up rig. You need to make a better impression than that."

She hadn't even thought about it, but he was right. "Okay, I'll call you when I'm on my way to pick you up." She gave him a quick kiss and hopped out of bed. He watched her as she dressed, then threw back the covers and paraded nude to the bathroom. His bare ass was the last thing she saw before going downstairs.

When Audrey arrived home, Jessica's van was in the driveway, as was her father's truck. Frowning, Audrey gathered up her things and went inside.

Jessica was at the stove, making what smelled like chicken soup. Isabelle was playing Barbies on the floor with her grandfather, and the little one, Olivia, was fast asleep in her mechanized bassinet, which gently swayed from side to side.

"What's going on?" Audrey asked.

Jess glanced at her, then at their father. "Mum's not feeling well. I took the day off to help out."

"I told you I can look after the girls," their father said from the floor, where he was dressing an African American doll in a hot pink jumpsuit. "I have helped raise three kids—you guys didn't turn out too bad." He pointed at Jessica. "'Cept for you," he joked.

Audrey set her bag on a chair. "I'm supposed to go to Stillwater today for my boss. Do you need me to stay?" She directed her question at her sister.

Jess seemed surprised that she'd asked. "No, I've got this." And then, "Are you okay with going up there?"

Audrey hesitated. She hadn't thought about it. Her time in Stillwater had been some of the worst and the best of her life. She had scars from the place—visible ones too—but she'd met Angeline there, and she had realized what she wanted to do with her life.

"Yeah, I'm good. Where's Mum?"

"Upstairs."

"She's sleeping," their father joined in, a warning in his tone.

Audrey turned to him. "Are you going to tell us what's going on with her?"

He looked her right in the eye. "What are you talking about? She's just got a bug."

Liar. She wasn't going to call him that, not in front of Isabelle, who was very interested in their conversation. "Jessica's soup will probably make her feel better." She smiled at her niece. "I bet it would make her feel really good if you made her some biscuits to go with it. You want me to show you how?" They'd always had biscuits with soup—like crunchy dumplings.

Isabelle's face brightened. "Yeah! That will make Grammie feel better. Is that okay, Grampie?"

John smiled. "Auntie Audrey's right. Grammie Harte would love that."

Audrey rolled up her sleeves, washed her hands, and got to work. Her mother kept all her ingredients in the same place, so she knew where everything was. She did the measuring, but let her niece do most of the stirring, taking over only to make certain it was blended enough. They rolled them out, and Isabelle cut them out with the cutter that had belonged to Anne's grandmother.

When they were in the oven, Audrey ran upstairs to pack for Stillwater. She stopped by her parents' bedroom and peeked inside. Her mother was asleep, the blankets tucked up under her chin. She looked peaceful but drawn. What was going on? Had she been to the doctor? This had been going on for a week now.

She was about to go inside, but she heard her father's footsteps coming up the stairs. He wouldn't be impressed to catch her spying, after telling her to let her mother rest. Audrey quietly closed the door and went to get a shower. Before jumping in she left a quick voice mail for Neve, telling her about Janis and leaving the woman's phone number. "I know you want to kick my ass for getting involved, but I need to know who killed her, Neve. I don't know if talking to Janis will help the investigation, but it's worth a follow-up." Then she hung up.

She was back downstairs thirty minutes later, greeted by the smell of warm biscuits and cooking soup. Isabelle and her grandfather were playing in the living room as Jessica tidied up the kitchen. The baby was still asleep.

"Do you know what's wrong with her?" Audrey asked in a low tone. There was no need to say who "her" was.

Her sister glanced toward the door. "No," she replied in a similar tone. "She hasn't said anything to you?"

Audrey shook her head. "Neither has he." They both knew their father was the one who had a harder time keeping a secret. "But there's something, isn't there?"

"I think so. She's been supposedly fighting this 'bug' for a month now."

They shared a glance that needed no words to go with it. They were both worried. "What about Dave? Has he said anything?"

"No."

"He's coming home for the weekend," Audrey said. "Maybe the three of us can corner the two of them before he goes back."

"He's bringing Seth. You know both Mum and Dad will put on a good face for that."

"I'm sure Greg or Isabelle can keep Seth occupied for a while. I'm not leaving until she tells us what's wrong."

"Weren't you supposed to leave tomorrow?"

"Yeah, but I can't walk now. I need to know what happened to Maggie. They frown on suspects taking off, you know."

"They can't really think you were dumb enough to kill Maggie after a public fight?"

Audrey laughed. "You know, that's what everyone's said. Not that they don't think I *could* have killed her, but that I would have been *smarter* about it. I think it's meant as a compliment."

"Well, you *would* have been smarter about it, wouldn't you?"

It was weird, having a discussion with her sister that wasn't fraught with emotion. "If I had to kill her, sure. But if I didn't kill her fourteen years ago, I wouldn't kill her now. Book or no book." She tilted her head. "Though I suppose I could have sued her for libel."

"Did she lie?"

"She would have." Audrey went to the sideboard and grabbed a couple of biscuits—still warm. She cut them in half, slathered the halves with butter, and wrapped them in paper towel. "I'm off. Do you have my cell number?"

"Mum's got it written down. I'll put it in my phone when I'm done here."

"Okay, I'll be back as soon as I can be. Call me if you find out anything."

"I will. Hey, Audrey?"

She paused, halfway out the door, and looked back at her sister.

"I don't like what you did. I still resent you for how your actions impacted my life, and I don't know if I can ever forgive you completely, but you're right—there's something going on with Mum, and I'm willing to put that in front of any issue you and I might have."

Audrey nodded. "Me too." Then she closed the door behind her. She hadn't seen that coming.

CHAPTER SIXTEEN

The sign at the end of the private road declared it simply as "Stillwater," leaving out the rest of the name that would give away the nature of the place, but the original sign still hung above the main door, the letters worn but legible: STILLWATER TRAINING SCHOOL FOR GIRLS EST. 1902.

It was a large, redbrick building with white trim in that classic Colonial style, with wings that extended toward the back, where smaller outbuildings filled in the courtyard. Audrey knew what purpose each and every one of them served—knew every detail of each and every floor of each and every building.

She pulled the Mini into the paved parking lot—it had been gravel when she'd been there. She removed the key from the ignition and stared at the building through the bug-splatter on the windshield.

"You okay?" Jake asked after a moment.

"Yeah. I'm good." She wasn't—not really—but there was no way to convey how it felt to be back at the place that had so completely formed her. Even if she had the words, she wouldn't dare make herself vulnerable to share them. Not with anyone.

She grabbed her bag from the backseat and got out of the car. Jake followed, walking beside her up the stone path to the front door. It had a modern keypad to the right of it, with an ancient intercom beneath that. Audrey pressed the button.

"Yes?" came a tinny female voice.

"Audrey Harte"—she cleared her throat—"to see Reva Kim."

"Come in." There was a loud buzzing sound and a green light appeared on the keypad. Audrey turned the knob—her damp palm slipping against the metal—and pushed the heavy door open.

Her sense memory was bombarded the moment her foot crossed the threshold, the sounds and smells and sights rushing at her with a host of emotions attached. She remembered the first time she entered through that door—and the day she finally left through it. It had smelled of lemon polish then, and it smelled of it now. The hardwood floor gleamed and the windows practically sparkled—each one washed and hand buffed by Stillwater girls. The walls were still the same shade of cream—fresh and unmarked. Reva had it painted every two years.

Audrey looked up. The cathedral ceiling domed above them, and the chandelier that hung there sparkled in the sunlight. Not a cobweb to be seen.

"This is quite the place," Jake remarked, his gaze slowly moving along the ceiling.

She didn't look at him but instead moved toward the security counter. "And this is only the front hall."

A woman of Native American heritage stood behind the sliding glass of the security office. Any visitors had to pass through this station to access the rest of the facility. Audrey and Jake both showed their IDs, stood to get their photos taken, and stuck the badges they were given on their shirts.

"Rosa will take you to Dr. Kim's office," the woman told them.

Audrey smiled at her. "Are you new?"

The woman drew back, as though insulted. "I've been here five years."

"I don't need anyone to show me the way—unless she's moved her office in the last fourteen years?"

"Nooo." The woman looked at her as though trying to put her in her proper place but having a hard time figuring it out. "It's where it always was." She probably didn't get too many visitors who had been former residents *and* psychologists.

"Thanks." Then to Jake, "Come on, I'll give you a bit of a tour on the way."

He followed after her, through yet another door that led to the inner sanctum of the building.

"I smell vanilla," he commented as they walked down a carpeted corridor framed by dark wainscot and more of the same cream paint. Photographs lined the walls on either side.

"Reva likes to make the place smell homey. It makes the girls calmer. Well, most of them, anyway." She stopped before one of the photographs. "My last year here."

His bicep brushed her shoulder as he leaned in to look. "Second from the left, back row." He grinned. "God, you were a baby."

"You weren't exactly ruggedly handsome at sixteen."

He shot her a sideways glance. "I'm not ruggedly handsome at thirty-two either."

"Well, I've never been a big fan of rugged anyway."

"Lucky me." He gave her that amused look, then nudged her with his shoulder. "Give me the rest of the tour."

"There's not really a lot to see. This is the gallery, as you can tell. Every year we'd get a group photo taken. There was a lot of turnover from year to year. Only a few of us were here for longer sentences."

"You liked it here."

"I did. I got into fights, and sometimes it was scary, but everyone knew what I was in for, so not too many people bugged me. Not unless they had something to prove. They had great teachers for us, and had lecturers come in. I met Angeline here. She came to interview some of us when she was writing a book on violent teen girls."

"*Sugar and Spice.*"

Audrey glanced at him. "You know it?"

"I read it. The acknowledgments said she talked to girls from Stillwater. Figured you'd be one of them. She called you Ivy."

"How did you know it was me?" There were a lot of girls included in that book.

He made a face that said, "bitch, please." "It wasn't hard. She said you had helped kill someone, and when she quoted dialogue I knew it was you."

"That's a little creepy."

"You like it."

She laughed. "Oh, here's the nurse's office. I spent more time here than I ought to have."

"I thought you said you didn't get much trouble."

"Sometimes I went looking for it." She stopped in front of the door at the end of the hall and knocked. A moment later it opened, revealing a gorgeous woman of Asian American descent. Her face lit up at the sight of Audrey.

"Thank you so much for coming up," she said, taking Audrey's hand and pulling her into the office. "When Angeline told me you were in Maine I couldn't believe it. How are you? You look fabulous."

Audrey had to stop smiling to talk. "It's good to see you, Dr. Kim."

"Reva. We're peers now." The older woman turned her gaze to Jake. She offered her hand. "Forgive me. I'm Reva Kim."

He accepted the handshake. "Jake Tripp."

Perfectly plucked brows rose. "Any relation to Grace Tripp?"

"Her grandson."

"She was quite the woman."

Jake smiled. "She was."

Audrey turned to him. "Do you mind waiting for me out here?"

"No."

Reva gestured to a small room off the waiting area. "You'll find coffee and soft drinks as well as snacks in there. Help yourself." Then, she gestured for Audrey to follow her into her office.

Reva closed the door and gestured for her to sit. "Audrey, thank you for coming up on such short notice. I need the opinion of someone with a forensic background, but who also specializes in troubled adolescent females."

That was definitely Audrey's area of expertise. It wasn't unusual to have psychologists assess some of the girls who came to Stillwater. Reva's background was in social work, so while she was more than equipped to care for and handle these girls—and understand them— she didn't always know what to look for when it came to criminal or court procedure.

"What exactly am I looking for?" she asked.

"She's a new girl. Brought in on criminal charges. She's been making claims about her mental state that I need validated in order to decide whether she stays here or is sent to a mental-health facility. I need to know if I'm correct in suspecting her of malingering or if she is actually being truthful. There was some mention of her being in a fugue state when she went to court, and reports of erratic behavior."

"How's she been since coming here?"

"Sometimes she's cheerful and other times she's on the edge of total despair."

"Her file doesn't say she was diagnosed as bipolar."

"No, though there have been issues with depression."

That wasn't a surprise. A lot of girls in trouble had mental illness, and even more had histories of sexual abuse, which could lead to more mental and emotional issues.

"Where is she now?"

"Her room."

"I'd like to talk to her there, if that's all right with you. It will make her more comfortable."

"Of course. I'll take you up." Reva stood and led her out of the office. Jake sat in a comfortable-looking armchair reading a book. He looked up as she passed.

"I don't know how long I'll be," she told him.

He held up his book. He had a cup of coffee as well. "I'm good."

The two women left the room and continued down the hall before taking a right, going through another door and then up a couple of flights of stairs.

"It's so strange to access the dorms this way," Audrey commented.

"I can only imagine how odd it must be for you to be back here. Are you certain you're comfortable doing this?"

"I am. This is like returning to my old high school. I have so many memories of this place—good and bad."

"Hopefully it will have been worth your time to come up here. The only person other than Angeline whom I would trust with this situation is you."

That warmed her heart so much. "It was worth the drive just to see you." Reva had yet to mention having heard about Maggie's murder, and Audrey wasn't about to be the one to bring it up.

"This girl, she's claiming to have DID?"

"Yes. My experience with the disorder is sadly lacking."

"There aren't many in our field who can claim otherwise. It's a hard one to diagnose, and it's been almost as sensationalized as satanic cults."

"I must admit, I'm tempted to say it doesn't exist, but then every once in a while someone comes along who fits the criteria."

"Mm," Audrey agreed. "Hard to prove—or disprove, depending on how you look at it. I'm afraid the Sybil hoax has made the entire psychiatric world skeptical. And careful in making a diagnosis."

Back in the seventies, a woman by the name of Shirley Ardell Mason had been diagnosed with what was then known as multiple personality disorder. Under hypnosis, Shirley, or "Sybil," as she was called in the book and the movies that followed, revealed sixteen separate personalities. The world went nuts over it, and MPD became the disorder of the day. And then it came out that Mason's therapist, Cornelia B. Wilbur, seemed to have planted these alters during hypnosis. There were audiotapes that backed the suspicion, but much of the research and the truth of the story was destroyed when individuals involved died. It was still considered controversial in the field to this day.

Audrey had seen DID—dissociative identity disorder, as it was now known—in a small percentage of Angeline's cases, and the kids they interviewed, but it was more common in adult females than teens, so that could account for her lack of experience with the disorder. However, she prided herself on her ability to tell when someone was lying, or malingering—faking symptoms of illness or the severity of it.

They climbed the stairs to the third-floor dorm, where the new residents were always housed. Audrey had spent the first six months of her sentence on that floor before dropping down to the second floor, where she'd remained until her release. At the third door down on the right, where a female guard stood, Reva stopped. "This is Melly's room." She knocked on the door. A second later they were told to come in.

Reva smiled at Audrey. "Come back to the office when you're done."

Audrey opened the door and stepped inside. A young woman with long black braids and a dark complexion was sprawled on the bed, reading. She barely looked up when Audrey walked in.

"Hi, Melly. I'm Dr. Audrey Harte. I've been asked to talk to you for a little while today. Are you okay with that?"

The girl's eyes widened. "Audrey Harte? You're the chick on that show."

Audrey cleared her throat. "Yes, that's me."

"Huh." The girl put on a smug face. "Don't I feel important. How much did they have to pay you to get you to see me?"

"I haven't been paid anything. I'm here as an associate of Dr. Kim's."

Melly's dark gaze took her in from head to toe and obviously she was unimpressed. "You look taller on TV."

"So I've been told." Actually, no one had ever said it to her before this visit, but she didn't want to say anything that might tip the balance of power in the room. This girl practically reeked of aggression. Audrey was glad for the guard outside the door.

"Well, you talk about murderers on TV, doc, but have you ever been in the same room with one?" The girl sat up, hands clenched into tight fists that looked like they could deliver a hard beating. " 'Cause your skinny ass is with one now."

Neve was surprised to find Lincoln's motorcycle parked behind Gracie's. She was even more surprised to find him up—even though it was one o'clock in the afternoon. A large truck was parked there as well—the sign on the side of it indicating that it was some kind of produce supplier.

The back door of the building was open, so Neve walked through, pulling her shoulder back to avoid banging into one of the deliverymen as he walked out. Inside, the place was dark, and smelled of cleaner, beer, and fryer grease. Her stomach grumbled.

Lincoln handed a clipboard and pen to a large bald man. "Thanks, Ed. See you next week."

"Say hey to your brother for me," Ed replied, and shook Lincoln's hand. He dipped his head to Neve as he walked by, but avoided her eye. *Ex-con*, whispered the cop voice in her head. She usually knew them and they almost always knew her, even though she'd been out of uniform for a few years now.

Lincoln watched her approach, arms folded over the front of his Rolling Stones T-shirt. His long dark hair was loose and tucked behind one ear. Shouldn't he have grown out of the whole rocker look by now?

"Detective Graham," he drawled in a vaguely mocking manner. "My brother's not here if you're looking for him."

Neve cocked her head as her gaze scanned the entire bar, making certain they were alone. "Actually, Lincoln, I'm here to see you. Got a minute?"

He seemed surprised—and a little nervous, but then most people were when a cop wanted to talk. "Sure. You want a coffee?" He gestured behind the bar where the coffeemaker sat, a fresh pot finishing its brewing cycle.

"I would, thanks." She followed him to the bar, sitting on the side so she could see both front and back entrances.

Lincoln set a mug in front of her—his black nail polish was chipped—and filled it with coffee that smelled strong enough to peel paint. He dropped some sugar packets and creamers on the polished bar top. "Is this about Matt Jones taking a swing at Audrey?"

"Thanks," Neve said, reaching for a creamer and peeling back the paper lid. "Did he grab her by the hair and threaten her?"

"Yeah."

She poured the creamer in her cup and reached for another. So much for Matt's story. "Then no, this isn't about Matt and Audrey."

He nodded, lips thinning. "Maggie then."

Neve ripped into a couple of the sugar packets. "She had hashish in her system. Since that's always been associated with the

Tripps around these parts, I figured I'd talk to you. Then, I heard you and Maggie had a more personal relationship."

Another nod. "We'd been fooling around for a few months, yeah."

"Did she get the hash from you?"

He hesitated.

Neve sighed. "I don't fucking care if you've got a brick of the stuff under the bar. I'm just trying to solve a murder. Did Maggie get hash from you?"

"Yeah. She did. We smoked the night she died." He poured himself a cup of coffee. His hand wasn't exactly steady, but he looked hungover. Lincoln always looked hungover. She couldn't believe she'd actually slept with him once. It had been years ago, back when his looking like a roadie had been cute—sexy, even.

"Before or after her altercation with Audrey?" She took a sip of coffee. It was actually very good.

"Before."

"So, you smoked a bit, got a little party going on, she performed fellatio on you, then what?"

"I told her she still had to pay for the hash and she stomped out. A few minutes after that, Audrey showed up."

"Did Maggie often offer sexual services as payment for drugs?"

Lincoln took a drink from his cup. "Sometimes. A lot of times I'd share my personal stash with her, but if she wanted her own, I charged her. Sometimes I'd take it in trade—only because she got off on it, not because I don't respect women."

Neve had to bite her cheek to keep from laughing. Of *course* he respected women. He respected anyone who had his dick in their mouth. "Got off on it. You mean like role-play?"

"Yeah. She liked to pretend she had no money and wanted me to tell her she could pay me in other ways. Normally I was into it, but she was drunk and weird that night. It didn't feel right."

"Weird how?"

He shrugged. "Needy? She kept wanting me to tell her I loved her. To tell her how beautiful she was. She never asked me to do that before. Afterward, her makeup was smeared—like she'd been crying. She looked like a young Courtney Love. It was kind of hot, but really weird. To be honest, I just wanted to get away from her. I knew asking for money would piss her off and she'd leave."

You're a real class act. A woman's crying and obviously hurting, but you'll let her suck you off and then kick her to the curb. "That's the last time you saw her?"

"Yes."

"How late did you work that night, Linc?"

"We closed at one. Jake and I cleaned up a bit and then jammed for about an hour before he left and I went upstairs."

"So, that would have been at about three a.m.?"

He nodded. "Probably. I didn't look at the clock. I just passed out. I had a couple of drinks after close."

The alcohol, paired with the hash, would have made him pretty mellow. It was unlikely he'd be able to summon the rage, let alone the dexterity, needed to kill Maggie without leaving evidence. Still, she wanted to be sure. "If I ask Jake about this, he'll corroborate?"

"Yeah. He can probably tell you the time too."

"Did you and Maggie talk much?"

He looked surprised. "Some. Not a lot."

"Did she ever mention if she was having trouble with someone?"

He frowned. "You mean, do I have any idea of who could have killed her?"

"Either-or."

Lincoln toyed with a lock of his hair, twisting it into a tiny braid as he pondered the question. "She told me once that she thought Gideon was screwing around on her, but Yancy hadn't heard anything like that. Maggie also used to say she was afraid of his temper. He wasn't impressed with her at all. There wasn't much love left there. I think he was embarrassed by her, y'know? I mean, she wasn't exactly subtle sometimes. And she was always flirting with everyone. Didn't matter if you were a guy or girl. Maggie just liked to fuck." He blushed again. "Sorry."

Neve smiled. "It's fine. So, Gideon was upset. Anyone else?" In the back of her mind she hoped he gave her another name.

"Isaac, Bailey's boyfriend, hated her. She was always trying to break him and Bailey up. Bailey was getting pretty fed up about it too. She'd been getting pretty rebellious lately. Maggie said Bailey would pick fights with her. Mags was worried she might get physical. She is—was—a lot smaller than Bee."

Bee. He knew Bailey well enough to use her nickname. That wasn't much of a surprise. Lincoln looked like a rebel and had the arrest record to back it up—nothing all that serious, mostly drug related. His access to drugs made him even more appealing to teens. He was musical and drove a motorcycle, and his face still had a bit of prettiness left to it.

"What about Matthew Jones? You and he are pretty tight."

"We hang out. He dates Yancy, so we see each other a lot. He's all right, but you never know if he's going to love on you or try to take your head off. He's a little fucked-up."

"Was Maggie afraid of him?"

Lincoln actually laughed. "I think she was the only one who wasn't. She'd talk to him like he was a retard or something. Maggie could wind him up like you wouldn't believe. I think she liked making him crazy. I guess it made her feel less nuts. That whole family's always been fucked—well, you remember. You were around it before I was."

She forgot that Lincoln hadn't lived in Edgeport his entire life. His mother had taken the kids away just before the Joneses had moved to town. Jake came back shortly after that, but Lincoln and Yancy hadn't returned for quite a few years.

"Yeah, I remember." Matt had plenty of reason to hate his sister, and if his attack on Audrey was any indication, it wouldn't take much for him to kill her. "Did Maggie ever talk to you about Audrey?"

"Not much. Once, she told me that Gideon wouldn't talk to her the way he did if Audrey was around. Another time she said she wished Audrey was there to help her deal with Bailey, but other than that, she didn't say anything. I tried to get her to tell me about when they killed Clint once, and she refused to talk about it." A strange expression came over his face.

"What?" Neve demanded.

He shook his head. "She said that what happened with Clint was something private between Audrey and herself. Something sacred. That was the word she used. That's fucked-up, isn't it?"

Neve didn't reply. It was a strange thing to say given that Maggie claimed she was going to finally tell the truth about that night. Or maybe Maggie simply intended to use the book as a way to force Audrey to deal with her. Maggie used to get so angry when they were teenagers and Audrey wouldn't do what she wanted. The more she tried to force her, the further Audrey pulled away. Having Bailey in the house, rebelling against her, probably brought back some of those feelings.

But that kind of hurt would explain Maggie lashing out at Audrey, not the other way around. Even if Maggie had published her book, claiming that Audrey had orchestrated Clint's death, it would be her word against Audrey's. At the time of the murder, Maggie had taken responsibility. Maggie was a hairdresser with a history of abuse and mental-health issues. Audrey was making a name for herself in her field. It wasn't hard to figure where public opinion would fall, but there were always going to be those people who loved a little scandal. They would still talk, and that could be damaging to a professional reputation.

No matter from which direction she looked at the murder, she couldn't find a way to make Audrey the killer. There was no way killing Maggie benefited her. But maybe getting rid of Maggie benefited Gideon or Isaac. Or Matthew.

She studied Lincoln over the rim of her cup. She hadn't scratched him off the list just yet. She'd check his story with Jake, though he'd probably say anything to protect his brother. Lincoln didn't strike her as being as smart as Jake—and she meant that in the sense that Lincoln wasn't as sneaky or devious. Maybe little brother hadn't been able to get to the beach in time to dispose of big brother Lincoln's mess.

She thanked Lincoln for the coffee and told him she might need to talk to him again. He nodded and let her see herself out.

In the car she checked her phone. She had a message from Audrey. As she listened, irritation chewed at the lining of her stomach. Neither her father nor Audrey seemed to think she was capable of doing her job without their interference or opinions. She was going to have a little chat with Audrey about what was going to happen if she or Jake-fucking-Tripp ever withheld evidence from her again.

She started the car, spinning up gravel as she tore out of the parking lot. It looked like she was probably going to have to take a trip to Bangor. The more she tried to narrow the list of suspects, the more it blew up in her face.

Was there anyone in Edgeport who *didn't* have a reason to kill Maggie Jones?

"Do you know what I find?" Audrey asked the girl.

Sitting on the bed, Melly frowned, some of the tension leaving her body. It was fairly obvious that Audrey hadn't reacted to her announcement the way she wanted. "No."

Audrey pulled the chair out from the small desk and sat down. One of the legs was shorter than the others and tried to pitch her forward. "A lot of people try to romanticize killing, like it's this daring deed. It's not. It's incredibly easy to kill someone. It's living with it that's the hard part."

The girl snorted. "I knew you'd say the same shit as everyone else."

"You asked me a question. I'm answering it. I've been around quite a few killers." Audrey paused, weighing whether or not she should continue in this direction. "In fact, I spent several years here at Stillwater when I was a teenager."

Now she had the girl's interest. "What were you here for?"

It was public knowledge now, so what did it matter? Plus, Melly was the kind of girl who viewed society as a food chain, and considered her delinquent self near the top of it. "My friend and I killed her father."

The girl's face dropped. "You're fucking with me."

Audrey shook her head. "It's not something I'm proud of, but it's true. I'm in some of the photos in the gallery, see for yourself."

"Why'd you kill him?"

"He was a monster. He had been sexually molesting her and we believed we were the only people who could stop him."

"Did you like it? Killing him?"

"No." And then, "Did you?"

Melly folded her arms, digging her short fingernails into her forearms. There were dozens of tiny, crescent-shaped scars on her skin.

"You don't need to punish yourself, Melly, or feel stressed. We're just talking."

The girl seemed to realize what she was doing and lowered her arms. She slid her hands under her legs. *How many scars does she have on the backs of her thighs?*

"I don't know if I liked it. I wasn't myself when I did it."

"Who were you?"

She shrugged. "Someone else."

"What can you remember?"

"It was like watching a movie. I couldn't stop myself. I kept screaming at her to stop, but she wouldn't."

"Who?"

"Me. One of the other mes."

Audrey nodded. "How many alters do you have?"

"I don't know. Too many to count." She shook her head, braids whipping around her face. "Look, I know they sent you to see if I'm lying."

"I've been asked to assess you so Dr. Kim and the people here will know the best way to help you, or if there's another place that might be able to help you better than Stillwater."

Melly shrugged. "Whatever. You won't believe me any more than they do."

"Try me. Can you tell me about the incident?"

"They say I cut my boyfriend's face off with a piece of broken mirror."

"In your file it says that he considered himself your *ex*-boyfriend. He filed a complaint against you. Claimed you were stalking him."

She looked confused. "No. That's not true. We were—are—still together. His mother made him say that."

"Why would she do that?"

"Because she hated me."

"If you and Ryan were together, why did you hurt him?"

She shook her head again—more violently this time. "I told you—I didn't. One of my other personalities did."

"Do you know why?"

"She was jealous. Jealous that I had Ryan and she didn't." Suddenly, the girl's face changed. She tossed back her hair and lowered her chin. "I wasn't jealous of that bitch. Maybe she'd put up with being slapped around but I wasn't going to."

Here we go. "I take it you're not Melly?"

The girl shook her head. "Na uh. I'm Jay. I look after Melly. I make sure no one ever hurts her again."

"Was it you who attacked Ryan, Jay?"

"Mm hm. He broke up with us. Told us we were sick and that he'd found someone new. He used us and tossed us aside, said we were crazy, but I fixed him. He won't hurt Melly or any of the rest of us again."

"Us? There are more of you?"

"A whole bunch."

"Jay, I mean Melly no harm. Do you think I could talk to her again?"

The girl closed her eyes, and shuddered. When she opened them again, she looked around in confusion. "It was her, wasn't it? You talked to Jay. She did it! She hurt Ryan! I knew it had to be her or one of the others."

"Melly, what was your childhood like?"

Suspicion narrowed her dark gaze. "Why?"

"I'm just wondering. Were your parents good to you?"

She shrugged. "It was just me and my mom."

"Did your mom ever date men that scared you?"

"No. My mother's a fucking dyke."

"Did she abuse you?"

"No."

"Have you ever been sexually assaulted?"

"No."

"Do you ever hear voices or lose time?"

"What the fuck is up with all the questions, bitch?"

There was a lot of anger in that young woman. "Melly, are you familiar with a woman called Sybil?"

"Who the fuck is she?"

"Her real name was Shirley Mason. She was diagnosed with what used to be called multiple personality disorder. It's called dissociative identity disorder now."

Big eyes got even wider. "Like me?"

"When did you first realize you had these alters?"

"I don't know. My mom told my lawyer that sometimes it was like I was a completely different person. She said it was the only way she'd believe I'd hurt someone."

"Why do you think Jay hurt Ryan?"

The girl gave her a disgusted look. "To protect me, just like she said. He hurt me, told lies about me, and Jay just wanted to stand up for me. I shouldn't be locked up because of her. I belong in a hospital. It's not my fault he's dead."

Audrey didn't contradict her. The girl was obviously experiencing guilt over killing her boyfriend, but she hadn't dissociated when she'd cut his face off. She'd known what she'd been doing the entire time. She just hadn't meant to kill him.

Most people who suffered from dissociative identity disorder couldn't just switch between alters in front of strangers. DID was a defense mechanism, and a secretive one at that. In Audrey's limited experience, the difference between alters wasn't so extreme, and they didn't publicly announce themselves. Also, DID was born in a childhood of trauma and pain. Melly hadn't seemed to experience anything that would cause her mind to splinter into different selves to deal with a situation, nor did she claim to experience many of the hallmarks of the disorder, such as lost time, or amnesia. If she had DID, she wouldn't be able to comment on something an alter had said, and she knew what "Jay" had said to Audrey.

"Do you suffer from depression, mood swings, phobias?" The girl shook her head. "Any sleep disorders? No? I notice you dig your nails into your skin. Do you do that when you're upset?"

"I like how it feels. I like the pain."

"Do you ever forget things?" As she asked the question, she thought of Maggie, who often had no memory of things they'd done, or no idea how she'd spent the past few hours.

The girl's gaze locked with hers. It was like looking into a well of hate. "I don't *forget* anything."

Audrey forced a smile. "Thank you for talking to me."

"That's it? You're leaving?"

"Yes. I was asked to visit with you, and I've enjoyed speaking with you, but I don't want to upset you any further."

"But I'm not done!" She jumped off the bed and came at Audrey, her body taut with rage. "You're not going to walk out on me. Sit the fuck down, bitch!"

This was the Melly who had killed Ryan, and she wasn't an alternate personality. She was a very, very angry young woman.

Audrey had already knocked on the door to be let out, but she didn't dare give the girl her back. When Melly swung at her, Audrey deflected the blow. It was the instinct to hit back that she had to fight.

"Melly, you don't want to do this."

"Yeah, I really think I do." The girl swung again, and this time, the blow hit hard against Audrey's ribs.

Something snapped inside her, and it wasn't a rib. It was her professionalism—awakening that part of her that remembered what it was like to be so *angry*.

Audrey grabbed the girl and thrust her against the wall, face first, pinning her arms behind her back. Audrey was bigger and stronger, and her own ignited anger was almost a match.

"You don't want to do this with *me*," she whispered, close to the girl's ear. "Now, calm the fuck down. You're already in enough shit."

Melly's muscles relaxed. Audrey let go of her just as the door to the room opened. She smiled at the guard and walked out, but her knees shook as she made her way back to Reva's office. She shouldn't have touched the girl, but there hadn't seemed to be any other way to settle her.

Reva took one look at her as she entered the office and rose to her feet. "Did she get violent?"

Audrey nodded. "That's one very angry girl up there."

"Did she hurt you?"

"No, but you're correct in your findings. She's definitely malingering. I think she genuinely regrets killing the boy, but she is terrified of what might happen to her. She wants to be sick, because she can't face the alternative. But DID? No. She doesn't have it."

"You're certain?"

"As much as I can be after reading her file and a short personal interview."

Reva's gaze turned concerned. "There's something else. What's wrong?"

Audrey shook her head. She even managed a smile. "Nothing. I'm fine." But she wasn't fine, and it wasn't because of Melly. It was because for the first time in fifteen years, she felt like she finally understood Maggie.

CHAPTER SEVENTEEN

Jake drove home. He didn't seem upset about not spending the night. He didn't ask how she was either, for which Audrey was grateful.

She ran it all through her head—from the first memory she had of Maggie Jones to the last. There were the pills Neve found in her purse—all of which could be prescribed to someone with DID. There was the abuse Maggie suffered—emotional and eventually sexual at the hand of her father. That was exactly the sort of catalyst DID needed. Maggie had always had a shitty memory, and her moods could swing so fast and hard. There had been times—even before killing Clint—that she hadn't known which Maggie her friend was going to be when she saw her. But after witnessing the death of her abusive father, which would be a trigger for anyone, Maggie had started "losing" time. It became more noticeable after Audrey came home from Stillwater. Most people thought Maggie was just spinny or stoned when she didn't remember parties, or having done something wild and reckless. Or worse, that she was lying.

Jesus. DID would explain so much.

"I have to talk to Maggie's therapist," she said. "Or Neve needs to."

"I don't know who that is," Jake replied, his attention focused on the road.

"Neither do I, but Neve does. His name was on the pill bottles in Maggie's bag." She pulled out her phone and texted her old friend: *Need to talk to you about Maggie. Have you interviewed her therapist?* She hit send and shoved the phone back into her pocket.

"Are you going to tell me what's going on? What did that kid do that freaked you so hard?"

"She got physical, but that's not what got to me. She was trying to fake having DID, and it made me realize that Maggie might very well have had the same thing. In fact, I'm almost positive that she did."

"DID? That's like multiple personalities or something, right?"

"Dissociative identity disorder, and yeah. A person has had so much terrible shit happen that their mind dissociates from it to protect itself."

"Well, being fucked by your father would be cause for that."

Audrey winced at his choice of words. Sometimes he was a verbal battering ram he was so blunt. "So could watching your best friend kill him."

He glanced at her, then back at the road. "You are not going to take responsibility for Maggie's mental state. No."

He was right, of course, and she knew it. That said, suspecting what she did about Maggie didn't change that the woman had been an absolute bitch to her at times. Maybe the "real" Maggie hadn't wanted to sleep with Jake and hurt her, but some aspect of her had.

"No," she said slowly. "Not responsibility, but maybe a little accountability. I'm sure it will go away. Most of my unselfish thoughts do."

Jake smiled. "Keep talking. Someday someone might believe you."

"You don't know what I'm like anymore. I could be an awful, terrible person." Hadn't that been why she got into psychology in the first place? Not just because Angeline had seemed so polished and smart to her young self, but because the older woman seemed to understand things Audrey didn't—like why Audrey killed Clint. That had been the true reason Audrey took up the field. Yes, she wanted to help messed-up kids, but the kid she'd most wanted to help and understand had been herself.

"I know you down to the bone, Audrey Harte. You're a bruise on my soul."

"That's a little dramatic, don't you think?"

"Yes." His smile widened. "But you like drama. I have more. Want to hear them?"

"I don't think you can top me being a bruise on your soul."

"No, that one is pretty good."

She smiled. They talked for the rest of the ride home, and there was no more assumption of guilt for things she couldn't change, and couldn't have foreseen as a teenager. But there was regret. Regret for so many things.

Alisha was at Jake's when they walked in. She looked disappointed to see them.

"I thought you were spending the night away."

Jake tossed his keys on the table. "Have a party planned for tonight, do you, Lish?"

"No."

He gave her the same look Gracie always used to give them when they tried to pull one over on her. His niece rolled her eyes. "Okay, so *yes.*"

"Have it back at the camp."

Her face brightened. "Really?"

Audrey shook her head. Only a teenager would think hanging out in an uninsulated building and peeing outside—while dodging june bugs—was more fun than a comfortable house with plumbing and air-conditioning.

Jake nodded. "Really. You're old enough, and the cops are done with it. Keep it to a dull roar, though, and stay in the damn woods. If I hear any complaints from people at the cottages, you'll never have another party on my land." It was a damn good threat, and Alisha obviously took it seriously. She dug out her phone and went out on to the veranda to call her friends.

"God, you're good to her," Audrey remarked.

He shrugged. "I treat her like Gran treated us."

"You don't worry about her getting in trouble?"

His expression turned wry. "You mean like getting pregnant? I think growing up like she has is deterrent enough. But she's not stupid. I can't stop her from having sex, but I can at least make sure she's smart about it."

She stared at him. The only light was the one over the sink, and it highlighted the planes of his face. Gracie used to say he had a poet's face and advised him to be careful how he used it when he got older. It had taken sixteen years for Audrey to understand what she'd meant.

Leaving him wasn't going to be easy. She wasn't even going to think about it.

After Alisha made all her calls, Jake and Audrey helped her gather up what supplies they were going to need: soda, cups, chips, bags of ice, sleeping bags for those foolish enough to bring booze and drink too much, lanterns, and matches, paper and kindling for the fire pit. She had a dock and speakers for her iPod. They loaded everything into the back of the truck and took it back the road to the camp.

Audrey handed her a bucket and a roll of toilet paper. Alisha stared at her.

"Ever peed in the woods before?" Audrey asked.

"Yeah." There was a silent "stupid" there, Audrey was sure of it.

"Your girlfriends will appreciate it. Trust me."

The girl shrugged and took the offering, setting off toward the back of the camp.

"When did you get so squeamish?" Jake asked. "You used to go in these woods all the time."

"Yeah, but after a few drinks a girl appreciates a bucket. Saves her from peeing on her jeans. Or her own feet."

He shook his head, chuckling.

"Yeah, you laugh. You can point that thing wherever you want. It's not so easy for girls."

Jake took her face in his hands and kissed her—right there, out in the open where Alisha could see. "You're crazy," he said, and went to the back of the truck to take more stuff inside. Audrey put the paper and kindling in the fire pit before going to the stack of wood at the side of the camp and bringing back an armful. She stacked a few sticks on top of the kindling and put the rest to the side.

"If you build a fire, make sure it's out before you crash or leave," Audrey instructed.

Alisha nodded. "I know. We have to check all the fire pits at the resort every night too. We give the guests buckets of sand to douse them with. Too bad we're peeing in the only bucket we have."

Audrey laughed. Alisha grinned, clearly pleased with herself.

"Hey, Lish. Can I ask you something?"

"Sure." The girl walked over to stand beside her. She was almost Audrey's height. "What's up?"

"I talked to Bailey the other day. Do you know if her father, or Maggie, or even Isaac ever abused her?"

"You mean hit her?"

Audrey nodded.

"Not Isaac. He's a jealous, possessive freak, but he treats her like gold. She loves her dad. I do know that she and Maggie used to fight."

"She has these bruises on her back and I was wondering where she got them."

"No problem. I'll find a way to look at them and ask her. She'll tell me."

"You are Gracie's blood all right."

The girl grinned. "Thanks. Oh, and tell Uncle Jake not to worry about me, please? I'm not going to drink and he doesn't have to worry about me having sex—every guy up and down the shore is too afraid of him to hit on me."

"Someday you'll meet one brave enough to risk it."

Before they left, Jake set an old tin bucket of sand by the fire pit. Audrey and Alisha shared a smile.

Jake turned to his niece. "Got your phone?"

"Yep."

"Jacket?"

"Yes."

"Knife?"

"*Yes*, Uncle Jake."

"What's the knife for?" Audrey asked.

"Whatever the situation demands," Jake replied, his attention still on Alisha. Audrey understood. He trusted the girl, but he didn't necessarily trust anyone else. Her own father had given her a knife for her birthday the year she turned fourteen. It was the way things were done around there. She didn't carry it anymore, but she still had it.

It was getting dark when they left Alisha there to do the rest of her preparations. A couple of four-wheelers pulled in just as they were leaving. Jake waved at the kids as they drove past.

Audrey's stomach growled. "I could go for some food. You?"

"Yeah. Takeout from Gracie's?"

"Sounds good to me. I want a cheeseburger and fries."

Jake called in the order and they drove down to pick it up.

Audrey waited in the truck while he went inside. She was scanning the parking lot for her father's truck, but she didn't see it.

Her gaze stopped on a woman leaning against an old black pickup that looked like the shocks were gone on one side—it was noticeably lopsided. The woman looked like Yancy. It *was* Yancy. Was she crying?

Audrey opened the door and hopped out of the truck. She glanced around the lot as she approached Jake's sister. She didn't see anyone else. "Yancy? Are you okay?"

The younger woman straightened at the sound of her voice, swiping at her eyes with her fingers. "Oh, hey, Audrey. Is Jake with you?"

"He went inside. Do you want me to get him?"

Yancy shook her head, wiping at her eyes again. "God, no. Thanks, though. I'm okay."

She clearly wasn't okay, but she obviously didn't want to talk about it. "All right."

"Don't mention this to Jake, okay?" Yancy sniffed. She had a red mark on her face, angry and swollen. She'd been hit, and Audrey didn't have to guess by who. "He's so nosy."

"Sure." No way was she keeping that promise. "I'll just go back to the truck then."

Nodding, Jake's sister looked up at her. "Thanks." Her eyes widened. "Matt, no!"

Audrey turned her head to look behind her and got a fist in the face for her trouble. She fell against the side of the truck, Yancy's shouts ringing in her ears. Her jaw throbbed. Luckily, Matt was drunk enough that the punch didn't have his full weight behind it. Unfortunately, he was drunk enough to try again.

Audrey moved just in time. He hit the truck instead of her.

"Fucking bitch!" he yelled, shaking his hand.

Running would have been the smart thing to do. She wasn't feeling particularly smart.

"You seem to have a really nasty habit of hitting women, Matt," she said, her hands curling into fists. "Ever had one hit back?" She punched him in the nose, feeling the cartilage give beneath her knuckles. Then she brought her left fist up hard into his jaw, knocking him backward.

Audrey hadn't been in a fight since Stillwater, but she boxed at her gym and had taken Krav Maga lessons as part of a self-defense course. What she lacked in physical strength, she made up for with sheer dirtiness.

She hit Matt again. He came back with a shot of his own, which landed high on her cheek, near her ear. She shook her head to clear it and managed to avoid another swing. She came up with a punch to his kidney and another to the gut. When he doubled over, she slammed her knee into his face. He lunged at her, arms out, grabbed her, and took her to the gravel hard enough to knock the air from her lungs.

Yancy was screaming, but Audrey couldn't make out what the foolish woman was saying. Matt was dripping blood from his nose, and it splattered on Audrey's neck as she tried to push him off. He pinned her arms, so she squirmed around, trying to get her legs up and around him.

She smashed her forehead into his when he got close. Damn, it hurt. But it hurt Matt more. She came up fast as he listed to the side and shoved him down onto the gravel. She straddled him, pinning his arms with her legs as she punched him again and again...

He bucked her. She landed hard on her side between his truck and another vehicle. His hand closed around her throat, pressing down hard on her windpipe as he punched her in the gut, robbing her of all air. Audrey clawed at the fingers around her neck as she gasped for breath.

A shadow appeared above them, and then Matt was off her, and she could breathe. She gulped air, tasting blood in her mouth. As she struggled to sit up, she realized they had attracted a crowd. Yancy's screams had been good for something after all.

She also realized that the person who had pulled Matt off her was Jake, and he had Matt up against another vehicle and was pounding his head into it.

"Jake, stop!" It was Neve. He ignored her.

Audrey staggered up to him and put her hand on his arm. He let go and Matt dropped to the ground. Jake stepped back.

Lincoln and Yancy pulled Matt to his feet. The son of a bitch was still conscious, though Audrey couldn't understand how it was even possible. Neve stepped up, pushed him over the hood of the truck, and handcuffed his hands behind his back. "You're under arrest, asshole."

Now that the fight was over, everyone was staring at her. Jake gathered her close.

Binky Taylor inched toward her, his weathered face full of concern. "Little girl, I am so sorry this happened to you."

Murmurs rippled across the crowd. Audrey could only blink at them. Her eyes felt wet, her vision blurry. Matt Jones had done the one thing more inexcusable than murder—he'd hit a woman, and in public.

Jake guided her toward the steps. "Let's get you cleaned up."

People stared as they walked in. Men stood up, their chairs scraping against the wooden floor. Women pressed their hands over their mouths.

Jake took her to his office. It was only then that she caught sight of herself in the mirror on the wall. Her hair was a mess, and her face was covered in blood. Her cheek was already swelling. Her shirt, was caked with a mixture of blood and dirt—completely ruined. Her knuckles were raw and bleeding, the skin scraped off by Matt's teeth.

Propping her against the desk, Jake ran his hands over her, checking for breaks and signs of serious injury. He took a handful of tissues from the box beside her and began dabbing at her cheeks.

Suddenly, Lincoln was there with a bowlful of warm water and a stack of napkins. Jake used them to gently wipe all the blood from her face. She could have done it herself, but she liked the attention.

"It looked worse than it is," Lincoln remarked. "That's good."

Jake barely glanced at him. "Take Yancy home, and make sure she knows she's done with that bastard."

"I think she already ended it."

He went still. Lincoln couldn't see his full expression, but Audrey could. "I said make sure she knows."

Lincoln nodded and left the room.

"I'm okay," Audrey said when they were alone. "Jake, really. I'm okay." She caught his hand in hers.

He was shaking.

Neve appeared in the doorway. "I've arrested Matt and I'm taking him in. We'll take care of the rest tomorrow morning. Give me a call when you're ready."

Audrey nodded. "Thanks."

The other woman hesitated, as though there was something else she wanted to say. But she looked at Jake, and then at Audrey holding Jake's hand, and obviously thought better of it. She turned on her heel and strode away.

Jake drew back. His jaw was tight, the muscle there standing out beneath his skin. His eyes were hard. Flat. His cheeks were flushed dark and high. He looked murderous. Audrey cupped her hand around the back of his neck and pulled him close again, bringing his forehead to hers. She was going to have a bruise from head-butting Matt.

"I'm okay," she whispered.

He nodded, silent.

"I would really like my cheeseburger now. And to go home. Can we go back to your place?"

Another nod.

He led her from the office with his arm around her shoulders. Donalda was behind the bar, looking like a frightened little kitten. She gave him a large paper bag that held their food and told him she'd take care of closing up. The bar was quiet—even the music was muted. Everyone stood up, like some sort of receiving line, as they walked past. And outside, there was still a small crowd gathered, talking. They stopped the moment Audrey and Jake appeared, parting for them like some kind of processional.

Jake took her to the truck and helped her inside. She was going to be so sore in the morning.

As they pulled out onto the main road, a four-wheeler drove by—it was missing a headlight, and on the back, behind the driver who was hidden by a full visor, was Bailey McGann. Audrey's gaze locked with hers, and then she was gone. So, her mysterious stalker had been Isaac after all. Why did he feel the need to keep tabs on her? At the moment she couldn't even bring herself to care.

Back at Jake's, she ate her cold burger and fries—it didn't hurt *too* badly to chew. Then, Jake ran a bath for her in the old clawfoot tub in the master bath. He insisted on helping her bathe, even though she said she could do it. He even washed her hair.

He still didn't speak.

Afterward, he patted her skin dry with a soft towel and wrapped her in his robe. He carried her to bed and climbed in beside her, cradling her to his side.

Audrey rested her cheek against his shoulder, feeling his jaw against her damp hair. "Why won't you talk to me?" she whispered.

The arm around her shoulders tightened. "There are too many words. I don't know what ones to say."

Neither of them spoke again until morning.

Jake was cooking breakfast when he heard Alisha's bike clatter to the ground outside. A few seconds later, her sneakers hit the steps, and the screen door flew open.

"Mom told me what happened. Is Audrey okay?"

He lowered the heat on the bacon and turned to look at her pale little face. If anyone ever treated her like Matt had done her mother, or Audrey...

He took a deep breath. "She will be." The bruises and swelling looked worse than they were, she'd insisted earlier that morning when she woke up. He'd already been up for an hour, watching her sleep, his heart writhing like a captured worm. When he'd seen Matt hitting her he'd wanted to kill him. He would have if she hadn't stopped him. He would have killed for her, and even thick-headed Audrey—who didn't know her own worth—had to know what that meant. He did, and it scared him. It scared him more than he would ever let her know, because she was going to leave again, and he was going to let her go.

And he wasn't going to think about it anymore because it pissed him off.

"Is she still here?" Alisha asked.

Jake nodded. "She should be down in a minute."

"He hit my mom, Uncle Jake."

"I know, sweetheart. I know."

"What are you going to do to him?" She had that same blood-thirsty look in her eye that his grandmother used to get.

"He got his ass kicked, and he was arrested. Right now it's out of my hands, but he'll pay for what he's done. First, we need to find out if he killed his sister." If nothing else, Neve had to now switch her attention to him instead of focusing on Audrey, or Lincoln.

His words did little to calm his niece. She was agitated, angry, and helpless against either emotion. There was nothing so overwhelming as the impotent rage of a teenager.

"You should have seen what Audrey did to him," he said, forcing a smile. It worked. She smiled a little too.

"Yeah?"

"His face was a mess."

"It wasn't in that great a shape to begin with," Audrey commented from the doorway.

Alisha turned to face her. Jake watched as his niece's eyes widened in horror, then filled with tears.

"Honestly, sweetie," Audrey said, seeing the girl's reaction, "I'm okay. Just a little sore." She walked into the kitchen—a little more slowly than usual, favoring her left side. With every step, Jake's temper inched up another notch. He watched her touch Alisha's shoulder as she moved to the coffeepot.

"How's your mom this morning? Is she okay?"

"She was crying a lot earlier. She said what Matt did to her was nothing compared to what he did to you. She wanted to come with me, but she's afraid you hate her."

That was all the more reason for her to come by, in Jake's opinion, but sometimes his sister seemed to have stopped maturing in high school. So afraid of what people thought of her.

"Of course I don't hate her," Audrey responded. "Nothing Matt did is her fault."

Jake hadn't noticed how anxious Alisha was until she saw her shoulders lower. Poor kid.

"I asked Bailey about the bruises."

"What bruises?" he asked, getting the coffee cream out of the fridge and setting it on the counter.

"Thanks. I noticed Bailey had bruising on her back," Audrey explained, pouring cream into her cup. "Alisha offered to ask how she got it."

Jake turned to his niece. "And?"

"Maggie pushed her and she fell back onto the stairs." Alisha's eyes sparkled with anger. "Bailey said she didn't mean it, that it was an accident."

"Does her dad know?" Audrey asked. Jake could practically see the wheels turning in her head, wondering if that would have been enough to drive either Gideon or Isaac to murder.

"Yeah. Isaac was so pissed off he told Gideon."

"Did either of them ever confront Maggie about it?"

"I don't know if Gideon did, but Isaac did. He called Maggie a bitch. She kicked him out of the house and told him she'd kill him if he came back."

"Jesus," Jake muttered. "I'm texting Neve." He turned to the stove to check on the food, used a fork to move the bacon in the pan to the pile already draining on a paper towel, and cracked six eggs into the pan. He wiped his hands as the eggs began to cook and picked up his phone. He typed quickly, telling Neve that Audrey was with him and for her to come by as soon as possible.

They were eating breakfast when Neve arrived. She took one look at Audrey and swore. "Jesus, girl. You look like hell. Are you all right?"

Audrey shook her head. "For the eighteenth time, it looks worse than it is."

"Mm. All the same, I want to get some photos of your injuries." Neve took out her cell phone. "Can we go somewhere?"

"Use my office," Jake offered. He watched the two of them leave the room before turning his attention to his niece. "If Matt ever comes around your place again, you call me, and then you hide. Understand?"

Alisha nodded. "Why would he do that to Audrey?"

"Some people are just bad. I wish I had a better explanation, but that's all I've got. Now, come help me make toast." Anything to distract the poor kid.

A little while later, Audrey and Neve returned.

"He's been charged?" he asked, as he handed Neve a cup of coffee.

"Mm. With the long weekend upon us, he won't have a bail hearing until Tuesday or Wednesday, so we won't have to worry about him until then."

"God," Audrey said. "I'd forgotten it's July Fourth weekend. No wonder Gracie's was so busy last night."

Neve nodded. "There's lots of traffic back the road," she said, looking at Jake. "You booked up?"

"Solid."

"Are you doing fireworks again this year?"

"We are. You want breakfast?"

She hesitated, then nodded and sat down at the table, across from Audrey. "I still haven't heard from Maggie's doctor. Thanks for the information about the ladies at Lipstick."

"You're welcome."

Neve smiled. "Now stay out of my investigation or I'll put you in jail just to keep you out of my way."

Audrey smiled back—it looked like a grimace. "Do a better job and I won't have to get involved."

Jake set a plate in front of Neve. "Woman," he said to Audrey, "have you ever thought how much easier your life would be if you didn't invite confrontation?"

She glanced up at him in surprise. "Not really, no."

"You withheld evidence so the two of you could run off and

play detective," Neve reminded both of them. "Knock it off. I know you want to prove you're innocent, but any evidence you hand me is going to be viewed as potentially tainted and untrustworthy. So from now on, no playing amateur detective, okay?"

Audrey nodded. "Okay, but when you talk to Maggie's doctor you need to ask if she was diagnosed with DID."

"Doesn't that stand for 'disassociative identity disorder' or something? Like multiple personalities?"

"Dissociative."

"That would be helpful if she was a suspect, or as a defense, but how could it be motive for murder?"

"Because it can cause significant personality changes and make her do things she wouldn't have remembered doing—things that were out of character. Had Gideon said anything about her having it?"

"I'm not discussing the case with you, so you can just stop." Neve's tone indicated that she was out of patience.

Jake sat down. "Matt's got a history of mental illness and violence. He's told various doctors that he blamed Maggie for how his life turned out."

Shrewd, dark eyes shifted to meet his. "How do you know about that?"

Jake shrugged.

Neve shook her head with a humorless smile. "Jesus Christ, I'm sharing a table with Sherlock and Watson."

Alisha laughed.

"Do you know where Matt was the night of the murder?" he pressed.

"Your sister said he was with her."

Jake looked at Alisha. She shrugged. "I don't know. I was here."

"Your brother says he was with you after you closed up that night," Neve said. "Is that true?"

He'd known she'd get around to asking sooner or later. Stupid fucking Lincoln. Couldn't keep his dick in his pants.

Alisha turned to look at him, her big eyes wide and worried.

"It is," he said, holding his niece's gaze. There was suddenly a very bitter taste in his mouth.

It was the first lie he'd ever told her.

CHAPTER EIGHTEEN

After breakfast, Audrey left to go home and change. She was up to something, and Jake knew it. Not even an hour after Neve told her to back off, she was going to go sticking her face in it again. He shook his head but didn't try to talk her out of it. She was a big girl.

Not like he was one to lecture on keeping promises or being honest. He'd lied to Alisha to protect Lincoln, and that went beyond fucked-up as far as he was concerned. His word meant something, and lying to that kid made him feel almost as dirty as screwing Maggie had.

So, when Audrey and Alisha left—on the heels of Neve—he got in the truck and drove to Gracie's.

His brother was still in bed.

With Donalda.

"Jesus Christ," Jake hissed at his brother in the living room. Lincoln stood before him in nothing but a pair of boxers. He was all pale skin, tattoos, and hickeys. "She's a kid!"

"She's twenty-one," Lincoln argued.

"That's still a kid. You're thirty-four, for fuck's sake." If he thought a slap would knock any sense into him he would have backhanded his brother. "She puked on your carpet!" The stain was still there.

"I like her" was his brother's only excuse. "And she likes me. It's none of your fucking business what I do."

"It is when I lie to a cop to protect your sorry ass. You told Neve you were with me the night Maggie was killed. Where were you really?"

"Here. With Donalda." When Jake raked a hand through his hair, Lincoln added. "You can ask her."

"I just might," Jake warned. "Why lie about it?"

"She's still seeing Andy le Duc."

Avoiding a fight with a jealous boyfriend was more important than proving he hadn't killed his other girlfriend? "Jesus, Linc. Is there a woman between twenty and forty-five in this town that you *haven't* slept with?"

His brother smirked. "Audrey."

Jake glared at him. "Funny."

"Hey, the one I haven't is the one you have—and don't try to deny it. You have that 'I just got laid by the girl of my dreams' thing written all over you. Bashing Matt's face in really declared your love."

"Fuck off." His brother was an asshole. "You swear on Gran's grave that you were with Donnie that night."

Lincoln nodded. He might not take their grandmother's memory to quite the same degree of sanctity that Jake did, but he knew better than to lie on it. "I was. All night."

"What about the blood on your shirt?"

"Gerald Pelletier's. He was in town for the weekend. We got arsing around and I hit him in the nose. Fucking gusher. He was at the bar last night and brought it up, that's how I remembered. I told you it was from a fight."

"Okay. Good." Jake sighed. "You should have told me about this." He jerked his thumb toward the bedroom door.

His brother shrugged. "We thought you'd be pissed. Besides," his voice dropped, "I *was* with Maggie earlier that night."

Jake actually laughed. Of course he was. "That's better than wondering if you killed someone."

Lincoln blinked at him. "If I killed someone you'd be the first to know."

"Really?" Jake waited for the rest.

"Hell, yeah." His brother grinned. "Who else would help me get rid of a body?"

For a kid, Isaac Canning was hard to track down. His mother was a woman who probably had been quite pretty in her day, but she had been slowly defaced by life. She couldn't have been much more than thirty-five, but she looked at least twenty years older. The cigarettes, tan, and gin didn't help.

"I don't know where he is," Mrs. Canning rasped when Audrey knocked on the door of their run-down bungalow. She blew a thin line of smoke right into Audrey's face. "Probably at that girlfriend's of his. That's where he spends most of his time. Or in the woods on that damn machine."

"Thanks," Audrey said, turning to go.

"What happened to your face?"

She paused on the bottom step. She could lie, but this woman would probably have more appreciation for the truth. "Fight."

"Not with my boy." It was said with the tone of a mother who thought she knew her son, and exactly of what he was capable.

"No. With someone else's. Thank you again for your time."

The door closed. Audrey walked back to the Mini, groaning as she settled into the driver's seat. Getting beat up hurt a lot more than she remembered. Of course, those fights had been against girls with anger issues, not full-grown men with anger issues. She was lucky Matt hadn't done much damage. By the same token, so was Matt. She'd thought Jake was going to smash his face right into his brain.

He'd lied to Neve earlier, when he said Lincoln had been with him the night Maggie died. She wasn't sure how she knew that, but she did. She had always seemed to know when he was lying, just as he knew when she did. It saved them the trouble of lying to each other.

She drove to Gideon's. His truck wasn't in the yard, but she stopped anyway. Visiting Bailey wasn't exactly sticking her nose in the investigation—it was a follow-up. Just like she was looking for Isaac to find out why he was following her, not to get information on Maggie's treatment of him or Bailey.

At that moment, discerning Maggie's mental health was so much more important to her than finding out who had killed her. Audrey *needed* to know if seeing her murder Clint had triggered Maggie's dissociation. And what had she done that deserved dying for it?

She rang the bell. A few seconds later the door opened to reveal Bailey, still in pajamas. She ought to have expected it. It was only shortly after twelve in the afternoon.

The girl frowned. "Lish told me you looked terrible, but wow."

"It looks worse than it is." Eventually, someone was going to have to fucking believe her.

Bailey shrugged. "If you say so. Do you want to come in? Dad's not here."

"If you don't mind. I wanted to come by and see how you're doing."

"Thanks." She stepped back to allow Audrey to come in. "Want a coffee?"

"Actually, I was thinking I'd take you to lunch if you want." The thought hadn't even occurred to her until that moment, but why not?

Bailey's face lit up. "Can I shower first?"

"Yes, of course." Audrey watched her run from the room with

youthful exuberance that made her feel so very, very old. It was probably due more to her battered body than her age.

She walked down the same hall, to the bottom of the stairs, where she stopped and listened. When she heard the shower running, she hauled herself up the endless flight of stairs. She knew which door belonged to Bailey, and it was the only one open. One of these other rooms would have been Maggie's. Had she shared a bed with Gideon still? Or had they opted for separate rooms as they began to lead separate lives?

The first room had an unmade bed and men's jeans tossed over the footboard. Definitely Gideon's room. No sign of anything feminine. The second room was the one she sought. The bed was covered in a cream chenille bedspread, and jewelry and perfume sat on top of one of the dressers. Audrey walked in and closed the door. She had to be quick.

The police would have already been through the room, but Audrey wasn't after evidence. She only wanted to get a mental picture of the woman Maggie had become. She looked in the dresser drawers but didn't find anything unusual. Maggie had some sexy underwear, and some plain and more comfortable items. She had flat shoes and stilettos, jeans and dresses. Even her jewelry was a mix of classic and fun.

On her bedside table was a photo of the three of them—Maggie and Gideon grinning, flanking a smiling, younger Bailey. There was another photo of just Maggie and Bailey taken a year or so later. They were smiling, arms around each other, looking every bit like a happy stepdaughter and stepmother.

In the drawer of that table were cards from Bailey and Gideon—birthday and Mother's Day kind of things. There was also a small black velvet box that contained an engagement ring and wedding band. That was telling. She picked up the address book beside it and flipped through it. The handwriting looked different on some of the entries, but that didn't mean it was Maggie's or one of her alters—*if* she had been living with DID.

"Do you ever just lose time?" Maggie had asked.

Audrey frowned. "What do you mean? Like, get caught up in something and not realize how much time has passed?"

"I mean, do you ever just kind of look up and have no idea what you were doing or how you got there?"

"Uh, no. Do you?"

"Sometimes. Maybe I should stop smoking so much hash."

They never talked about it again. Audrey forgot all about it for the most part; the conversation had taken place shortly after her release from Stillwater, just before her friendship with Maggie began to fall apart.

When she smashed Clint Jones's head in, Audrey hadn't dissociated. She'd been firmly in that moment, aware of what she was doing, making certain he wasn't going to get back up. She thought she'd been saving Maggie, but Clint had already done his damage. She couldn't stop wondering if his death had made that damage even worse.

Maybe she liked thinking she was to blame for the suffering of others, like some kind of twisted martyr complex. Or maybe it was a bizarre kind of egotism, as Jake liked to point out.

Audrey left the room. It might have been where Maggie slept and dressed, but it didn't feel like her. There didn't seem to be any personal touches—nothing that claimed any kind of ownership.

She was in the kitchen, sitting at the table checking her e-mail on her phone, when Bailey joined her. Audrey put her phone away. Grant had e-mailed her, asking her to call him. She couldn't put him off much longer, but with everything else going on, getting fired—or not—wasn't high on her list. She liked to avoid unpleasant things, and she was just about at her limit with this trip home.

"Where do you want to go?" she asked Bailey.

"Fat Franks is really the only choice," the girl replied. "Unless you want to go to Gracie's."

"Let's avoid Gracie's. Somebody might jump me in the parking lot."

Bailey's eyes widened. "Lish said that her mom said Jake lost it on Matt's ass."

"Jake never loses it," Audrey replied. "And Alisha might have exaggerated a bit in her uncle's favor." If Jake had "lost it," Matt wouldn't be alive.

"Alisha said you beat Matt up. Did you really fight him?"

"Let's talk on the way to lunch," Audrey suggested, moving toward the door. "And yes, I defended myself when Matt attacked me."

"Where did you learn to fight?"

"Stillwater, mostly. Teenage girls are dirty fighters. You probably already knew that."

Bailey laughed. "Yeah."

"Have you ever been hit?" Audrey asked, as they got in her car. She slipped the key into the ignition. "Or been in a fight?" Neve would be so pissed at her right then.

"Not fights. I did punch a girl in the throat once. And..."

Audrey glanced at her as she started the engine. "And what?"

She shook her head. "Nothing."

Shit. There was something, but the girl didn't want to share it. "Isaac doesn't hit you, does he?"

"What? No! Oh my God, he would *never* hurt me. No. *No.*"

"But Maggie did, didn't she?"

Bailey glanced out the window. "I don't want to talk about Maggie."

"Sure, sweetie. I'm sorry." The girl was clearly uncomfortable with and agitated by the topic. Audrey believed what she said was true. She wondered if Gideon hadn't figured out how bad it was.

Protecting your kid from abuse was grounds for murder. So was protecting your girlfriend. If Audrey had to choose, she'd bet on Isaac. A teenager was more likely to act on impulse than an adult. Gideon would more likely push for a divorce, and maybe take legal action, than bash his wife's head in with a rock.

"So, did you go to Alisha's party last night?"

"Yeah. It was a lot of fun. I was so glad there was a place to pee. I hate going in the woods. Silly, huh?"

Audrey laughed, even though it hurt. "No, I don't like to pee in the woods either. We used to have parties at the camp all the time. It was our summer hangout."

"We were looking at the photos. I saw you and Jake and Maggie. There were some of my dad too. It was so funny, you all looked so young and grunge."

"We *were* young and grunge."

"Do you ever regret leaving?"

Audrey pulled out to pass Binky Taylor going twenty miles an hour in his old Chev. "Not really, no. There are people I miss, but I needed to go."

"I'd like to leave. I can't wait for college."

"Where are you going to go?"

"FIT in New York—I hope. I want to work in the fashion industry. I want to design shoes."

"I have a thing for shoes, especially boots. Maybe someday I'll own a pair of yours."

Bailey grinned.

Since Fat Franks was one of the few options for food, it was busy, but they sat outside and ate. Audrey kept the conversation light—music, movies, the lack of things to do in Edgeport when you're under the age of seventy. It wasn't solely to get Bailey comfortable and trusting with her; it was because the steady chatter kept Audrey from noticing just how many people had stared at her since their arrival. Yes, she was a mess and looked like she'd been trapped in an elevator with an NFL player, but she couldn't help but wonder if—and maybe secretly hope that—people recognized her as "that girl that helped kill that guy."

It was not a good realization to discover that part of you had come to like, and even crave, notoriety. That news story had brought her past back to haunt her, but it had also freed her in a way. No more hiding.

They had ice cream for dessert and then got in the car to head back to Edgeport. Audrey waited until they were back in Bailey's driveway to finally ask the question she needed answered.

"Bailey, I need to ask you something."

"Okay."

"Do you have any idea why Isaac is following me?"

Suddenly, she was a deer in the glare of headlights. Her mind clicking and whirling as she sought out a lie was almost audible. Audrey waited.

"He's overly protective," she blurted. "He knows we've been talking and he knows you used to be friends with Maggie. He also heard people saying that maybe you killed Maggie. He's just looking out for me."

Okay, that actually made some semblance of sense. He wanted to keep an eye on her and make sure she didn't do anything that might hurt Bailey. "Maybe you should tell him that for the last fourteen years, Maggie and I didn't like each other much either, and that he doesn't have to freak me out by sitting outside a house I just happen to be in."

The girl blushed. "I'm sorry. I'll tell him to back off. You know, any time Maggie talked about you it was what great friends you used to be, and how you saved her. She told me she'd hurt you once and that she'd do anything to fix it."

"Let's just say that she never actually tried to fix it."

"Figures. That was kind of her move." She smiled. "Thanks for lunch. It was nice hanging out with you."

Audrey returned the smile. "Same here. I'll see you later."

Bailey hopped out of the car. Audrey watched until she was inside with the door closed before backing out onto the main road.

If Maggie had gotten physical with Bailey, Audrey didn't blame Isaac for being protective. The question was, would he kill to protect her? To her, the answer was obvious, but then again, when it came to murder she probably wasn't the best person to ask.

The holiday weekend rolled along without any mishaps. Audrey spent most of it at home with her parents and David, who had come home from New York for the weekend with his boyfriend, Seth. She and David hadn't been home together twice in the same week since before she left for Stanford.

"I wish Matt Jones wasn't in jail so I could fuck him up," he told Audrey when their mother wasn't in earshot. They were at the table, having tea and biscuits slathered in molasses while Seth took a shower. He'd made a fuss over her face just like everyone else, but the swelling had gone down pretty quickly and the bruises were fading. She could cover them with the right application of makeup—which she did if she was leaving the house, simply because she was tired of having people tell her how awful she looked.

"I'm glad he's in jail," she replied. "He needs to get some psychological help."

"Seriously? You're all empathetic toward him now? Or are you buying into his whole 'you ruined my life' bullshit? 'Cause that stuff's old. That would be like me telling Dad his drinking is the reason I can't form lasting relationships."

Audrey smiled. "I thought the fact that you're a fickle queen was the reason you can't form lasting relationships."

He made a face at her. God, he really did have incredible eyebrows. "You told me once that we could only blame Dad so long. That eventually, we have to become adults and take responsibility for how we go forward in life."

"Wow." She poured molasses on half a biscuit. "I'm so incredibly smart. That's good advice."

"So you can't carry any guilt for how Matt Jones turned out."

"But self-flagellation is so fun." When he didn't laugh, she sighed. "I know, Dave. I'm working on it."

"Good." He eyed the last biscuit. She could see him struggling with whether or not to eat it.

"Oh for God's sake," she said, pushing the plate toward him. "Take it. It's not going to affect your waistline that much. You're worse than a teenage girl." That made her think of Bailey and Alisha. They seemed like fairly well-adjusted kids—Alisha especially, which was odd because her mother had little to no self-worth. It had to be Jake's influence, which was even odder, because in the grand scheme, he wasn't a great role model.

But then who was *she* to judge?

Her brother reached for the molasses. "Have they found Maggie's killer yet?"

"Not yet. I've tried to help, but Neve's told me to stay out of it." So far, she'd done just that if she didn't count talking to Bailey and Alisha and reading Matt's prison file.

"Yeah, well, even if you weren't a person of interest, you still have way too much of a personal connection to the case." He arched one of those perfect brows. "Oh, look who's the smart one now."

Audrey smiled, then it faded. "I just want it to be over. I want to go home."

"That didn't sound so convincing, Auddie. Has Edgeport finally got you in its fiendish grasp?"

She shrugged.

David's handsome face brightened. "Oh my God, you slept with Jake."

Audrey shushed him. This was not a conversation she wanted their mother, who was in the next room, to hear.

Her brother leaned forward, resting his forearm on the table. Nosy delight shone in his eyes. "Details. Now."

"No. You are not living vicariously through me."

He pouted. "At least tell me that he was as good as I've always suspected." She raised a brow but remained silent. David clapped. "He was!"

Laughing, Audrey shook her head at him. "You're a nut. Seth seems like a love." Not the most subtle of switches, but it would do.

Pink filled David's cheeks. "He is. He really is."

"I'm happy for you."

"I want to be happy for you too. If you finally have Jake Tripp in your clutches, why are you in such a hurry to get back to L.A.?"

Wasn't it obvious? "That's where my life is."

His face took on a sympathetic expression as his hand touched hers. "But, sweetie, everyone you love is on the opposite side of the country—and the opposite end."

"And that's probably for the best. For all of us." Funny, that didn't have the bite she thought it should. "I don't want to live here."

"Why?"

"Because I don't like who I am when I'm here." She gestured to her face. "I got into a fight, Dave. I haven't been in a real fight since I left for college."

"To be fair, what you did to Maggie wasn't a real fight. She didn't even try to fight back."

"Don't remind me. I don't want to be that girl again."

"How about you just be the woman that girl grew up to be

instead of the person you pretend to be in L.A.? I've seen you out there, babe. The only time I felt like I truly saw you was when I watched you defend a girl who went to prison for killing her rapist."

"I love my job, and L.A. is where my job is. I won't give that up—not for anyone."

He just looked at her—like he was disappointed. She hated that look. "You're going to die alone, and your fifty cats are going to eat your corpse."

"I'm going to will the cats to you."

The conversation was put to an end when Seth entered the kitchen. David's face lit up at the sight of him, and Audrey didn't blame him. The guy was gorgeous, twenty-five, and built like an underwear model.

"Oh my God, are those biscuits?" he asked, pointing at what was left on David's plate.

"There's more," Audrey said. "Do you want some?"

"I shouldn't, but yes, please. Just point me in the right direction."

A few moments later he joined them at the table with his own plate and a cup of hot tea. Audrey asked him what he did, and he replied that he worked in the theater. He did wigs and makeup on Broadway. She was fascinated—who wouldn't be?—and she listened as he told her stories about some of the productions and the actors involved. The stories ranged from silly to touching to downright ludicrous, but they took her mind off the fact that there was a killer somewhere in their tiny little village.

John arrived home an hour later. David and Seth helped Anne in the kitchen while Audrey assisted her father in setting up the picnic tables and canopies outside. They wheeled out the massive grill he'd bought the year before when they went on sale, and got it ready to cook.

Jessica and Greg and the girls were the first to arrive. David fussed over Olivia while Audrey and Jess helped their mother make salads. Their new and uncertain truce had held so far, though there was still tension between the sisters. Still, it was better than fighting all the time. Greg took Isabelle outside to "help Grampie" finish setting up while Seth proved himself a love by making iced tea and lemonade.

Audrey kept an eye on her mother, who seemed to be feeling much better and like her old self. There was something going on with her, though, and Audrey was beginning to worry about it. She and Jess had talked to David about it earlier when the three of them managed a moment alone, and he was as much in the dark as they were, but trying to get their mother and father cornered was like trying to herd cats.

Some of their guests began arriving around three. Mostly aunts, uncles, and cousins from both sides of the family. Her father had invited Binky Taylor to one of their barbecues twenty-three years ago and the old guy kept showing up every year after. Audrey was surprised to see Jake's truck pull into the yard, and he and Alisha get out.

"Figured you might want someone here just for you," came her father's voice from just over her shoulder. She glanced at him, surprised.

"You invited Jake?"

He shrugged. He'd already opened a beer, she noticed. "He's not so bad. Plus, maybe he'll give us good seats at the show tonight."

Audrey laughed, then walked toward Jake and his niece. Alisha was carrying a large covered bowl. "Great-Gran's potato salad," she announced proudly.

"The one with mustard?" Audrey glanced at Jake. He nodded. "Go put it on the table over there."

Jake joined her. He wore jeans that had been rolled up over his ankles, a white T-shirt, his ever-present suspenders, a black fedora, little round sunglasses, and flip-flops. It should have been a ridiculous combination, but he made it work somehow. She knew the flip-flops wouldn't last long anyway. He had a plastic container in his hand. "What's that?" she asked.

"Brownies," he replied smugly. "With fudge icing."

She stared at him. Another of Gracie's recipes, but it was more than that. "Are you trying to get on my mother's good side?"

"Her name was at the top of the list."

Gracie kept all of her recipes—the ones she hadn't stored in her head—in a book. On the page for each recipe, she kept a list of locals who had let her know how much they liked that dish, so that she could make it for them if the occasion arose. Her mother had talked about Gracie's brownies for years, and sometimes Audrey would be sent home with a pan of them just for Anne.

"Hey, Mom!" she called as they approached. "Jake brought Gracie's fudge brownies."

Her mother's face lit up. "She left you the recipe?"

He nodded and offered her the container. "She wrote in her book that you liked them. I hope they're as good as when she made them."

Anne smiled at him. "Thank you, Jake. That was very thoughtful of you. Do you know everyone?" She drew him away to make introductions to the remaining family and Seth.

David appeared beside her. "Well, he's in. It takes confidence to own an outfit like that."

"He's not lacking in confidence," Audrey drawled.

"No, he is not. Who would have thought he'd turn out so damn pretty?"

"Not you, apparently."

He slanted a shrewd glance in her direction. "I'm just glad

you've finally done something about it. Carrying a crush into your thirties is so chick-lit."

Audrey wasn't quite certain what that even meant. She didn't ask. She just watched as her father offered Jake a beer from the cooler and took another one for himself. And so the July Fourth Drunk was officially under way. Fabulous. She couldn't wait to see him staggering around the beach later singing disco songs at the top of his lungs.

"Seth made white sangria," her brother said. "Want one?"

"Yes, I do."

He poured the fruit-filled drink into three plastic cups and gave her one, taking one for himself and another for their older sister, who had wandered over to them.

"So," she said, looking at Audrey over her cup. "Jake Tripp, huh?"

She'd roll her eyes if this new peace with Jess wasn't so delicate. Her sister was trying, and the least she could do was try too. "I've been told that carrying a crush into my thirties is very chick-lit."

Jessica laughed and turned to David. "I think I read that one." And then, to Audrey, "He seems to have a good relationship with his niece."

"Yeah."

"Bet she doesn't think as much of Lincoln."

"Didn't you date him once?"

"Don't remind me. God, he was so...sloppy."

Audrey choked on a mouthful of sangria. But she was her father's daughter, and she managed to swallow without spilling a drop of alcohol. Jessica smiled—rather smugly—and David laughed.

Isabelle played with some of the other kids like they were old friends—even Alisha had found someone she knew. As Audrey looked around, everyone was talking and laughing. Even Seth, who was a stranger, was engaged. There were faces that looked familiar, though she hadn't seen them in years. Alisha and Jake knew her family better than she did. That was the price of living somewhere else, of having dreams that were bigger than Edgeport could sustain. She'd missed birthdays and Christmases. Her own nieces were practically strangers. How long before Audrey saw them again?

At seventeen she would have dug a fucking tunnel to get out of that place. Couldn't wait to run away to someplace bigger where no one knew who she was or what she'd done. Where no one judged her.

But there was no one who loved her either.

At that moment, Jake lifted his head and looked at her. He reached up and took off his sunglasses, so she could see the question in his gaze. Audrey forced a smile. Instinct told her to run away like she always did. *Just turn around and keep going until you hit water.*

She took a step toward him. Then another. Her heart clamored in her chest. It didn't want to do this. Didn't want to ask for everything she'd walked away from before. Just a few more steps.

He met her halfway. "Having some trouble, Aud?"

She nodded. "A little, yeah."

"Want some help?"

"Would you mind?"

He put on his sunglasses and offered her his hand, cheek creasing with a lopsided smile. She entwined her fingers with his. He drew her toward her family, all of whom were happy to let her in.

CHAPTER NINETEEN

The crowd for the evening's fireworks was insane. Way bigger than Audrey remembered as a kid. Jake had set up parking in a field not far from his house and had vans driving people out to the beach from there. Some people walked back the road rather than take advantage of the ride. Others came via the beach on four-wheelers and handmade contraptions for checking weirs and back-road adventuring. The beach—normally practically empty in the summer at night because of the cold water—was littered with blankets and folding chairs, milk crates, and other inventive objects that could double as chairs.

Jake had to leave the barbecue earlier to go oversee things with the volunteer firemen who were taking care of the fireworks, so Audrey took Alisha with her. They stopped and picked up Bailey as well. Jake told her to go ahead and drive all the way down to the camp and park her car there; that way there'd be a vehicle nearby if they needed one.

When they pulled up next to the camp, Isaac was waiting. He was a handsome kid, with blondish hair that was a little long, and a brooding set to his shoulders. No wonder Bailey liked him—he was the archetypal bad boy.

He watched Audrey as she got out of the car. She recognized

something in that gaze. He was a kid who had been in trouble, and he had the attitude to go with it. Bailey ran over to him and grabbed his arm. "Say hi to Audrey."

Audrey raised her hand in greeting, offering a tentative smile. Isaac didn't look impressed. "Hi."

He lifted his chin. "Hey."

"I'm going to get a couple of chairs out of the camp," Alisha announced. "You want some, Audrey?"

"Yeah, I'll get one."

It wasn't totally dark yet, but the trees and shadows made seeing difficult. Alisha used the flashlight app on her phone so Audrey could see to find the key and unlock the door. Inside, she let the kids go and find the chairs, since they would have had them at the party a couple of nights before and knew where they were. As she stood in the darkening gloom, thinking about the nights spent in that building, her gaze fell on the floor planks where an old camp stove had once sat—long before she ever stepped foot in the place. One afternoon, while their other friends were swimming at the beach, Audrey and Maggie had discovered one of those floorboards was loose. They never told anyone else about it, and used it as a private storage space for pot and booze, or even tampons. Once their friendship fell apart, Audrey stopped using it. She hadn't thought of it since.

Curious, Audrey moved toward the spot. Using her own phone for light, she crouched down and pried up the plank with her fingers, trying to avoid splinters. Beneath it, in the small cache, wrapped in a clear plastic bag, was a leather-bound journal. She picked it up and unwrapped it, opened it to the first page.

Maggie Jones was written inside the cover.

Audrey's breath caught. Trembling fingers opened it to the first page. No date, but all she had to do was read the first line to know the book was important. *Dear Audrey,* it read.

"What's that?" Alisha asked. She was little more than a shadow near the door, holding a white plastic chair.

"It's an old diary," Audrey replied vacantly as she stood up. "Of Maggie's."

"That's weird. If you see Uncle Jake, will you tell him we'll leave the chairs near the front steps when we leave?"

"Sure thing." Distracted, she barely glanced up. "Enjoy the fireworks."

The three teens left. For a moment, Audrey thought she felt Isaac's eyes on her, but when she looked up, she was alone. She put the journal into the messenger bag slung across her torso. It had some water, a couple of beers, and some snacks in it as well as a sweater in case it got cool.

She didn't care if the book gave her insight into Maggie's death. She was honestly more intrigued by the insight it might give her into Maggie herself. As someone with a keen interest in the human mind, the opportunity to study a primary source that was candid and unfiltered was intriguing and exciting. And if she was completely honest, there was something very ego-stroking that Maggie had written at least one of her entries as an open letter to her.

Audrey grabbed an old folding chair that had seen better days, its plastic canvas frayed in spots, and went outside, locking the door behind her and replacing the key. Her phone buzzed—a text from David letting her know where on the beach they had set up. She walked in that direction, taking a path through a bit of forest to get to the beach, where several families had already spread their blankets and placed their chairs and coolers.

She stopped, there on the edge of the sand, and looked back over her shoulder. It was already dark enough that people were little more than blobs of shadow, unless illuminated by lanterns or cell phones. She would just be another shadow to everyone else, but she couldn't shake the feeling that she was being watched.

Her phone buzzed in her hand. She jumped. Then, cursing, looked down. It was from Jake. *People coming over after show. Come by.* She texted back that she would be there, and if he was lucky she might stay. Smiling, she slipped her phone into her pocket and set off toward where her family had made camp. She didn't look back.

Even though she wanted to.

Next to the fireworks of Audrey's youth, the show that night was like comparing Cirque du Soleil to a kid doing cartwheels in their backyard. There just wasn't any contest. The sky over the beach had been alight with every shade imaginable, plumes of pink and blue, purple and green, gold and red. There'd been starbursts and trails of light like weeping willows between bursts of sizzling sparkles and whistling rockets. It must have cost Jake a fortune. He told her that Gracie had loved fireworks and that was why he did it, but it wasn't all about sentimentality. It was PR. Everyone on that beach was going to leave thinking how great it was that Jake did this every year—and how good he was to the town. He was the Lord of Edgeport. What did that make her? His consort? Harlot?

The show lasted for half an hour. Afterward, Audrey helped pack up her parents' belongings and carried them to the vans that were lined up to take people back to their cars. They took their time, knowing they'd only have to wait in the rush. Jessica had Olivia in a carrier strapped over her chest. David carried a sleeping Isabelle while Seth and Greg carried their blankets, bags, and chairs.

"Jake's having people in, if you're interested," Audrey told them.

"We have to get home," Jess replied. "I'm beat." She looked moody. Maybe it was the crowd, maybe it was Audrey, maybe it was Mercury in retrograde. Audrey wasn't going to waste time guessing. Their peace, though tentative, felt good and she didn't want to jeopardize it.

"We'll come," David said. "We'll meet you there."

Once they were on one of the vans, Audrey walked back to the camp and put her chair by the ones the kids had already returned. They had probably walked out to the house, or all crammed up on Isaac's four-wheeler. She got into her car and began the slow and tedious trip out to Jake's, sandwiched between two of the vans. There were so many people walking along the road that they were a hazard—especially the drunk ones.

Jake was already there and had a full house by the time she arrived. He'd left the truck at home and used an ATV instead. Smart.

Inside the house, she said hello to the people gathered in the kitchen and took the overnight bag she'd brought with her upstairs to Jake's room. She'd put Maggie's journal in that bag because it locked. Paranoid—she preferred extra cautious—she shoved the small suitcase under the bed and set her messenger bag on a nearby armchair.

Downstairs, she found Jake in the kitchen mixing a drink. There were a few people sitting in the living room, and a few around the kitchen table, but the crowd had seriously thinned out.

"Where is everyone?" she asked.

"Fire pit," he replied, handing her a rum and Coke. "Lincoln's getting the guitars out. You going to join us?"

She hadn't heard him play in years. There'd been a time when sitting around the fire singing and laughing had been a weekly occurrence—one that she had enjoyed, because she and Jake would sing together. And Maggie. There was always Maggie, singing and dancing and flirting with all the boys—and some of the girls. It would be weird sitting out there without her nearby, just like it had been strange to watch the fireworks without her constant chatter in Audrey's ear. BC—Before Clint—Maggie's face had been alight with joy at every burst of color. That joy had dimmed considerably by the last fireworks they watched together.

"Yeah," she said. "I'd like that."

Guests gathered thickly around the fire, but it was a big fire and there was room for everyone, even though some spilled onto the grass. It had been updated since her last visit as well. Now it was a large rock circle on top of a flagstone base. Citronella lanterns hung from posts around the perimeter of the patio. People sat on the ground, in chairs, and on benches. Some stood around the outer edge. It was a warm night, and there weren't any neighbors to upset. This kind of thing would just never happen in L.A.

Jake and Lincoln sat where they always had—on two large rocks set a couple of feet back from the fire. Lincoln had a guitar on his lap and was tuning it as Jake opened the case beside him and took out a familiar black acoustic. His father had given him that guitar when he turned thirteen. Audrey remembered, because she'd been at his birthday party. As far as she knew, it was the only gift Brody Tripp ever gave his younger son. Jake had treasured it—especially after his father died.

Jake gestured for her to sit in the empty chair next to him. A few people spoke to her as she sat. She smiled at the others. Not one of them asked about the bruises on her face—most of which she'd covered with makeup—and no one looked at her as though they were weighing the sins on her soul. It was nice.

David and Seth sat on the opposite side of the fire in the second row. Her brother looked comfortable and happy. That alone was reason to smile. Alisha plopping down on the ground beside her was another. She was becoming pretty attached to the girl. "Where're Bailey and Isaac?" she asked.

"They're on the porch. I think they're having a fight."

"What about?"

She shrugged. "Bee says he's been really clingy lately—and jealous. I don't know. She doesn't tell me much about their relationship."

And that stung—Audrey could tell. There had been a time when she'd been jealous of all the attention Maggie got from boys, back when she confused drama with romance, and sex with being worthy.

"Where's you guitar, Lish?" Jake asked.

"In the house. Why?"

He plucked a string, tuned, and then strummed it again. "Go get it. You can play with us."

The kid looked as though he'd offered her the world on a platter. She jumped up and ran toward the house.

"She spends too much time worrying about her love life and not enough time actually having a life," Jake commented. "Sometimes she reminds me of you—I can practically see the restlessness coming off her in waves."

"Really? I think she's like you—she's got this place in her bones. If she goes away, she won't stay gone for long."

"I'm going to hope you're right. Whatever she wants, I'm going to make sure she gets a chance at it."

"Are we going to play or what?" Lincoln demanded, taking a swig from a bottle of beer. He winked at Audrey. She laughed. He was such a dog—it was almost cute.

On cue, Jake began to play "Take It Easy" by the Eagles, drawing hoots and hollers from their audience. It was practically the anthem of summertime parties in that hemisphere. At that moment there was probably some kid in rural Canada, sitting around a fire or in a gravel pit, singing that song at the top of his or her lungs, thinking it was written just for them, long before they were ever born.

They sounded good together, the Tripp brothers. A verse in, a female voice joined them. It was Yancy. She sat down next to Lincoln, her sweet voice mixing perfectly with theirs. Audrey tried to imagine herself, David, and Jess singing together like this and just couldn't do it. If it was movie dialogue, they might stand a chance. It was a family trait to be able to quote a movie after only one viewing and retain those words for years to come. Their parents did it as well. Sometimes it was awful, but it was fun, and it was their thing. Or at least it had been, a long time ago.

Alisha returned with her guitar, drawing enthusiastic applause when she sat down and jumped right into the song with her mother and uncles. Audrey cheered her on before taking a drink from her glass. Eventually, she joined in and sang along—like almost everyone else gathered around the fire. For the first time since she came home, she felt lighthearted. Like she was part of something, not a stranger looking in. A much-needed reminder that Edgeport wasn't always the hell she'd made it.

Eventually, her drink ran dry, and Audrey got up to fix herself another. When she walked into the kitchen, she found Bailey sitting at the table. "Why aren't you outside?" she asked.

Bailey smiled, but it looked forced. "I'll be out in a minute."

Audrey glanced around as she opened the bottle of rum on the sideboard. "Where's Isaac?"

"Bathroom." The girl rose from her chair and came to stand beside her. She handed Audrey the Diet Coke. "Can I talk to you?" Her voice was low.

"Sure. What's up?"

"Isaac didn't hurt Maggie. I need you to know that."

Audrey nodded, not at all convinced. In fact, Bailey's pale cheeks and the circles under her eyes made her suspect Isaac had been very much involved in Maggie's death.

"You know Neve—Detective Graham—can protect you."

Bailey frowned. "I don't need to be protected. Not like she protected you from Matt Jones, is it? You should be more careful, Audrey."

Her brows rose. "That sounds vaguely threatening."

The girl shook her head. "I just don't want what happened to Maggie to happen to you."

"Who are you afraid of, Bailey?"

The girl never had a chance to answer, because suddenly Isaac was there. "Want to go outside?" he asked his girlfriend.

Bailey nodded. "Yeah. Lish is playing her guitar." She cast a pleading glance at Audrey as she walked away to join the boy. Audrey watched them walk outside, her chest tight. Was Bailey afraid of Isaac, or afraid *for* him? Regardless, the girl should know better than to warn her off. It only made Audrey more determined to find the truth.

Armed with a fresh drink for both herself and Jake, Audrey went back outside. Bailey and Isaac stood on the fringe of the crowd as she took her place between Jake and Alisha. For the moment, she pushed her conversation with Bailey to the back of her mind and let herself enjoy the party. There would be time for questions and looking for answers later. Where was Neve when she needed her?

They sat around the fire singing for hours. Four rum and Cokes later, when Audrey was pleasantly tipsy, wrapped up in a blanket, Jake declared the gathering over. Audrey sipped at another drink as he said good-bye to the last guests, waving at those who said good night to her.

Finally, he came back. He sat down and glanced at the dying fire. "That was a good night."

"I forgot how musical you Tripps are," she said. "I always envied that."

"You can sing."

She made a face. "Some stuff, sure. But you can actually *make* music. That's pretty fucking cool."

He grinned. "You're drunk."

"No, I'm not. I am, however, feeling very relaxed." She'd always had a high tolerance for alcohol, thanks to a long ancestral line of alcoholics.

Jake reached out and took her drink as he stood. "How relaxed?" He held out his hand.

"*Very*," she reiterated, letting him pull her to her feet. "So, if you're thinking of taking advantage of me, I suggest you do just that."

They walked into the house to find Alisha, Bailey, and Isaac at the kitchen table finishing off a bowl of chips.

"Thought you two took off hours ago," Jake commented.

Bailey smiled at him—a little too brightly. Audrey cocked her head to one side and watched the girl's body language, her expression, and the movement of her eyes. She was nervous. No, more than that—agitated.

And Isaac was tense. His hands were fists, his back poker straight. Only Alisha seemed comfortable, but also confused. Poor thing really was a third wheel.

"We wanted to listen to Lish play," Bailey said. "We're leaving now. Thanks for letting us come over."

"Anytime," Jake said, but in a tone that warned not to push the validity of the invitation. "You can take Alisha home?"

"Sure." Isaac was already on his feet. "Thanks again, Jake. C'mon, Lish."

"Good night," Bailey chirped, following after him. The boy didn't even look at Audrey on his way out—an obvious snub.

"Bye, Bailey," Audrey replied. "See you later, Lish. Good night, Isaac."

He nodded. He was a cold little bastard.

The car—not the four-wheeler as she thought—had just pulled out of the drive when Jake said, "That boy's going to pop someday. I hope Alisha isn't around when he does."

"Bailey said some strange things to me tonight. I think Isaac was involved in Maggie's murder. Hell, I think he might have been the one to kill her."

Jake frowned as he dumped a bowl of chip crumbs in the trash. "What did she say?"

"She warned me off. Said she didn't want to see me get hurt."

"Fuck."

"My thoughts exactly. I'll tell Neve about it in the morning. Meanwhile, come upstairs. There's something I want to show you."

"It's not you naked, is it?" he asked with an expression of exaggerated remorse.

She grinned. "There's something *else* I want to show you."

Jake locked up, leaving the brunt of the mess to clean up in the morning. Together, they went upstairs to his bedroom. Audrey went to retrieve her overnight bag and found it partially sticking out from under the bed skirt. She frowned as she crouched. She had pushed it all the way under when she first arrived.

What was that on the carpet next to it? She reached down and picked up a pen. "The Beharrie Centre" was printed on the side of it.

She glanced up at her messenger bag on the chair in the corner. It was buckled up wrong. When she set it there, the pen had been inside it. She unbuckled the bag and reached in where she normally kept her pen—it was empty. She looked over her shoulder at Jake.

"What?" he asked, pulling his T-shirt over his head.

"I think someone went through my bag." And tried to get into her suitcase. Fortunately, she had locked it.

He balled the cotton in his hands. "Why would someone go through your bag?"

"I'm not sure. Nosiness, maybe?"

The shirt was dumped into the wooden hamper by the closet. "I'm not fucking thrilled at the idea of someone letting themselves into my bedroom. Are you sure?"

She held up the pen. "This was in my bag. I just found it on the floor. It's not buckled the way I normally do."

"Is anything missing?"

She checked. "No. Just the pen." Maybe she was paranoid, but it looked like some things had been moved around a bit—nothing completely in the wrong spot. Whoever had searched it was cautious.

"What do you have that someone would risk getting caught looking for it? And who knows you have it?"

Audrey looked up at him, pen clutched tight in her fist. It couldn't be, could it? But it was the only thing that made sense. "A journal with Maggie's name on it, and Alisha, Bailey, and Isaac."

Jake ran a hand through his hair. "Fuck." He reached for his cell phone and swiped the screen before putting it to his ear. A few seconds later he said, "Are you home? Are you alone? Did you see either Bailey or Isaac snooping around the house tonight...? Are you sure?...Okay...No, nothing's wrong...I'll see you tomorrow...Good night." He hung up. "Lish doesn't know anything."

"No, Bailey or Isaac would be careful not to include her." She sat down on the bed. "When I came into the house to mix drinks earlier, Bailey was in the kitchen. She said Isaac was in the bathroom, but I don't remember hearing a flush. She was acting strangely—she asked me to be careful, to stop looking into Maggie's murder."

Jake sat down beside her, his expression grim. "We'd better take a look at this journal."

Dear Audrey,

I don't want to tell you this, but I've done something awful. Something terrible, and I can't fix it.

No one can.

CHAPTER TWENTY

The whole thing's a letter to you?" Jake asked, pouring her a cup of coffee. "Every entry?"

Audrey was at the kitchen table, Maggie's journal open before her. They'd looked at it briefly last night, but Audrey wanted to be fully awake and totally sober before giving it a serious read.

"It looks like. I've only read the first few pages. It looks like she started keeping the journal when she was in the hospital after Clint's death." Audrey had gone straight to Stillwater, but Maggie had been put in a juvenile psych ward for a few months. The court had figured she needed help healing from what Clint had done to her and, in turn, what she had done to Clint.

She flipped through some pages. The paper crackled beneath her fingers. She loved that feeling of paper that had been written on, pressed hard by a pen. Maggie used several different colors of ink over the years. Audrey stopped at an entry where the handwriting looked different and read aloud, "Dear Audrey, you ignored me tonight. At the camp you sat there and talked to Neve and Yancy. You even hung out with Lincoln, whose only interest in you is a fuck. You'd picked them over me—your supposed best friend. I *lied* for you, you bitch, and this is how you repay me? I could make your life miserable, you know. I *should* make your life miserable, maybe then you'd feel as awful as me."

Jake pursed his lips. "A little light reading, then."

"Look at how the cursive is different on this entry, though. It's like it was written by someone else, but it *is* her writing. It must be one of her alters. It's fascinating."

He sat down and picked up a piece of bacon from his plate. "She's not a case study, Aud. She wrote this to you. Even if she never sent it, she meant it. That's not fascinating; that's hate."

"Obsession, actually," she told him bluntly. "Using my name at the bar, this diary, it's all indicative that Maggie used me as a focus for a lot of her shame and anger. Even love. There are some entries in here that break my heart, and others that chill it. Jake, she had a baby—Clint's baby. There's even a photo of her in here. She named her Audrey. I have to look at this professionally and distance myself from it, otherwise it's too awful. So, for now, she's a case study." And it was awful. And strange. And disturbing. For Maggie, it always seemed to come back to Audrey.

Fitting, because for Audrey, it always seemed to come back to Maggie.

Jake shook his head. "What would she have been when she gave birth, thirteen? Fuck. I'm so glad you killed that bastard. You think there's going to be something in there about who killed her?"

"I'm not sure. I looked at the last page, and it was written the night she died, but there's nothing there other than how upset she was that I pushed her. The letter before says that Gideon was going to divorce her. I think the best course is to start at the beginning and read the whole thing."

"You sure you're up for that?" There was nothing but concern in his voice.

"I have to be. I knew Maggie better than anybody. I realize now that's not saying much, but I stand a better chance of reading between these lines than anyone else." She reached for her mug. "If I find anything that might point to her killer I'll turn the journal over to Neve." She should turn it over anyway, but she wasn't going to do that until she read it herself. This was her only chance to really look inside Maggie's mind and find out just how much of that chaos and instability was her fault.

"Even if there's stuff in there you don't want her to read?"

Audrey shrugged. "It hardly matters now. I served my time for what we did to Clint."

"She probably wrote about me and her."

Audrey's coffee turned sour in her mouth. "Yeah, I know."

His expression was neutral—carefully so. "I don't imagine it will paint a flattering picture of either Maggie or me."

"It was a long time ago."

He just looked at her.

"It is what it is, Jake. What do you want me to say? I am an adult, you know. I can handle it."

"I know you can handle it. I just don't want to hear about it. I don't want to know."

So really, what he was saying was that he didn't know if *he* could handle it. "You won't." She gave him a slight smile and closed the journal. "I'll read it later."

"You don't have to stop reading it for me."

"I'm not. I stopped reading because I want to have breakfast. With you."

He was scowling now. "There might be something in there that clears your name and gives Neve someone else to look at."

"She has other suspects." Audrey studied him. He was coiled as tight as a snake. "Is there anything I could say or do that will avoid an argument right now? Or are you spoiling for one? We're about due, aren't we?"

Jake looked down at the table. "I hate this."

"This what?" she asked. "The murder investigation? Or us?" It was too good to be true, wasn't it? Had either of them expected that reality would actually live up to years of fantasy? Neither of them was perfect, and neither of them was exactly great relationship material. Plus, as soon as this was over, she was going back to L.A., and it didn't matter that it didn't hold the same appeal as it did even a few days ago.

"The investigation," he replied, lifting his gaze to hers. "I have no problem with us, except that you're going to run away again."

"And you'll let me because you're too proud to chase."

"Yes."

It wasn't an ultimatum, because she knew he didn't want to make her choose. Audrey picked up the journal and stood. Her bags were already by the door—she'd placed them there earlier. "I'm going to go."

"Running already?" He barely glanced over his shoulder. "That's quick. Even for you."

"I'm not running anywhere," she replied, slipping the messenger bag over her shoulder. "You know where to find me."

The screen door rattled as it snapped shut behind her. He didn't come after her—she didn't expect him to. She tossed her luggage into the Mini and climbed in, digging the keys out of her bag. She started the engine and reached over to open the glove compartment to get her sunglasses.

They weren't on top where she'd left them but underneath the insurance and rental paperwork. The little bastard had gone through the car as well.

If trading digs with Jake hadn't pissed her off enough, this did. It had to have been Isaac. She couldn't think of anyone else who would have reason to go through her car and her bag. He'd been there when she found the journal and stupidly announced what it was.

So had Bailey and Alisha. Bailey could have been trying to protect her boyfriend, and Alisha...Well, maybe she was trying to protect Lincoln. Maybe Jake was just trying to protect Lincoln. Maybe that's why he'd decided to sleep with her and get close to her, so he could see how close she came to finding out about his brother.

Audrey put on her sunglasses and backed out of the driveway. It could have easily been Jake who went through her things, but he wouldn't have dropped a pen, or forgotten where her sunglasses had been. No, this was a kid. A kid trying to be sneaky and careful, but nervous enough that he—or she—forgot the exact placement of things and hadn't noticed a pen falling to the floor.

Vilifying Jake, or getting pissy at him wasn't going to solve Maggie's murder, and it wasn't going to make leaving any easier. It just made her petty and foolish. They both were.

She fished her phone out of her bag and dialed his number. She wasn't even around the bend from his place yet, and already calling to apologize. Either she'd gone soft, or she'd grown up a bit during this trip.

He picked up on the second ring. "Hello?" His tone was cool, but she thought there was a hopeful edge to it.

"I'm sorry," she said, checking her rear view as she slowed down to talk. There was a dump truck a fair distance behind her, but it was going fast enough to have a dust cloud behind it. She pulled over onto the shoulder of the dirt road.

"Who is this?" Jake asked with mocking gruffness. "I think you have the wrong number."

She laughed. "Yeah, yeah. I know. I've lost my edge."

"I was going to call you. We're too old for bullshit, Aud. Come back to the house. We need to talk—honestly."

Was that anticipation or dread flapping its wings in her gut? "Okay. I just have to let this truck go by." She checked her mirror again. The truck was almost upon her. She watched as it swerved—but not to avoid her.

It was coming right at her. "What the fuck?"

"Aud?" Jake's voice was sharp in her ear. "What's wrong?"

"This dump truck's coming right at me." She put the car in drive and stepped on the gas, but it was too late. Just as she started to move back onto the road, the truck slammed into the rear of the Mini like a sledgehammer hitting a tin can. Audrey screamed, the impact sending the little car toppling. It rolled once. Twice.

Her bag hit her in the face—her suitcase smashed into her arm. The seat belt felt like it crushed her ribs as she hung upside down for what felt like forever before crashing back down.

Her door opened. Hands reached inside, groping. They grabbed her bag and started pulling, dragging the suitcase over her. Then they reached for the messenger bag. Audrey pushed at them, but her head was ringing and her heart pounding so fast she couldn't think. There was blood in her eyes. All she could think about was the journal. She wrapped her arms about the bag and held with all her strength.

"Let go, you fucking bitch!" It was a male voice. Audrey hung on all the tighter. A fist slammed into her face—right where Matt had hit her only days before. She cried out but refused to let go.

And then she heard someone shout, and suddenly the hands fighting her were gone. Something slammed against the side of the car hard enough to rock it. She whimpered, tried to wipe at her eyes to clear her vision. She blinked at the blood, tears diluting it until she saw the world through a pink haze.

Was that a police siren? It couldn't be. There were never any police in Edgeport when you needed them. She fumbled for her seat belt, wet fingers slipping on the latch. She couldn't get it undone.

"Help!" she cried, but it was nothing more than a hoarse rasp. She tugged at the seat-belt strap, still struggling with the buckle.

And then warm hands touched her face. "It's okay, Aud. You're safe. Just be still." It was Jake.

She tried to focus on him, but he was behind a thick red film. She did what he said, though, and went still. "Jake?"

"I'm here, babe. I've got you."

"Take the journal," she said. "Don't let anyone else get it."

"Fuck the journal."

"Please." She tried to turn toward him to give him the bag, but it hurt too much. "Jake, take it. *Please.*"

"Jesus wept." He reached in and grabbed the bag.

Audrey smiled. "Thank you."

And then she tasted blood and everything went black.

The local fire department was volunteer only, but they were trained EMTs and had an ambulance as well as a fire engine. The three who responded immediately to the call were Gideon, Albert Neeley, and Rebecca Pelletier. Gideon took one look at his daughter's boyfriend in the back of Neve's car and turned his bewildered gaze to her.

"Get Audrey out of that car," Neve instructed. "Then we'll talk." She stood back with her father, who had insisted on coming with her. Since she didn't have any other guys in Edgeport at the moment, she let him come, just in case she needed backup. When Jake had called her she didn't know what to expect. "Audrey's in trouble" could have meant almost anything. She had not expected to find her old friend seriously hurt and a seventeen-year-old boy responsible for it. How in the hell had he gotten hold of a dump truck?

To be honest, she'd been surprised to find Isaac alive when she realized what he'd done. Jake had been the first on the scene, and he'd hit the kid hard enough to knock him out but restrained himself from doing further damage. When the first responders arrived, Jake immediately joined them as part of the volunteer department and was now helping to get Audrey out of the car and onto a backboard. Neve waited until they had her secure and on the way to the hospital before she called Anne and John.

"John? It's Neve Graham...I'm fine, sir. There's been an accident...Yes, sir, it's Audrey...She's alive. She's on her way to Down East...No, I don't know how serious...Jake Tripp is with her... We're not sure exactly what happened, but I will meet you later at the hospital and tell you what I can...You're welcome." She hung up and let her phone dangle from her fingers for a few moments. Then she turned to Gideon, who had stayed behind, letting Jake take his place as a first responder in the ambulance with Audrey.

"What happened?" he asked.

Neve pointed at the dump truck. "The name on the key tag in that truck is yours. Did you know Isaac had your keys?"

Gideon shook his head. He was pale and had a smear of blood on his cheek. Audrey's blood. "I've been doing some contract work for the DOT. I hired Isaac to work with me for the summer." He glanced at the boy in the back of her car. "He did this?"

"Yeah."

"Why?" He looked genuinely confused as he stared at the wreckage of Audrey's rental car. It looked like a soda can that had the shit kicked out of it. "It had to have been an accident."

"Jake was on the phone with Audrey at the time of the incident. He said she told him a truck was coming right at her. When he arrived at the scene, Jake said he saw Isaac struggling with Audrey."

Gideon shook his head. "Jake had to be wrong. Isaac was probably trying to help her. Let me talk to him."

Neve put the flat of her hand against his chest when he tried to approach her car. "Sorry, Gideon, but no."

"You can't think he did this on purpose!" He rubbed the back of his neck, his expression contorted into horrified disbelief. "Jesus Christ. Did he do this on purpose?"

"I don't know, but I'm going to find out. Where's Bailey right now?"

"At home. She was still in bed when I left."

"Good. Keep her there. I'll be by to see you later today. Do you need a lift home?"

"No, Jake told me to take his truck."

"Mind giving Dad a lift?"

He nodded absently. "Sure."

Neve turned to her father as Gideon walked away. "Dad, Gideon's going to drive you home."

"What?" He looked offended. "I'm going with you."

"This isn't your case, Dad. It's mine. And Mom will kill us both if I let you come along. I have to take this boy in, and then I'm going to the hospital to question Jake and Audrey—if she's conscious. You need to go home." And then, so only he could hear, "I need you to keep an eye on Gideon, even if it's just for a little bit. He's in shock, and I don't want him wrapping his truck around a tree."

Her father's rugged face lit up at the idea of being useful. "Okay. You'll let me know how this works out?"

She nodded. "Sure."

"Guess I was wrong about the girl."

Admitting he was wrong wasn't something her father did easily. Neve gave him a small smile. "I'll call you later."

He returned the smile, and for the first time in years, Neve thought she saw admiration in her father's gaze. If she lived to be a hundred she would never figure that man out.

She opened the door of her car and climbed in. Isaac was hand-cuffed in the backseat. He was going to have a black eye that he wasn't going to be able to see out of for a few days, and he was covered in blood—some of it his.

"What's your mother's number, kid?" she asked, glancing in the rearview mirror as she started the engine.

He didn't respond.

"It doesn't matter," she said. She'd already informed him of his rights; now she had to take him to county jail in Machias.

"I did it," he said, when they were headed west on the main road.

"You probably shouldn't talk to me," she advised him. If he wanted to confess, that was lovely—made her life easier—but people got very concerned about doing things by the book where juveniles were involved, and Isaac was just at that tricky age where he could be tried as a kid or as an adult.

"I don't care," he replied. "I did it. There's no point in lying anymore. I killed her."

"Audrey's not dead, kid." At least not yet.

"I didn't mean her." Neve met his blank gaze in the mirror. "I mean Maggie. I killed Maggie."

Jake had seen Rusty Harte so drunk he cried, pissed himself, and beat someone senseless—sometimes all in the same night. He'd seen him angry, sad, and more than a little crazy, but the look on his face when he walked into the hospital waiting area scared Jake more than any of those things combined.

It was the face of a man afraid his child was going to die. He took one look at Jake and the blood on his shirt and turned white. Jake jumped out of his chair and went to him, taking his arm and guiding him to one of the ugly chairs. Why did hospitals always seem to pick the absolute most ungodly and uncomfortable upholstery?

"Where's Anne?" Jake asked. Everyone knew she was the emotionally stronger of the two of them, no matter how gruff her husband seemed.

"With the doctor. Jess and David are with her. They said you were with Audrey when she came in, so I wanted to talk to you. What the hell happened, Jake?"

"I don't know, exactly. When I got there, she was still in the car and struggling with Isaac Canning."

The older man frowned. "Caroline's kid?"

Jake nodded. "I grabbed him. He was trying to get Audrey's purse." He looked down at his scraped knuckles and flexed his hand. It was sore. "He put up a fight."

"Little bastard's lucky it was you who came along and not me." There was no bravado in his odd-colored gaze, only hard fact.

"No. He was lucky I was more concerned about her than I was with kicking his ass."

Rusty nodded. "She's been through a lot since coming home, my girl has."

"She won't be back any time soon."

Those same unnerving eyes turned to look at him, so much like Audrey's. "Worried about that, are you?"

Now was not the time for lies and saving face. It took more guts to be honest than to lie. "Yeah. I am."

"Good. I like you better for it."

Jake angled his head. "You remember how much you like me next time I kick you out of Gracie's."

"Don't kick me out and I'll remember it just fine."

He chuckled—a release from the tension of waiting. He'd held Audrey's hand all the way there in the ambulance. Feeling her fingers go slack as she passed out had almost made him puke.

Anne, Jessica, and David entered the waiting area. Jake and Rusty stood. Anne looked drawn and thin—older than she was. Her children stood on either side of her. Jake wondered where Seth and Greg were. At home with the girls, probably, though why it mattered eluded him.

"She's going to be fine," Anne told them. "The doctor says we can see her now."

Rusty clapped him on the back. "Come on, boy."

Jake hung back. He had Audrey's messenger bag—dotted with blood—in his hand. "I'll see her later. You go."

The other three turned and walked away, but Rusty wasn't done with him. "Caring about someone doesn't end with letting them chase their dreams, kid. It's hard and awful, and sometimes it breaks your heart, but if you can't be there for the bad, you don't deserve the good. Understand?"

Jake arched a brow. "Not really, no."

The older man gave him an exasperated look and grabbed his arm. "Smart-ass."

He didn't try to pull free—he wasn't certain he could, despite being thirty years Rusty's junior. Dread hung heavy around his shoulders as he accompanied the family into the emergency room. He hated hospitals. In his family people usually didn't go to one until they were dying, which as a child had made the hospital a thing of fear—those who went in never came out. The one exception was when Yancy gave birth to Alisha.

Jessica asked a passing nurse where Audrey was. The man pointed to one of the curtained-off areas. As they parted the fabric, it was like stepping into a circus tent, tentative and a little fearful of what might lie ahead.

The reality was nothing like he'd imagined. Audrey reclined in the bed, a sheet over her legs. She had some small cuts on her face and arms—a few had been taped closed—but she looked otherwise whole, though still wearing the fading marks of Matt's assault.

Her family rushed her, each desperate to touch her and make sure she was indeed alive and well. Jake stood back, letting them have their time with her. When they were done, they all drew back like a bird opening its wings, two on either side. Suddenly, he had nowhere to hide.

Audrey gave him a soft smile. Did she have any idea just what that simple gesture did to him? Probably not. Hopefully she never would. That was too much power for anyone to have over him.

"Hey," she said. "Thanks for coming when I called."

Jake stepped forward, his legs moving of their own volition. He didn't stop until he was right beside her. He tossed the bag on the floor, took her face in his hands, and kissed her. He didn't care if her family was there, or anyone else for that matter. Fuck his pride.

"I think I'm going to swoon," David said.

Audrey broke the kiss by laughing. Then she groaned. "Don't make me laugh, Davy. It hurts."

"The doctor said you're going to be sore for a while," her mother said, giving Jake an assessing look as he straightened. "Bruised too."

"Better than dead," Audrey quipped. She laced her fingers with Jake's. With her other hand, she touched the raw skin over his knuckles. She didn't ask. He didn't volunteer.

"How long do you have to stay here?" he asked.

"I think they want to do a few more tests to make sure I'm not more banged up than I seem. A few more hours at any rate."

"We'll stay with you," Anne promised. "And then we'll take you home."

Audrey looked up at Jake. "What happened to Isaac?"

"Neve arrested him." He didn't tell her that Isaac had tried to run, or that it had taken more effort than he wanted to admit not to beat the kid to death.

"I knew he was a messed-up kid, but I never thought he'd do something like this. Matt, yes, but not Isaac."

Matt. Fucking bastard. He had unfinished business with Matt. "He popped," he said. "Wish I'd been wrong about that."

She frowned. "I guess." She squeezed his hand. "You don't have to stay. I know you have work to do."

Yes, he did. "It can wait."

"Go," she insisted. "I don't want Alisha to hear it through gossip. She needs to know what really happened before Bailey finds out. Bailey will need her."

She was right. He didn't want to leave her, but he was grateful for the excuse at the same time. "Call me when you get home."

She nodded. "I will."

He kissed her on the forehead, said good-bye to her family, and slipped through the curtain. He called Yancy to come get him and then went to the lobby to wait.

He dialed a second number. He listened to the voice-mail message—the usual banal crap. When the beep came he said simply, "Kenny. We need to talk."

CHAPTER TWENTY-ONE

Audrey was released from the hospital later that day, sore and battered but lucky that her injuries hadn't been worse. She was told to rest and take it easy on herself. She told the doctor that wasn't the issue. "It's other people who aren't taking it easy on me." She'd gotten more battered in the week and a half she'd been home than in her first month at Stillwater. Hell, maybe even her first year. Back then she'd given even better than she got.

Jess and her mother had left a little earlier—Anne wanted to get home and make sure the house was "right" for her, and that there would be her favorites for dinner that night. Telling her not to go through the trouble was futile, and Audrey understood that her mother needed to feel like she was doing something helpful. That left her father and David to take her home. They fussed over her more than her mother ever would have. It was annoying. Infuriating. Wonderful.

"I'm fine," she told them as they drove home. "Dad, you can go more than thirty miles an hour."

"I don't want to jostle you."

"Yeah, well, I'd like to get home before the end of the summer." She shifted on the backseat, trying to get comfortable, but such a position didn't exist. She'd never thought it was truly possible for a body to hurt all over, but it was.

"She's like you when she's not feeling well," David remarked. "Like an old bear."

"Smart-ass, huh?" her father asked. "You must have recovered from your *swoon*."

Audrey laughed. It hurt, but breathing hurt too. The pills helped. "What was up with that anyway?"

David glanced over his shoulder at her as she half-lay, half-sat across the backseat. He looked like he couldn't believe she had to ask. "It was like something out of a movie. He just grabbed you and kissed you, and it was obvious how scared he'd been and how relieved he was. If you didn't feel it then you do not deserve that man. Just saying."

John peered at her in the rearview. "Never thought I'd say it, but Davy's right. That boy's got a serious jones for you, kid."

The Percocet made stoicism impossible. The smile that stretched her lips felt rubbery and ridiculous. "If you say so." He had come running when she called. Jake had always been there for her when she needed him. And she had come home when he needed her, but he'd walked away from her first because other people had decided it was for the best, and she couldn't stand someone thinking they knew what was best for her better than she did. Not her mother, not Gracie, and not Jake.

Their relationship had always been like the tide—a lifetime of drawing each other in and then pushing away. It was poetic—in a pathetic adult-children-of-alcoholics kind of way. Dramatic gestures were easy. It was the little things that were hard.

She closed her eyes—being stoned made her a little motion-sick—and leaned her head back against the seat. They were going a little faster at least. Maybe she'd make it home without puking.

She slept, and didn't wake up until they pulled into the driveway.

There was a welcome party waiting for her when they arrived, and it wasn't Jake. It was Neve. Audrey went into the house and walked past her, straight to the little bathroom at the end of the hall. She used the toilet, washed her hands, and splashed cool water on her face to clear the drug-induced fog. Then, she went back out and sat down at the kitchen table, where a cup of tea was already waiting for her, along with a plate of biscuits and a container of molasses—the cure for any ailment.

Neve's cup and plate were already empty.

"How are you doing?" Neve asked.

Audrey arched a brow—it hurt. "Just dandy. You?"

A small smile. "I've been better. I wanted to apologize to you in person."

"For?" *God, those biscuits look good.* Her stomach growled. She'd left Jake's without finishing her breakfast and hadn't eaten since.

"Everything."

Audrey shrugged as she reached for the biscuits. It hurt. "Okay."

Neve moved the molasses and butter closer to Audrey's plate. "Isaac Canning confessed to Maggie's murder earlier today."

She made a figure eight with her molasses on top of the butter. She wasn't even all that surprised—the drugs had robbed her of that. "Did he happen to say why he felt it necessary to take a stab at killing me before making this confession?"

"He figured if you were hurt you'd stop looking for the real killer. He thought you'd be unconscious, and that he'd be able to get away before the cops arrived."

"He didn't realize that hurting me took suspicion off me? He had to know you'd look at other suspects." She took a bite. Actually, she shoved the entire biscuit half into her mouth and chewed. It kept her from mentioning that he'd also wanted Maggie's journal, which made her wonder what Maggie had written about him.

"I don't think Isaac thought it through quite that far. He said when Jake got there he knew he couldn't escape, and that it would be better if he confessed. He said he couldn't live with the guilt anymore."

That she could understand. Guilt was a hard thing to live with. "Why'd he kill her?"

"He said he Maggie hit Bailey once. Then Maggie tried to break them up. Apparently, she'd threatened to tell Bailey and Gideon that Isaac attacked her."

"Did he?"

"He says he didn't. I called Gideon, but he didn't pick up."

"He was probably comforting Bailey."

"Probably. I'm going to stop by when I leave here. Talk to Bailey and get her version of events. Isaac said Maggie made her threat after they picked her up at Gracie's. When she took off on her own, he followed her. He confronted Maggie on the beach that night and when she told him he wasn't good enough for Bailey, he didn't think, he just picked up the rock and hit her with it."

"You believe him?"

"He knew details about the crime we didn't release."

It seemed oddly anticlimatic. "I guess that's it, then." Why hadn't Isaac mentioned the journal? If he had, Neve would have asked. What secret was he afraid Maggie might have told? The book was still in her bag—which Jake had given back to her at the hospital. There was more going on here, and the answer was probably in that journal.

She wanted to be the one to find it.

"For now," Neve said. "I'm going to want to follow up with you in a day or two, but I don't imagine you're going to jump on a plane anytime soon, are you?"

As soon as she fucking could. "No, I'm not going anywhere." Angeline didn't need her, and the show . . . well, she should probably give Grant a call. Maybe after a handful of Percocet. And a bucket of rum. She smiled at the thought.

"I'm glad you weren't seriously hurt."

Audrey nodded. "Me too." If the next thing out of the other woman's mouth was that she'd only been doing her job, and no hard feelings, she was going to punch her in the mouth and enjoy it.

But Neve merely rose from her chair, thanked Anne for the tea, and said good-bye to the rest of the family before walking out the door.

"I'll give her this," John remarked once her car had passed the window, "she's a damn sight more courteous than that bastard father of hers."

Audrey took a bite of the other half of the biscuit. Suddenly, she wasn't so hungry anymore. "She is. I think I need to lie down for a bit."

"It's time for another one of your pain pills," her father reminded her. "Take it now with some food and then go to sleep."

She eyed him. Was he getting some kind of vicarious drunk from getting her completely wrecked? "Dad, if I take another of those things I won't wake up for a week."

"Your father's right," her mother joined in. "You have to stay on top of the pain or next thing you know it will be on top of you, and that's not good. Take your pill."

Sighing—and feeling like she was four—Audrey took the bottle of pills from her purse, opened it, and fished one out. She took it with some tea, and then finished her second biscuit. None of her clothes were going to fit by the time she returned to L.A., not with the way she'd been eating.

Her mother fussed over her for a bit, detailing the menu for dinner—which was basically a laundry list of her favorites—before finally allowing her to go to her room.

David and Seth had gone out for a drive to Eastrock, but they'd be back for dinner. Audrey had the upstairs completely to herself.

She gingerly staggered—why did they give her enough drugs to take down a horse?—to her room and sank onto the bed with a noise that was caught between a cry and a sigh. She opened her bag and took out Maggie's journal, opening it to the page where she had left off. It was a little beat-up from its tumble in the car but otherwise okay. The bag she tossed on the floor. It was ruined.

She would read until the pills kicked in and knocked her into a drooling, catatonic trance.

Jake had been right—the things Maggie said about him weren't easy to read, and not just because her vision was starting to blur. Mostly, it was insults, but every once in a while she wrote something meant to twist that knife, and Maggie knew just how to twist it.

I know I've said awful things about him, but to be honest, Jake was the only guy I ever slept with who made me come.

A couple of weeks, and a few painkillers, ago, that remark would have stung. It did sting, but it also made her feel sorry for Maggie. Maybe it was a sign that she was finally moving past what Maggie had done to her. Or maybe it was the drugs. Whatever. Audrey had dated a few jerks, but her sex life had been pretty decent. Some guys were better than others, but she almost always got where she needed to go.

Then again, she hadn't been violated by the man she ought to have trusted above all others.

So, when she read the line in another entry, *Audrey, I think I'm falling in love and it scares me*, she wanted to stay awake to find out what happened next. Her eyes, however, had different plans. The lids were so heavy it was a chore to keep them open, and then the words on the page started to shift and blur completely.

Audrey drifted off with Maggie's writing running and smearing across her mind:... *it scares me.* That was strange. The only person Maggie had ever been frightened of was *her.*

*   *   *

"Neve, have you seen Jake?"

Neve turned around, her braids bouncing off her bare shoulders. It was late summer, and humid, but Neve always looked fresh. She never had mascara under her eyes or hair that stuck to her scalp. Her dark skin always glowed, whether she had makeup on or not. "He went toward the old cottage."

"Okay, thanks." Audrey wanted to say good-bye to him before she left. She had to work in the morning, and it was already too late.

"I think he's with Maggie."

She stared at the other girl. They'd been friends once, but Neve's father had been the one to arrest Audrey and Maggie for killing Clint. It had put an end to their friendship. No cop wanted his kid hanging out with a killer. "What do you mean?"

Dark eyes met hers. "I thought I saw her follow him." She shrugged. "Maybe I was wrong."

No. Not Jake. Anyone but Jake. Audrey walked up the path toward the old cottage. The moon was full, casting the woods in silver and black. Audrey knew this place like she knew her own face. Every step was sure, the ground beneath her feet exactly as it should be.

Music from the camp followed her, growing fainter with every step. When she reached the front of the cottage—empty for years—she heard a different sound. She froze. It was Maggie, moaning and crying out—just like she had been the night Audrey found her with Clint and bashed the bastard's brains in.

"You sounded like you liked it," Audrey said, teeth chattering, every inch of her shaking. Clint's body lay at her feet.

Maggie shrugged. "Sometimes I did. I couldn't help it."

Audrey took another step. Her legs shook. Her hands clenched into fists. There was a light inside the cottage—not much of one, but it was there. Maggie liked to see what she was doing.

She climbed the steps, avoiding all the places the wood creaked or groaned. She pushed in on the door as she turned the knob, lifting so the wood wouldn't scrape on the threshold.

Grunts. Groans. Pants. Louder. Faster.

She stood just inside the door and watched them. The cottage was only one room, but they were on the sofa. Maggie was on top, her back to Audrey. Beneath her were denim-clad legs, and dirty bare feet. Long and skinny just like Jake was. She'd know his feet anywhere. He hated shoes—always had since his mother made him wear ones that were too small for him.

Maggie cried out, shuddering, shoulders slumping. Audrey was still a virgin, but she knew that sound—knew how it felt. There hadn't been much privacy in Stillwater, and girls learned to be quiet, or shouted it for all to hear.

"Get off me," Jake said.

Maggie didn't move.

He gave her a shove. She laughed and hit the floor on her feet. He sat up, zipping his jeans. He saw Audrey first. His eyes widened, and for a second, she imagined she saw regret there, but then it was gone. "Aud," he said.

Maggie turned around, hauling her dress on over her head. She didn't look surprised to see Audrey at all. "If you'd shown up a few minutes earlier you could have joined in."

"Shut up, Maggie," Jake said, swinging his feet to the floor and standing. He took a step toward Audrey.

She turned and walked out. She didn't run—she couldn't. She couldn't think, couldn't feel. All she could do was put one foot in front of the other. She had just made it back to the small clearing where the camp was when Maggie caught up with her.

"I did you a favor," Maggie called.

Audrey turned. Was this when the humiliation started? She

walked up to Maggie and looked her in the eye. "How's that?" she asked. Her voice sounded weird in her ears—low and flat.

Maggie tossed her head, all that blond hair spilling around her shoulders. "Well, obviously if he fucked me he couldn't care much about you, could he?"

"No," she replied. "Neither of you do, apparently."

Blue eyes widened. "That's not true. I did this for you, just like I lied for you. I told the police that I killed my father. I did that for you."

"I never asked you to lie. I was going to tell the truth, and you stopped me. And I sure as hell never asked you to fuck the one guy in Edgeport I like." She looked up in time to see Jake standing there, staring at her. Had he heard what she said?

Maggie smiled. "Come on. We both know he pretended I was you. Hell, I pretended he was you."

She shook her head. "What?" She couldn't have heard that right.

Maggie—at one time her best friend, now a stranger—leaned closer. She was smiling that smile she used to get her way, only this time it was bigger, more genuine. "You heard me. I just closed my eyes and pretended you had your fingers inside me."

Audrey's breath caught. Her lips parted, but not a sound came out. Even her mind—that thing that never fucking left her alone—was silent. What was Maggie trying to achieve by saying this shit? Did she mean it, or was she just messing with her like she always did?

The smile faded, and there was the old Maggie. She looked young and vulnerable. "Dree," she whispered, "you're scaring me. Don't you know I love you?"

"Love?" Audrey growled. She'd threatened her, slept with the boy Audrey loved, bullied her and manipulated her every chance she got. She was trying to manipulate her at that moment. "What the fuck do you know about love?" She turned to walk away, but Maggie grabbed her arm. That was when something inside Audrey snapped, just like the night she killed Clint. The only difference now was that she'd had almost four years of Stillwater behind her—where you learned to fight or you got beat.

She whirled around, planting her left foot, and pivoting her right for momentum. She drove her fist into Maggie's jaw. Some girl screamed. Maggie didn't make a sound. She just staggered backward, but then, getting hit wasn't anything new for her.

Jake took a step forward. Both Maggie and Audrey glared at him.

"Fuck off," Audrey said. His eyes widened, but he backed up.

Maggie smiled at her with blood in her teeth. "There's my girl. C'mon, Dree. If we can't fuck, we can at least fight."

It wasn't a fair fight. Maggie was smaller and didn't have the rage behind her that Audrey did—that she always did—but Maggie could take a punch. She had Maggie on her knees before anyone intervened. It was one of Neve's older brothers—Patrick—who got Audrey's arms behind her back and held her until she calmed down. Neve tried to help Maggie to her feet, but the battered girl pushed her away. She'd never liked Neve, and it wasn't because Neve was black—it was because Neve had captured Audrey's attention when she moved to town.

Maggie staggered to her feet, weaving. Jake's brother, Lincoln, caught her when she started to collapse.

Audrey pulled free of Patrick's grasp. Everyone was staring at her, but no one would hold her gaze except Jake. He tried to stop her as she walked by. "Aud."

She yanked her arm back, smearing Maggie's blood across the front of his T-shirt. "Don't fucking touch me," she snarled. "Don't, Jake. Just don't."

He stepped back and let her go. She got into her father's car and backed out onto the gravel road. She drove home on autopilot. It wasn't until she was in her own dooryard, sitting on the same step she'd been sitting on the first time Maggie ever came to her house, that she buried her face in her bloodstained hands and cried.

Audrey woke up to soft little hands combing through her hair. She opened her eyes to find Isabelle next to her on the pillow—so close her sweet face was out of focus.

"You're all black and blue with bits of red," her niece informed her as she stretched out beside her.

"I was in a car accident."

"I know. Mommy told me. She said I could make you feel better."

Audrey smiled. "Your mom was right." And it was nice of Jessica to say it. She and her sister weren't going to be getting pedicures together any time soon, but the truce was nice.

The child nodded, pushing her own hair back from her face. "She usually is. Everyone is downstairs waiting for you. Do you want to get up? It's almost suppertime."

A glance at the clock revealed that it was almost six, an hour verging on late for dinner in these parts. "I should get up then, shouldn't I?" Oh, but she wasn't looking forward to moving. Not at all.

It took some effort, and it hurt, but she managed to haul her ass out of bed and run a brush through her hair. Then she put on some mascara and lip gloss, because she didn't want to look like *complete* hell. Isabelle was very interested in the lip gloss, so Audrey put a sheer coat of a much lighter color on her little lips. She immediately puckered them into duck lips and admired herself in the mirror.

"Do you mind if I take your hand when we go downstairs?" Audrey asked. "I'm afraid I might fall down." Of course, she wasn't afraid, but Isabelle didn't know that. She nodded gravely and took Audrey's hand when they came to the top of the stairs. Those little fingers around hers did her more good than any pain-killer ever could.

When they made it to the bottom, and Audrey had thanked Isabelle for her help, she found Jessica, Greg, and the baby in the living room with David, Seth, Alisha, and Jake. Alisha took one look at her, made a noise that sounded like a sob, and rushed her.

"Lish," Jake cautioned, slowing her down with just his voice. When the girl put her arms around her, it was a gentle embrace. Audrey pressed her cheek against Alisha's hair.

"I'm okay," she whispered. Inside, her heart ached. This girl had come to mean so much in such a short period of time.

Alisha pulled back, her face damp with tears. "I didn't know. I swear I didn't."

"I never thought that you did." If they'd been alone she would have questioned Alisha right then and there, trying to make sense of it all. Instead, she smoothed the teen's silky blonde hair and smiled. "You have nothing to feel bad for."

Alisha nodded and hugged her again. Audrey met Jake's gaze just over the top of her head. He watched her with an expression she couldn't quite decipher. When Alisha released her and went back to the sofa, Audrey sat down in the nearest chair, which was her father's recliner. She grimaced as her body tried to do what she wanted but managed not to groan out loud.

"How are you doing?" Jess asked.

"Stiff. Sore. It'll be worse tomorrow, I imagine. It could have been much worse than it is."

Seth reached over and touched her arm. "I'm so glad you weren't seriously hurt." He was such a love.

Audrey thanked him, her attention drawn to Isabelle, who was staring at Jake. They'd met at the barbecue on the Fourth, but something about him had obviously sparked the little girl's interest. She wandered over to him and plunked herself down on his knee.

"Iz," her mother chastised. "You don't just sit on people without asking."

Isabelle turned to Jake. "Can I sit on you?"

He smiled—he would have been heartless not to. "Sure."

She smiled in return. "You're pretty." It was the same thing she'd said to Audrey her first night home.

His laughter was unguarded and genuine, carving lines around his mouth and eyes. "Thank you. I think you're pretty too."

The little girl nodded, as though this was an established fact. "I look like Aunt Audrey. I have the same eyes, see?" She opened her eyes very wide and stuck her face so close to his they were practically nose to nose.

"Yes, you do," Jake said. "Audrey eyes."

"That sounds like some sort of procedure," Greg remarked as he gave the baby a bottle. "You've been Audreyized." Audrey smiled at the absurdity of it.

"What would that entail, exactly?" David asked the room.

"Side effects would include disorientation and the realization that no matter what you say you will be wrong," Jess quipped, giving her sister a tentative smile. There was the faintest edge to the words, which was oddly comforting.

"And the feeling of having been insulted, but not exactly sure how," David added.

Audrey rolled her eyes. "Thanks, siblings. Really, I mean it."

Isabelle joined in the laughter, even though it was obvious she didn't quite get it. She turned to Jake. "Your turn."

"Yes, Jake," Audrey challenged, hoping her speech wasn't

too slurred. "What side effects have you experienced from Audreyization?"

"Definitely the disorientation and being wrong," he replied, smile easing into a faint curve. His gaze locked with hers. "And the growing realization of how much I'm going to miss feeling disoriented and wrong when I'm no longer Audreyized."

It was as though he'd hit her in the chest with a brick.

"Oh!" David pressed the back of his hand to his forehead. "I feel another swoon coming on." Seth grabbed a magazine from the coffee table and started fanning him with it with exaggerated swoops of his arms.

"Suck-up," Jessica said to Jake in a teasing tone that turned it back into a joke, but he'd still said it and everyone heard it. How could he say something like that in front of people and not look the least bit flustered or embarrassed? God, if she were to say something like that, she'd be terrified of being mocked for it—or rejected. Or having it come back to bite her on the ass.

Jake hated being vulnerable, she knew that. Never give anyone something they could use against you later. Then again, he'd never been big on shame and self-doubt either. Just honesty. Neither of her siblings or their significant others seemed the least bit bothered by his words, nor did they say anything more about it. Audrey didn't know what to say at all, so she just looked at him, wondering what he saw when he looked back.

When her mother announced that dinner was ready, they all filed out to the sunporch, where John and Greg had set up a long table surrounded by mismatched chairs. The table in the kitchen simply wasn't big enough to accommodate them all. Jake helped Audrey out of the recliner and she let him assist in getting her onto a chair at the table.

There was so much food on the table it was ridiculous. Audrey dumped a mountain of garlic mashed potatoes on her plate and reached for the grilled steak. David speared one for her with his fork and dropped it next to her potatoes. It made her think of her grandfather, dead with his steak. Oddly enough, neither that thought nor the pills curbed her appetite. She was starving.

"John and Anne, thank you for the invite," Jake said, as he spooned buttery carrots from a bowl.

"Yeah," Alisha joined in, a little awkwardly. "Thanks."

Anne smiled at both of them. "Alisha, it's lovely to have you, and, Jake, you have always been such a good friend to Audrey."

"Yes," Audrey agreed, her gaze locking with his as he smiled and handed her the carrots. "You have." Her oldest and most faithful friend.

How could a TV show, or a job, be more important than that? Maybe it was the pills talking, or all the emotional upheaval of the last week and a half, but she couldn't think of an answer.

After dessert—apple crumble, another of her favorites— Audrey walked out with Jake and Alisha. The teenager didn't have to be told to wait in the truck. She gave Audrey a hug and climbed into the cab, busying herself with checking her phone.

Audrey turned to Jake. The sun was sinking on the horizon, bathing the sky in a pink-orange glow. The breeze lifted his hair, dropping it over his forehead. He looked young.

"I was scared this morning, Aud. I thought I'd lost you."

His honesty unsettled her. "I'm going to have to go back to L.A. sometime, Jake. I'll be gone then."

He shoved his hands in his pockets. "I can live knowing you're in L.A. I've done that for fourteen years. Living in a world without you in it is another story."

She thought about how she would feel if he died. The pain was crushing—suffocating. Pushing him away or running back to L.A. wouldn't change that.

"I know that look," he said with a chuckle. "Now I've scared you."

"Not like I can run, though," she joked. "I can barely walk, so good timing."

Smiling, they looked at each other. He put his arm around her shoulders and pulled her close, kissing her forehead. "How about neither of us runs?" he murmured.

She glanced up at him. "But that means we both have to behave in a mature, rational fashion."

"You up for it?"

"I like to try new things." Why not? What was the worst that could happen? Her foggy brain couldn't even form a response to the question.

This time he kissed her lips. "I'll call you tomorrow."

"I promise not to get involved in any drama before then."

"Woman, that is not a promise you should make." Then he sauntered down the steps and to the truck.

"Thanks for wearing shoes!" she called after him.

"Anything for you, Aud." He climbed into the cab, started the engine, and drove down the lane. Alisha waved. Audrey waved back. She watched them turn left onto the main road before taking her cell phone out of her pocket. She dialed Grant's number. He picked up on the third ring.

"Audrey?"

"Hey, Grant. Sorry to take so long to get back to you. Things have been crazy here." She was queen of the understatement.

"So I gathered from the news. Are you okay?"

"Yeah. Someone's confessed, so it looks like I'm in the clear."

"Oh, good." He paused—it was just long enough to be uncomfortable. "Listen, Audrey..."

"I'm fired?" She really didn't know which answer she wanted to hear.

"There are those who are worried about our credibility."

"And others who think I'd be great for ratings." The words came out so dry she could spit sand.

"We can talk about it when you get back."

"Actually, Grant," she began, looking out across the field that then dropped thirty feet to the beach. In that moment, it was the most beautiful thing she'd ever seen, and with it came a clarity she'd never felt before. "I think it's better for everyone if I simply quit."

"Really?" He sounded like it was the most outlandish thing he'd ever heard. Why would anyone walk away from a TV show?

"Really. I don't want to talk about kids who have done horrible things. I want to help them. That's what I've always wanted."

"Well, if you're sure..." He sounded so relieved Audrey almost laughed. The network must have been giving him a hard time.

"I'm sure. Dinner when I get back?"

"Of course. Carrie would love to see you."

Carrie, who she'd thought was her best friend, but whom she'd neither thought of nor heard from since her arrival. Was that what she thought friendship was? "I'd like to see her too."

"And, Audrey? I'm glad they found the real killer."

"Yeah," she said. "Me too." They said good-bye and she hung up. She ought to have done that days ago—it felt like an anvil had been lifted from her tired, aching shoulders.

Losing the show would mean a decrease in her income, but she—and her shoe closet—could learn to respect that. Now she'd have more time to put into her own research, and maybe write her own book instead of helping Angeline with hers. There would be those in the psychology world who would snub her for what she'd done in the past, but most of them would be intrigued by her past and find her all the more interesting for it. Anyone who went into the field and stuck with it was someone who found the human condition fascinating, and she would be just another puzzle to solve.

They were more than welcome to try to solve her riddles. Maybe they'd be good enough to share their findings. God knew *she* hadn't figured herself out yet.

But she was willing to try.

CHAPTER TWENTY-TWO

Two days later, Audrey was still stiff and sore and had bands of bruising on her chest and stomach in the shape of a seat belt that were the most attractive shade of aubergine.

The entire town was still in shock that Isaac had confessed to killing Maggie—though Jeannie Ray had always known that kid was up to no good—and it was as though a blanket of silence had fallen over Edgeport. The murder had gotten everyone worked up, and now that it was over no one knew what to do with themselves. It was like dead air in the middle of a TV show.

Audrey sat on the front porch with Jake, who had his laptop open and was doing up paperwork for his accountant with his feet crossed on top of the veranda railing. They'd had breakfast together. The day before, he'd come to her parents' house with lunch. Her mother had been impressed by his kitchen skills. At the moment, Audrey was impressed by the fact that he could lift his legs that far. She was lucky she could walk.

While Jake worked, she read Maggie's journal—finally reaching the end. Some of it had been disturbing to read—especially the entries that appeared to have been written by one or two of her alters. Other than the mention of this mysterious person she'd fallen in love with—and shouldn't have—there were no more clues as to who might have killed her. She'd thought maybe the lover was Janis, but why treat her the way Maggie had if she loved her? Then again, Maggie had a fucked-up way of showing she cared. Some of her writing indicated that if Audrey had been there for her, Maggie wouldn't have fallen in love, which made zero sense.

It's your fault I did this. If you had been here to stop me—if you'd been here for me—it never would have happened. You have to claim at least partial responsibility.

Yet, throughout the journal, Maggie claimed to have loved Audrey—and not in the platonic sense. It really hadn't come as a surprise—not after finding out about the women at Lipstick. She'd always kind of suspected that Maggie's affection for her was not just friendly, but she'd focused on the obsessive and possessive aspect of it. Even when Maggie came out and said it to her the night they'd fought, Audrey hadn't truly believed it. She had thought Maggie wanted to control her, but really Maggie had just wanted her, and to keep Audrey in her life.

I tried to show you how bad Jake was for you, and you treated me like the villain. He wanted you to find us. But then again, so did I. He even said your name. It made me feel like you were there with us. I wish you had been. I wish just once that I'd had the balls to tell you how I felt, or to kiss you. But I was afraid you'd reject me. I shouldn't have been surprised that you acted the way you had that night at the camp, but I thought what we had was strong enough to survive it. That was when I truly realized you would never be mine, and that I had ruined things forever.

Maggie mentioned being jealous of Isaac and Bailey because the boy so obviously doted on Bailey, and Bailey believed in it. She'd written that she didn't believe Isaac's faithfulness, and that he could be persuaded away from her stepdaughter. Had she set out to make that happen?

Maybe Isaac had done it after all, but why try to take Audrey out and then confess? It seemed more likely that he'd run her off the road hoping to get the journal and protect the secrets inside it rather than kill her. Had Isaac been the mystery lover? He certainly wouldn't want Bailey to find out about that. Maybe his mother had found out and confronted Maggie. Maybe Bailey or Gideon had confronted her. That didn't add up, though. Gideon and Bailey both said they had been home with each other after Maggie walked out. Only Isaac had left the house—supposedly to go home.

Why was she spending so much time on this? Isaac had confessed to the murder. He didn't seem to be much of a planner, so maybe he hadn't thought through what he was doing and when he got caught decided to cooperate before the situation got any worse. She knew what it was like to carry the memory of murder throughout life, and it wasn't easy. How long would she have lasted if Everett Graham hadn't shown up at the house and arrested them that night? If not for Maggie, Audrey would have confessed to the whole thing—even the planning of it—right then and there.

"Still staring at that thing?" Jake asked, snapping her out of her thoughts.

"No, I'm done." She set the worn journal on the table. "I guess I thought there'd be some magical explanation that would just wrap this all up in a bow and lay it at my feet."

"Life rarely goes that way. You know that."

"Yeah, I do. Did you know that Maggie had a thing for me?"

He turned his head to look at her. "You didn't?"

"Not really, no." Was she the only one who hadn't noticed? Or was Jake just a little more observant?

"A lot of the guys used to wonder if the two of you were sleeping together."

That wasn't a surprise. "Did you?"

Jake smiled. "Yeah. Teenage boys are horndogs, you know that. I used to think about walking in on the two of you and joining in."

Audrey returned the smile. "I used to think about a threesome with you and Lincoln."

That took the smirk off his face. "Seriously?"

She laughed. "No. My fantasies were usually just of you." There was little point in lying about it. "And sometimes Gideon." She grinned so he'd know she was joking.

"I think every straight woman in a thirty-mile radius has had fantasies about Gideon."

"And yet he married Maggie."

"Yeah, I never got that. He had to be lonely. And she was really good to Bailey when they first got together. Alisha told me Maggie was always buying Bailey gifts and doing things for her."

"When I realized Maggie had hit Bailey I wondered if Gideon could be Maggie's killer."

"Nah. Gideon wouldn't do anything that might cost him Bailey, no matter what Maggie did. He would have gone to the cops if he'd known."

"Neve should be happy it wasn't him. She still has a thing for Gideon."

"I'm just glad it wasn't my brother." He closed the laptop and set it on the table as well.

"You think he'll think twice before jumping into bed with a married woman again?" From what Jake had told her, Lincoln had moved on to a younger, single demographic. At least now she didn't have to wonder if Jake would fall for Donalda and her perky boobs.

"Maybe, but he'll always pounce on crazy. You know he's watched *Girl, Interrupted* almost twenty times?"

That was a little surreal. "Really?"

"Honest to God. He and Alisha have watched it together at least three times. He's got a thing for Angelina Jolie because of that movie."

"Who doesn't?" she retorted with a smile. "Well, I hope his next crazy chick doesn't end up dead."

"That's it? You're not going to ream me for using the term 'crazy'? I thought your type hated labels."

"Are you serious? The entire field is built upon labels. Crazy might not be the most PC description, but it implies that wild-card factor that anyone with real mental illness has. And my 'type' isn't always politically correct either. In fact, sometimes, we're twisted as fuck. A lot of people go into this field wanting to fix themselves."

"Is that why you chose it?"

"When I was a kid, hell yeah. I wanted to know myself better. As I grew up I realized other people were way more fascinating than me."

"That must have come as a blow to your ego."

She gave him an arch look. "I think you're confusing your ego with mine. I don't have much of one."

He flashed an indulgent smile. "No. Not at all, Miss 'Everyone is talking about me.'"

She laughed. Yup, still hurt. "Asshole."

They shared a smile, but it soon melted off her lips. "I'm flying back to L.A. at the end of the week." Maggie's funeral service was the next day, and there really wasn't any reason to put off returning to the real world, and her life. By the time she left, it would be two weeks since Maggie's murder. It was the most time she'd spent in Edgeport since she left for Stanford.

Jake sobered. "I know."

As she opened her mouth to say something—anything—her

phone buzzed in her hand. She looked down and saw that she had a text. She didn't recognize the number. She opened the message center.

HE DIDN'T DO IT.

Her heart thumped hard. He who? Isaac?

"What is it?" Jake asked. She showed him the screen. His brows lowered. "Whose number is that?"

Audrey pressed her thumb to the little green phone symbol by the number and brought the cell to her ear. It rang three times, then went to voice mail. When she heard the recording, she almost dropped the phone.

"Hi, it's Maggie. Do what you've gotta do after the beep." The beep that followed echoed in her head like the screech of a smoke alarm.

"It's Audrey," she whispered. "Call me." Then she hung up and looked at Jake. "It was Maggie."

His eyes widened. "Didn't Neve say the police hadn't found her phone?"

Audrey nodded. "Yeah, it wasn't in her purse. And they hadn't been able to track it because it wasn't on."

"Aud." There was an entire conversation in that one word.

She looked at him. "I know. I just got a text from Maggie's killer."

Jake decided to barbecue that night and invited Yancy, Alisha, Lincoln, Gideon, Bailey, and even Neve—when they got in touch to let her know about the text Audrey had gotten—to join them. Audrey knew what it was—it was her good-bye party. Her family was probably going to do the same damn thing to her.

She stood at the sideboard, cutting tomatoes for salad, when

Lincoln came in. There was a moment of tension when he and Gideon came face-to-face, but then Gideon offered his hand and Lincoln shook it, and that was it. It had always amazed Audrey how conflict was resolved in Edgeport—either with violence or silence.

Both Audrey and Jake hugged Bailey when she came in. The poor kid looked heartbroken, and she probably was. She and Alisha went to the living room to hang out while Jake got Gideon a beer.

"How's Bailey doing?" Jake asked, handing the other man a frosty bottle.

Gideon shook his head. "Not good. She's either crying or looking like she's on the verge of it. I have to admit I was shocked as hell. I knew Isaac and Maggie butted heads, but I never thought the kid was a killer."

"Everybody's a killer given the right circumstances," Lincoln remarked. "Sorry, Audrey."

She waved her hand at him. "No need, Linc. I agree with you."

"It must be hard on Bailey, though," Neve commented, taking a drink from her own beer. "Losing her stepmother and then finding out her boyfriend did it."

Audrey was going to have to show Neve the text she'd gotten, but she wasn't going to do it in front of Gideon, or Lincoln.

Gideon sighed. "Bailey and Maggie used to be close, but that changed when Bee started dating Isaac. Maggie tried to spend time with her, but Bailey was always gone. I think she felt left out when Bee started dating."

"Girls and their mothers," Neve commented. "Did your mother do the same thing, Audrey?"

She shrugged. "I think every day I didn't come home in a police car was a win for my mother. Though when I came home from

Stillwater we went through a few weeks where poor Mum didn't know what to do with me."

The rest of them were quiet, until Jake said, "At least your mother didn't drop you off at your grandmother's and say, 'He's your problem now.'"

"That's harsh," Gideon said, lifting his bottle.

Yancy poured a glass of wine. "I think she might have said the same thing to Dad when she brought me back here when I got pregnant."

And then Lincoln added, "First time I got arrested Mom hit me with a frying pan."

"That's horrible!" Audrey gasped.

He shrugged. "It was Teflon."

They all laughed. And then Audrey raised her glass. "To Gracie Tripp, patron saint of troubled kids."

A surprised smile curved Jake's lips, and his eyes brightened. "To Gran," he said.

"To Gracie," they chorused as Jake pulled Audrey close and kissed her hair. Lately he didn't seem to care if people saw him touch or kiss her. It was odd because she thought he'd be as private about their relationship as he was about everything else, but he didn't seem to have any such reservations.

They ate outside on the back patio near the fire pit. Citronella candles and bug spray kept the mosquitoes at bay as they enjoyed the sinking sun. They ate and talked and laughed. Even Bailey didn't stay sad faced throughout the entire meal. She even ate a little. Audrey watched the subtle flirtation between Neve and Gideon. Those teenage crushes were powerful things if allowed to linger.

After dinner, they sat outside with coffee. Audrey walked over and sat down in a chair next to Bailey. "How are you doing?" she asked.

Bailey shrugged. "Okay, I guess."

"I can't imagine what you're going through."

"Can't you?" The girl gave her a pointed look.

"I had no emotional attachment to Clint." Blunt, but true. "Like Isaac, I saw myself as protecting someone I cared for. And like me, Isaac has to pay the consequences as well."

The girl's jaw tightened. "It's not fair."

"Are you saying Maggie deserved to die?"

"I'm saying Isaac shouldn't be in jail."

"Isaac hit my car so hard it flipped. He could have killed me."

Bailey's expression turned sullen. "He didn't want to hurt you; he just wanted Maggie's journal."

"He could have asked." Silence. "But then I would have asked why."

Bailey nodded.

"There wasn't anything about him in it. Only that Maggie didn't like him much."

"What did she say about me?"

"That you infuriated her sometimes. That she thought you deserved better than Isaac. That she loved you."

Bailey looked surprised. "Really?"

Alisha joined them. "You know what? Sitting together like this you guys look alike."

Audrey and Bailey looked at each other. They did have the same face shape, and Bailey's eyes were almost the same shade as Audrey's brown eye. Their hair was a similar color as well, and they were almost the same height. She looked down at Bailey's feet; they probably had the same size shoe.

"I'll take that as a compliment," she said, and stood up—stiffly—so the two friends could sit and talk. She set her coffee on the table with Jake's and limped through the side door into the house. After using the bathroom, she came back through the addition known as the summer kitchen and paused at the door, looking out at the small group. At first her gaze went to Jake, who was laughing at something Gideon had said, but then her attention went to Alisha and Bailey. The two of them sat with their heads together like she and Maggie used to. Bailey did look a little bit like her—Audrey could see it now. Had Maggie noticed?

Of course she had.

Audrey froze as thoughts snapped and flew through her head. When Gideon and Maggie got together, Bailey would have been about the same age they'd been when they killed Clint. Of course she noticed the girl looked a bit like her former best friend and partner in crime. She'd probably been drawn to Bailey before she was drawn to Gideon. They'd been close until Bailey started dating and then Maggie got upset. She had lost Audrey; she didn't want to lose Bailey.

Bailey's feet were about the same size as hers. Size ten. The size of the print at the scene of Maggie's murder.

Fuck.

How could she have missed it? She'd been trained for this, for God's sake.

She went to her purse and got her phone before returning to the door. She found the text from Maggie's phone and selected the call icon again.

Audrey held her breath. Outside, Bailey reached for her purse and took out a cell. She looked at the screen. Maybe it was a coincidence...

And then she looked up at the house—and right at Audrey. They stared at each other. Audrey slowly lowered her phone and disconnected. She stepped back from the door as Bailey stood up. She was in the dining room when the girl found her.

"It was you," Audrey said, toneless. How could she have been so blind? So much of her career had been dedicated to kids who killed. She had been one herself. She should have seen the truth immediately.

But she hadn't, because no one wanted to believe little girls were capable of murder. Young boys were another matter.

A tear trickled down Bailey's cheek. "I guess we've got more in common than you thought. We're both killers."

CHAPTER TWENTY-THREE

Audrey took Bailey to Jake's office so they could have some privacy. She closed the door.

"Why?" she asked. "Was it because Maggie hated Isaac? Or because she hit you?"

Bailey shook her head, wrapping her arms around her torso. "It wasn't either of those things. Not really."

"Then tell me what it was. Make me understand why Isaac took the blame for you." It was important. "Did you ask him to?"

"No!" She looked completely offended by the suggestion. "I wanted to confess. He wouldn't let me."

"So he's protecting you."

Narrow shoulders slumped. "Yeah."

"Tell me what happened, Bailey. You'll feel better." Confession was good for the soul and all that.

Surprisingly, the girl responded, "When Maggie and my dad started dating I thought she was awesome. She used to do my hair all the time. She taught me about makeup and took me shopping. She was everything a mom should be. She told me I reminded her of you sometimes. She used to talk about you. A lot.

"Then, after the wedding and she moved in with us, I started noticing things. Weird things. Sometimes she was like a different person. She'd get angry, or she'd be mean. And then, when she was herself again, she wouldn't remember what she'd done."

"So Maggie verbally and physically abused you. Bailey, why didn't you tell your father?"

It was like the girl hadn't even heard her. "The first night she came into my room I was fourteen."

The words struck like a bullet. How many terrible stories had started with similar words? *No. No, no, no, no, no.*

"She kissed me and put her hands under my shirt. She touched my breasts, told me I was becoming a woman. Two nights later, when Dad was away on business, she crawled into bed with me, and touched me again. This time she asked me to touch her. And I did." Tears filled Bailey's eyes. Audrey moved toward her, but Bailey stepped back.

"I knew it was wrong, but it felt good. No one had ever taught me about sex or how it felt. She told me she loved me and that there was nothing wrong with what we did. I believed her. I *loved* her. As I got older, I started coming to her. Then, one night she started crying and said that what we were doing was wrong. That she was sick, and that we couldn't do it anymore. She rejected me. That's when I met Isaac. He asked me out, and I dated him because I wanted her to see that I didn't care about her—that I could be normal. I knew she was jealous and I *liked* it." Tears streamed down her face.

Audrey stared at her, helplessly. She'd heard horrible stories before, but this one was somehow worse, because at the core of it was an element of something that at one time had been pure and good—the affection between a parental figure and a child. Maggie had totally twisted it.

"I told Isaac that she had touched me. He got so mad. He called her sick and a pervert. All I could think was, what would he think of me if he knew I'd liked it? When we had sex, it was all right, but it didn't feel like it had with Maggie. I didn't feel like I had with her. I started thinking there was something wrong with me. Like I was being punished for liking girls more than guys. For falling in love with a woman."

Audrey's heart broke. "Honey, she was your stepmother. She took advantage of that. You can't blame yourself."

"The day you were coming home—she heard about it from Yancy—we were alone in the house. I confronted her—told her how I felt. She kissed me and we ended up in my bed. She told me she was leaving my dad, that we'd have to be careful. I thought everything was going to be okay—and then, she called me your name."

Oh, God.

"She was in bed with me, and she was thinking about you! And then she started crying and begging me to forgive her. She said it was a mistake. I believed her. And then she got shit-faced and we had to go get her. When I saw the two of you together, I knew she had picked me because I looked like you. When we got home, Dad didn't want anything to do with her, but I went to her room. She told me she was going to leave, and that we couldn't see each other anymore. She told me she was sorry for what she'd done, that she needed help. She thought *you* could help her. She told me to go away, that she didn't love me. She said she was a monster just like her father—that she deserved what he got."

Audrey pressed a hand to her chest. It hurt. She didn't want to hear the rest. *Oh, Maggie. What a mess you made.* "So you followed her to the beach and gave it to her."

Bailey nodded. "I called Isaac. I was so scared. He came and got me. He tossed her purse and I took her phone. There were things on it I didn't want anyone to see." She began sobbing so hard her body convulsed. "I loved her and I killed her. She's gone, and I won't ever get her back." She fell to the floor.

Audrey knelt beside her and put her arms around her. "It's okay, sweetie. It's going to be okay." But it was an empty promise and they both knew it. God, how did someone even start to repair this kind of damage?

Oh, Maggie. Look what you've done.

The door opened, and there was Jake. He looked at Bailey, and then at her, and Audrey saw the moment he figured it out. His face fell.

"Get Gideon and Neve," Audrey said, still holding the sobbing girl. Tears welled in her own eyes. "We need them to come in here."

Maggie was buried on a bright and sunny Thursday, almost two full weeks after her death. Fluffy white clouds hung in the sky and birds sang in the trees.

Gideon and Bailey stood closest to the small grave, and the urn beside it, along with his family. Maggie didn't have anyone left, except for Matthew, and he was still in jail. Gideon was stoic and dry eyed, and Bailey was drugged and exhausted. Audrey had managed to convince Neve not to arrest the girl until after the funeral. "Let her say good-bye." It wasn't like Bailey was going to run. Neve had agreed, a fact that probably owed more to her attraction to Gideon than any regret she had about accusing Audrey of the murder.

No one else knew yet about Bailey's confession. For once, Yancy kept the information to herself. She stood beside Alisha, her arm about her shoulders. Jake was on the other side of the girl, holding her hand.

Familiar faces made up the small crowd of mourners. Most of the town was there to say good-bye, though some—Audrey was certain—had come out of morbid fascination. Her mother and father stood with her, and her mother's expression had a slight smugness to it, as if looking forward to those who had thought Audrey guilty eating crow.

Audrey had called Janis to let her know about the service, and the woman stood at the back of the crowd, somber in black. It wasn't a surprise to discover that she was a brunette. Maggie had a type.

Audrey stared at the urn that held Maggie's remains. How was it possible to feel so sad and angry and . . . *vindicated* all at the same time? And guilty. She couldn't forget the guilt, even though every bit of her training knew she was faultless. She hadn't turned Maggie into a sexual predator or pedophile. Clint had done that. And it wasn't her fault Maggie had developed DID. It was her fault that Clint Jones was dead, and she accepted that responsibility. But torturing herself trying to figure out what she'd done to make Maggie love her, or what she could have done differently, was exhausting and fruitless. She killed the man who molested her friend, and she didn't regret it. She'd done it to protect Maggie, but she hadn't saved her like she thought, and it broke her heart.

Bailey had said that the last thing Maggie said to her was, "I'm sorry." In her manuscript she'd asked Audrey to forgive her. Maggie might have been searching for absolution, or some kind of clemency, but she sure as hell hadn't known how to go about earning it. She'd probably never meant to hurt Bailey, and her feelings for the girl had probably been genuine, but she'd had no right acting on them. Maggie ought to have known the damage she was sowing—admitting it was wrong and still doing it didn't count. And now Bailey was going to pay the price. Maggie had made her a mess and left her with blood on her hands. Clint Jones's legacy lived on, and that was the real pisser.

The urn was lowered into the ground. Almost everyone in attendance had been given a white rose or lily, and as they passed by the grave, they dropped their flowers on top of the urn before moving on to Gideon and Bailey. Fortunately, most people were brief.

Except for Jeannie. She went on and on about Maggie to Gideon. If Bailey stabbed her in the eye with a rose, Audrey wouldn't blame the kid. Fortunately, Anne stepped up behind the old crone and spooked her into moving on.

Audrey and Jake held back, waiting for the end of the line.

"What's going to happen to her?" he asked. Behind his sunglasses his gaze was fixed on Bailey.

"I don't know. Therapy. Lots of therapy. She'll probably end up in a hospital. Depending on the judge, she might even end up in Stillwater. I'm going to do everything I can to help her and make sure she doesn't get tried as an adult. If I can, I'll get her sent to Reva. She'll look after her."

He squinted against the sun. "I told Gideon I wanted to help with whatever treatment or legal fees they needed."

"You're a good man," she said, taking his hand. There was strength in his fingers, a grounding force that made her feel centered.

"Sometimes. Bailey's Alisha's best friend. I have to do something to make my girl smile again."

"That breaks my heart."

"Mine too." He squeezed her hand. "Stay with me tonight."

Audrey nodded. There were so many things left unsaid between them, and they were going to stay unsaid for the time being.

They moved along in line for what felt like forever, finally stepping up to the edge of the grave. Jake opened his fingers and dropped a lily into the hole. "Rest well, Mags," he murmured.

Audrey's fingers tightened around his as she threw her rose. A thorn pricked her finger just as she let go. "Good-bye, Maggie." *I forgive you.*

They joined Yancy and Alisha and Neve, who stood with Gideon and Bailey. Bailey pulled away from her father to hug Audrey, and Audrey hugged her back. Jake went to talk to his niece.

"We have to go to the police tomorrow," Bailey said. "Will you come with us?"

Audrey turned from her beseeching gaze to Gideon. He looked like he'd aged ten years. "I think having you there would help Bailey not be so afraid."

"Of course I'll go with you," she said, giving the girl a squeeze.

As they walked away from the grave site, Audrey glanced over her shoulder, at the hole where Maggie had been put. She might not have been able to save Maggie from becoming like her father, but she was going to do everything in her power to help Bailey.

I promise you, Mags. I will *save her.*

"Oh my God," Yancy said, clutching her phone so tight her knuckles were white.

"What is it?" Jake asked. They had just returned from the cemetery and were still in his truck.

Wide green eyes turned to his. "It's from Jeannie. She says she just saw on the news that Matt was killed during a riot in prison."

"Jesus," Jake swore. "There's none of them left. You okay, Yance?"

She nodded. "It's horrible, but it's not like I was in love with him. He wasn't the kind of man who was easy to even like. You're right, that whole family is gone now."

"Good," Alisha said, her voice hard. "They've caused enough trouble."

Yancy turned to her daughter, who sat between them in the truck cab. She opened her mouth and hesitated. Jake expected her to admonish the girl, but then his sister nodded. "They have, my dar. They have." She sounded so much like their grandmother that Jake's throat tightened.

The women got out of the truck and Jake watched them enter the bungalow before backing out of the driveway. Audrey had told Alisha to call her if she ever needed to talk, and he suspected his niece just might have to do that once or twice. But at least he didn't have to worry about his sister mourning Matt Jones.

Jake picked up his own phone as he drove out the road and dialed his cousin Kenny. He picked up after the first ring, his voice low. "Did you see the news?"

"I did. Consider your debt paid," Jake said, and hung up.

Audrey returned home the next day after a mostly sleepless night at Jake's and an emotionally exhausting trip to the police with Bailey and Gideon. She'd called Reva for names of some of the best juvenile lawyers in the area and managed to find one able to take Bailey's case. The woman had met them at the station and was there to guide Bailey. It all went very smoothly. Still, there was nothing smooth about a sobbing teenage girl having to tell the story of her sexual awakening and abuse and how she'd killed the woman responsible, whom she'd also believed herself to be in love with. And there was nothing smooth about sitting there, watching her father suffer through the story once again.

Maybe it was penance for her own sins.

The lawyer—Candice Fiddes—believed that after Bailey was assessed by a psychologist it would be recommended to the court that she receive therapy and possibly a hospital stay rather than long-term jail time. The murder hadn't been premeditated, and the situation was a delicate one. Worst-case scenario would be a stay in Stillwater or another facility. Audrey told Gideon she'd do whatever she could to get Bailey into Stillwater if it came to that. Reva would do what she could on her end as well.

So, when she walked through the door and saw her parents, Jess and Greg, and David all waiting for her, she almost cried. What now?

"What are you doing back here?" she asked her brother.

"Mom called me," he said. "Told me I needed to come home."

Her mother gestured for Audrey to join them at the kitchen table and poured her a cup of tea. "Sit, Audrey. Your father and I have something to tell you."

"You're not divorcing, are you?" Jessica demanded.

Anne laughed, her eyes bright. "Of course not."

John reached over and took his wife's hand. "Mum?" Audrey said. "What's going on?"

"There's no easy way to say this. I have cancer."

"What?" That was David. Both Audrey and Jessica were silent. They shared a look. They'd each been afraid of something like this, Audrey thought.

Their mother glanced at their father. "It's in my cervix. Now, they think they caught it early enough. The treatment's made me feel a little sick, which I know you've all noticed. I'm probably going to have to go in for a hysterectomy, but my doctor is very optimistic. She believes we've got it in time, and that it hasn't spread to any other organs. There's a very good chance I'll still be here when Isabelle starts having a family of her own." She smiled brightly at her children.

Audrey's first impulse was to scream, flip the table, and then kick a few walls. Instead, she took a drink of tea. "What do you need from us, Mum?" That ought to have been Jessica's line, but her sister just sat there, white faced. Was she worried about their mother, or was she thinking about her own chances of getting cancer? Or her daughters'? Maybe all three.

Her mother turned that loving smile on her. It was the smile that made her believe as a child that everything was going to be all right, but coming from Bailey's meeting with the lawyer, Audrey knew that there were no guarantees that things would ever be all right again.

"I need the three of you to be strong with me." She looked at David and Audrey. "And I need to see the two of you more often. I know that's selfish of me, but I can beat this if I have my family supporting me."

Suddenly, losing the show wasn't such a bad thing. "You've got it." She didn't know how she'd work it, but she would. Angeline had an office in Boston that she used as her East Coast center. Audrey could probably work out of there for as long as necessary. She'd have to give up her apartment in L.A., but that wouldn't be hard. She would do whatever needed to be done so that she could be there for her mother—the one person who had always been there for her.

"Yeah," David agreed. "Anything you need, Mum."

Audrey looked at her father. She had despised him for so many years, but actually seeing him had reminded her that he wasn't all bad. "What about you, Dad? What do you need?"

He looked surprised that she'd asked, but her mother looked at her with such love that Audrey almost declared herself the favored child right then and there. "Patience," he replied. "Patience and strength. I don't have much of either, and I know there have been times the three of you haven't had much patience for me. Or respect. I hit the bottle pretty hard when Annie was first diagnosed, and it's tempting to hit it again, but I need to be here for her. I'm going to need some help with that."

It was the most honest thing Audrey had ever heard the man say. "Does that mean I'm not going to have to drag your sorry ass home from Gracie's anymore?"

"I don't know, but I'm going to try. There's an AA chapter in Eastrock. I went to my first meeting last night."

It was not going to be easy, Audrey realized as she watched him. He was going to stumble and he was going to get pissed and fight and puke and pass out. He was an alcoholic, and the road ahead of him was not going to be an easy one. Part of her wanted to smack him for waiting until his wife was sick to get help, but that was only because he had never even tried to get sober for one of his kids. He would try for their mother, though, and that was worth a little something.

"I want to talk to your doctor," Jessica blurted. She looked at each of her siblings. "And I want the two of you to come with me."

"All right," Anne replied. Audrey and David nodded. "I'm not keeping anything from you, Jess."

"It's not that. I just...I just want to hear it from her with my own ears. I want to ask her questions and get answers."

"You should talk to her," John replied. "She answered all of my questions and made us both feel really good about your mother's prognosis."

Audrey watched her parents. If her mother died, her father was going to be a wreck. They all would be. He was going to need their support during this just as much as their mother would. It was funny. She'd spent so many years being bitter and angry at her father that she hadn't realized just how much they were alike. Because sitting there, after all she'd been through in the last couple of weeks, what she was thinking about wasn't her parents or her past, or even Jake.

All she could think of was how much she could use a drink.

Jake drove her to the airport, since the Mini hadn't survived the encounter with Isaac. It held up well, cabin-wise, but the rest of it was in pretty bad shape. That was going to be a nightmare to deal with. Thank God she had insurance. She still came out of that situation better than Isaac had. The kid was going to be in juvy for a while, and all because he'd been trying to protect his girlfriend. Maybe he thought the consequences were worth it. Audrey was still thinking on the fact that consequences often had ramifications of their own. It hurt to think of Bailey, and to think about Maggie. If she hadn't turned her back on Maggie all those years ago, would things have turned out differently for either of them?

Probably not, but she still had to wonder. And it made her want to get back to work. There were so many kids out there who needed someone to speak for them, to help them. If she didn't do it, who would?

"When will you be back?" Jake asked, lifting her suitcase out of the back of the truck. She had her carry-on already in hand.

"Miss me already?" she teased.

He shoved his hands in his pockets. "Last time it took you seven years. If you're going to do that again, I'm not going to wait."

"Jake, I don't expect you—"

He kissed her—hard and fast. "Shut up, Aud. Stop analyzing everything. You and I are what we are. I don't have any expectations, but I would like to know if I'll still be in my thirties when I see you again."

She smiled. He was making this as easy as he could for her, but she didn't have any illusions. If she was willing to do the work then so was he, but if she ran away again . . . well, she was on her own.

"Yes. I have to make arrangements with Angeline, but she's happy to have me in Boston. Apparently she thinks it will increase our productivity and enable us to expand. I'm a little frightened of what that entails, to be honest. It sounds like a lot more responsibility." She was also a little thrilled at the change. Angeline trusted her and was obviously grooming her to become a partner, not just her assistant. "But it will let me be in the same time zone as my mother, and I'll be able to get home more often. Think you'll get sick of me?"

"Probably." He smiled. "I think you'll keep things pretty interesting."

"What a nice way to put it." She laughed. "Have you been reading *Psychology for Dummies* again?"

"Actually, I had to lend it to Alisha. She's decided she wants to be a psychologist. I think you've made an impression."

"She drank the Kool-Aid. Want me to talk her out of it?" All joking aside, she was thrilled the girl wanted to be anything like her. Maybe she wasn't such a mess after all. Or, Alisha took after her uncle and liked messes.

"There are worse people she could want to emulate than you."

"Flatterer."

"Hey, I'm just glad she wears shoes."

She glanced down at his feet. He was wearing sandals. They'd be off the second he got back in the truck. "Maybe Alisha could come visit me in Boston."

Jake's brows rose. "Ouch."

"Are you saying you'd actually come all the way to Beantown? For me?"

"I drove to California and back."

"I still can't believe you did that."

He just smiled, as though he knew things she didn't. "Call me sometime."

"I will." Then, because the conversation was so foolish and purposely dancing around the issue, and she was just so tired of lying and not being herself, "Jake, I'm going to be back on the East Coast by the end of September, and if you don't come to Boston the first weekend I'm there, it will break my fucking heart. And I plan to call you. Probably a lot, and I expect to be called in return, and told just how much I'm missed. Do you have a problem with any of that?"

His smile grew. "You just had to ask." He kissed her again—slower this time. "Go. I'll be here when you get back. I'll always be here."

Grinning, Audrey took hold of her suitcase and wheeled it toward the terminal door. She didn't glance over her shoulder to see if he was still there. She didn't need to.

She wasn't going to spend her life looking back. Not anymore.

MEET THE AUTHOR

Photo Credit: Sarah Kolej

As a child, **KATE KESSLER** seemed to have a knack for finding trouble, and for it finding her. A former delinquent, Kate now prefers to write about trouble rather than cause it, and spends her day writing about why people do the things they do. She lives in New England with her husband.

INTERVIEW

When did you first start writing?

When I was eight. I wrote my first *book* at twelve. It was all longhand and very melodramatic. There was always someone who posed a threat to my long-suffering heroines. I read a lot of Sidney Sheldon as a kid, and watched far too many soap operas. I was all about the intrigue and deception.

Where did the idea for *It Takes One* come from?

I'll try to answer this without sounding unhinged or blood-thirsty. When I was twelve, a very good friend of mine was raped by her father. When she told me about it, I said, "We could kill him." We plotted it but of course did nothing. He went to jail and she went into a decent foster home and that was that. Many years later, a friend and I had a discussion about the lengths to which people would go for someone they cared about. I shared the story about my childhood friend, and it made me wonder, "What if we had done it?" I decided then that I had to write it. I want to say that Maggie in the book is *nothing* like my actual friend. Maggie is an amalgam of several good "frenemies" I've known over the years.

How did the characters of Jake and Audrey take shape?

I grew up in a town like Edgeport and I wanted to write a heroine who rejects where she's from and make one of the most important people in her life someone who has embraced that same place. Audrey has tried very hard to make herself into the person she wants to be, but she knows deep down that she can't change everything. Jake doesn't want to be anything other than what he is. I like using him as a kind of mirror for Audrey. Plus, I love their relationship. Since childhood they've always just accepted each other for what they are. They genuinely love each other, and not just romantically. It's funny, because the more I got to know Audrey, the clearer Jake became in my head, and the more I got to know him, the more I learned about Audrey.

How much research did you have to do in preparation for writing *It Takes One*?

A LOT! I probably missed things too. I'm still researching as I go along with the series. I've read and am reading a ton of psychology books, and books on crime. I've watched videos and documentaries. I'm even hoping to take some classes. I need to add to my primary sources, so if anyone out there is a psychologist, police officer, or someone involved in forensics and is interested in having me pick their brain, please contact me!

The research into Maine has been fun. My husband and I took a drive along the shore where I set Edgeport and it was so great to see it—and to know that it looks just like I thought it should. Of course, I've taken some liberties, for which I hope the people of Maine will forgive me.

There was a wide-ranging cast in *It Takes One*. Who is your favorite character?

Gracie, even though she's long gone. I just love that old woman. Among those who are still alive, I guess my favorite would be... Jake. Jake says what he thinks and does what he wants. He's a very gray character—he doesn't see things as black or white—which will come out more and more as the books go on.

What is one piece of information that you know about the story or characters that you loved but couldn't fit into the book?

There's history between Anne (Audrey's mother) and Jeannie Ray that I would have loved to flesh out, but there was just no place for it, and I couldn't figure out how to reveal it without Anne bringing it up. Since Anne isn't a gossip, there was just no place for it. However, it might come up again, so I'm going to keep it to myself just in case I can use it, or it changes! However, I would have loved to elaborate on the brief romantic history between Neve and Lincoln, but it didn't happen. I actually think Neve might have been Lincoln's first—which he would be mortified to have get out seeing as he thinks of himself as quite the player and is a couple of years older than her.

Do you know what's next for Audrey?

I do! Audrey's story continues in a book that is tentatively titled *The One That Got Away*. I believe it's a fall 2016 release. Audrey will find herself up against a serial killer who sees her as a suitable adversary, and goes after someone Audrey loves. In the first book, you find out how far Audrey *has* gone for someone she loved. In book two, the question is, how far will she go now that the stakes are so much higher?

INTRODUCING

**If you enjoyed
IT TAKES ONE,
look out for**

Two Can Play

An Audrey Harte novel

by Kate Kessler

Ian Monroe didn't look like a serial killer.

Audrey Harte stared at the mugshot in Monroe's file. He didn't have a vacant expression like Gacy, or Bundy's crazy eyes. He didn't have that seventies gay-porn-star look like Dahmer, or the full-on nut-job vibe of Ramirez. He looked preppy and stylish—smart, like he was posing for his high-school senior photo.

In fact, Monroe had been out high school for only two months when he was arrested for the murders of five girls in Portland, Maine. The yearbook, in which he wore a smile much like the one in his mug shot, had been dedicated to the memories of four of his victims. He'd gone to their funerals, the little prick. Someone had given him the title of Maine's youngest serial killer—like it added prestige to the violence done by the then seventeen-year-old. Monroe, a fairly textbook psychopath, didn't need his ego stroked.

He was finally going to trial, and the prosecution had asked Audrey to be an expert witness. They said it was because she was from Maine and understood the people there, but when a tabloid magazine ran a photo of her next to one of Monroe with the caption *Killer Doc to take on "Boyscout" Monroe at trial*, she wondered if the D.A. wasn't trying to stir up some publicity of his own.

If someone had told her that having committed murder when she was thirteen would actually make her professionally desirable, Audrey wouldn't have believed it. But, with the murder of her former best friend and partner in crime, Maggie Jones, that summer, Audrey's past had bit her on the ass so hard she still had a bruise. She didn't like to think about Maggie, or the particulars of her murder, but she couldn't deny it was partly responsible for her having her own office at the Beharrie Centre. Her boss, Angeline Beharrie, had put her in charge of the East Coast office—a position in which she felt like a fraud at thirty-two. And she was well aware that there were those at the Centre who didn't think she deserved the promotion.

Which meant she was going to have to prove that she *did* deserve it.

A knock on her office door—which was open—made her lift her head. It was Lauralyn, who ran the front desk and handled appointments, calendars, and client concerns for the clinical psychologists in the office. Basically, no one there would know what to do without her. She was fortysomething with curly blonde hair and a youthful, round face. She smiled as she stuck her head in.

"It's two o'clock."

Audrey glanced at the clock on the wall. She'd asked Lauralyn to remind her that she wanted to leave early. Traffic around Boston was horrible at the best of times, and she didn't want to turn a three-and-a-half-hour drive into five by being stupid enough to leave at rush hour.

"Thanks," she said, closing the folder. "I'm staying at that B and B in Rockland, right?" It wasn't far from Warren, where Ian Monroe was incarcerated, and a hour and a half from Portland, where the murders had taken place.

"Yep. I emailed you details and the Google map, and here's your travel mug." She set the tall mug on the desk. "The coffee's fresh and I added that Italian Sweet Créme that you like."

Fetching coffee wasn't part of Lauralyn's job; she was just that nice. "You are an angel," Audrey told her with a grin.

The older woman winked. "I'll remind you that you said that at my review." Then she left the office.

Audrey stood, gathering up Monroe's file along with several others and the binder in which she kept her notes. Her hand hesitated over the latest *People* magazine, which had an article on Ian and the victim who escaped him, leading to his arrest. The writer spoke in depth to Victoria Scott—"the one that got away"—and several other people close to the case. Since a good part of her involvement in the trial consisted of assessments and interviews, the article would be a good one to have as a reference. Plus, it mentioned her. Audrey tossed it in her leather computer bag before putting her laptop inside as well.

She slipped into her dark red peacoat and wrapped her scarf around her neck before slinging her bags over her shoulder and grabbing her coffee. She turned down the heat, shut off the lights, and locked the door behind her.

The clinic was located in Cambridge, a bit of a walk from Harvard. Angeline chose the five-story building for its location, and for the fact that its redbrick facade was both academic and inviting. The first time Audrey had seen it, she thought it looked like money, and vaguely pretentious, but she wasn't the one paying the rent. She had to admit, though, it was a nice place to work.

And she had been working. A lot. Mostly to avoid going home.

And because her work enabled her to continually psychoanalyze herself without anyone noticing. Of all the killers, violent offenders, and victims she'd interviewed, the workings of her own mind were what confounded her most.

She had a reserved spot in the parking garage attached to the building via a covered walkway, which helped her avoid the damp cold that had settled over the city for the past couple of days. As she approached, she hit the remote starter for her Prius so it would be nice and warm for her. Jake had laughed at her for getting the remote, but he hated to wear shoes, even in the winter, so obviously he was a freak of nature. A guy with that little body fat should not be warm all the time.

The drive to Rockland was uneventful except for the thermometer dipping a few degrees the farther north she drove. In another couple of weeks it would be Halloween. She remembered it would sometimes snow while she was trick-or-treating as a kid.

She wasn't prepared for a New England winter. She wasn't even prepared for fall.

It was getting dark when she pulled into the B and B's drive. Hers was the only car in guest parking. This place probably did extremely well in the summer, given its picturesque view of the water. The trees had turned color, and most of them still had an abundance of leaves. It might be colder than L.A., but the air was clean, and it was a hell of a lot prettier. Not that L.A. didn't have its moments.

Pulling her coat closed, Audrey got her bags out of the backseat and locked the car.

The door was opened by a smiling woman who looked to be in her sixties. "You must be Audrey."

"I am." She returned the smile. "Mrs. Fletcher?"

"Indeed. Come on in. It's going to be a nippy night, I think."

Audrey stepped inside. The interior was very English countryside—plush and rich but inviting. And was that roast beef she smelled? And apple pie? Her stomach growled.

Mrs. Fletcher showed her the dining room and common areas before taking her up to her room. Decorated in shades of plum, cream and dark green, it had the same relaxed opulence as the rest of the house. It had its own bathroom as well, complete with large, claw-foot soaker tub. *Much* better than staying in a cheap hotel.

"It's lovely," she told Mrs. Fletcher. "Do you suppose I could trouble you for some ice and directions to the nearest good restaurant?"

"I can bring you an ice bucket. And you needn't worry about going out again after your long drive. If you like roast beef, I'll bring you up a tray of our dinner. I always make too much."

The inherent kindness of this part of the world always surprised her, even though she'd grown up with it. As a kid, though, it always seemed intrusive, and was counterbalanced with the nosiness and gossip-mongering of small-town life. "That's very kind of you. If it's no trouble, I'll take you up on it."

Mrs. Fletcher smiled. "No trouble at all! It's so nice to have someone else in the house. Did I hear that you're part of the prosecution against Ian Monroe?"

Audrey froze as she set her bags near the bed. And there was the flip side of small-town hospitality. "Yes." She met the woman's pale blue gaze. "I am, yes."

All the mirth drained from Mrs. Fletcher's round face. "Terrible business. Do you actually have to see him? Is that why you're here?"

Was there any harm in being honest? Audrey couldn't tell, but she also couldn't think of how this nice woman could possibly make trouble for her since she would be leaving the next day. "Yes. I'll be interviewing him tomorrow."

Graying curls bobbed as she shook her head and clucked her tongue. "I'm going to bring you a slice of pie as well. Do you like ice cream?"

Do bears shit in the woods? The voice of her father rang in Audrey's head. "I do. Thank you."

The older woman's smile returned just before she closed the door, leaving Audrey alone. She took her toiletries from her overnight bag and set them in the bathroom. Then she took her suit for the next day out of her garment bag and hung it up. It was simple and well-cut and had cost more than some people made in a week. It had been a worthy investment, though. With a crisp white shirt she looked professional, put-together, and slightly intimidating, but not like she was trying too hard. She called it her *Grosse Pointe Blank* suit.

She had just kicked off her boots and taken off her coat when Mrs. Fletcher returned with a tray bearing dinner, a bucket of ice, and a bouquet of flowers. Audrey quickly took the heavy tray from her and set it on the small table near the window.

"I forgot that those were delivered for you earlier today," the older woman told her, her face a little flushed from carrying the tray up an entire flight of stairs.

Audrey checked the flowers. "Really?" No one but work and Jake knew where she was staying. "They're very pretty." Actually, white roses always made her think of funerals, but they still smelled nice.

"Well, I'll leave you to it. Just leave the tray outside the door and I'll collect it later.

After thanking the woman once again, Audrey put the bottle of wine she'd brought with her into the bucket of ice and sat down to eat. It was as delicious as it smelled—and way too much food. Cooks in Maine seemed to operate under the thought that every meal was for a lumberjack—or a teenage boy.

When she finished the last bite of pie and melting vanilla ice cream, she set the tray on a table outside her room and went back to the flowers. There was a small card inside a white envelope. She opened it.

Looking forward to playing with you.

What the hell? That wasn't cryptic or creepy at all.

The card wasn't signed, but the phone number for the florist was embossed in silver on the bottom. They could be from Jake. Though, she couldn't imagine him picking white roses as a gift. He had more color to him than that, and he'd probably go for something more exotic.

Like a carnivorous plant. A pretty one. And he'd tell her it reminded him of her.

Audrey smiled at the thought of him, even though her stomach fluttered like a hive of neurotic bees. It wasn't a new sensation. Jake Tripp had fascinated her, scared her, and held a firm grip on her heart for almost twenty years. They'd been friends for even longer. His grandmother, Gracie, had appointed herself Audrey's fairy godmother even before she and Maggie had been arrested for killing Clint. Audrey wouldn't be where she was if not for Gracie. God only knew how she might have turned out.

She ran a bath and called Jake while the tub filled.

"Are you in Rockland?" he asked when he picked up. The sound of his slightly scratchy voice loosened her muscles more than any bath ever could. He was like her grounding wire. Always had been.

"Yeah. Got here a little while ago. Hey, did you send me flowers?"

There was a pause. "No. Was I supposed to?"

"No. But the owner gave me a bouquet that had been delivered earlier with my name on them."

"What did the card say?"

Now she was the one who hesitated.

"Aud?"

"It said 'looking forward to playing with you.'"

"That smacks of unoriginality. I'd never send you something like that." He sounded offended that she'd even asked.

"I didn't think so, but I wanted to ask before I let paranoia set in."

"You think someone related to the Monroe case is trying to unsettle you?"

"I don't know. At least I know they didn't come from Monroe. I can't imagine they let you send flowers from prison."

"He could have paid someone to do it. It's a classic taunt."

Oh, shit. "Not helping with that paranoia."

"You want me to tell you it's nothing? That you're imagining things?"

"Yes."

"Can't do it. It's weird, and you should look into it. You should also tell the prosecution. Take a photo of the flowers and the card."

"I will." She took a corkscrew from her bag and opened the bottle of wine. "You still want me to stay at your place this weekend?" Though she spent most of her time in Edgeport at his house, she did occasionally stay with her parents. She didn't want him to get tired of her, and she didn't want to let herself buy into the happily-ever-after scenario her inner teenager wanted so desperately to craft for the two of them. So far, their longish-distance relationship was running smoothly, but there was bound to be a hitch eventually. It was inevitable.

"You get a better offer?"

She smiled at his teasing tone. "No."

"You just want to hear me say it, is that it?"

"Would it kill you?"

He laughed. "Yes, Aud, I want you to stay with me. It would fair render me distraught if you hung your hat elsewhere."

Audrey's brow pulled as she poured wine into one of the glasses on the table. "I've heard that before."

"Gran used to say it to Gramps when he accused her of trying to get rid of him."

Gracie and Mathias Tripp had one of those loves that they made movies about. The sort that ran down to their bones and even death couldn't shake. "Good thing I packed a hat, then."

They talked for a little while longer and then hung up. Audrey took a photo of both flowers and note with her phone; sent both to Will Grant, the prosecuting attorney; and then headed for the bath with her glass of wine. She soaked for almost an hour before getting out, her skin gone pruney. She dried off and slipped into a T-shirt and pajama pants. She slathered on her nightly skin care and climbed into bed with her tablet and another glass of wine. She read for a couple of hours before deciding to call it a night.

But before she went to sleep, she climbed out of bed, picked up the vase of roses, and put the creepy arrangement on the table in the hall. They were not going to be the last thing she saw before going to sleep, and they sure as hell weren't going to be the first thing she saw in the morning before heading to Maine State Prison to interview its most dangerous inmate.